SPACE MYSTERY

"Something is not right with the ship," said Heglit. "We're dead in N-space."

"We'd better see," said Jade.

Silence out in the corridor. The floor, somehow cold and alien, jarred Jade's heels as he headed for the captain's cabin.

There was no answer to Jade's knock so he had to palm the plate and slide the door back. Turloz sat in his chair. He did not look up.

"Captain," he said quietly.

Turloz screamed, both hands covering his eyes. He cowered in the chair, moaning, "—mub-mub-mub—go—stop—" Or something sounding like it.

With a quick heart-thudding look around for Heglit, Jade moved toward the man, touched him—Jumped back as he screamed and lept away, knocking the chair away. Turloz ran full stride into the wall and collapsed, moaning thick mushy sounds.

For Jade, it was the bizarre beginning of a mystery—and before it was solved, he would be the most wanted man in the universe.

STAR WEB
JOAN COX

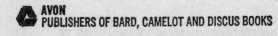
AVON
PUBLISHERS OF BARD, CAMELOT AND DISCUS BOOKS

STAR WEB is an original publication of Avon Books.
This work has never before appeared in book form.

AVON BOOKS
A division of
The Hearst Corporation
959 Eighth Avenue
New York, New York 10019

First Avon Printing, July, 1980

1

Spun-out, brain-glazed, flying on the wings of the tiny silver grains, he sat in thick brown shadows bemused by the subharmonics of the tabletop singing against his arms. Soft rainbows of talk helixed across the joyroom, bubble-bursting against his shadows but not penetrating. Always like this, he thought, interesting sound-color. He knew this territory of Shiva Pearls. He was thirsty, he recognized the dusty feel-taste of his thirst, but no more Z'Atua. Wait until the rainbow dance of noise flattened. Dangerous territory. *I could get lost here.* Knowing that was a Lursteak richness shuddering through him. A fight beyond the helix shimmer was an almost sensual itch along his flanks. He wondered briefly how he knew it was a fight, but resisted the urge to self-analysis. He'd remember and figure it out later.

"Jade." The sound exploded sleek and glossy blue through the sensory mix, splashing against his face like warm foam. Me, he thought, recognizing his name by the taste. Damn. For a minute he tried to focus everything properly, and dove through glass webs of confusion. Never mind, then, he thought, damn him, he can wait.

But the soft singing table bubbled up on the far side, shaping a chorus of taut melody. Heglit. Great.

Heglit sat down, quiet, watching the flushed lean face, the metallic yellow eyes. Chem-linking. Again. "Jade. You still here?" He kept his hard voice quiet.

Jade blinked, shadowed lids falling over bright gold, struggling up again. Out of the jumble of otherness happening in his head he dredged up memory, looking for the known face, Rafalan face, bronze-hued and more like metal than skin, cast by some forever angry sculptor. Almost like a rept. But more man than rept, he remembered, behind swinging shimmering visions of sound. Warm-

1

blooded, cold-hearted, strong as twelve-point. He looked for the black eyes in the melange of feels and flavors, knowing they were all there somewhere but not finding them. He scrabbled around in the shadows inside himself and tried to build word-sound, shaping it like thick wet clay.

" 'glit," managed, mumbled, exploding slow gold-red flashes before his face. "Away me."

Heglit nodded, a G-minor chord, distracting. The bright yellow eyes slid away to watch the revolving colors of conversation below the table. The Rafalan watched a moment from unmoving black eyes. Too far out. So. It couldn't be helped. He slipped a dark hand into the pouch hung against his chest inside his blouse. The black dust was ultra-fine and ultra-secret, but there were no eyes in the noisy dimness of the joyhouse fast enough to catch the expert flick of thumb across finger, directing the tiny cloud toward Jade's face. It was a brutal thing to do, and he knew it.

Jade inhaled on schedule, drew a dozen or so tiny grains into his nostrils. Moisture effervesced, the spore dissolved, melted into warm membrane.

Kaleidoscope exploded into murderous shrieks of color, violent raw brain-violating extremes climbing into impossibles, driving him back into his head whimpering, as black splashed perception into nothing.

. Heglit was ready. As the man folded, he scooped him up, tossed him over his left shoulder, and made his way out of the joyhouse.

At night the port was a collection of ship shapes in hard blue light, tangled and knotted together with black shadow. Heglit walked easy with the coiled-spring stride of his race, untroubled by the weight of the man. Nothing of what he might be thinking or feeling showed on his dark face. But nothing ever did.

He was well out on the field before the expected command halted him. He waited until the two figures stepped into the light. Algorans, he recognized the race, squat thick shapes, manlike, but not quite. They croaked a demand for identity and his business on the field.

"Centra Zar, signed tonight," he said, looking down at them, knowing they were armed and liked to kill, and no one would say too much about a dead Rafalan in this sector. He let his speech drop into the common lowspeak. "Turloz Captain is. Signed us, him." He pulled the papers from the neck pouch, knowing they couldn't read and wouldn't admit it to him. Jade stirred slightly on his shoulder and subsided.

"Alive him?" the right-hand Algoran croaked, rising on his toes for a better look.

"Alive being. Sick him."

They backed up a step in unison and Heglit noted it. He had heard the race had a morbid fear of disease, something to do with a long-ago plague on their homeworld. These ones wanted no more to do with him. He was free to go. He made sure to get his papers back.

The Centra Zar sat in a blaze of light, and there was a lot of activity around her, sign of an early lift. Approaching from the shadows, Heglit catalogued the shapes and activities. None of his kind moved here, nor did he expect them to. There was another Algoran standing near, a sheaf of papers in one thick hand. That was a new thing, an Algoran trained to read. Could be interesting. He stepped into the blue light with his burden, and the Algoran came over to him, taking his time, held out his hand for papers without speaking. Heglit gave them over and watched the eyes moving to piece together the few words.

"Heard Turloz signed Rafalan, Heglit you. What's it?" He indicated the figure draped over the broad shoulder.

"Clate. Work-mate being."

"Drunk being." The laugh sounded like gravel sliding on iron. "Dump it. Turloz workers needing, not—"

Heglit's head moved slightly, expressionless eyes staring down at the squat form, just looking, but in the violent light his glassy black eyes damned up the hoarse voice. He waited a silent minute, and none could tell what he thought. When he finally spoke, it was quietly. "A team us, small one. Togetherness."

"Can't work him." He couldn't give in easily with so many workers standing around listening.

"The work he signed for doing him. Other chores will do me. Until wakes him."

The Algoran nodded, glad to have it settled. He had never seen a Rafalan, but he knew what was said of

3

them, that they had no feeling and would kill cool and easy and with no reason if they felt like it. He showed Heglit the quarters assigned to them, and let the Rafalan stow the sleeper before putting him to work carrying crates marked "fragile" into the huge hold and spraying them with plastic buffer foam.

Heglit knew the foreman had seen the qualifications on the sign-on slip, knew that he and Jade were Linkers, necessary to take the ship through the freaked-out arteries of the Star Web, that they were the means by which this ship would get where it was going. But he worked, silent and efficient, cool while the others sweated, knowing the foreman watched, doing no more or less than necessary. It had happened before. He was a Rafalan, a Restricted. He was less than the others until they needed his special talents. It was never tried with Jade, who was to both the eyes and lists a Clate, a Class A type.

The Centra Zar lifted from the port as night lifted from C'Erit, and was as much noticed. The Linkers, raised to true status as the ship gained space, shared special quarters, answerable now only to the captain, and then only outside their own work. And Jade was mad. Hung over as he couldn't believe possible, and sure with his own special brand of sureness that Heglit was the reason.

"Remember it, me," he groan-growled from the couch where he lay curled against the pain riding zoar-dragons along spine and into head.

"Talk like a man, Jade." The hard flat voice touched nothing but sound. Another time (maybe later this time) Jade would laugh at Heglit telling *him* to talk like a man. Now he hurt. But he knew the Rafalan would ignore him unless he obeyed.

"What did you do to me?"

"Brought you down. I will not tell you how, now. Once you eat, the pain will go."

"Eat?" Jeff grimaced, shutting yellow eyes. "Can't. I'm sick."

"You will eat."

He did. They were standard rations, tasteless but nourishing, and the beverage was the standard tea from Santo. As usual. And Heglit was right. As usual. The pain evaporated. But not the mood, entirely.

4

"Where're we bound?" He ran long fingers through his fine dark hair with distaste. Down and straight, he was careful about his appearance. He was a mess and he knew it.

"Get clean and comfortable. The captain will ask to see us before skip one. He knows you are a linguist, so don't play games."

Jade made a gesture, lost on the Rafalan but satisfying to his inner self, and stripped off the clothes he had slept in.

Lean and taut as the dancer he had once been, he stepped into the washer, sluiced in warm detergent and cool rinse. He spread arms and legs as the warm air blew him dry and pumps sucked up the moisture to return it to the system. Hair, flowing finally clean, wove a silk screen to his hips, and he moved his head to enjoy the texture against his skin, an unconscious gesture as familiar to Heglit as the yellow eyes, telling him the man was returned and himself. Dark tights were drawn over long legs, a green tunic pulled over the head, leaving chest and arms bare, belted snug about the lean waist with a wide belt of scarlet fnat leather. The feet were left bare, Jade's way on board ship. He sat on the couch to brush his hair, ready to hear his companion. It was ritual.

"The ship is the Centra Zar, bound for TaLur Sector. A ComUn special run. Fast."

"Why TaLur?" Jade asked around upraised arms, not meaning only the ship's business.

"There is a cargo of plague serum." And the other answer. "No Rafalan has been so far in on this limb."

In. Toward Centra. Looking through the veil of his hair flowing across the brush, Jade watched his companion. Always in. Why? Only to go, as far as he could tell. Because it was there, maybe. Gleest, who could tell what anything meant to a Rafalan? He wouldn't ask again. The first hundred times he had, as they moved in, down the spiral arm from the Rafalan Sector, he got the same answer. "We are restricted, held to our home space, while the galaxy goes on without us, though we are of human stock. We need to know. You cannot understand because you are Clate."

Clate. Class A type. Typed by what, or who, he didn't

know. But Clate's were (if tradition meant anything) authors of the Federation, founders of the farflung Commerce Union that wove a million worlds (Clate and marginal Clate) together in economic interdependence. So what was a Clate? He didn't know. He was only himself, drifter, worker, happy being. One of thousands of young men and women from hundreds of worlds, unfamilied, conceived (probably) in some ComUn port joyhouse for the price of an hour's fun, deserted at some forgotten age, growing up untethered as a starsail, learning any trade for food and shelter. He had been lucky, he supposed, when he thought about it. He lived, learning dancing and acrobatics as a child, and later trading on a hard-edged beauty, feeding his hungers and learning to understand (by necessity) the hungers of others. He lived. He learned. He even enjoyed. Until he left ship on Oren (already a bonded Linker) and the port jobber tried to kill him for no reason he could tell but signing on the available list. And Heglit had come cool and quiet and broken a neck in one hand and looked at him a while without asking why.

On Everwait Twin it had been a ship's captain. First the attack, then the alarm, and the miracle of Heglit (twice murderer now) being there, taking him on to the Rafalan ship to outwit the authorities. Making a debt. And an offer.

"You're a Linker." The Rafalan said the obvious, making some obscure point. "And Clate."

"Listed me. Yes." Staying with the lowspeak until Heglit told him hispeak was easier to understand and more natural to him anyway.

"How could you tell?"

But Heglit ignored that. "What do you know of Rafal?"

"Nothing. Just came out from Togol because there was a place on ship for a Linker. I've heard you Rafalan are master Linkers."

"Yes. But we cannot outsector. Unless we are partnered Clate."

The point was no longer obscure. "I'm a loner."

"Long skips, the hot ones, are only open to teams."

Yeah. Well, that was true. True too, that for no reason he could think of (unless it was personal, he had not always been nice to his patrons) someone or two out here near Rafal Sector wanted him dead. And he had no reason not to team with the Rafalan.

"Ship Linkers to captain's quarters."

The unexpected voice brought Jade up, hair knotted smoothly against his nape. He didn't let it hang loose any more in public. He followed Heglit out into unfamiliar territory. He hadn't seen anything but their quarters so far. It was, he thought, a rather large ship, with a crew of probably no more than the minimum ComUn seven (five of them superfluous). But it was well-kept and clean.

The captain was more obviously Clate than Jade, with his straight-set blue eyes and pink skin. Typical career ComUn, Jade thought. And he didn't like Rafalans. Only once, when they came in behind the steward, did he look at Heglit, blue eyes widening, then going unfocused, and there was just enough of a bump in his formal movements to say he was jolted. From then on he looked at Jade, or the floor, or the three ringed fingers of his right hand. His hair was short, a cluster of tight curls fitting his round head.

"You work as a full team, Linker Jade?"

"Yes." And, feeling Heglit's flat eyes, "Sir. Watch on watch, with full shared privileges." He got that in, anyway. They were invited to sit, after a slight hesitation, and he waited one beat, prolonging the motion of sitting so Heglit was actually seated first, and dammit, he was doing it anyway. He could feel Heglit knowing it. He missed nothing. Ever.

"You understand we have a priority run to TaLur Sector. Tel IX has reported two suspicious deaths, so time is a factor. We have a choice of skip channels to that sector. I'd like to take the hot one."

That was Linker choice, and he knew it. But, with two Linkers rostered, if he had to ask that meant the hot one was a real bastard. Cocky Jade was, and knowing it, but not stupid. "How hot is hot?"

Turloz shot him a look, then played with his rings. "Very hot," was no answer, and his little fidgety movements said there was more. It came slower. "In fact, we don't know. For sure. Two shippers have recently reported a new channel that gates in TaLur Sector."

Heglit reacted to this, head lifting a fraction, and for some reason Jade felt a chill across his lower back.

"New channel?"

"Yes. Just reported in the last few stanmonths. It cut eight hours off the first run, and either eleven or eighteen off the second. There was no other run as far as we can tell. The gate was found equidistant to the gates for Malhil and Rohdin sector channels." He turned to his table for a folder. "This is the data I was able to get. I'd like you to read it and give me your answer as soon as you can."

He stood up, and so did the Linkers. "We take the regular channel skips to the sector breakout in M2LH. I'd like to know by then."

"You'll have it." Jade could feel a frown creasing his forehead and he forgot to open the door for Heglit.

"M2LH is in the wrong quadrant," he said in the passageway. And Heglit looked at him calmly. "Well, isn't it?"

"It's not the usual breakout point for TaLur runs."

"Heglit—" Shrugging, he kept quiet until they were back in their quarters. "There can't be a new channel just like that," he decided, reaching up to dislodge the knot of hair, shaking his head quickly, telling Heglit he was upset. The Rafalan, thinking nothing visible, watched the cascade of hair and took up the folder.

Jade was annoyed, and made no effort to hide it. A feeling started somewhere in him that there was something not right about this run-skip. This gleesting bit about a new channel just didn't make any kind of sense, unless he was completely misinformed. The channels were detectable lines of force, like gravity or magnetism, a frequency of something that permeated the galaxy like light, but had bonding lines in a sort of three-dimensional web linking areas of balanced energy. By matching that frequency, the ship could travel through the flow from one point to another. The theory was only vaguely understood, as far as he knew, and he had never really made an effort to study it. But the whole idea seemed to demand the channels were part of the natural structure of the galaxy. And so far that had held true. Therefore, there could not be any new channel. Unless they were something else entirely.

8

Heglit was reading the papers, and would not talk to him until he had something to say, so Jade prowled about the confines of their cabin, began finally to exercise, forcing his supple form into tortuous unnatural postures, a habit formed before he was a Linker when he depended on his grace and looks for support. Besides, it felt good when he stopped. He lay on his couch finally, breathing deep, enjoying the mild euphoria of his own warm flesh.

Heglit broke his silence finally. A new channel was possible, he decided. Two ships had gone into the Star Web expecting to get someplace else and ended up in the TaLur Sector. One of the ships was one they had worked on just in from the Rafalan Sector.

"Channels don't just come and go," Jade protested.

"As far as we know."

Jade lay back on the couch, drawing one foot up close to his face to examine the nails. He knew he could argue about the channels and get whatever answers Heglit had, but he knew also that anything important had already been considered by the Rafalan, or he would still be talking. So he let it be.

"Last night, or whenever," he mused, changing the subject, "you hijacked me, ruined a good trip." He didn't have to look to feel the weird black eyes on him. "You said you'd tell me how."

"I said I would not tell you about it then," Heglit corrected calmly.

"If I was skipping into a super you'd tell me just like that, wouldn't you?" Annoyed again, and curious.

"I would tell you." Heglit was reasonable and predictable for just that long. "Jade, why do you try all the chemical links?"

That brought the man up to sit crosslegged, facing the Rafalan, golden eyes narrow. Heglit just didn't ask questions like that that often. "I guess it's for the territory, a whole other place to be. Why?"

"Why what?"

"Why do you ask, I guess. You don't usually."

"To make you aware of it. You're flying every port now. On edge spot. What does it do for you?"

"Pleasures me." Fake and brittle he grinned, twisting up his hair. Heglit only looked at him. Jade let the question drift back into his head where he knew it would hang

9

around to ambush him. He read the notes the captain had given them on the new channel and thought about the skip. Something in him not concerned with safety and survival began to get excited. A hot channel, wild. Eagerness was spinning a ball under his ribs around a bright little core of fear. Always like this, the expectation building until— His muscles tensed slightly and he breathed deep and slow, conquering reaction, began stretching slow and hard, just to the point of pain, pulling out the excitement until the rush of blood was caress pleasure inside out.

"Hey!"

Heglit looked up from wherever he had been in his quiet.

"I was going to rent me some joy-skinner in port. You owe me."

"You made the wrong first choice." A man would have smiled; Heglit simply went back into his quiet.

"Linkers, skip one, first call." The flat voice heard a thousand times on a hundred ships spoke into the room, putting them back on the job. Heglit stood up.

"The captain will want to talk to you. I'll take first skip."

Jade shrugged, but followed along. "I want to see the Link-room first."

It was good, better than most, quiet, and equipped with new insulation and soft color-change lights that could be dialed to fit the mood of the Linker. And there were two Link-chairs.

"Teaching or watch-dogging," Jade guessed, walking around the massive chairs to face the Rafalan. He'd never been in a Link-room with two chairs.

Heglit looked at the man rather than the chairs. "I haven't heard of using them on standard runs in channel."

"What would be the point?" The chairs were the best he'd seen, adjustable for size and position, the Link-masks delicate filigree of platinum and jewels. Seeing them brought the cool-warm feel over the skin of his face and throat.

"Jade." Heglit's voice pulled at him and he saw the Rafalan was, as always, checking the connections. Their sanity, if not their lives, depended on them. Now he

10

fingered the unobtrusive cables leading to the computer that linked the chairs with the sensors of the ship. "Jade, the chairs are cross-linked."

"To what?"

"One another. Not by-pass, but complete circuit."

"But that would mean—" Jade frowned, yellow eyes flashing from the chairs to his companion. "That can't be right."

"Probable shared Link." The hard planes of the face altered slightly. "Possible. Or it could only be to back up the on-Linker to avoid lapses. It's a hot channel he wants."

Jade relaxed something in himself he hadn't known was tight. Heglit must be right. But the question was there. And he asked it. "Would it be possible? Could we share-Link, know how— I mean, well, share it?"

The barest pause made the nod hesitant. "In theory."

Theory. Because it had never been done, not that either of them knew. Not that it couldn't be tried, but who would want to? It was too private. A Linker—as far as he was concerned while in Link—skipped alone. Through his link with the ship's sensors he became the ship. The experience of the channel was his. The rest of the crew depended on him to know what was danger, to keep the ship clear, keep them safe in their ship-womb where walls and air and light and temperature and gravity held them until they were back in N-space and they could believe that was all there was. But the Linker (watcher-feeler-taster-be-er) lived that other place. He alone knew the—

"Skip call two. Techs in ten. Identify Linker." Standard call from the speaker telling them the Link technicians were coming up to adjust the masks and explain the system. Familiar procedure on well-run ships. Many times they were called on to handle the whole thing themselves.

Two techs, one male, the other passable female but skirting the edge of Clate classification, came in. The female talked, giving a clear precise explanation.

"For dead-shipping in channel," she told them, "the code is 'kill.' All systems stop. With no external energy loss. Go-call gives an instant response of eighty percent total capacity."

Jade relaxed a little more. Dead-shipping in channel

was an emergency procedure to be used only when some disturbance set up a reflexive flow in the channel that threatened the ship, or if the Linker felt himself losing control and had to come in to get a fix on being human again. Of if he simply got too damned scared to stay out. Time spent dead in channel gave control to the flow, putting the ship elsewhere with very few indications of just where that elsewhere was. To have eighty percent control of the ship's reflexes and sensory imput in the first instant of Link was as good as could be handled. If it was true, he thought, lying back in the chair so the tech could fit the mask to his face and throat, this was one good ship. The web tingled slightly, pulling him toward ship union, but he knew Heglit was taking it this time.

"Linker Jade to captain when you're free. Report to central command section. Cue me if you need any help finding it." The growing-familiar voice had managed some humanity that time, Jade thought, keying off the clingy Link-mask. He slid out of the chair, glancing at the mask-shielded face across from him, but it was too blind to talk to, so he followed the tech out, knowing Heglit had heard and knew where he was going.

The sight of Heglit in the chair linking with the ship stayed in his mind as he set out for the captain's quarters. Link sharing, he thought, and his belly went tight and strange again. I don't think I could do it, don't think it can be done at all.

He had talked to other Linkers, wondering what it was like for them, especially in his early days. He had their words, words they all used—". . . getting away from that black hole on the Dagon run . . . the twist through the Triffid . . ." Words from out here to talk about the alienness of inside the Star Web where everything was metaphor. They simply had no language for the actual experience. *He* knew a black hole in there, knew how it pulled strands out of the channel web so directions went someplace, trapped, then released unexpectedly. He knew the way a ship skipping a congruent channel could make his path sticky or slick or turbulent enough to toss them toward the (to him) blazing blue of the channel edge and instant disaster. But he didn't know how to talk about it so anyone else could say, yeah, that's how it is . . .

The captain was alone, and there were cups and a TaLurien stone bottle on the table. The outview screen was showing a kaleidoscope pattern, slow soothing folds of color, rather than N-space. The ship was skipping down the channel groove already. Heglit was—

"Ah, Linker. Checked out?"

Jade nodded. "How long's skip?"

"Four hours, max." Turloz was looser, more comfortable without the disturbance of the Rafalan, inviting Jade to sit, offering him a cup of the innocuous but exquisite baDant juice. Jade picked up the cue with the cup. A social visit.

"The Link-room is good."

"Yes. New. Some ideas from ComUn research down in Centra. We picked up the contract to try them out for commercial use."

"Tested?" He'd never heard of any research on the Link system, but it was a big galaxy.

"Of course. We have the test assurances in writing. Even picked up full insurance for this run."

You're lying, Jade thought suddenly, watching the round face. He wanted to ask about the chair link Heglit had discovered, but was suddenly not sure he would be told anything like the real purpose of it. He didn't like Turloz again, but he wasn't sure why. He wished Heglit was here to watch the man talk. He had a feeling something was going to come up, and he didn't think he was going to like it.

When it came it wasn't anything he had been expecting. "You've made an unusual partnership," the captain said, pouring more of the juice.

"We've done all right. Rafalans are the best Linkers in the galaxy, by record and longevity."

"Yes. That's partly why I picked you. You know how important this run is."

"Because it's medical."

"Yes, of course. A lot depends on you. The ship I'm sure about."

"But not me." Jade built a smile and saw the response to it, but he didn't trust it. There was some reason for

13

his being here, getting the soft treatment, and he wanted to know what it was without having to guess at it.

"The run is going to be difficult," the captain told his cup, casually. "Anything I can do to make your time out easier, let me know."

"Like?"

"I thought you might prefer quarters for yourself. I've never bunk-shared with a Rafalan, but I understand they're—" The gesture was delicate and distasteful, and funny coming from him. Jade bit down on his tongue and kept his face straight, not sure if he was going to laugh or get mad.

"They are from human stock." He heard himself say that and wondered a little. He thought he was still undecided about it, for all he'd heard Heglit say it, and even seen him skin out. He was pretty well standard Clate male, all right, except for a slightly strange skin tone, and pretty enough to buy a sponsor. But maybe non-functional, as far as he could tell.

"I assume you are his friend." The voice was cool but there was some other phrase in the eyes, and a lot of curiosity. For some reason that made Jade madder than anything else. He thought of making up something, then controlled himself.

"He's no rodman like a lot of shippers. There's no skin play between us. But there's friendship and life debt. He saved my life twice. I will continue to bunk-mate with him."

"We allow our Linkers their preference by ComUn contract." Frost brittled the lips and Jade wondered suddenly if Turloz had been in the process of suggesting a more personal relationship. "However, I will ask you not to associate with the rest of the crew. Some are not so lenient with Rafalans."

That suited Jade fine. He had only seen one female, and she wasn't enough to make him think any warm thoughts. Anyway, one didn't on a work run. Nothing ran competition with the Link.

The Link. He had to ask about the chairs. Whether he wanted to or not. They had to know.

"The link between the chairs," he said, putting his cup down, "looks like a new system. Is it for watch-dogging?"

"Could be. But with this system it should be possible

14

to share-Link with the ship. The thought was that two heads could be better than one in a really hard channel. And this one is that. The techs would have brought it up before the main skip. ComUn wants to know if it can be done. There's a large bonus in it if you care to try. It should, so I'm told, be quite an experience."

"Quite." Jade didn't smooth out the nastiness in that but Turloz didn't seem to notice. "Have you tried Linking?" he asked.

"Me? Hardly."

"Didn't think so." He stood up, knowing his irony was lost on the man, and not really caring. Turloz nodded slightly, dismissing him, and he made his way out the door. By the time the door slid shut behind him he was already thinking about the Link. Shared. And was suddenly balanced between hilarity and rage. Turloz was too much. Don't bunk with the non-Clate, but please crawl into his head, his feelings, his senses out in the channel. His sudden laughter ran down the corridor ahead of him.

It took a lot of bending and stretching to work out the energy of his anger and he was sweating when Heglit came in.

"How's she handle?"

"Good. The sensors are powered up. I couldn't find any lag."

That, Jade translated, meant she was exceptional. Anything less would have brought forth a simple: "it works."

"You had a social visit with the captain."

"How'd you know it was social?"

"His tradition calls for baDant juice."

"Oh." He wished he knew how Heglit did that.

"You let him make you angry."

"Yes. But he doesn't know it. He forbade me to mix with his crew because I refused to accept separate quarters." He wished Heglit would get mad at that, or smile, or something. He didn't. "It's not just that. He's not telling us something. And then there's the freaking chairs. I don't know. It's a bad run. Oh, and he said the chairs were linked for sharing in channel." He tried to sound casual, but he never knew how much Heglit could tell of what he felt anyway. "Said ComUn wanted to

15

know if it was possible to double link. There's a bonus in it if we do."

Heglit didn't answer that for a long time. He watched the man, picking up his own kind of signals, letting information build.

"It's not the run or the captain. You've not thought about it, Jade," he said finally. "You take the next skip and think about it."

He took it, letting the tech fit him in, blocking out external messages from skin and nose and ears over a core of expectancy, secure with the feather pressure of the mask against lids and cheeks and throat. He heard the door slide shut and lock in a burst of warm glad. It was always like this, the set up, then the wait until the tech cleared. He felt the stud under his finger, and it was the most real thing for him, waiting for the timer to cue him.

He never really heard it. His ears sent the message to his finger and pushed. He gasped, exploding into sight-sound-feel-taste-smell, rushing out through the ship's sensors, bigger, higher, freer, feeling for balance and learning all she was, in the intimacy of this supersensory expansion. The universe shivered, parted, as the ship skipped over the threshold of N-space and leapt into the channel. He dove down, slashed up the slow curving glide, and energy squeezed lush pastels against thighs-hips-sides. Firefly flakes of silver topaz streamed against his up-turned face, through spread fingers, over chest, belly, and groin, and power surged, lifting him. Always this, but seldom so clean and sweet. Joy, he thought, curving his body fluid and clean about the pressure of pale blue sliding up beneath him. A ship counter-skipping, his mind said absently as he began the super-free sky-dance, feeling for the currents and eddies that elsewhere were solid planets, a chaos of dust, blazing nuclear pits of suns. Twisting, diving, racing in free sensuous curves and rolls, he swam the center current of silvered amber thereness until the current parted and he flashed free, open, into black quiet and drifted, complete, replete, and buoyant.

The end-tone was still vibrating in his ears as he moved to key the mask loose, and as it dropped away he still tasted laughter in his mouth. UnLinked, he sat in the comfortable chair, replaying it in his head. She was super. The best he'd ever had. Sheer unadulterated joy.

Then, think about it. About Link sharing. Having someone else with you when— Would you know they were there? Would Heglit know how it was for him in Link?

Then the other question hit, and he blinked. Would he know how it was for Heglit? The big wild rush, the joy laughing ballsy fun of it? Heglit who seemed to feel nothing, not joy or hurt or needs or— What was it like for him?

He left the Link-room thoughtfully, knowing there would be no more regular skips until they reached the new gate and went through for TaLur Sector. And they had to talk about that.

One thing, Heglit was easy to talk to. He never reacted enough to make anyone pull back. Jade laid out his thoughts about the possibility of sharing a subjective experience.

"Possible. To some degree," Heglit agreed quietly. "Otherwise even a watcher would not know if there was trouble in the Link."

Until the ship died, Jade thought. "But there's a question, isn't there? Like how different are we?"

"That is a question." Black eyes held him for a moment saying nothing he could hear. "If the differences are extreme might we not get tangled in that and lose the ship."

"Huh-uh. *I* could get tangled up. Right?"

"Jade, do not mistake me on purpose."

"But you have the controls—"

"Of a kind. As you have physical discipline and graces. And you use it in Link. The Link transmits to the brain, which interprets the channel physically as subjective reaction."

"For you?" He couldn't have kept the surprise out of his voice with a chair in his mouth.

"Of course. Linkers actually run the channel in their own experience, they don't consciously take a ship through."

All right. True. Still— Questions tumbled around in his thoughts, but he didn't ask. Two years of Heglit didn't gift any freedoms he knew about.

"What if—" He stopped, frowning, and Heglit waited,

17

watching him marshal his thoughts. "Wouldn't it bother you? I mean, my reactions?"

"Or mine you?" The dark eyes didn't drift as he let his knowledge of the question become common property. "There is no way to know until it is done. We do have the right of refusal."

Jade folded himself up on the couch, pulling bare feet into his lap, thumbs stroking the high arches. "Be smarter to try in an easy channel."

"There would be more time and attention to put on the process of linking." Heglit pressed the button that would bring the steward with their meal. "I think sharing the Link would give us more ability in a bad channel. The mind should react automatically to it, without defining authority."

Logical. But Jade couldn't get laid back. This thing was going to change the skip for him, that was the big thing. And he didn't want that.

The meal came and he ate around the tightness that kept trying to take over his middle. He was a little surprised when he talked again.

"Heglit, do you enjoy it? The Link?" He hadn't meant to say that, looked like the words had spilled out onto his plate. He dared, finally, to look up at the Rafalan.

"Yes," Heglit said. Calm. Always calm. Like: of course.

Jade was quickly annoyed. "So do it us. And maybe fail. What then?"

Heglit ignored the intentional slip into lowspeak. "Failure is a possibility. If anything goes bad the system will dead-ship and one of us can draw out. We will have learned something by trying."

And learned nothing by not trying. He didn't say that, it didn't need saying. Jade knew it. But knowing it didn't make him feel any better. He looked at the Rafalan and knew they would not speak of whether or not to try again. If he said anything more Heglit would only ignore him. Unless he said either yes or no. That would be all of it. And he couldn't say no unless he had a reason, something he could talk about. He couldn't say yes, either. So he didn't say anything, just let it go. Knowing that was the same answer.

He stayed on his couch while Heglit read, not talking, not sharing anything. And then the light was off, giving them time to get the sleep they would need. And in the dark it was worse, all the thoughts the light kept out came to bother him. Like burnout. It happened to Linkers. And the sharing—try it once, he thought. Sure. But it was his head. Try it once, and maybe never do it again. Ever. He lay in the dark knowing Heglit lay across the small cabin. Soundless. Always. Never a snore, an unconscious night sound. He never dreamed, never ran scared of phantoms, or got jerked off by his fantasies. But I'm scared. I don't want to Link with him and get laughed at. Or maybe worse.

"It's the unknown, Jade. You're fighting maybes."

The unexpected voice made his thighs and belly jerk and then he heard his heart beating slow and hard in his ears. Was Heglit lying awake thinking like he was? *No. My restlessness woke him. And why am I scared?* Because the Star Web skip was the most important thing in his life. It was what he was always hungry for. And it was his, more even than the outside him was his.

2

Heglit watched him come into the Link-room. Just black eyes watching like they always did. But Jade's neck tightened. Heglit doesn't want me to Link with him, he thought, surprised. Then double surprised because his own not-wanting was the strongest non-erotic straight feel he had ever felt out of channel, and his face felt red and hot. He actually hesitated at the chair.

"Skip in sixty." The boxed-up voice grated against the tension.

"We should Link before skip, Jade. Or the search for differences could throw us off."

"Right." Those damned black eyes nailed him to the floor.

"Jade. Don't start out angry. It could hurt us."

How did he always know? But the mild chastisement worked. Anger fell into warm contrition, and to show he could handle it he moved into the chair, pulled the mask over his head . . .

Cool-drift, quiet feel of N-space fell over him like fog. His brain automatically adjusted; the drift of free atoms like stray drops of rain on bare skin, hair loose and cool-soft on back, stirring over buttocks— Remembering there should be differences, lazing here in the cool jeweled black, he let occassional thoughts dirft by, dust motes in the glory of the universe—

His hair was gone.

No. It flowed, photon-waved, as usual.

Wait. Hair/no hair. The mutual exclusion stretched him wider, larger— What the Rim—?

Jade?

Oh. Wait a flash. Heglit? Say again.

Jade.

20

Thought so. Heglit's voice. Except— Rich-warm, sigh-singing inside out. Where was the hard flat sound?

"Heglit." He talked from someplace that had no mouth he could recognize, but it seemed to work. "Did you say my name?"

"Yes. Strange (interesting) verbal sense. Not using outside (mouth-lips). Telepathy?"

"Can't exist in pure verbal form."

Heglit laughed. *Laughed?* Wonder clasped the ship-skin Link so he faded, came back quick.

"Sorry."

"The hair. You skip with it loose?"

"Guess so." Heglit did not ask questions like that. "You feel it? I can't feel anything different."

"I feel it. Interesting. I'm not very body-conscious in cool-drift maybe."

All the warm should-be qualities wove into the voice. Amazing. "It's not so bad."

"We're not responding yet, Jade. I feel your agility like some kind of balance, a difference."

Then they were in and there was no time for acquaintance. Like shooting lava rapids, heavy, hot and fast. And blue veils of danger sweeping into the rush so he ducked, twisted, dove down, over, around, and it's the crookedest damn channel— Purple blazed up, cymbals against his silver shipskin, and a laughter big as the Core God— Nowhere to go—

Duck, Jade! Watch! Power crushed his quivering torso, kicked legs hands scalded shoulders bunched, heaved, leapfrogging the nothing cloud that snapped too late hungry for the silver ship.

Hot Damn! How—?

Later. Blue veils smoking along sweated flanks— Twist, slip— Fall a million years into—

Banshee chorus of strings and crazy horns screaming either danger or safety.

Run, Jade! Laugh-bellowing, muscles flexing, he/they swam up/down naked skin(s) sweated with fear excitement, crashing through cinnamon clouds . . . *A cappella* choirs of drift— Further faster than he could skip had skipped— Colors overturned, became sound shrieking male bass happy groaning hornings and Heglit's words sang and shouted cascades of—

21

STOP! Stop stopstopstopstop—

Wrong wrongwrongwrong—

Down in the belly of the metal ship he groaned and stirred against the web, wanting to scream, but the ship had no mouth he could find—

Jade?! Surf-racing, concern drowning channel twists, pressing him down and down to black.

Heglit's skipping, he thought, echoing an emptiness. He was overriding me. God, I can think in words. I'm okay. Just turned off, somehow. Where the hell had Heglit put him anyway? He reached out, feeling for his legs, hips, ribs, felt the shuddering silver shipskin melt, thrust him out to the roar of energies screaming blue, close to sweating elbow. He twisted away to the chill-hurry of channel center. Rough! Eddies tried to curve him back to the blue shore. Muscles tensed, held—

Thanks.

Don't leave like that— Jade— *Dive!*

Command irrelevant to the situation, Heglit dove— Down. A tongue of black flame roared out narrow, curling about the streaking shape(s) hot. Heglit sang, roaring laughter, and the tongue lashed— Instinct took over. Jade lept, twisting, reaching, bending double, snapping straight, curved, slid through the spiraled energy to a still-water float space.

That was me, he thought. I did that. And he knew the Heglit-shape of him could never have done it. The mind learned from the body's ability, too, and Heglit wasn't that pliable . . .

Or was it Heglit knowing that? No matter. Truth was.

Currents tugged, non-directional but conflicting, too many areas— A protest shaped itself in muscular denial, power to hold, to maintain, rose up, countering his fluid grace. Obstinate power. Good. He would have had to ride the currents, feeling his way. This was better.

The ship steadied, quivering but unmoved, held— Dropped sickeningly into a gulf bottomed vivid blue. Jade spread out, curved, swandiving, skimming heat across chest and belly and thighs, planed, gliding, using the hungry power to swing up, away, safe—

Again and again, endlessly trading, merging, wrongside outs until he felt he wore Rafalan skin and flesh, knew

22

the body-feel strange-familiar— There were times of chaos, of not knowing, just doing, gestalt, creating impossible combinations of strength and pliability, and coming apart, spent and gasping, dizzy, until the burning blue veils burned—

Sometimes Jade thought he couldn't continue, muscles relaxed a moment, jerked, his lower back ached dull and heavy beneath the silken flow of his hair—

Rest. Jade. Get out a while—

"No" washed against his throat. He could rest here a little, ready, lulled by the bobbing current, floating in Heglit's strength, dozing even, like being held safe.

He didn't know for real when they burst the membrane into N-space— Heard-felt Heglit's soft sound of relief and they fell apart weak and limp like spent lovers— He jumped away from that thought and heard rich laughter racing down the halls of normal space. Nonsense. Rafalans didn't laugh—

Of course they do. And cry and—

Sweat-soaked muscles aching with a phantom pain born in a brain that said it was all real, he realized he was sitting in the Link-chair, mask sticky against skin. A bath. Yes. Oh yes. His hands tried to come up and take off the Link-mask but shook too hard.

"Jade?" Hoarse solid sound.

Yeah, he thought, remembering when that worked like talk.

"Jade—" Closer, and feel of being touched made him flinch, oversensitive all over, bruised and burned from the blue fires, the shrieking black sound reaching—

The mask peeled back from his face, letting cool canned air touch him. He opened his eyes and light brought a tiny residual reaction, then he saw Heglit, big and lean, bending a little, reaching to touch—

"I hurt, Heglit—" he whispered, and tasted blood on his lips and started to see. The Rafalan face drawn tight, sunken and gray, black eyes glassy with fatigue.

"Okay. I'm okay." Except for cramping muscles and tremors that wouldn't let him move, would knock him down if he tried to stand up. "You. How—?"

"I'm all right." But he was leaning on the chair, and the mask in his hand whispered softly, trembling, and his shirt was dark-striped with sweat.

"I didn't know you could sweat," he thought-said, surprised, then ashamed because he heard himself say it.

"All human stock perspire—"

"Shut up!" Hissed, and he was shaking violently, teeth clenched, skin iced by another sweat.

"Breathe deep, Jade. What was the last port?"

"C'Erit. You— Were there—"

"The last chem-link?"

"Thana— No, wait— Shiva Pearls. Right." It was a trick, but it worked, making him think, respond. The shaking eased and he started to warm up.

Heglit moved, began to walk back and forth between the chairs. Loosening up. Jade tried, but felt hurt and beaten up. It was work. He made his muscles flex and stretch against the stiffness.

"Twenty-four hours," Heglit said, looking up at the blue glow of the chronometer.

"We made it."

"What scared you?"

The question slammed him out of the ordinary and he stared at the Rafalan. He always meant something— What had scared him? Something he remembered— "Oh." Wide-eyed, shivering, he hugged himself. "I— uh, I heard you laugh." Stupid dumb thing. "No. I felt— I know how laughing feels to you. Once there—"

"You thought I could not?"

"Well, I mean, you never do. Out here. Now I think maybe you laugh a lot in there where you live—"

Heglit looked at him a little. "Skip-sharing is more union than sharing. We will not see one another as before."

"So. I kind of liked you in there." And that was honest enough to make him want to cry. He wanted to get away from that, fast. And Heglit made it easy for him, not saying anything, knowing he didn't want to see anyone else for a while, not until he was really back from the skip. They were used to doing for themselves, there was no need to call for the techs. Heglit logged them out on the comp and they left the room, going back to their shared quarters. Tired, more tired than from any skip Jade could remember. All he wanted to do was lie down and not move.

He drifted, looking for sleep, but thoughts kept chasing

through his head, pulling his eyes open to look at the ceiling, and he tried to avoid getting too close to that freaking shared skip, the immense power and pleasure of it, the mind blowing *ability*, totally without fear. He had been in his element. And (for all his earlier fear) shared it so easily with—

"Jade." The familiar voice jerked him awake. He sat up, groggy, feeling gummy with sleep and not showering.

"What?"

"Are you awake?"

"Yeah. About." He looked around over his hand, stifling a yawn, and even before Heglit spoke he sensed a trouble. "What time is it?"

"You slept an hour. Something is not right with the ship. We're dead in N-space."

"What? Damage?"

"Not from skip. We would have known. But I can't raise the techs or the captain."

That brought him awake, made him start thinking. Turloz might ignore Heglit, but— "We better see."

Silence out in the corridor, and, like never before, feeling the big metal bulk of the ship around them, a thing that could not, should not, be still, not out here where only movement by intent implied life. The floor, cold and somehow alien, jarred Jade's heels as he headed for the captain's cabin. And he wasn't going to think about whys.

There was no answer to his knock and Heglit stood big and solid behind him so he had to palm the plate and slide the door back. Turloz sat in his chair. He did not look up.

"Captain," he said quietly.

The man jerked, one hand slashing up to his eyes.

"Captain." Louder.

Turloz screamed, both hands covering his eyes. He cowered in the chair, moaning, "—mub-mub-mub— go— stop—" Or something sounding like it.

With a quick heart thudding look around for Heglit, Jade moved toward the man, touched him— Jumped back as he screamed and leapt away, knocking the chair back. He ran full stride into the wall and collapsed, moaning thick mushy sounds.

"Rim," Jade whispered. "He's spaced out. Or sick. What'll we do?"

"Leave him. Come."

They ran now, down the empty corridor toward the tech's quarters, heard whispers and swearing, two-voiced nonsense. They looked at one another and did not go in. The Algoran, first met on the field, was unconscious. Steward—

"He's dead," Jade said, sounding mad because that was better than yielding to the terror he felt flitting around the corners of his mind. The steward had been fairly young and he had apparently beaten himself to death against the plasteel wall. His forehead was dished in and felt like loose gravel when Jade touched it. The eyes stared up like painted glass around a dried-blood stiff strand of hair.

"And the rest—"

"Are mentally non-functional." Heglit looked at the corpse with his usual expression. None.

"Now what? The aid-signal?" It was the universal and solitary survival feature of all ComUn skip-ships. If they were lucky enough to be in N-space when trouble struck, they could holler for help on a wide broadcast beam and hope someone heard them before air and water were used beyond reclamation.

But the Rafalan was thinking other thoughts. "This should not have happened. The danger should have been ours."

True. They were the ones exposed to the unfiltered fact of the channel. In here the shielding of the ship should have kept it like N-space. Somewhat sluggishly, Jade began to think, to see the inside-outness of the mystery. There was, in both theory and practice, no way for the Web channel to affect an unlinked crew. It simply couldn't touch them. So what had happened inside while they were hooked up to the ship?

A sudden thought touched him as they moved back down the corridor. "Hey." A chill pushed down his flanks and he looked at his companion. "How do we know this is real?"

Heglit thought that over for a minute looking back toward the crew quarters. "We assume, Jade. But I

26

think you would be more qualified than most to recognize illusion."

"Oh." Sure. As long as he knew it *could* be. All right. He could accept that and watch for clues. "So what do we do?"

"Nothing. Until we have more information. I think the captain had more than he gave."

"But that's against ComUn regs," Jade protested, and felt the silent look reminding him that he hadn't trusted the captain.

Turloz lay against the wall, curled tight and fetal. Jade had seen that before. He was withdrawing from something, from everything. Heglit ignored him, searching the room quickly for papers and finding none. They went out, toward the control room.

"The way he reacted to your voice," Heglit said, thoughtfully.

"Crazy. He acted scared. He—" Then he remembered the thing Heglit must mean. "He covered his eyes." Sensory confusion. Blown cortex. Reacting to sound as visual stimulus. And the steward, reacting to physical sensation as maybe sound, or smell, even taste—

"But that's the stuff we handle in channel." The sensory mix that Linkers somehow had a talent for manipulating intuitively. Something a part of them that so far could not be taught. It just was.

Heglit nodded and entered the nerve center of the ship. Here were all the signals of their mechanized existence, showing the ship was alive but without order or direction. Outview screens reported a visual image of the outside the way it was now, the diamonded black of N-space. This was a place Jade seldom visited, now. Once, long ago, Reese had let him stay in the control room, let him learn and practice and ask questions . . . He looked around with interest as Heglit slid into the command chair before the command-comp and asked for a report. A casual voice, male, reported a successful breakout to N-space, gave various reports on ship status (not involving the crew) and position, correcting for drift, and asked for the coordinates for their destination.

"Shouldn't that be programmed already?" Jade asked.

"Not if he wasn't sure of his breakout point." Heglit punched in a request for exact spatial relationships, using codes Jade had learned so long ago he had nearly forgotten them. The navicomp flashed a map on one view panel and traced their position, first in a major segment of the galactic arm, then fining it down, giving them a complete picture of their present position relative to both C'Erit and TaLur Sectors.

· A long way, Jade thought, bemused by the moving lines and simulators. They'd apparently skipped by four major sectors.

He watched Heglit program the new coordinates and order a hold, then lean back in the chair.

"The ship is, except for us, derelict," he said, watching the outviewers. Jade agreed, wondering. "Under law a dead ship is salvageable by first claim."

"Claim and cost of grounding," Jade corrected. Then the idea flashed. "Us?"

"We can bring her in. You were apprenticed pilot." Tactful. "Was, yes. But we aren't authorized—"

"Sector watch should pick up our signal with an hour time-lag."

Jade thought about it. It sounded so wild— But only because he'd never thought of it before. Still, if the crew was non-functional— It could happen. Realizing that took his breath a little. There would be an investigation of course, but— "They could correct our coordinates and tag us down. Verify the situation for us. They could even register the claim for us," he said, soft, holding his excitement. "The standard value claim is—"

"No value claim, Jade. The ship." Solid.

"Ship." Dumbly. But inside something leapt up shouting yes, oh yes, the *ship* . . .

"It would be easier. They do not like value claims beyond real cargo worth."

True enough. And medical cargoes were not worth all that much. It was possible. He had once registered his apprenticeship with ComUn shipper Captain Reese, and Heglit— "You know enough to qualify, too, don't you?"

"Technically. But restricted." Flat.

"Right. But how, I mean, if you never expected—?"

"We were taught young and well, on the chance that one of us might outwit ComUn law and be able to take advantage of the opportunity."

Jade looked at him and shook his head. There was so

much he didn't know about him (and so much now he did).

There was no more discussion. Heglit never hesitated. The signal went out requesting aid and information, and they waited.

Two long hours later the voice spoke, wispy with galactic static and TaLur-accented. Their message had been received and a watch-ship was homing on their signal. Did they need a pilot?

Jade acknowledged the communication, giving his qualifications and making claim on the ship. His position as Linkman placed him outside the crew proper, so he was acceptable. He stated his intent to ground the ship himself and agreed to follow a pacer to avoid trouble.

By the time the conversation was finished the lag-time had dropped to short minutes, and by the time the requested coordinates were fed into the navicomp they had visual contact.

They followed the pacer in quick and clean. Coming in, swinging around to tail down in the grab-beam was a little tense, but the commandcomp was good. They came in quiet and easy and got a good word from the pacer that set down behind them.

The claim for salvage was standard, witnessed by the Falleen Dal, the sector watch-ship, and the ComUn port authority caught the claim as it came in, signalling the Centra Zar to remain in lift status until someone could get out to investigate. There was always the danger of some unexpected and virulent organism aboard, or, more likely, someone trying to rip off a cargo.

The ComUn official was a Centra standard Clate, light hair and blue blue eyes. Very official. And he would not speak to the Rafalan.

"You came out of link and found this?" He indicated the crew, seen once and briefly, with a flick of his hand. "What was your Link-mate about?"

"Linked him. In channel." Jade never blinked. "Watch-dogging me. Double-chaired ship." He felt Heglit's eyes on him but he kept up the character, offering to show the Link-room. The ComUn official declined. He only called for medical personnel to come to the ship to examine the crew and transport them to a quarantine facility, and told Heglit and Jade to stay around the port.

The ship would be thoroughly inspected, the crew examined, and they would be notified of ComUn's decision on their claim in four days. Standard procedure, he assured Jade. Then he was gone.

Jade wanted out to breathe the new air, see the new port, to really be on TaLur Tel IX. Heglit said nothing. He stayed on board.

The port, like ComUn ports on most worlds, had been built so long ago no one remembered when it hadn't been there. There were some different kinds of people, natives of this sector, but not different enough to claim Jade's attention. He was caught up in realizing this wasn't really like every other port. He had come here changed. Already in his thoughts the Centra Zar was theirs. He was no longer a free-lance Linker looking for a good run. He was a shipper. A Free-shipper at that. One of the elite. And knowing that was an already excitement getting in the way of his usual urge toward the standard pleasures available. This was new and big. He wandered about the sameness of the port district, looking, thinking a new kind of dream, and saw no one he knew for sure. *Their ship*. And the growing dream brought him back while the yellowish sun still hung above the rugged inland peaks.

The ship was empty of crew and cargo and he found Heglit in the command center, sitting before the commandcomp.

"Been here looking yet?" he asked, pulling him away from a readout.

"Some. They will be back tomorrow. Early."

"Find anything?"

"They did not. I did." He got up, leading the way to the Link-room. "The time is wrong. And there are other things that are not as they should be. Turloz did not tell us the truth."

"She is—wasn't fit?"

Heglit shook his head. "More than fit. But different. And maybe he did not know how different."

"He paid. Did you find out what flashed them?"

Again the head shake. "There was no physical damage to the ship. No malfunction. I think the answer is in the chronometer. But I don't understand it yet."

Jade looked at the time band on the face of the Link

system comp. "It's wrong." He echoed the Rafalan's earlier statement. The glowing numbers read eight-twenty-seven-eleven. The port time, remembered because it was new and different to him, had slipped from the standard double-barred one to a blocky two while he watched it. That would mean a twenty-three-hour difference in the standard thirty-hour ship day used on all ComUn ports. And the port time was automatically coded into the ship comps when the beam picked them up for grounding. Twenty-three hours . . . Unless he was going the wrong way. Maybe it was only six hours off. Trying to juggle the numbers confused him slightly and he gave it up, looking at Heglit, feeling the hard eyes locked on him.

"It's not wrong, Jade."

"Sure it is. The port—"

"Look at your wrist timer."

He had nearly forgotten he wore one (picked up on some port or another because he had the credit) because he never paid much attention to the time unless he had to make ship. He glanced down to see the tiny green numbers flicker to eight-thirty-one-oh-one. "But—"

Heglit held out his own wrist. Jade looked and his belly went cold for no reason he could name.

"How come they're all wrong?" His yellow eyes begged for some kind of sense he could handle.

"Not wrong. I checked the Link-timer. And all three agree. Not wrong. But different. I wanted you to see before I changed it."

"Why?"

"So the port authority won't see it."

"I mean why are they like this?" His voice was a little tight, and something in his head felt stretched, almost like hurting, but different. He didn't like it.

"I don't know yet. Only that somehow we lost twenty-three hours."

"Lost—" Ready to laugh, he was nailed down by the dark eyes and something in his head that stretched tighter.

"I ran back checks all the way to departure time logged off C'Erit. Everything tallies until we logged into the Star Web on skip three, forty-seven hours before breakout into N-space. But we only spent twenty-three hours in channel."

31

"Impossible." His mouth felt dry and his head really started to hurt. "There's a mistake in—"

"Jade—"

"Dammit, you can't rod around with time!"

"The facts stand. We, and the ship, are twenty-three hours younger than—"

"No."

"Yes, Jade. It has to be. It's the only answer. We could not have survived over forty hours in channel. Somehow, when we were in channel—"

The tightness in Jade's head snapped. "Crazy you!" he yelled, twisting the sudden gut-wrenching fear into rage, running out, away from the dark eyes, the seeing mask that never said anything but words. Running to the familiar, the tumultuous smoke-wild half-light of the joyhouse, and Z'Atua bright flames over his tongue while his yellow eyes ran, seeking corners and quiet talk-islands in the storm of hurry-up fun. Experience guided, and the squat blue-leather shape of a baDant shipper held the purse, the vial, the quick silver grains.

He dropped flight into the churning fear in his throat (wasn't Heglit always right?) and found a corner away from the light that would get loud too fast. And remembered Turloz. That scared him more. He got up, fast, trying too late to change his mind. But the taste of the hard wooden floor oozed treacle over his lower lip and a hard word of warning as he bumped someone flashed smoky loops of glistening green against his face, bursting into his nose like dry pepper. He fought it, not remembering he shouldn't, standing taut and stare-eyed at the sounds, the multi-colored shafts spearing the expanding space around him.

"No—" Tried to say. But his tongue, turgid and sensitive, butted the walls of the cave that trapped it, escaped slowly to rub a minor discordancy against his lower lip. He lifted a hand to hide the strangeness his tongue had become, but the glowing skeletal frame came up too fast from the aurora of someone's laugh.

"Stop—!" He tried. But the ess flew out scalding, drawn out and out, flickering dragon-flame, smoking, and his lips scorched, flaked, blowing ashes into his eyes. He shook his head, hard, to clear it. A mistake. He felt his brain slop around in the viscous boiling blood inside his skull, dizzying him, revolving until he could only see out of his left ear, watching tiny red and blue worms of sound wriggle over and into the wall beside him.

"Bad skip!" The words, understood somehow, tumbled at him, square solid pillows of color . . .

Movement clanged gongs in his ear, blinding him, so he only vaguely felt the black flames circle-scorching his arms. Then night-cool air laced string-solo wires through his head, pulling his brain back out through his eyes. A pin-prick on his shoulder tasted sour, and the sour spread, leaving a sweetness like baDant juice, flowing, flowing, nice, easing the idiocy of his terror, leading him to a safe dark where he could curl up and go to sleep.

3

He woke quick, some distant alarm saying time had passed, a big forgotten block of it. Important. If he could remember—

"You wake, Linker Jade. Or is it Free-man now?"

The voice, cool, mock-polite, startled his eyes open. He sat up, tried to, but his wrists were bound against the bed, jerking him back. A minute more he struggled before he understood he could not move. Then he looked around.

The man, nearly classic Clate, stood near his right shoulder, robed in electric green.

"What is?" Jade growled, more puzzled than alarmed. "What's doing you?"

"Games. Even now." The pale face smiled to show perfect white teeth, blue eyes wrinkling narrow with humor. "You made it so easy for me, young man. I appreciate that. Maybe my luck will hold, and you will speak with me of a thing or two." The gentle quizzical expression was a touch overdone.

Jade stared, trying to make some desperate sense of this, wondering if it was real or—? You would be able to tell, Heglit had told him last time he asked that question. So. Maybe. But where was he? How had he got here? And why?

"You may, after our talk, wish to extend our acquaintance," the stranger said, moving down a little so Jade could see him without twisting his neck. "I am Lurz, of Adlistr VII, Burkoze Sector."

Lurz. The name meant nothing to him. He said as much.

Lurz shrugged. "No matter. You will know me."

"Where am I?" Jade asked finally, starting to actively dislike the handsome face. "And why?"

34

"So. It does hispeak. My questions first, Linker. Then we can discuss yours. Agreed?"

Jade ignored that.

"Well then, question one. What do you know of Sarn?"

Expecting something to do with the Centra Zar, Jade was only further confused. "Sarn? What's that?" The wrong thing to say. Lurz didn't look so mild.

"I see. Then number two. Does Barmalin Tas know?"

Barmalin Tas. That name he knew. "ComUn Chairman Tas? Does he know what?"

"You really should cooperate, Jade. You can't be too comfortable like that."

"Right. I'm not. But first you've got to make some kind of sense to me. I don't know what a Sarn is." This was idiocy. He'd laugh if he wasn't flat on his back. "And I sure don't know what Tas does or doesn't know."

"Very convincing, Jade. Except I already know he tried twice to kill you. In two sectors. No one hunts a Linkman through the arms without good reason." Long fingers tapped upper arms thoughtfully, and the eyes went hungry and unfocused. "He hunts and I find. One day Tas will know me. Well. And the Free-men will be free." His attention snapped back to the recumbent man. "You could be a part of it, Jade. If you wish. Free of the ComUn."

But Jade was not hearing him, he was still listening to something said before. *Barmalin Tas had tried to kill him?* No way. This Lurz was brain-sick.

Perhaps Lurz mistook his silence. "You will tell me what I want to know. I already have a part of it. I know it's about Sarn. If you don't talk now you will later. And I have you. That's more than Tas can say." He nodded and turned to leave.

"Hey, Lurz," Jade called him back. "How about letting me up?"

"As soon as you tell me about Sarn." And he was gone.

This felt like a bad chem-link. He lay still looking at the ceiling. Sarn. He had never heard the word. It simply left him blank. And that glis about Tas. Couldn't be. Why would the chairman of the ComUn Council, a hundred skips in to Centra, want to kill him? He might have made a reputation for himself on a few worlds, but nothing that would get the attention of someone with the clout of Barmalin Tas. Lurz was unLinked from real-now and caught in a channel of his own fantasy. It had to be.

The more he thought about it, the easier that was to believe, and he finally started to think of his own here and now. His body protested the long stillness. He shifted, pulled with his arms, but nothing gave. His bladder was complaining, and the need to sit up became his one worthwhile goal. He found, after a while, that he could grab the edge of the cot on the right side, and, with that as anchor, by placing his weight on his forearm, he could slide himself up, raising head and shoulders. It wasn't easy, but his body was trained to answer his demands and he kept at it, pulling his legs up through the bridge of his arms and shoulders until he was actually sitting, bent nearly double, but able to see the bindings on his wrists. It was some kind of plastic, too elastic to break by pulling. He thought of biting through it, but he couldn't bend far enough to one side. He tried to stretch the stuff and discovered, by pulling, that his hands were actually bound together under the cot. If he raised his right arm, his left was pulled down, stretching him out. There was no help there.

Sweating, he held still and thought about it, finally began to slide his buttocks further up, pulling his legs along, lifting his weight by holding the edge of the cot. One knee cleared, then both, and he was kneeling. And now he could reach the bindings with his teeth. It was like chewing zoar leather, but he kept at it, shredding the stuff until he could bite through the narrow strips.

He nearly ran to get out, then got hold of himself and stopped to think, to look around. The room was square and windowless. Standard light-globes drifted near the ceiling. He could be anywhere, even underground. The door—opening really, there was neither door nor drape—led into a dark corridor that looked like cut stone. He entered cautiously, but there was no alarm. He moved into darkness, stopping long enough to relieve himself against the wall and coil his hair, tucking it into the neck of his tunic.

Distant light showed, finally, in the long straight walk. There was a draped doorway leading to a bright wide-windowed chamber, fancy with a high-pillowed bed and rich chests, table, and mirrors. Sleep room or joy-crib, he thought, moving to the window.

It was a long way down, but it was still TaLur, and not too far from the port. It was nearing sunset. Sooner or later someone would come into this room, and there was only one way out. Through a heavy-looking carved door. And he had to get out. Heglit would be worried about him. If he worried.

But he didn't hurry. He stopped long enough to find a comb in the jumble of personal items on a high chest, and deftly combed and knotted his hair. Not vanity, particularly; his hair would mark him instantly and from a distance among the usual crowd of shippers—supposing he got that far.

It took another minute or two to open the door. Too many autos. Then the round knob turned with a click and the door swung in. There was a wide hall, soft-rugged, and a stair. And an open room to his left. He went quietly and quickly, not looking into the open room. Down. To voices and the smell of food. That, more than the voices, halted him. His belly hurt with the reminder that he had not eaten in a long time.

The room at the foot of the wide stair was rich in color and furnishings, but he had seen richer. The voices came from the left. He moved close enough to know they were all men and the tongue wasn't fedstanspeak hi or low, but a sector speak heard only down the west limb near Mann and Burkoze. And there was laughter.

He crouched on the stairs, half-listening, looking around. Maybe they hadn't set a guard on him because there wasn't a whole lot to worry about. He had no idea where he was in this maze, or how many people (of one kind or another) were around. Then he heard a familiar voice, Lurz, talking above the others, and in the staccato babble he caught the word ComUn. He started to listen, picking up the few words that sounded familiar. Something about pay or bargaining, a question for Tas, and several times the word Sarn. But nothing made as much sense to him as the painful hook of hunger beneath his ribs. A brief flurry of what sounded like argument rattled through the open door with Lurz's voice one of many, and he ignored them, wondering, remembering Lurz had linked Tas to the attempts to kill him. Nonsense.

37

But who was Lurz, and why would he believe it? And if he was from Burkoze Sector what was he doing here in TaLur? And what was Sarn?

Heglit, he thought briefly. Maybe he would know something. But Rafal Sector was in the north and they had been restricted so long— He would have to find out what he could for himself. And without wasting a lot of time. Heglit, a Rafalan, could be in trouble here in spite of his half claim to the Centra Zar.

The babble of voices rose, then grew quiet with distance (he hoped). The windows were darkening with the winy blue twilight, and Lurz would be wanting to see him again. He had two options, he thought, and the one least likely to succeed at this point was escape.

Shrugging slightly, he moved down the stairs, soundless in his soft boots, and strode through the open door. His heart thumped a little with the success of finding it empty. The remains of a large meal lay about and he examined a few dishes before selecting a helping of Lursteak (most familiar) and Drul'za (learned to like a long time ago in some pleasure villa owned by some forgotten patron). There was rich red Rill wine and Z'Atua for added zest. He took the ornate chair at the head of the table and began to eat with good appetite, keeping an eye on the door.

He wasn't disappointed when the immaculate-robed figure swept in, handsome face scowling, seeing nothing.

Lurz turned to a sideboard, poured a jeweled goblet of something and, raising it to his lips, turned—

"Ah, Lurz," Jade said jovially, raising his own glass, leaning back, posing a little. "I was looking for you." He chose to ignore the violent purple stain splashing down the white robe as Lurz's hand continued a motion his gaped mouth forgot.

"Wha— But how—?" Lurz sputtered.

"Missed breakfast," Jade explained, spearing a morsel of steak. "Hope you don't mind."

Lurz shook his head, hard, glanced at the door, then seemed to collect himself. "No. Of course. Help yourself."

Jade's nervousness evaporated, leaving him high and brightly glad. Better than drink. "I hope I didn't startle you."

"Nothing. I—"

"But you left me a little confused earlier," Jade broke in smoothly, patting his lips with a napkin.

"Confused," Lurz repeated. Jade could see him scrabbling desperately for a hold on the situation.

"Yes." He got up. "If we could talk."

"Talk. Of course." The host recalled his duty. "The comfort room. We will not be disturbed there." With a flourish only slightly marred by the stained robe, he led the way into the room Jade had watched through the other's long meal. He gestured to twin chairs.

"Nice," Jade commented, gesturing at the room. "I would guess you furnished it yourself."

"I did." Lurz was looking less confused and more alert. Jade decided he better keep it moving.

"You offered me a position with you. I think. But you didn't say what it would be, or how it would benefit either of us."

"I should think it obvious. Considering your position with ComUn. My organization could offer you sanctuary."

"From Barmalin Tas." He said it with the eerie feeling of having uttered some alien speak. Lurz nodded.

"We have to avoid the cluster sectors within a large radius of Centra for the time being. But the outer sectors are becoming more and more dissatisfied and more eager to join me. Even Tas will have to admit our claim before long."

Jade nodded, not understanding any of what that had to do with anything. He didn't even know what questions to ask to keep from getting himself in worse trouble. Then inspiration struck. He looked at Lurz a moment, unsmiling, then let his gaze fall.

"I—" He sighed slightly. "I supposed you meant a, ah—a rather more personal position." The slightest touch of embarassment and regret touched his voice and he glanced up to see color rise in the other's face. "I thought you had heard—" He shrugged, managing to look uncomfortable. "Forgive me." He got up.

After a moment Lurz also rose. "Not to forgive, Linker Jade. There is no loss of honor in honest admission." He all but preened, coming close. "To be honest, I have only thought of my struggle with ComUn for too long. There has been small time for personal thoughts. But perhaps we could come to know one another. You could return to Burkoze with me."

"Would you want that, Lurz?" He brought faint hope to his face, turning to look at the man, seeing the hope of double victory in the blue eyes, the patronizing smile.

"Yes. I rather think I should."

"If you wish it then." With a long-practiced gesture Jade raised his arms, shook the cascade of dark hair about him, managing both arrogance (natural) and submissiveness (practiced) in his look and posture.

"Extraordinary." Lurz all but licked his lips, reaching to lift the long hair.

For no reason, Jade remembered another hand, dark bronze, reaching so, fingers exploring the weight and length of his hair, impassive eyes following the hand (obedient to the challenge in Jade's voice asking if he wanted to touch it) saying yes,˙ silently, it's hair and nothing else.

Coming now, that memory brought unexpected and irrelevant anger, schooled out of his face but fully present in the lean hand that lifted to Lurz's shoulder, the simple caress lasting long enough to find the correct pressure point. Then thumb and index finger pressed with more than necessary force. The blue eyes went blank, lips peeled back, silent in the minor convulsion. Lurz folded.

A good trick, relic of wilder (he used to think) days in Holsher Sector, learned from a fellow joy-skinner. It would keep Lurz down for a while, and he wouldn't move his head comfortably for several days. But he deserved it.

The building, whatever it was, was a maze, and several times he felt completely lost. But finally one of the doors opened out into soft-scented garden air. The glow from the port gave him direction, but it was a long way back, and he had to be careful. He didn't want any local authorities clipping him.

Heglit said nothing when he came into the ship, but the dark eyes watched him, learning, while Jade bathed and dressed and finally sat on the couch slow-brushing his hair.

"Who took you from the joyhouse?" he asked finally.

"Crazy named Lurz. Nerve-blocked him and ran. How'd you know I was taken?"

"The chem-dealer. Said he was paid to bad-link you."

"Set up? I thought—" He didn't say what he thought, thinking suddenly of Heglit in the ComUn port, finding the dealer, questioning him. "Have any trouble with port?"

"No. I remoted our bid on runs. The share code is registered to us both. We can load and lift in four hours."

"The claim stood?"

"Stood."

The simple word was the beginning of excitement in Jade, enough to dim the events of the day. "We'll have to get—"

"Free-shippers don't need the standard crew. I can Link while you pilot, or you can Link. With a little time and equipment we could both Link and auto-run any channel."

"I never heard of that." And remembering. "I can qualify on one run. Need that for insurance."

Heglit nodded. "They might not qualify me."

"I could." Jade grinned and knotted his hair. "Once I'm listed I can test and qualify on my own. You'd have to lay one skip but that's registered in port. You code out on a single run from departure and code in successfully on arrival, with my report and confirmation from the commandcomps that you handled programming. It's automatic. You get listed qualified captain."

"Reese taught you well," Heglit said, meaning just that or something else. But he was never personal.

"What'd we bid on?" Jade asked, yawning.

"Luxury and medical for Roc I."

"Still up the limb." But that was all right, going and doing the thing they could do. Without orders. Free-shippers. That was good. Their own ship to—

"Jade." Heglit's voice brought him back from the edge of sleep. "We must talk about the ship."

"Tired me," he protested. "No thinking. We'll talk after lift. Okay?"

Heglit looked at him long and dark and saw that he was tired. He decided to let it ride. "Yes. Sleep now. I'll have the load made up and set up the run."

41

4

When he woke, the Centra Zar was moving out from the central sun of the TaLur Sector, threading her automatic way through the local sector web according to coordinates punched into the navicomp in port. Once beyond the busy space of planets and close suns she would be free, moving out into the big space where gates to the Star Web channels lay, plotted and waiting. They were on their way. A good right feeling. He joined Heglit in the control room, found him calculating time and distance to first skip. There would be three this run, made interesting by the increasing density of traffic as they ran in toward galactic center. With two or more days between skips it would be an easy run. He let Heglit work out the math and went down to the galley where the well-planned stock reminded him his partner had had a lot to do while he was off playing some weird's idea of a game. He heated the trays and took them back to the control room with a couple of containers of Santo tea.

He checked over the figures, logged times and places while they ate. "Where'd you learn?"

"Rafal." Heglit had other things on his mind. "Turloz had papers in his quarters. Special orders. I did not turn them over to the ComUn."

"Special orders for what?"

"The TaLur run. He did not tell us the truth."

"What did he lie about, the channel?"

"Many things. There was no plague serum on board, only special ComUn order items for port stores. And the channel had only been run by drones, remoted through with a special pick-up signal so they could be found after breakout. This run was experimental. I think it was on a different frequency."

He had Jade's full attention now. "But how would that

work? I mean, the channel frequency is standard everywhere, from Centra to the Rim."

Heglit reached into his neck pouch, drew out an oddly faceted crystal that glowed blue in his palm. "The resonator was wired to include this in circuit. All else is standard, but new-built. I disconnected this before we grounded. I think it somehow adds a harmonic or amplification."

"Never got into the mechs of the ships," Jade admitted, taking the crystal. It drew his eyes with a strange fascination, seemed to swell, to pull him, twisting, down into some spacious otherness where—

Heglit's dark hand, covering the glow, unlocked him, and he looked up, slightly wrenched, to meet the penetrating watch of dark eyes. Heart beating a little, he shook off the sensation. "So we were expendable. Only it didn't work that way. And the ship's really okay."

Heglit nodded. "The resonance was probably changed to the point it no longer matched the interior shielding. Another thing. We were to be detained on grounding, shipped to Hazor Cluster Blue G for study. The order was hand-signed and ret-printed by Barmalin Tas himself."

At the name Jade's middle tensed. "Tas. I— Lurz said Tas had tried to have me killed."

Heglit just looked at him.

"He said twice. And someone did. If he was right— Could this have—?"

"Even Tas could not know we would Link on the Centra Zar." Almost absently. He might have said more, but a melodious tone from the control board turned him toward the chronometer. A calm voice told the crewless ship that skip one was scheduled in ten.

Jade went down to the Link-room to check Heglit out, then, envying him a little, went back to the control room and watched the outview screen until it blanked and began to flow with soothing colors. A five-hour Link. He rechecked the log, went over bid price and profit expectations, but everything had been done. There were tapes to read, or have read to him, or music, but he sat in the contoured command chair and let his mind wander over the strangeness of the last few days. Lurz and Tas. Nothing figured. Except maybe the few words he had

43

picked up before getting away from Lurz. They implied that he was to have been a bargaining point between Lurz and Barmalin Tas. For something. But why would anyone think he had value to someone like Tas, who, in effect, controlled all the worlds united in the ComUn?

Watching the colors dance sedately across the screen, he nearly smiled. Someone had made a mistake. If he were in a slightly different position he might enjoy seeing Tas's face when he was handed a down-limb Linker.

He was dozing when the tone said they were breaking into N-space. He stretched, pulling over-relaxed muscles tight, and was glad to see Heglit come in with a bottle of baDant juice. There was traffic, he reported, but nothing the ship couldn't easily handle. Jade could take the next skip.

He rested in his singular Rafalan way, staring at nothing, very still, but there was a feel of thoughts racing behind the stillness, and he held the strange blue crystal in his left hand like a talisman, thumb rubbing lightly, rubbing until Jade wanted to ask what it was telling him. He kept the silly thought to himself and enjoyed the elegant juice, talking instead of the possibilities of their new freedom, now that they were Free-shippers. He kept up the constant chatter until Heglit turned his attention full on him.

"Jade, what is it you don't want to talk about?"

Damn him, again. He hadn't really been thinking about it, but there it was, solid and cold in his mind and throat and no place to run to. "Did you— What was wrong with the timers?"

"Nothing."

"Impossible."

"Yes. Until understood," Heglit agreed mildly. The stone in Jade's throat dissolved and his thighs relaxed.

Heglit noted the reaction, filed it away with other items that one day might add up to something intelligent. He was patient. For now, he too wanted to get familiar with freedom, with having the whole of the galaxy to choose from.

The long N-space runs gave them time to learn the system and think up answers for the questions likely to be asked when Jade filed for pilot's status on the strength

44

of the run from TaLur. Then there was the last gate, a long N-space run, shuttling through mild diversion currents on a course automatically broadcast from Roc Sector ComUn beacon, and permission to ground.

Roc I was bigger and heavier than most ComUn port worlds, the port busier and richer, indicating that they were moving into the denser central sectors of the ComUn.

The business of the claim and qualification took two days, and Jade handled it himself, not sure what problems might stumble them if it became known his partner was Rafalan. Fortunately, this close in, requests for qualification were fairly common, and the authorities were only interested in his ability as proven by the successful run down from TaLur. He was even offered an application to join ComUn. It was tempting. Insurance rates were automatic, charged to the Union to be subtracted from the dues. But he was a Free-shipper and wanted no one saying where to go and how to run his ship.

"Not many Free-shippers on it," the non-Clate clerk chatted, brushing round furry cheeks with nervous delicate fingers. "Big in out-arms, with small runs and not too many choosings of places."

The registration cards were finally completed, somewhere in the complex innards of the computer, and popped out onto the counter, freeing him to go. He palm-printed the credit charge against cargo price and went out to look at the activities. Not pleasure-seeking this time, but business. He found Heglit at the bid center, standing back against the wall.

"Bid?"

The Rafalan head shook no. The eyes were not on the board, but scanning the tiers of bidders, mostly Clate. The list of cargoes and destinations flashed on-off, on-off, in eye-catching yellow, and the slender bid-pillars glowed green with the slots for ID cards, the numbered bid-buttons bright red. Jade handed over the papers and one of the cards to Heglit.

"Where do you want to go?"

"In." Always the same.

On the board the listings blinked, yellow to red, jumping to the left to make room for the listing of the successful bidder; ComUn Pake, ComUn DeArmin, ComUn— Always ComUn.

"See any Free-shippers?"

"No."

The listed cargoes were still mostly period runs, popular items with rigid quotas set by ComUn, fabrics, cosmetics, scents, a few rare spices and local items from distant worlds well down the limbs that traded up in value as they moved in. The runs were mostly short, but in toward Centra the worlds were closer.

"That." Heglit slipped his card into the slot in the bidpole. Jade looked up, saw the name Grio. T'ChkTic, des. Rio Del, health. He wasn't sure what it was. The listing glowed a long time, there were other bidders, and he forgot to watch Heglit's fingers. Then the board flickered, the words slid aside to accommodate F. S. Centra Zar.

"We got it!"

Heglit retrieved his card without expression. "We can't get information on load before morning. We can leave the ship now. Go eat."

They moved through the loose crowds that took note of them without comment. There was a wider variety of non-Clate, most more strongly alien than usually seen close to ComUn ports, furred or scaled or what looked like feathered but might not have been. Jade amused himself by watching them, and found that the urge to put eyes and ears and mouths where they belong (in his opinion) made them hard to really see unless he looked at them sideways.

There was a carnival of sorts in the street, with acrobats, and he stopped, caught by the sight, the unexpected reminder. There were five in the troupe, all good and all very young except maybe the tallest male (not quite man, certainly not Clate, the body was too boneless, the skin dull red) but he was graceful and his gestures and attention on the crowd hinted at more private and expensive services. Once, his eyes (red around blue) met Jade's and he stiffened with a curious inside-out feeling, broken when someone jostled him from behind. He stepped aside, looking for Heglit, saw the tall frame and started toward it when a familiar word came to him through the babble. *Lurz.*

He stopped quick without turning and traced the voice with suddenly-awake ears, chasing it through the multi-speak noise. The speak was rough Dagon, but he knew enough to follow it.

"What's Lurz and Free-shippin'?" The voice was to his left and slightly behind him.

"Free's buyin', him." Another, more cultured, voice answered in lowspeak. "Favors trade to Free-ships, him. And high credits."

"And local runs them. Sameplacin' for life."

"Not. Saw it, me. Even ComUns comin' out to him. Signs 'em, him. Insures too."

"Like ComUn?"

"Like."

They started to move away and Jade followed, curious, losing part of the conversation.

". . . down by Tas and ComUn, them. Restricted be. And no far-run goods for sellin'."

"Seven sectors. For Lurz all. Bad thinkin' because only Clates gets authorization, and more trade from out goes into Centra than comes down. Free-ships not given quotas."

"Goin' you?"

"Needs techs, him. And Linkers."

"Tas mad gets, eats Lurz, him." A rough laugh sounded more bitter than amused.

"Try him and all down-limb sectors goin' with Lurz. Watch you."

They were moving down a narrow alley, unpeopled, and Jade left off following, turned back to find Heglit waiting a little away from the crowd, leaning against a wall, arms folded. Jade had the strange feeling the Rafalan had watched the whole thing, maybe even knew what had been said.

They chose an eat-house further away from the port than most of the shippers found, and sat down to a meal of local meat, some orange cheese, dark bread, and a sort of foamy grain beverage that was only mildly euphoric.

"I would talk," Jade said finally in the complex speak of Rafal.

Heglit seldom seemed surprised, but there was a suggestion of question in his look. Jade only spoke Rafalan

47

when there was something important to say. "I listen," Heglit replied finally, in the same tongue.

"There was talk of Lurz on the street. From shippers." He told what he had heard. "Lurz wanted me for something beyond pleasure."

"We did not speak of him before," Heglit reminded quietly.

"I thought he was space dreaming. Now I think he is trying to form a ComUn to compete with Tas."

"Evidence?"

"He thought having me was a point against Tas because Tas had tried twice to kill me."

"Tas." Heglit clasped his hands about his cup, looking at him.

"A mistake, yes. But evidence for his activity, if they are talking of him even here."

"Why would Tas want you?" Heglit stuck to the other part of the subject.

"A mistake," Jade repeated. "Only, if Lurz is forming a Free-shippers union not bound by Centra's quotas, we should find out more."

"Lurz had you once."

"I did not know—"

"Think, Jade. What would he have done with you?"

"I think he wanted to use me to bargain with Tas. He thought I was important to him."

"Evidence."

"None."

"Perhaps you are important to him."

"No. Tas is after one who knows about Sarn."

Heglit straightened slightly, hands turning to lay flat on the table. "Sarn?"

"He said. I don't know what a Sarn is, but he thought I did. That's what Tas wants."

Heglit looked at him a long time, like trying to decide something, then he looked down at his hands. "I forget sometimes that what is on Rafal is not necessarily so outside."

"What?"

"Sarn is not a what. He's a— Eat. Then I will show you."

Jade looked at him, yellow eyes puzzled, but he didn't ask.

When they left Heglit turned away from the port to the gentler lights of the surrounding port settlement. It was a long walk through the unpeopled dark separating the port from the living area of the port workers and the town built for them. Then there were travel strips that carried them into the Study and Information center, a standard feature in all ComUn settlements in sector capitals. Jade knew about them but he had never visited one before, preferring to spend his free time in the pleasure centers crowding the port proper. Their identification as shippers got them in, and Heglit asked for history information, Federation, and a study booth. A soft female voice gave instructions in fedstanspeak.

Lost, Jade followed him down long halls of silence until they came to the designated booth, a small room with a large readout screen and coded keys for material selection. Heglit adjusted the light and punched out a rapid selection. There was a brief wait while the screen flashed a standby pattern, snowed out, cleared to show a color portrait of a man.

"That's Sarn?" Jade glanced at his companion, catching a look so strange he drew back. "Heglit—?"

"It's— Looks like you."

Jade looked at the screen, at the lean face, dark hair, yellow eyes. "Yes. A little, maybe—"

"Not a little." Annoyed, Heglit's arm jumped out, brushing Jade's as he touched the stud. The screen went dark, reflecting Jade's face. Then light, and Sarn's.

Jade stared, then his own hand reached, dark, light. His skin roughened. Like on like. But older, sterner—"Me." Eyes wide, and a little scared, he turned to his companion. Heglit nodded briefly and turned to leave.

"So Lurz, and maybe Tas, think I'm Sarn," Jade said, when they were back on the ship and Heglit was quiet too long.

"Jadriel Sarn was captured and executed in Rafal Sector three hundred and two stanyears ago. During the Traveler invasion." He said it flat, and his eyes stuck on Jade's face, hiding thoughts he wouldn't try to guess.

"Three hundred and two stanyears. Then what was Lurz on about? I never heard of Sarn." He felt lost, like things were getting away from him. "What's he to Tas? Or Lurz?"

"Sarn was of TreAsh. One of the oldest man-claimed sectors. It was Sarn's death that brought the Federation to restrict our sector."

"You killed him?"

"We gave him sanctuary. And it was found out. Rafal refused to take part in the war. It was a mistake. TreAsh knew that better than all the Clate worlds and sectors. They, and we, knew the beginning of it."

"Everyone does," Jade broke in, interested in spite of the lack of connection to his problem. Heglit just didn't talk about the things of Rafal all that much. But the beginning of the Traveler War was common knowledge. "The Travelers, wherever they came from, destroyed Obere in Kazzan Sector. That started it."

"Only because a sector patrol destroyed a Traveler ship, out of fear, without knowing what they were destroying. It could have stopped there, but war happened because of panic before it was known the Travelers were from outside."

"Out?"

"Yes. Only TreAsh knew. And Rafal. We shared many things with TreAsh. We were not very close sectors, but we were both old, and when TreAsh found the first Star Web channel it led them to our sector. We were the first union, before it was known there could be travel between all sectors."

"TreAsh found the Star Web?" That was another thing Jade had not known.

"They designed the ship-Link and Rafal built the first large ships. Before the Federation. The TreAshal were thinkers and Rafal has always been a sector of craftsmen."

"They don't talk about that." Jade said, loosening his hair. "I thought they were built in the center. Never heard of TreAsh. Where is it?"

"Gone."

"Travelers?"

"Federation. The TreAshal were masters of communication; some on Rafal think they discovered the Star Web through their work in that field. When the Travelers appeared, they learned to speak with them, I think. Anyway, they learned something of them. Then they tried to take a message from them to the new-built Federation, but before they could arrange a meeting in Centra a

Traveler ship was taken out in the northern limb. Six adult TreAshal were found aboard, but no Travelers. And the ship was different, alien. There were rumors; a panic that spread, and the TreAshal were called traitors to the Federation. They were ordered to ground all their ships and cease all communication. They refused. Shortly after, another Traveler ship was taken and it, too, had TreAshal aboard. The central military coalition, what later became ComUn, attacked TreAsh. It was totally destroyed with the entire population, except Sarn and some few in Rafal Sector. When they were discovered we were held responsible."

"So Rafal was restricted. But if all this happened so long ago, why should my likeness to Sarn interest anyone? Or does it?"

Heglit waited a little before answering, thinking. "I don't know. I think— The TreAshal were a knowing people. Some worlds called them wizards, even thought they built the Star Web. They didn't, of course, but they knew more about it than any other people. That, the Star Web, was Sarn's interest, I think. That and the Travelers." He fell silent, looking at Jade, and his hand went to his neck pouch. "Tas found something, maybe. Something of TreAsh. Perhaps something taken from Sarn. Yes. And then he learned of your resemblance. That would make sense of it. But there are too many things I don't know. I feel I should return to Rafal and— But I'd better not leave you alone."

"Don't trust me?"

"To do what?" Heglit was serious.

"Anything." Slightly annoyed.

Heglit saw that and ignored it. "We've run a long way, but if Tas is after you—"

Heglit's believing that made it serious, even if it didn't make any sense. But Jade was enough of a survivor to play it safe.

"So then, let's go."

"Go?"

"To Rafal Sector."

"The restriction, Jade. No contact except on Iron. No non-Rafalan ship goes further in."

"But why? I mean you're— There was a Rafalan ship bound for Azee out of C'Erit."

"Personal request of Tas. With a tracer in it. He has his secrets too. And we are still known as master builders and craftsmen."

"But you Linkers— Right. Have to be Clate partnered." He knew that, but it suddenly angered him. He wanted to get to Rafal. And not just for safety. "Tas has no right to keep traffic out."

"It has nothing to do with ComUn. We closed our sector to outsiders after the restriction. And it is sealed. We will not go as easily as TreAsh. They refused to fight."

Jade folded himself into the chair, pulling his feet into his lap, soles turned up, thumbs stroking absently. "Heglit, I don't understand what's happening. But if Tas is trying to get me killed for no reason except I look like someone dead three hundred stanyears, I'm ready to get scared. I mean, Tas, he damned near *owns* space. At least the Star Web. Maybe the only place safe for me is Rafal. And you say I can't go there. So what do I do? Go tell Tas I'm not this Sarn or whatever?"

"Maybe you are." Heglit's fingers felt the outline of the crystal in the pouch.

"Not funny."

5

Morning came busy, crowding the thoughts in Jade's head. There was no time for quiet talk or prowling the port like in ones before this. They were shippers now, and Free-shippers didn't rate the scheduled ease of the ComUn. Mostly it was hurry up and wait, for transfer information on cargo, for insurance and bonding (and that came high), for the port crew to ready the ship and load the ordered supplies.

Jade was new at it, but he learned, and his hard-earned knowledge of people told him there were games they kept for Free-shippers. He threaded his way through the confusion, hanging onto his temper with both hands, and played his own games.

He celebrated the experience with Z'Atua before returning to the Centra Zar to see how Heglit was faring.

"We lift at dawn." Heglit was outside, watching the loading of the last of the stores.

"How long's the run?"

"Long." Heglit watched the non-Clate field men impassively. "They do not like Free-shippers," He observed finally, turning toward the personnel ramp.

"Some do. I heard talk of Burkoze again."

Heglit nodded and said nothing, heading for the captain's quarters.

"There are two bio-techs on board to monitor and care for the cargo."

"Hired already?" Jade paused in the act of stripping.

"On board. We need no more delays. As captain, you should speak with them."

"Oh." Nude in the cloak of his hair Jade looked at his partner, remembering he was, indeed, captain. Remembering also something he had thought during the hectic day. "I'm going to log you out apprentice with

53

the port. It's my option." At the end of the run he could qualify and get his papers. It was a major step for a Rafalan, but if it meant anything he couldn't see it in the dark face. Shrugging, he stepped into the washer. He liked the idea. It felt right to him that Heglit should be a qualified pilot. Besides, with him handling the run Jade could Link every skip, and that was good too, smoothing the frayed edges of his nerves.

Heglit was gone when he came out of the washer, probably in the control room. Pulling on clean clothes Jade wondered what the bio-techs were like, and why two. Knotting up his hair he keyed the crew-com asking the cargo-techs to report to him. Then he settled himself with the cargo and run briefs to find out just what the expensive stuff was and why it needed special handlers.

T'ChkTic, he learned, was a spore collected on Grio II, a nasty little hothouse of a world famous for a number of effective (and outlawed) sentient toxins and a few exportable pharmaceuticals The one they carried was refined to a general-use base for inoculations and other medications distributed through ComUn Health. Fragile in its natural state, it had to be kept alive, which meant optimum environment and continual applications of nutrients. The maintenence schedule was listed, but the technical codes meant nothing to him, except it was complicated. He hoped, considering the bid-price, that the bio-techs knew their business.

A light tap at the door pulled him away from the schedules. He stood as they entered and lost the purpose of the meeting in vision. Metallic rather than flesh, pure poured gold with eyes of green-flecked gray startlingly vivid in their dark gold faces. Benjo, he thought. He had never seen pure Benjo before, but he had heard of them. Every joyhouser in the galaxy knew of the legendary beauty—

"Techs, us, captain." The male's voice sang low and on the edge of something that could have been laughter, but it was the female that held Jade's eyes, a slender dark gold flame scant-clad in silver felspun, a riot of honey gold hair up-clasped with bright green gorocks.

"Techs," he said, finally hearing, and the sound of his voice woke him slightly to look at the male who was as beautiful, but flat-muscled, perfect mouth slightly curved,

54

gem-eyes dancing, seeing all of Jade and flashing to—Who? Mate? But the slight smile made a challenge and he would not be made a fool, even by perfection like this. He gestured them to sit on the couch and resumed his seat, taking the plastic ID card from the male.

"Both techs?" He addressed neither of them directly.

"Together us, captain. All times." Her voice sang a softer song than the male's. "Lista, me being, and him Borget. Of Benjo Sector."

The code on the card he had taken marked them Clate, with a small mark that said borderline. Their authorization code was five. High, and registered ComUn. He asked it of the male, frowning slightly.

Borget nodded. "Was us. Off-listed, so free-lancing, us."

Off-listing was a heavy penalty. It was almost as hard to get off the list as it was to get on. Beautiful as they were, that probably meant trouble.

"Why?" It was his right to ask.

"ComUn shipmaster did," Borget said, looking at the floor. "So to buy me, him. I would not."

Lista watched, close, then leaned to touch the closed golden hands. "He is Free-man." The sweet flute song of their native speak sang sense to Jade. Benjospeak was the pleasurespeak of the joyhouses on a thousand worlds throughout the limbs, his life before Reese and Linking.

"Free I am, Lista." The words shaped themselves like good taste on his tongue, pulling their eyes to him. He smiled. "Do not fear me. I wish only success for my ship and cargo, and need to know my position if you join me."

"Lord," Lista made the slight nod seem a bow. "Your words call truth from us. There was no crime, but justice. The shipmaster took us from Jonli. We are not many listed with ComUn for ship work, and so little is known of us in other limbs. The captain was of Centra, and when he saw Borget, my brother, he desired him for skin-gaming, and hoped to profit from him in Centra. He placed a charge against us to remove our authorization, and claimed ownership. Of me to sell on Dagon, of Borget to use and keep until Centra."

"We will not be separate," Borget added. "It is our birth and fate to be always joined. To him we offered our

55

togetherness, but he laughed and sold Lista and threatened me with chains."

"Yet you have your freedom."

Borget reached to take Lista's hand. "We gave him pleasure and long sleep through T'Chan'Za. He ceased."

Ceased was a unique way of putting it. Jade looked at them a little differently. He knew T'Chan'Za, another product of the mean little world of Grio. Called Wif in the outworld joyhouses, T'Chan'Za was the ultimate skip, pleasuring one beyond the brain's ability to sustain life functions. The blissful death. They were not only off-listed, they were murderers. Wif was outlawed in every port he had ever touched. Any dealer was executed without appeal. Leaning back, looking at them, he didn't know what to do. He wondered if Heglit knew.

Borget might have read his thoughts. "It was said, when we grounded on Jader, that the shipmaster had died of natural causes, as indeed, he did. But the off-listing could not be reversed." He smiled slightly and Jade knew where the legends began. "The dark cool one who speaks for you asked only of our knowledge of your cargo."

Telling him they had spoken with Heglit. He pulled one bare foot into his lap, rubbing absently. There were few, if any, questions about free-lancers in port, he knew; they were simply assumed to be less capable, or were non-Clate, and so were last hired, or were taken to fill out the mandatory seven-man crews of the ComUn ships, as cheap help to leave a larger profit for the captain. He couldn't see any real trouble coming from hiring them.

"Lord," Lista's voice pulled his eyes up. "We have good knowledge of T'ChkTic. Our people work the seasons on Grio. The living seed has a liking for us and is happy to have us near."

Jade smiled at her. "I have heard the Benjor are pleasure masters," he said. "I did not know the art reached even to plants."

They looked at one another and the look became soft laughter uniting them. Borget spoke. "All life yearns to pleasure, shipmaster, giving or taking. Your cargo lives—" He spread his hands in a graceful gesture.

"So it does." Jade let his foot slide to the floor as Heglit came into the cabin, dark and silent; he moved across the room like shadow. Used to him, Jade glanced greeting and turned back to the Benjor and the game building between the female and him. "How do you pleasure the seed life?"

"By being pleasured among it," Borget answered the question, unsmiling.

Heglit did not know Benjorspeak, but he watched the three, unmoving, dark eyes gathering, saying nothing.

Only after they were gone to see about the cargo space did Heglit come and sit, accepting a glass of Z'Atua. "They will work well for you."

Jade looked to see if something else was meant, but the dark face told him nothing. "They were off-listed by ComUn. Killed a captain, but it wasn't found out." If he hoped for a reaction he was disappointed. "Never seen Benjor before. They are as beautiful as I heard."

Heglit let silence make a space before changing the subject. "We have eighty-four hours run before first skip. There will be six altogether."

"Why so many?"

"Web complexity. The denser the systems, the more options. But only two are close, ten hours apart. Three are coded red."

Heavy traffic. He hadn't run a channel busy enough for a red since his first year as Linkman. "Traffic control?"

Heglit nodded. "We may be held back a few hours."

"You will pilot?"

"Yes." He looked down at his outstretched legs a moment. "Jade, after—"

A light tap on the door interrupted him. Borget came in with their meals. Galley duty had fallen to them on other Free-ships, he explained. As there was no other crew here, they would be glad to do the same. Jade agreed, glad to have some sort of structure forming. He watched Heglit as the Benjor leaned to hand him tray and cup, wondering what he thought of this, and if he felt anything at all. Then a quick unbidden memory flashed, surprising him with recall of a closer knowledge. He thrust it aside, annoyed, and began to eat.

"After Rio Del," Heglit continued, when Borget had gone, "we can no longer travel in toward Centra. Not until we know why Tas wanted you killed. If he did."

The reminder of Tas brought back the other problems,

the ones Jade had almost managed to forget. "So it's Rafal?"

"There is only the one world, Iron, that has any contact with the outside. And that is restricted to port."

But it was in Rafal Sector. And Heglit had been thinking about it. A quick thought struck Jade as he pushed his plate away and pulled his feet into his lap. "You could go. Leave me."

"Yes. I could."

He wanted to ask the obvious, but somehow he didn't. Maybe scared the flat voice would tell him. He shook down his hair, relishing the freedom as Heglit took their plates and slid them into the trasher. At the next port all discarded material would be removed and reclaimed or discarded, depending on the world.

After a while he thought of going to find Lista. But he did not.

Before lift, Jade notified Departure of intent to qualify an apprentice. Pilot of record this run would be Heglit D'Othiel. Departure confirmed by standard code, assigning a list number to be used on board, and according to regulations the commandcomp on board was notified to so code all commands identified by Heglit's voice-print. Any other commands or overrides would be flagged for identification when Arrival ran through the program at the Rio Del port.

A final run through ship-watch comps, including external sensors, and they were clear. Berth arms slid them out to the beam path, lift engines pushed the floor up against their feet, then the beam took over, throwing them up into the dawn sky. And it was good to be in the control room again for that. Exciting.

They broke away from the beam, from gravity, hooked into the local web, and began the complex series of three-D chess moves programmed by Departure, avoiding traffic as they flashed out away from the sun toward the first gate.

Borget reported the cargo in perfect condition, read technical information into the ship-watch sounding business-like and almost ordinary through the sort of lowspeak he used. Then Lista brought their meals, meeting Jade's look with a strange blend of bold shyness. But there was the run to become familiar with, records of the standard Star Web channels he would Link through, with places and approximate times between breakin and breakout (approximate because for no reason the skips varied occasionally in duration by as much as half an hour). It was all standard ship procedure, but he had been away from this part of it for a long time.

The hours slipped away and the course steadied as they broke out of the system proper and headed for gate one. And Jade's restlessness grew. He went down to check the Link-room, though there was no need. Then he gave it up and called control to tell Heglit he was going down to cargo, wondering who he thought he was fooling.

She was waiting for him, meeting him in the corridor as though she knew he was coming to her. Her eyes danced over his face, see-saying things he hoped for. Perfect lips lost their smile as she reached to take his hand. "Come."

The cabin was scented with some subtle perfume, maybe her, and this was a new thing, unlike other bought or sold unions. It was free and offered, and that surprised him with differences he didn't expect. "Lista—"

"It is a joy-sharing thing you wish Jade."

"Yes. Joy-giving." Pleasurespeak made explicit sense and goodness of it. Her skin sang against his palms, warm silk music rousing harmonics and subtle rhythms in his blood. Her shocking bold hand cupped him, warm, measuring, encouraging exaggeration. And she was wise, tease-yielding, letting his hands fumble her out of unfamiliar garments. Nude she was exquisite, retreating from him, singing the delightful pleasurespeak as she reached to dim the light to warm red, came to offer a yielding hungry mouth, twining supple legs about his still-clad thighs, then insisted on disrobing him, finally reaching to his knotted hair, loosing it to fall about her arms and perfect dark-nippled breasts, drawing him down to the couch but outmaneuvering him, feeding his heat with his urgency until a wildness built in him and he knew she knew the game better than he did. But his strength was greater. He forced her down and mounted her, but she yielded, making it her victory, drawing him in, holding him with knowing strength.

59

The sudden hand on his thigh shocked him and he would have jerked away. "No."

"Borget, Jade. Together we are in all things. It must be." Her legs loosed him, giving him choice, and he looked down into wide eyes and saw truth there and desire, and maybe hope, pulling soft words from his throat like surrender. The warm, slightly moist, hand stroked his inner thigh, filled itself gently, caressing— All right, he knew that game too, and it didn't matter. Not now. He raised himself to let the hand have its way with him, and knew a different excitement as it frustrated reunion briefly in the crowded dark. A deeper song breathed against his shoulder, stranger hands learned his shape and reality, teaching lessons he thought he had already learned, until what was known once as ability and expertise became pleasure, and more, leading to a give-taking done-doing link beyond anticipation.

He lay spent, a little stunned, against hard warmth, held safe by soft arms, all tangled in his sweat-damp hair, and wondered how he had got here, supposing he should feel used and maybe he would later. Now he only knew that buying and selling was different from sharing.

"Joy-skinner, you," she said against his chest, damp and breath warm, making shocking transition to low-speak.

"Was, me." Annoyed, wanting her to be quiet, wondering why she said it now and how she knew. But his mind was awake suddenly, erasing euphoria more than her sliding away.

"Pleasure-sharing is more," Benjorspeak stroked against his unease, confusing him. "Not skin-sharing for fast joy and self-pleasing. We are not skin-mates sharing you."

"Not complaining." But he felt vaguely ashamed. Pulling away from the hard silent warmth behind him, he sat up, legs folded, and she sat by his right knee and Borget by his left.

"Our thought was you understood our togetherness, pleasure-made Jade." Direct and intense in the red glow, Borget's eyes held him, the deep voice weaving a newer intimacy. "Because it is a known thing to our people, perhaps we suppose all know of it."

"That you and she share pleasure-mates?"

Borget's face betrayed unexpected embarrassment and he shook his head.

"Because you know the ways of joining and joy-skinning you see it so," Lista said, sounding sad. "Our togetherness was first, before one birth gave us real-life. So we share oneness."

"Twins, then." He began to understand.

"Two of one." Borget nodded. "But our realness is all shared, mind-being, feel-being. It is one between us. You looked on us with joy and pleasure-thoughts. This is a Benjor knowing thing. In our ignorance we made a different thing than you chose. It was not our right."

"I was not displeased, only surprised." He looked at them both and felt a laugh building under his ribs. Here he sat, naked, with two of the galaxy's most beautiful creatures, and they were apologizing for something most people would pay a fortune for, even kill for. Obviously they saw something quite different between skin-sharing and pleasure-sharing. They thought they had wronged him.

"Lista," he said, finally. "You said I was a joy-skinner. And I was. But how did you know? Are we that different?"

"For Benjor flesh-joinings are only pleasure-sharing, not a doing thing, like a thing for pay, a performing. But a—" She gestured, looking for words. "A fulfilling. A coming together to share all closeness and pleasure and become more. You were not glad when Borget joined us."

"Surprised only, lovely one. Not angry. I could have gone away."

"Letting is not wanting," she grinned, becoming a golden imp.

"You are one in two." He smiled, feeling a game beginning. "Wanting you," he touched her thigh, "is wanting you." He laid his left hand on the firmer thigh. "Only I did not know it was so."

"Lord Jade," Borget's voice drew his eyes, and the Benjor's eyes were direct and honest and totally serious. "Is it so?"

Jade held the look, wondering what this was, really, and finally nodded. "Yes, Borg, it is so."

They each took a hand, turned them and bent to press

61

their lips to his palms. "It is good between us, for you are easy to love," Lista murmured.

It was several hours more than he expected before he returned to the captain's cabin. Heglit was there, sitting in a chair, looking at the crystal he had found in the ship. He looked up to watch Jade a moment.

"I could have told you they were bound," he said.

Jade's head jerked around. How the Rim did he *know?* "No secrets, me," he growled, pulling off his tunic, needing to wash and sleep, and wanting to tell Heglit something of what had happened and not sure why. And that annoyed him, too. Then he wondered why Heglit had said anything at all. "Wanting to join us, you?" he challenged.

"Do you want me to?" Cool, like a serious question.

Expecting to be ignored, he took the question like a fist in the belly, losing his breath. He retreated to the washer in confusion. Did that mean he would? Or could? Gleest! He let himself think of the possibilities in that for about one second, then tucked it way down out of sight, letting the warm wind caress him dry.

6

The skips were pure clean joy, letting him leap out of himself, fly through the wild glory of the Star Web playing with it, flexing muscles, laughing down the amber rapids through the blue-flared traffic, coming out loose and happy to join Heglit in the control room to talk of it. And when the N-space runs were long and lazy he would go down to the cargo hold, made clean and good-smelling and somehow restful, and talk with Borget or Lista or both, and they would tell him tales of Benjo and Grio, and the unknown ways of their people. And he would spend long hours in the good-scented cabin losing irony and bright joy in the long slow pleasuring, coming away thoughtful, tamed, and somehow different than he had been.

Heglit watched him, marking the subtle changes, thinking his own thoughts. Sometimes the Benjor would speak with him and he would answer, and more often they would speak about him to Jade, wondering as much as he did.

Then there was the last skip and breakout into an N-space like Jade had nearly forgotten. Four large clusters blazing like frozen fireworks against the silver-dusted black; yellow and blue, red-orange and green, blue-white and deep violet. An automatic beacon signal held the coordinates to each of the four sector beacons, and Heglit sent the code request for Rio Del, then sat before the out-viewer looking at the wonder of the galaxy. The dark face shared nothing, but Jade wondered, thinking that as far as he knew no Rafalan had seen this for three hundred stanyears.

There was a lot of traffic, and as Free-shippers they were held back, dead-shipping on the edge of the sector until Arrival found out what their cargo was. The spore was special cargo, and they were programmed into Del VIII direct, keying on the beam, swinging around to drop softly into the busy port.

Before Arrival completed run checkout, the portmen were unloading the cargo into special environmental containers. It was examined and cargo credit plus eighty percent of insurance fee reimbursement was coded into the Centra Zar's commandcomp log. The total was nearly six times the bid price. Jade was impressed.

Jade made a standard request with the port authority for Heglit's qualification and pilot ID. It was granted without questions. All information on the qualifying run was obtained from the ship's commandcomp. It took time, but Heglit's palm print and retina pattern were recorded and the necessary papers and card were produced and presented. Jade wanted the four of them to go into the off-time district to eat and explore and celebrate, but Heglit refused.

"There will be other ships in from Roc I," he said, looking out over the port. "We will be remembered. There are not many Free-shippers here." He ordered the ship's stores replenished and headed for the bid center, where they learned that cargo headed out into the limbs was offered later in the day. Jade was just as glad. He had something else he wanted to talk about.

"A crew," he suggested as they returned to the ship.

"The Benjor." Heglit looked at him.

"Why not? They're good. The off-listing was a trick against them, but it stuck. And we have enough credit."

"You want them with you."

"All right. I do." He felt his face go warm, but tried honesty. "It's not just skin-gaming, they're more than that. I like them. Both."

"Did you talk of this?"

"No. I wanted— You're my partner."

That got nothing but a thoughtful look. "Tas," the Rafalan said finally. "We may find trouble. He knows this ship. He sent it out himself and will wonder what happened to it. And he might want you."

That again. Jade shook his head, dropping into a chair, watching Heglit key a request for the out-sector run program. He was tired of the thing with Barmalin Tas. It made no sense, had nothing to do with him, so far as he knew. He finally saw what Heglit was doing. "What's that for?" He gestured toward the coordinates flashing on the readout, showing what was going into the navicomp. "We don't even know where we're going."

"We go out-sector first." Reasonable.

"Borg and Lista?"

Silence.

"There's no reason we cannot hire them. They would like to stay."

"Yes. They would."

"They bother you?"

"No. Should they?"

Overturned again, thinking he meant something else. "How the Rim should I know? You don't want them with us."

"Being with you could bring them trouble, Jade."

"With me. From Tas."

"Perhaps."

That meant (maybe) there was something more that could mean trouble. "I wish you would tell me what you think is going on."

"I do not know, Jade. Or I would tell you."

Not at all sure of that, Jade prowled around the control room. "I'm going back to the district," he decided suddenly. And to the quick dark look, "Looking over shoulders, me. Right?"

"Outbound cargo goes up in two hours."

"So I'll meet you at the bid center."

Heglit nodded.

Three ships had grounded since their berthing, and the port was bustling under the soft red-gold sun. There was a breeze, faint-scented with unfamiliarities, making contact with Jade so he knew it was a new world to him. He wished there was time to get out away from the ComUn sameness of the port. There were things to see and feel and taste, different people and ways. Moving through the swirling crowds of ship-men and port-workers he wondered what pleasures were favored here, what things he had never known before. And he wondered where Borget and Lista were.

He smiled, thinking of them. He would, he thought, ask them to join the ship. They had said nothing, but since the last skip of this run he had felt their desire to stay with him.

Having them with him would be a good thing, a new thing. They touched him in a way he hadn't even thought about before the run to Roc I.

The joyhouses were larger, fancier, mysteries with many dark corners and several-scented smokes drifting, some well-known. But he did not see the two Benjor. Once, turning into a narrow tunnel-like entrance, half blind in the sudden light-to-dark, he thought he saw a familiar face, but when he could see clearly there was no one he knew. He bought Orziel, a rare and expensive joy-drink out beyond C'Erit, but common as Z'Atua here. Looking over the hushed-noisy crowd he poured the cold-steamy liquor over his tongue, closed his lips and let it trickle back. Breathing in slowly through his nose, he inhaled the vapor it became, felt it explode gentle rushes of pleasure along his nerves. One more thing learned long ago. He watched the games, picking up signals automatically, wondering even as he turned them down how he would have fared here before Reese and Linking and ship-work. But it was idle thought. The ones he wanted to see were not here. He pushed his way through the crowd and back onto the noisy street. It was time to go to the bid center.

Ship-mates and jobbers filled the wide entrance to the center, making a rumble of tongues from a hundred worlds orchestrated by the chorus of fedstanspeak. He was about to step through the pillared gate when a strong hand fell on his shoulder, pulling him back. Instinct ducked, twisted, slid him aside before he recognized Heglit. The dark eyes flashed, covering the milling crowd.

"To the ship."

He didn't hear that tone often. He went. Wondering. Heglit led the way up the ramp, stepped aside to let him enter and see—

"Borg?"

The Benjor sat, bent forward, bare to the hips. A small non-Clate, maybe Roccer, stood near, doing something Jade couldn't see, didn't really try to see. All he really saw was that familiar dark gold back marred by triple bands of dark glistening red. Blood—

"What—?" He moved forward. "Borg?"

"It is not known, Jade." The non-Clate did something behind him, and his breath hissed in between clenched teeth. He trembled. "Jade, Lista— They took her. Please—"

"Took her? Borg, I do not understand."

"Nor I." Again the pain, the quick breath, the trembling. "I tried—They left me at the door of Zoar-Dragon House." He straightened a little and the great dark bruise along his ribs was visible, swollen and darkening. Kicked, Jade thought, and something in him went bright and cold.

The med-tech finished, and Borget's breath sighed out his relief. But he was pale and shivering.

"Borg. Tell me what happened."

It made little sense. They had gone to the district for food and exploring, to see it. It was no different from most ports this far from Benjo, they were noticed, but left alone; Borget's beauty did not look helpless. Then they were stopped on the street by two Algorans and a true Clate who asked Lista to go with them. She refused, thinking it a game request and nothing more. So they took her. Borget fought, but he was no match for the Algorans. They had beaten him, left him on the street unconscious. When he could move again, he made it back to the port, where Heglit found him, collapsed near the ship.

"Left him for dead," Jade said, hurting from the look in the gray eyes. He stood up, looked at Heglit. "It's like the shipmaster."

"I must find her."

"You cannot. Not now." Jade touched his arm. "I will find her."

"No." Heglit's voice fell between them, hard.

"I will—"

Heglit ignored him, looking to the med-tech. "Are you done with him?"

"Am, me. Hurt him, and bleeding. But not dangerous. Strong him being."

"Then you will go. And not speak of this." The hard voice promised retribution. The Roccer went, scuttling, cowed.

"Heglit, I will go for her. They cannot be separated."

"No. It is a trap. The Algorans did not kill him. They wanted you to know. To follow."

He wanted to protest, but Heglit was right. Algorans

did not hurt, they killed. It was the way they were. They had wanted Borget to come to him. "Then it's me they want. They will let her return if I go to them."

"It is Tas, Jade. You cannot."

Tas or not didn't matter. Only that Lista and Borget were not part of it, could not be made to suffer in his place. And he was resourceful. Getting him to come to them was not the same thing as keeping him. He turned to leave.

"Jade." The voice slapped across the cabin, surprising him. He turned. "Will you fight me to go?"

Fight? Heglit didn't fight. But he had no rights here, this was a thing that must be done. "Yes, then, if I must. But I will go."

He watched Heglit come close to the boarding door. A mistake. He should have run, he was the quicker. Instead, he attacked, feinting sideways as if to slip past, then striking, throwing all his weight in a blow aimed for the throat. Heglit seemed not to move, only his right hand leapt out, captured Jade's, and his left hand reached out to press the straining shoulder lightly—

With no change of expression he caught the boneless weight, lifted Jade to his shoulder and turned to the frozen Benjor. "You will come."

"I— Lista, I must find her."

"You will come. Now." Soft and lethal, the voice leashed Borget, pulled him toward the captain's cabin.

Heglit placed Jade on the couch. "Watch him," he told Borget. "You will not leave."

Dumb, Borget nodded, sat stiff in the near chair, staring at the unconscious man.

Now Heglit hurried. The ID card was registered, qualifying him, but he didn't know how much authority he had, even if he could lift without cargo. Probably not. But all he could do now was claim charter and two passengers. He took the chance without option, knowing they were discovered. And it was Jade who was quarry.

Departure logged his request without question, relaying the standard request for destination. He picked TomLeest, in toward Centra, and received the run coordinates. It took an hour for clearance in the busy port, and he held himself still, expecting some command from the port Authority. None came and the distant casual voice alerting him to lift seemed lightyears away from his increasing tension.

Once they were up, headed out, he relaxed. He requested a complete printout of their run from the navicomp and went to see to Jade.

He was sitting up holding his head when Heglit came in and the look he threw him was unimportantly hostile. "Now you. Just like them. Everyone doing to me and hurting others. It's enough."

"It was a trap. You would have done what they wanted." Calm. The always Heglit.

"It was my choice. She—" He could not say, even to himself, what she meant to him, or why. "You had no right."

Heglit ignored that, turned to the pale and silent Borget. "They will not harm her, knowing you are with Jade. They need her to buy him."

"How do you know it was Tas? It could—"

"Logic. Now come. I need your help. Both of you." He walked out, and after a little Jade got up, rubbing his neck.

"Come, Borg, he would not ask unless he needed us." He held out his hand and the Benjor took it. His fingers were icy.

Heglit sat before the control board studying the printout. There was Santo tea on the table, and he gestured to it.

"Where are we going?" Jade asked.

"Rafal." Heglit didn't look up.

"Just like that." Quick sarcasm.

"Like this." Heglit indicated the printout. Jade leaned over his shoulder to read, and just once, as he looked at the strong neck, dark satin over the hard tendons, he was tempted. But maybe it wouldn't work anyway.

"Says TomLeest," he read. "That's in."

"Four standard skips. First breakout to N-space is 021LV. We can reprogram there."

"Re— Oh." Make up their own run, override the program punched in at the port. He knew the possibility was built in for things like that when a skip went sour, but to plan a full run without the necessary help from ComUn's standard Star Web chart— He frowned. Unless Heglit knew a lot more than he did, they could get them-

69

selves more lost than he liked to think about. He scanned the blocky figures, trying to make sense of something he hadn't paid attention to in a long time. "Rafal Sector is a long way from here. Down the limb."

"By standard run. There are a minimum of fourteen sectors to cross. But there is an ultra channel." Heglit crossed his arms, swung the chair slightly to look at Jade. "It isn't used because the function of the Web is commerce and by-passing sectors is non-profit. But the channel is there."

"Charted?" He'd never heard of an ultra channel.

Heglit looked at him a moment. "No. But run. Long ago. The gate in is a day's run from 012LV."

"Tell it all."

"It is not the same as the standard channel; the distance is longer. I think the first skip is nineteen hours. There is a forty-nine hour N-space run, then skip two is longer. Perhaps as much as twenty-three hours."

Jade shook his head.

"We have run as long as twenty-four in channel."

Jade's back and thighs roughened, scared more by that. He looked to Borget but there was no help there.

"There are two chairs, Jade. A timer could key one in, one out, split the skip."

Relief weakened him. "Why not the standard channel, Heglit? If we stay out-sector we could—"

"Too many chances to be seen. And the automatic ComUn gate beacons will recognize our signal, give it to anyone asking. In the old channel there is no traffic and no beacons."

"What difference? Unless they could do something to us in channel."

"Is." Borget's soft voice pulled them both around. "Want you bad," he said, using lowspeak so Heglit could listen. "They can. Pushing drones or unmanned into channel. Squeeze up. Drone breaks out, send in again."

"Would work," Heglit said.

Jade pushed down angry surprise, amazed by his down-limb ignorance. "You know this for real?"

Borget blushed, but his eyes were steady. "Did, me. A down-limb ship from Burkoze run private and un-cargoed for Centra. Linkman SheelDan had her. ComUn shipping stopped two days, then went. But later same

70

ship broke back dead. Only SheelDan lived. Burned out, him. From eighty hours in Link. Talked to him, us."

A Linkman would know traffic in channel. Heglit said nothing, but Jade believed Borget. They had no choice. Now Tas, or whoever had Lista, would be surprised, not expecting them to lift. And when they found out, they would follow to TomLeest. Once they lost them and checked the beacons, the chase would be on.

While the Centra Zar ran the short shuttle-weaving course out of the busy sector, they worked on the new run. The math was complicated, the standard ComUn maps and skip charts almost worthless. Heglit said (and there was nothing else to believe) that the first breakout was into un-sectored N-space outside the limb proper, cutting across the curve to the north limb. A binary, green and orange, formed the Web break. They re-entered, according to Heglit, somewhere on toward the limb and would skip down past Rafal Sector, a long way past, breaking out near a dull red super-giant that no longer cradled planets.

Borget, moving stiffly from his injuries, surprised Jade with a sophisticated knowledge of the limbs and a talent for plotting runs, charting a way back to the Rafalan Sector. He and Heglit studied the charts, seldom talking, and Jade watched, did galley duty, and tried not to think about Lista.

"Skip one in ten." The automatic call spoke to a nearly empty ship, pulling Jade toward the Link-room. It was a relief to have something to do. Heglit joined him, automatically seeing to the system. They would, he said, respond to the beacon as usual, then break the pattern and run north. The gate they wanted was un-beaconed, but lay in the center of a triangle of three distinctive stars. It should take them about fifty-seven hours from breakout. Time to rest, and maybe be chased a little if they were noticed.

Then the cool clasp of the Link-mask, dark, the sound of the door sliding shut, the sweet alone feel— He was tense, but broke in clean and crisp.

It was a busy channel, but all soaring dives and sweeping curves, easy and exhilarating.

He came into the control room while they were still receiving the automatic program from the beacon. Heglit

71

watched the complete series, keyed the standard response, then turned to the control board where Borget waited. The golden hands played quick and sure over the keys, overriding the program, feeding in new coordinates. The spangled view on the outview screen began to drift down and to the right.

They ran, looking back, but no ships broke from the ComUn traffic pattern to follow. Cut loose from the charted run, Jade watched the outview, thinking of bigness and getting lost, wondering how Heglit knew so much, and offering himself the hints from Heglit about TreAsh and Rafal for comfort. He washed, sat alone in the cabin brushing his hair, wanting to rest, but thinking of the skip. A new channel. Like Turloz gave them. Only no Sector Watch at breakout. Nothing there. He wanted to go tell Heglit no. But he didn't.

Borget came, subdued, feeling his nervousness, and they talked of nothing, passing time, not speaking of Lista. And finally he slept.

Then it was time. He went down to the Link-room and Heglit was there. But he kept his what-ifs to himself, waiting for the door to close on his blindness, for the timer to key his finger and push him out into the photon-sparkled dark. They were in closer to the dense sectors, and the million-starred galaxy shimmered with light, pouring feather-torrents of energy against his skin, good—

Then the gate. They came into it obliquely, he knew by the violent twist, the searing violet yell against his shoulder and left leg as he fought scared toward the amber flood of channel center, thinking ship-thoughts now, not self-thoughts, using agility and instinct, running from the hurts. It was a wild channel, narrows deepening, dropping him to wide spiraling pools, trying to throw him into howling discords of black-laced blue. Hair snapping, trickling violet sparks of excess energy against back and flanks, he reached, dove, curved, leapt, soared into violence, hanging onto the elusive siren-solo of amber safety. Until fatigue slowed him, cramped and weakening. Confusion made response harder. He slid toward the edge, stretched, jerked back and fell and fell and fell down a long horn note into big amber space, bright and safe. Resting, heart thudding. He searched for the flow, reaching, felt movement— Four ways. Great black bubbles oozing out of amber, pushing up from the bright depths, red-flickered, pulling— There was nowhere to go. He froze against his own answer to the insideout impossibility of being pulled all directions at once. He was not strong enough to hold, stretched—

Black flickered, but warm quick strength flowed like prayer-answer, pulling him back into himself. Relief met abrupt termination, black staccato silence ringing in his head . . . What—?

"Jade."

Wordsound made him flinch. Touch let him trade ship-feel for skin-feel, and he would have cried out, but hands pulled away the mask. He covered his eyes.

"Jade. You are unLinked."

"Yes." His eyes opened to see Borget beside him, "What—?" flashed to the other chair where Heglit sat faceless behind the jeweled mask.

"Eighteen hours, Jade. You were hurting."

Not his strength, then. He wanted to be angry but he knew he had reached his limit in the channel. He might have lost them all. Even out here where things felt slow and simple, he felt confused. It was good to let Borget take him to his cabin, to lie still and let the knowing hands knead away the tension.

Breakout tone woke him, and Heglit was already in the corridor, heading for the control room. It had been three hours since he took over.

Jade's eyes jumped to the outview screen. "Where are we?"

"Here."

"Here where?"

"There is no name for here. It is the place between gates."

The place between gates. Black and empty, the distant galactic limb a silver-dusty arch across the screen. Heglit did something to the controls and a bright point slid onto the screen, drifted across, then another, and finally three. A triangle of blue, green, and yellow. The next gate. After the brilliance of the inner sectors this loneliness was too cold, too big. He could feel it outside the Centra Zar squeezing them small. He turned away.

"How long?"

"Forty-nine hours to skip. Perhaps longer." The skip had gone longer than planned. Maybe things were different here.

A dark bronze hand keyed the frequency-scan, the sensitive ear that listened for the local web of short channels that threaded the space around each stellar family, binding it into the larger Star Web. These quieter channels were usually preprogrammed by Sector Watch comps and fed into each ship as it broke into N-space, directing traffic into and out of the system. Here there was no traffic, no watch—

"There is nothing here," Heglit said, not looking up. "We can feel our way in."

Feel their way in. "Heglit—" Jade shook his head, watching the readout, the nearly idle hand responding to the projected figures, wondering about this Rafalan who seemed suddenly to know so much, wondering how much he did know that he kept to himself. And why.

"Last gate we came in sharp. Nearly took my leg off." Saying it did not feel as good as he thought it would. He felt Borget look at him. Heglit said nothing. Naturally. He shrugged and left, going to the galley to fix their trays, uneasy with the outside emptiness, feeling scattered, like everything was getting away from him, and he couldn't anticipate the future. Just caught up, like in the last skip.

He ate alone in the cabin, then sat brushing his hair, trying to build a pattern of the past weeks. Longer than that, if he included the two attacks Lurz said (and apparently Heglit believed) Tas directed against him. Tas, Lurz, Sarn. They had nothing to do with him. He had no plan, no need beyond freedom to go where he pleased and be no more answerable to anyone. The ship was his (and Heglit's). He was free. And he had Borget and Lista. Had had. Then nothing but trouble. Trouble for him, trouble for them, trouble only Heglit seemed able to read. And it meant nothing he could understand.

The door slid open and Borget came in, stopped when he saw Jade cloaked in dark veils of hair. He looked drawn, hurting someplace, and Jade could only guess at his secret feelings.

"Are you well, Borg?"

"I am well." He came, finally, and sat, watching the

74

hair-brushing ritual pensively. He had not spoken of his sister since the first hours away from Rio Del. Jade sighed and did it for him.

"You are worried for her."

"I am afraid for her. But if it is her fear or my own, I do not know. It is a strange thing, being so far apart from myself. I do not know where she is, only that she lives."

"You know that?"

"I know it. When she ceases, so shall I also." He said it easily, like an of course thing. That shook Jade. True or not, Borget believed it.

"You will find her."

"Perhaps. Or I shall lose you also." The gray eyes measured him, accepting even that. "This is another kind of adventure with you and dark Heglit. He runs to save you."

"And the ship."

"I think the ship is nothing to him, only a way of doing the thing he must do. It is you, and a greater area of action. He has a will to know, to understand the whys of it. He does not game, but he watches and learns. And he knows many things beyond other non-Clate ship-workers."

"He knows many things, Borg. But he will not speak beyond this time. He does not feel fear or gladness." But he thought of a time when he knew the other side of that dark coin, and his hands were like angry protest jumping up to coil and knot his hair.

"You wish to be angry."

"No. I wish—" He relaxed, chin cupped in palm. "I wish to be done with unanswered questions and Web-ghosts. I want it done, to be safe all together. Then we will have Lista and maybe laugh together again."

"Perhaps."

Maybe Heglit didn't trust this outer Star Web so much now. They flashed in and out of the local web, vectoring on a visual goal, and he spoke to Jade of the next Star Web skip, saying they would stagger the Link. No more than twelve hours in for either of them.

"When you broke in," Jade said, remembering, "there was something in the channel like I never felt before."

Heglit had seen-felt them. He did not know what they were. "There was a feel of gates," he suggested.

"Four together?"

Heglit shrugged and Jade thought. There had been that feel, the untranslatable impulse to approach holding back, until the tension burst, thrusting the ship out into N-space. But four? Equal in pull? He had felt he might burst through all four at once. Impossible. But the feeling had been there. He wondered what would have happened and was glad he didn't know. The Star Web was used, but it was not really known. And it was not for gaming with.

The second skip was straighter, faster, less eventful. But Heglit broke in in twelve, bringing a flash of new dimensions and knowings before the slap of unlinking.

He and Borget stayed in the control room, not knowing when they would breakout to N-space, or where. If it was near a ComUn beacon they would have to identify themselves and move fast.

They had nearly eleven hours. And breakout came simultaneous with a ComUn beacon signal. Borget recognized the code. They were four sectors down from Rafal. And now that their ship's signal was being automatically recorded, they dared not run straight in. Thinking fast, Jade opted for the beacon program, then overrode with a program Borget had charted. He punched in a skip one warning and received a green from Heglit, who had stayed put.

They shuttled back and forth, darning the limb together, but approaching Rafal, avoiding all but the most peripheral channels of the sector webs. Three weeks. And they were tired, completely out of touch with what was happening in the sectors of ComUn. Then they broke out to N-space and the beacon read the code for Rafal.

Jade left the Link-room, tired and hungry, joining Heglit in the control room. Borget was asleep. The sector lay ahead, a loose cluster of seven stars, five with life-supporting planets. The beacon itself gave evidence that this was a different sector. The first contact was standard code, feeding itself into the comp-system, but it was followed by a verbal request for personal, not ship, identification, first in Rafalspeak, then in fedstan. Jade looked at Heglit in surprise, but the bronze face (sharper now than when this run began) showed calm as he replied in Rafalspeak. "Heglit D'Othiel. For Iron. Object sanctuary clearance. No cargo, no ComUn bond, or run record. Relay message to Port Coordinator Tarf."

"Heglit, welcome. Request monitored and coded. Straight run coming in on signal."

"They know you?"

"Possible. But Rafalspeak is not common. It tells them much."

They came in straight and easy, the beam swinging expertly to draw them to ground and into a waiting berth. They all sagged a little, hoping for a stillness and an end to running for a while.

Heglit left the ship alone, returning shortly with another Rafalan, as dark and hawk-faced as himself, who welcomed them in hispeak, offering them the hospitality of the port.

"There are things I must do that are held away from outsiders," Heglit explained. "You will be safe here, and perhaps I will return with some answers."

"In?" Jade asked, knowing this was what they had come for, but not liking Heglit to leave them.

"In to Rafalpha, yes. Tarf knows of Tas. You can speak with him if necessary."

Jade wondered why that might be necessary, but he kept quiet. They would do as he said. There was no choice.

7

The run into Rafalpha would have surprised Jade, had he known. Heglit did not leave from the ComUn port, but from a place screened and hidden from any curious off-worlders who might wander away from the port. He walked through a place of quiet efficiency and was greeted by name by tall bronze men who reported his ship ready for him. Unlike ComUn vessels, she was small and slim, speaking to the eyes of speed and purpose, black as space itself but for the design of three linked circles on her flank.

He entered the ship alone, spoke briefly to the ground crew, did things to the control board and lay back as the ship came alive, poised, leapt into the twin-mooned sky. Not pushed up, like the ComUn ships, but leaping with her own secret muscle. Heglit tested her, examined all sensors and responses, then relaxed, hard mouth softening a little. With good cause. She was his ship as no other could be. Sweet and secret, known only here in this sector, she knew him through a special Link-system, became him in the flash-runs along the local Web-lines. It had been a long time.

Six fast hours later, the port on Rafalpha picked up his signal and flashed back clearance. He was expected.

And they were waiting in the flat golden light of late afternoon. The old man and the woman. And it was on her the dark eyes rested, for her the hard mouth smiled.

"You did not forget, Zendra."

"Nor you, Dariel-Heglit." Warm laughter wove about them, and pleasure sharing breath and touch, and he was home. But the hardness learned into him was not so easily softened. He turned to the old man, holding her pliant body against his side.

"Varon. You are well?"

"Yes. And you, Dariel. Leaner, more tired, perhaps. Tarf said you came with business to interest the Academy, and maybe the Council."

"Yes. It may be urgent. Can you convene them?"

"All?"

"The question touches many areas, Varon. We will talk together. You can decide who is needed."

Varon nodded. "Tomorrow is soon enough." He smiled and led the way to his ground car. And there was time, moving through the deepening dusk, to speak with the woman, quiet, touching a time past, and a life.

There was the wide airy home, the comfort of the heated pool and icy spray, the flowing scarlet robe not chosen by accident. And a night to share and be, and know what he had given up.

She came to him, woman of Dariel, as was her right, strong-soft, bringing laughter and ways of taming his learned severity.

But she could not, in one night, undo the years of training and discipline that made him what he was, one of the elite of Rafal, one of the Outgoers. Long after she slept warm and moist against his hardness, he stroked her back, feeling it yield beneath his hand, pleased by the new lethargy of his body, but already wondering how he would speak with the Council to tell them what he thought to be true.

Varon was there when he woke before dawn. They bathed together and talked.

"There is change coming, Varon. ComUn will soon know pressure from the out-sectors. There are more Freeshippers liking to be free and joining together."

Varon nodded. Nothing, he knew, lasted forever, not even ComUn and its rigid economic control of all sectors with space-reach ability. "Will there be conflict?"

"Sooner or later." He floated on scented water watching high clouds blush, red-glazed with sunrise.

"This is not all you returned for."

"No." Pulling himself out of the water, Heglit leaned against the stone wall, arms folded. "There are three things. All linked somehow. First is the Free-men coming together against ComUn under a man named Lurz, from Burkoze Sector. We have known from the beginning that the power of the ComUn would be challenged and fall. That it should happen now is only a thing that happens. But there was a ship, controlled by Tas himself, sent to run a channel between C'Erit and TaLur, and it was modified to run the Star Web differently. And there is a Clate, unparented, from the Rim Sector worlds as far as memory takes him. Tas has tried more than twice to have him terminated, though he was only a free-lance Linkman, and a joy-skinner before."

"Ah— Your Link-mate."

"More now. But important here is that he has the identical appearance of Jadriel Sarn."

"Exact?"

"To the eyes. But younger."

Varon pinched his lower lip, thoughtful. "Three separate items. How are they joined?"

"I am not sure. Time perhaps. The ship— There have been no new skip methods since the Traveler War. We have watched for that, but only we have developed the in-ship beams and freed ourselves from the port system."

"That does not necessarily connect the other two items."

"Not obviously. And perhaps, I hope foolishly. It is one of our faults. Is it not?"

Varon did not smile. He knew too well what was done to prepare the Outgoers, the mental discipline that made them expert observers, and pared away wishful thinking. "What do you see?"

"As Outgoer I do not have access to certain knowledge, but it is my belief that TreAsh foresaw the rise of the ComUn from the military union of the war."

"They did. Correctly."

"And could they not have forseen the time of this new conflict within the union?"

"Say what you suspect, Dariel."

"I found a device in the ship Tas had modified. It is probably TreAshal. And Tas must know it. He saw Jade's resemblance to Sarn, or something more. If the TreAshal knew of this time coming they could have planned for it. The device could be for some TreAshal purpose, and Jade could be involved."

"You have the device?"

"Yes. With me. The ship is on Iron. And Jade also."

"You brought him?"

"Tas would have found him."

Varon looked at him a minute, then nodded. "I will tell Gandar. He chairs the Council now. The device will be studied." He turned away, then turned back. "You believe the Clate is connected to TreAsh."

"I do."

"Evidence."

"None. But Jade is Clate, and he has Linked into the Star Web for six stanyears. Most do not complete a third before burnout."

"Do not hope for too much. Tas could fear his resemblance to Sarn might rally the Free-men." Then, watching the schooled face, "There is more."

"Yes. We share-Linked the run to TaLur."

Varon's reaction to that showed only in his eyes. Heglit looked at him a moment, then turned away and went in to breafast. The woman watched him, saw the closed face, the controlled bodyspeak, and kept silent. He was no longer home.

A brief call broke into the morning. Expected. Bring Jade to Rafalpha. Drug of choice was chai, so he would know nothing. It was ordered by the Council. He called the port, found Varon had already alerted them to have his ship ready, and sent down the vial of sleep-drug.

The flight out was more careful, coming in to the dark of Iron, following a path screened by Rafalan technique. He came fast, hitting the down beam below the horizon line. No other run was so exhilarating, or dangerous. He liked it.

8

Iron was a closed port. No open listing for free-lance ship-workers, no brawling joyhouses, only food and lodging and shelter from the cold wind that blew always from the bleak and sterile peaks surrounding the port. And the tall dark men like Heglit, moving about the houses and shops. But there was Z'Atua, and comfort during the long cold dusk. Borget accepted everything, sitting still, watching Jade and the other Clates in the warm room, face pensive.

Missing Lista, Jade thought, feeling his middle loosen and warm with liquor. He missed her too, like a hard knot of hunger inside where the Z'Atua could not reach. And he did not like Iron. He felt restricted, hemmed in by the sobriety and the always-there Rafalans. What was Heglit doing? Why was he being hounded by Tas? Too many questions scattered his thoughts. He frowned at his hands, linked around the bowl of Z'Atua, and thought of that last run out from Rio Del, wanting to speak of it, afraid of it, but wanting more to go back, to run it again, to feel—

He shivered, looked up, found dark eyes watching him through the confusion of Z'Atua.

"Watching me, Borg," he said quietly. "Not liking it me."

"Knowing you from Heglit." The Benjor shrugged, reaching for a slice of dried zrill-fruit. "No friends of ComUn them." Then, switching to Benjorspeak, "Jade, why did that one bring us here? To be safe from Tas he could have run to Burkoze Sector, where the numbers are against ComUn and there is help from other Free-shippers."

"Jade did not know. He only vaguely sensed the difference between what Rafal was supposed to be and

82

what it was. But there was a feeling in him that he didn't want to get involved in whatever Rafal was. Something more than simple unknown warned him.

They shared a small chilly room above the eating house, lying together for warmth. But dreams troubled Jade's sleep, jerking him awake with a memory of Heglit's laughter echoing through the dark.

"You are troubled." Borget's warm voice returned sanity and he grasped it, shivering.

"A dream," he breathed finally. "Of him laughing."

"The dark one." Borget was comfort and knowledge, but not selfless, and they slept finally. Warm.

Then Heglit was back, unannounced, one of the always-there dark men that Jade ignored. Only Borget saw him, watched him come into the warm room seeing them already or knowing where they were, seeming no different than two days ago. Borget held silent, wondering what would be said between these two who were (or were not) friends.

"Jade." Heglit pulled the man's attention to him. "Come. It is time to learn why Tas wants you."

"Where have you been?"

Not answering, Heglit turned toward the door. Jade made a short explicit sound, then, glancing at Borget, got up to follow. It was night and very cold, and Heglit turned toward the great shadowed building about the port. Jade caught up with him, angry, and knowing enough to keep it to himself. "Where?"

"Here." Heglit stopped. One hand moved to his chest, then reached to Jade. Following close, Borget saw the small pale flash as something popped softly near Jade's face. Jade jerked back, caught a breath to question or cry out, then slid into Heglit's arms. Lifting him easily, the Rafalan turned to see the forgotten Benjor.

"Kill him then, you. For Tas." The Benjor softness had a different quality, a threat and determination.

"No." Heglit thought a moment wondering what to say. He could not take Borget to Rafalpha.

"Why sleep him, you, Rafalan?"

"To learn of him and keep him from greater dangers, only. We will return here soon, and he cannot know where and how we go. I must take him now. Go to Tarf, at

83

the port. Tell him you are of the Centra Zar. He will give you lodging and safety until we return."

"Wish him well, you?" The quiet lowspeak demanded truth and Heglit wondered how he knew Borget would know it.

"I wish us all well."

"Stay with you, him, after this thing you do?"

"Perhaps I will not wish to stay with him." Heglit looked down at the pale face, the dark hair, undone, falling over his arm to brush his boots, and he wondered how the Benjor demanded of him such specific honesty. When he looked up Borget was moving away toward the port.

Jade slept deep and dreaming, unaware of the journey or the ship. Once he stirred, rising toward consciousness, and his companion pressed a small silver cube against his neck, watched carefully a moment, before turning back to the control board.

Varon was waiting at the port with two others who took the sleeping man to a waiting ground car. Heglit would have gone with them, but Varon stopped him.

"They go to the Academy. We will follow, but there is talking needed."

Heglit did not answer. If Varon said talk was needed, he would talk. They climbed into his ground car and floated away from the port.

"I spoke with Gandar. He has called Councilmen from History and Physics, and they have the option to call others at need. But it is you I must speak with. You know your choosing as Outgoer placed you under restriction that must last as long as you go out."

Heglit nodded. It was the price Outgoers paid. Knowing that and always wondering what they did not know. But it was their greatest security, and Rafal's. What they did not know they could not tell or imply.

"If this question should move into those restricted areas, and you wish to follow, you will have a choice to make."

"I?" This surprised him. He had thought all decisions of this nature were made by the Council. He wondered how he would choose between going out, Linking through the Star Web toward Centra and the dense shimmering skies, or remaining here, tying into whatever research areas were involved. He was of Rafalpha, the scientific research center of the Rafal Sector. He had always supposed he would return to stay and apply what he had learned to their continuing studies. But so soon?

"What is to be done, Varon? To Jade."

"A genetic history, and as complete a profile as is possible without his full knowledge and cooperation. He will not know."

They were good in bio-search and diagnosis. Better than any Heglit had found outside Rafal Sector. But then, anymore, he was only surprised at what was not known outside.

There was no time wasted here. The Council knew he was back and was convened, waiting for him. He felt conspicuous among the vari-colored robes, somber in his loose dark blouse and tight dark pants and boots. Gandar greeted him, a familiar voice. "Dariel, you bring us interesting news of ComUn. Does your question concern Rafal?"

"I do not know, Gandar. I believe the thing I bring has to do with Jadriel Sarn, last of TreAsh."

"Evidence."

Standard reply. He told of Jade's resemblance to Sarn, of the device and the hunt by Tas.

"You see a connection between these incidents?"

"None I can explain," he admitted. "Only that Tas had reason to think of Sarn and became aware of Jade at the same time. And gave orders to test a ship that had been changed by the device I left with Varon."

"It is being examined." Gandar looked about the bright airy room. "Questions?"

"How shall the problem be stated?" A blue-and-gold-robed someone spoke. Not to Heglit.

"There is no one statement yet," a red robe responded.

"Correct." That was Varon, and, as head of the Academy research coordination department, his words had weight. "First we learn what we can of this device and the Clate Linkman. Then we can define the problem and its possible connection with ComUn and Rafal, if any."

"Agreed." Gandar leaned back. "And you, Dariel. Will you stay and learn, or leave us again?"

"The man is friend, Gandar. He shared his fortune with me. And we are contracted partners. I will stay a while. There is another on Iron I have bonded by my word that Jade will be unharmed."

"Clate?"

"Benjor. Marginal class A. He is staying with Tarf." He thought also of Lista, but that was a thing of outside and not the Council's problem. His duty here was to Rafal.

"Outgoer Dariel-Heglit." Someone spoke into the silence. "What do you suspect we will find to be true about the Clate and that device?"

It was this he had expected. He was ready. "That the device is connected to Sarn, perhaps taken from him when he was discovered in Rafal Sector. And that the man is TreAshal."

Silence fell, loud with the pressure of the eyes turned to him.

"Evidence." Gandar's voice slapped.

"There could be none. Not for the man. Sarn and his were the last of the TreAshal. He knew—" The voice haltered in mid-stride as the speaker remembered the restriction on Outgoers . . .

"This news of tension between ComUn and the Freemen," someone suggested, and the Council turned to more concrete areas of speculation, querying Heglit about the current situation and other Federation matters. He answered as completely as he could from his observations outside. It was a long session.

Two days of being home, of exchanging his sober Outgoer dress for the colorful garments of his homeworld, of long talks with the heads of various departments at the Academy always hungry for news of the outside. It was Rafal's only contact, and a way of measuring growth. Two days and nights of seeing Zendra and not seeing Jade. Impatience had been schooled out of him, but not curiosity, so he was pleased when he asked again and was given permission to go to the area of the Academy where Jade was undergoing tests.

He expected a sleeper, unaware. He found Jade sitting on a narrow bed brushing his hair. And he was angry.

"Cage, me," he snapped when Heglit came in. "Saving from Tas by you is flash-dust. His cage or yours for me."

"Talk like a man, Jade." Automatic words slipping into fedstanspeak as though he had not been speaking Rafalan for four days. "We are trying to find out why Tas wants you."

"I am trying to find out why everyone wants me. Tas, Lurz, Rafal. And no one tells me why. I cannot go out and no one speaks to me. What are they doing to me here?" That was fear.

"Trying to find out who you are." Wondering still why the man was awake.

"I am me." Sharp, staring down at his up-turned feet, then looking up. "I am only me, Heglit. I cannot stay here, closed and locked, waiting for them to come and sleep me. I need—" He gestured vaguely. "Out. All the out there. You are Linkman and shipper, you know this. Grounding crushes us down."

Heglit looked at him like Heglit always looked at him, and he thought maybe he didn't know. Maybe he had never needed. Except— He shook his head. "How long, Heglit?"

"Not long, Jade. I will speak to them. Do not be angry."

But they would not speak to him. The study of the Clate, they said, had moved into restricted areas. He did not argue; he was too much of Rafal. But there were other ways of learning than asking direct questions.

It was late when Varon found time to join him at the house. He had been kept busy. "You bring us much to puzzle about, Dariel-Heglit."

"I am puzzled also. Why is Jade awake? He is Outsider and you said he would not know of this."

"True. But unconsciousness interfered with suggested studies when it was prolonged. He needs the normal sleep-wake pattern."

"This cannot have to do with identification."

"No. We know what he is. There is no doubt possible there. But that gives other questions, perhaps more important. We must know why he is."

Heglit could make no sense of that, and Varon saw it, calming him skillfully. "In your position, without full knowledge, it is impossible to understand."

"Accepted. But Jade is—"

"The Clate is well. I myself am involved in his studies."

"He suffers from being caged and alone."

"As you suffer from curiosity. No more." Varon poured a refreshing drink and changed the subject. Heglit noted it and waited to ask what he wanted.

"Will he be released?"

"He is not captive." Varon smiled. "But he is important to us."

"What of the device?"

Varon shook his head, still smiling. "Dariel-Heglit, you should have done as other Outgoers and brought the problem for solving, then returned to your work outside. You ask questions we cannot answer for you."

All areas of the study on Jade were classified. Why? He pondered unknowables after Varon left. Perhaps he should leave, go back to Iron for Borget, take the Centra Zar out to the long runs toward Centra and learn of ComUn and the Free-men. But would Borget go and leave Jade here? He doubted it, remembering the voice and posture of the Benjor when he took Jade. And he had bound himself by his word.

He was as accepted in the Academy as any Rafalan, wandering the maze of halls and departments until he found where the crystal was being studied. He spoke with the technicians, telling them of outside, answering their questions. They were learned men, but not trained in the ways of the Outgoers, not suspecting his questions.

"Have you studied the TreAshal Web device?" He asked the question without pause, watching eyes and reactions.

"We have. A strange device. Not built, and not quite natural."

"Crystal."

"But specific. Only to what is difficult to determine."

"Modifier perhaps. To change the Link frequency?"

"Certainly. But the resonances have no function. It must have been a prototype, and the use was lost with Sarn."

He spoke a while longer, but already had what he wanted. The crystal was TreAshal, and linked to Sarn. As he suspected. And Sarn had been taken by the Federation. And executed.

88

The work on the Clate was not so accessible. He was not welcome in that section, by Varon's order. The excuse was that his familiarity with the Clate would interfere with the work. He did not like that. But he did not argue.

As though aware of his unease, the Council kept him busy. He had been gone from Rafal a long time, and visited many sectors. There were questions, they said. But he could not forget Jade, or the accusation of the Benjor. His patience was long, but not infinite. After four days he called Varon, insisted on seeing him.

"What are you doing with Jade that I may not see him?"

"Seeking answers. There is that in him which fights us, so our work is more difficult."

"What are you doing, Varon?"

"Dariel, there is so much you cannot know as you are. It would be easier if you had a fuller knowledge of our science." He gestured, a single hand raised, palm out, pacifying. "This I can say. The TreAshal had knowledge of more than flesh. They linked mind and body, and taught us their methods in a small way. We have studied the Clate. We know, somewhat, who he is, that he is linked to Sarn. Now we must know why and if he is a message of sorts to us."

"To Rafal?"

"Yes. It would be no real surprise. Sarn is the reason for the Outgoers who keep watch on the actions of ComUn, waiting for the time we will be able to use our knowledge. When Sarn was last here he spoke of a future when Rafal would complete the work he had begun, and he charged us to maintain our growth and understanding of the sciences."

"What was the work we were to complete?"

"The work of TreAsh, of course. They knew there would be a time when the menace of the Travelers would be forgotten, when the bounds of the union would weaken and it would be possible for Rafal to go out as TreAsh did before the war, to Link the worlds together in understanding."

That had more the ring of ritual philosophy than history. "What work did Jadriel Sarn do here?"

"He was Linkmaster and Master communicator. He

came to us last to leave a message of hope. Already they knew TreAsh was doomed."

"That period of history is not fully taught Outgoers," Heglit said, reaching to fill their goblets.

"There is much they have to learn, and little time. That was long ago. Your training deals more with the Star Web and practical knowledge. And long before Sarn we worked with TreAsh on charting the Web, from the time they learned we had a form of mind that could work well within the Web without strain. They taught us much."

"And Sarn was one who worked with the Star Web?"

"The last of TreAsh. He came that last year to collect the Silvron ore of Rafaldel as they had done every year. It was expected by the Federation. And he came here to Rafalpha to make payment and study our charts of the Web. We had been working with TreAsh to create a complete map and investigate the nature of the Star Web. But he came most importantly to leave a message, to guide us through the time of the Restriction, though he did not say it."

Heglit paid polite attention, but was not really listening. He had been well schooled in logic and what Varon was telling him defied common sense. He knew that here on Rafalpha, site of Sarn's last contact, TreAsh was a legend, revered for its martyrdom. But he had also been schooled out of hero-worship. There had to be a reason for TreAsh to allow its destruction, and a reason for Sarn to come here on the eve of that destruction. Something more than a message of hope. The fact that he had come here and been taken in this sector hung in Heglit's mind, irritating, trying to tell him something he could not hear.

The complexities of his problem shifted slightly after Varon left. He sat a long quiet time watching the breeze break stars over the water's gloss. They knew what Jade was. Connected to Sarn, he was certain. But the nature of that connection was kept from him. Why? And why was the who of him not enough? What more did they hope to learn? He began, finally, to understand that he could not learn all he needed to know by manipulation and observation.

How much of his decision was made from the fear for

Jade he didn't know, but it looked like the only way to the truth. He understood and accepted his own arrogance in believing the Council had blinded itself by mythologizing a long-dead people, but intuition was a stronger force in him now.

Gandar welcomed him early in the private study, perhaps expecting him. "Varon has spoken to me of your interest in our current problem, Dariel-Heglit."

"He has correctly shown me my lack of knowledge, but I would like to participate in the Council's study."

"Then you must make a choice."

"I have chosen. I will relinquish my position as Outgoer." He said it carefully, knowing he was lying, half expecting Gandar to know it too. But the old man only nodded, looking pleased.

"So we expected. You will notify the registrar and be classified researcher."

"Immediately." And he wondered suddenly if this, after all, was why Varon had kept him from the answers he was seeking, perhaps because Varon was father to the Lady Zendra.

Status change for Outgoers got notice. For Heglit, the Academy opened up. He was invited (and counselled) to study those things restricted, and so his visit to the history department was welcomed without comment. But even he could not have said what he was looking for. He received the standard history tapes for the period of the Traveler War and Sarn's last grounding on Rafalpha, meaning to take them home to study at leisure. Only the one, the last message taped for the people of Rafal, did he listen to in the library. And he was disappointed, or expecting too much. Sarn was indeed like Jade, not the meta-human hero worshiped for three hundred stanyears. The address was banal, touching humor at times, praising the industry and science of Rafal. And it rang false. He stared at the screen, watching the face, not really listening to the words, seeing vibrancy and excitement beneath the assumed dignity. That should not be, not when this man and all his people faced death and knew it.

"The pattern of this fabric of events cannot wholly be changed," the voice said in his ear. "But you can and must remain what you are: our hope for the future of the Federation. Do not yield to the warriors of the Union. Their time has come and will pass. Do not be driven in on yourselves through your unwillingness to join in their battle. Buy your way out into the galaxy, and watch and wait for the opportunity to continue my work. The Star Web in time will provide you with answers and perhaps pose even greater questions . . ."

Impatient, he snapped off the viewer, collecting the tapes he had ordered, wondering what he had hoped to learn. The other students in the library watched him as he strode out, still moving with the silent arrogance of the Outgoer. He did not notice.

It was nearing dusk, the quiet hour before the evening meal, usually reserved for meditation on the day. But his curiosity itched. Impulsively, he turned toward the bio-research area. Unencumbered by restrictions now, he could ask to see Jade. The uncanny resemblance to Sarn stuck with him, and he wondered if the researchers studying the man had noted it.

As he half-expected, the senior was absent, already gone to his home. But a student, aware of his status change, welcomed him, telling him the Clate was depressed and angry. Heglit only nodded, thinking the student would also be depressed and angry if locked up and not told why.

The man lay on his bed, face to the wall, dark hair weaving a tangled mass over the pillow. He did not move when the door slid shut.

"Jade."

"No more." The words whispered, as if the voice was out of reach. "I cannot—" The hand on his shoulder brought him over on his back, staring up, uncurious.

"Jade. What are they doing to you?"

"Dreaming me. No more. I cannot reach them— All gone. Even Borg. He will die of losing her."

"He will not die."

The man sat up violently, thrusting the hand away. "You, cold life. Rafalan. He will die, I tell you. You who have no feeling, no need, no hurts here on your cold hurting world. You do not know." Fast and angry Rafal-speak, face flushed now. "They are trying to change me."

92

Heglit looked down at him, thinking invisible thoughts. He had seen this Jade before, sick and hurting. But not here, with the best care in the galaxy. Some decision made, he turned toward the door. "I will be back."

It was night, the corridors soft-lit and quiet as he strode toward the senior's office. The student sat at a desk writing something in a file. He looked up, recognizing the Linkman.

"Greetings, Dariel-Heglit. Madian left word you had joined us, he was pleased with your status change."

"And I. There is much to learn and do. I have known the Clate long. I believe there is a mistake in his studies."

"And I. But Madian insists. Have you seen the work?"

"Not yet."

"Now would be a good time. Then you can speak better with Madian tomorrow."

It was that easy. To please the student he went over the first tests, let them be explained to him. "The conclusion is obvious. We have records here of tests done, both ours and TreAshal, when we were seeking some key to the Linker types, and Sarn was among them. As you see, the genetic pattern holds. Proof that the Clate is first generation. Jadriel Sarn's son. Quite impossible, of course, because of the time."

Time. Stunned by the identification, he held his face still, waiting for his thoughts to clear. But a phrase, waiting, scattered them. ". . . Star Web in time . . . complete my work . . ." *My* work. The TaLur run. Three hundred stanyears. Time. Too much time. *A reason for that last message.*

The idea had lain full grown in his mind. Now it rose up, blinding. He thanked the student, walked alone back down the hall. Sarn had told them in such a way they would only understand if they had all the pieces. Jade, the crystal, the history, a practice run in the Star Web. No wonder the Council was confused. They knew the last address too well, had heard it too often. They could not hear the calculated message.

Asked, he could not have supported his knowledge with evidence. But he did not doubt it. Nor did he doubt that Varon would listen sympathetically and smile to himself.

And if he did convince them?

93

He stopped walking, stood staring at the door. They had waited three hundred stanyears for the Federation to weaken, believing in a prophecy from Sarn that they would one day rule wisely and well. But he had not said that either . . .

He turned away from the door, went back to Jade's room. "Come, Jade."

The man shook his head. "No more. I will not."

"Jade. We are leaving now."

There had been too many dark faces, too many confusions and things done and said he could not understand. His head felt like after chem-linking with Djin-glow. "Leaving? Going out?" But he did not believe it.

"Yes." The dark hand reached and he took it, found it warm and unexpectedly strong. He let it pull him up.

No one watched, no one could imagine this being done. Not by a Rafalan. Heglit helped him down the dim hall, out the door. Jade stopped here, looking up, shivering, breathing fast against the star-rich dark. Relief spread through him like laughter, making him weak.

"You will stay here. There is a thing I must get." Knowing already what he planned he did not let himself be surprised. The crystal was part of this. He must have it.

This was Rafal; no one here feared for the security of objects in the Academy. He simply walked in and picked it up. Gambling for time, he punched in a request to the library, asking that a complete Star Web chart be sent to his house immediately. Then he returned to where Jade sat, still looking at the sky, still shivering.

Leaving Jade in the ground car he went into the house without waking the woman, pulled on the familiar dark Outgoer clothing, clasping the neck pouch so it lay heavy against his chest with the weight of the crystal. The chart lay waiting on his desk.

The little ship was a wonder to Jade, bringing him a way out of his stupor.

"That lifts?"

"It lifts, Jade. Come." He got the man aboard, then called port control, not wanting to lift into a downshipper's pattern. There was interest, but no surprise, when he requested clearance, and it came quickly.

Then they were away, fast and sure. Jade watched a

while, then slept, not the heavy chai sleep, but the sleep of one carried beyond exhaustion and finally allowed to relax.

An hour out from Iron, Heglit called Tarf, asking him to have the Centra Zar lift-readied immediately. Again there was curiosity, but no suspicion.

9

It was disconnected and dreamlike to Jade, remembering
after, the moving when he was told, the warm golden
embrace of the Benjor who had half-trusted the cool one.
But relief at being free was a narcotic, and he slept
warm and secure in the cabin of the Centra Zar, to wake
hungry, feeling the subtle message of life in the ship,
wondering if it had not all been a bad chem-link. He ate
alone, and went to find Borget and Heglit and learn
where they were going.

Only Borget was in the control room, and the outview
screen played the kaleidoscope of channel skip.

"What channel?"

"Down-limb to Ergon."

"Out."

Borget nodded. "To the uncharted ·channel. Heglit
is—" He paused, seeking the right word. "A thing happened to him on his world."

"They were keeping me. He took me to them. Then
he brought me away, secretly."

"He did not like what they did to you. They are like
him?"

Jade thought about it, then shook his head. "Different.
Not so cold. But less kind." Though he had never thought
of Heglit as kind, exactly.

They ran straight for the gate to the off-chart channel,
and after three skips in less than forty hours, Heglit
joined them. To Jade's familiar eyes he looked finer-
drawn, tired.

"I take the next skip. You're tired."

"Yes, then. If you are well."

"Well enough." He turned to go down to the galley,
but Heglit's voice stopped him.

"Varon told me you would not wake on Rafalpha. I did not know they meant to keep you there."

Heglit apologized almost as often as he looked tired. Jade looked at him a little. "Why did they? What did they want me for?"

"We will talk when we are safe, with time to understand."

Teeth clenched, Jade nodded and left, annoyed that even now Heglit would put him off, always cool, keeping it clean and straight. But that was his way.

The skip shook him out, dusted his mind free of confusion, giving him joy and speed, so he forgot to ask where they were going and why this way, until the last N-space breakout before the new channel.

"There is no place for us that ComUn touches. And Rafal will not grant us sanctuary again," Heglit answered.

"Because I—"

"They will know I broke faith with the Council and disobeyed their law."

"They lied to you."

Heglit reached for a gate chart and said nothing. If he was more like Borget, Jade thought, I would ask him how he feels, if he has been cast out. But he wasn't like Borget, and one did not ask Heglit private things.

He took the first half of the run, ten hours of wild violent gaiety, wrenched away when Heglit came in and Borget broke him out. But this time there were only fourteen hours in the channel. Freaky channel, he thought. But they broke out near the triangle, through the right gate. Heglit moved them in, away from the gate, then deadshipped, safe and more alone than Jade liked to think about. And there was time to talk.

"They were trying to learn why Tas wanted me, or wanted me dead. Did they?"

"They examined the crystal I took from the ship in TaLur, and you. Both are TreAshal."

"I?"

"You are Jadriel Sam's son."

"And you are Borg's father." Jade grimaced and pulled his feet up into his lap as Borget joined them, bringing Santo tea.

Heglit ignored the remark. "That was why they kept you. The genetic identification was questioned, but every physical study produced the same result. You are the first generation offspring of Jadriel Sarn and Glovin."

"Then there was a mistake. Or Sarn lived three hundred stanyears to breed me. I'm not that old."

"You are his son." Calm.

"Impossible."

"Only not understood. It is, therefore it is possible. The Council was seeking a reason, a way of believing it. The device, also being here, and of TreAsh, is a clue. The TreAshal knew the time of the future, in pattern; those happenings more or less probable. Sarn must have arranged that the device would be found when you were able to use it."

"Use it for what? Heglit—"

"Listen. Do not think of possibles or not. Accept for now what cannot be explained." He waited for Jade's reluctant nod. "The device is linked to you, by being here, tested as a new thing, when you are here in a place to find it. To do whatever it does."

"And if I do not want to do what it does? I am not a device or a Rafalan. Will it help me find Lista, or run into Centra, free to do the things we were beginning to do?"

"I do not know."

"There are too many impossibles, Heglit. You wish to believe I am his son. But there have been three hundred stanyears. And to bring one man and that small device together in the galaxy—"

"Through Rafal. We were pledged to remain what we were in Sarn's time, to always be Master Linkmen. Sarn would have known we would be chosen to link with the new device. And on Rafalpha, more than any other world in the galaxy, the device would be known as TreAshal."

"And me?"

"How long have you Linked?"

"You know that."

"Yes. More than three times the expected limit for all but Rafalan. You would mate with a Rafalan sooner or later."

All logical, all coolly laid out. But disbelief stayed there with questions of the three hundred stanyears. "You speak of things you know, Heglit, of Sarn and

TreAsh and Rafal. I've nothing to do with them. But why would Sarn arrange this thing you want to believe in. And if Rafal knew—"

"The time is long enough to forget, or to change meanings and memories. We came to the Rafal Sector out near the Rim. The reason for it is no longer clear, but it was long ago. We built our worlds, and fought for some of them, and learned. But we did not have the secret of interstellar travel except through the cold sleep. TreAsh was first to discover the way of the Star Web, and they found the channel and gate that led them to us. We did not know, for a long time, that it was more than just the way between TreAsh and Rafal. When we learned together to build the ships and the Link system, we found other channels and began to learn the gate pattern. Then, through the plan of TreAsh, we began to teach others to use the ships, and they taught, and the skip-ships brought together the life worlds of the galaxy."

"Then you began the Federation?"

Heglit shook his head. "We were teachers and students. The Federation grew out from the Center, where the suns are close and were already joining together in each cluster. There was trade for a time, then the Traveler War bound them together."

"And TreAsh was flashed," Jade finished. "I can't believe they knew and let it happen. The whole system—"

"Only world, Jade." Borget broke a fascinated silence. "Linkmen of Benjor run up the south limb past the restricted sector, called Burn now. But stories are told in the joyhouses, and it is heard out there how the one world, third out from the yellow sun, was gone, unsettling the balance and scrambling the local system channels. Eight of the worlds remain, unlived, and it is said now the system is making itself stable, for the star is strong and wills it."

The sector, he said, was forbidden, and ComUn had posted the channels once used as dangerous and changeable. And there was a watch, remnant of the Federation war fleet, set to watch that no one broke the restriction. It was planned, or so the story said, that when the channels were stable ComUn would run in to check the worlds about the star, to learn if anything of TreAsh had been left.

Heglit leaned back on the couch, one leg drawn up, arm resting on his knee.

"Perhaps they believe not all were taken," Jade suggested.

"Legends are made of how all came home but one."

"Came home? For what?" Jade shook his head. "Crazy, them."

"Perhaps." Borget shrugged. "On other worlds mates of joy or mind or life choose to be so close, to share the dying."

Stung, Jade blushed. "But *all?*"

"They were not insane, Jade. They all knew. The Federation offered sanctuary and high position to any who would come and tell of the Travelers to help the Clate worlds against them. None did. They did not even tell Rafal what they knew of the Travelers."

This picture of TreAsh was as impossible for him to believe as his own parentage as proclaimed by Rafal, and Jade said so.

"Because we do not understand," Heglit reminded. "We have talked of TreAsh and Rafal as much as we know. But we must decide the thing among ourselves. We cannot stay here."

He did not move, but Jade was suddenly aware of the blue crystal in the neck pouch. Decide. There weren't that many options. He felt penned up again, and wanted to be angry.

"Ideas," he said. "There was no proof, and no way of proving. But the thing Rafal claims to be of TreAsh has lost us our freedom. Even you." He looked at Heglit. "Rafal is no longer a place of safety from ComUn. We have a ship but every ComUn port will be against us."

"Tas was after you before we knew of the device. Or your link to Sarn," Heglit reminded.

"Then we have nothing but the Free-men—" But even as he said it he remembered that Heglit and Rafal linked the new union of Free-men to the discovery of the device, somehow. So, they could run maybe a while before getting caught. Or they could try to learn what the TreAshal device was. Big choice. Commonsense logic made deciding easy. But feeling overcame it.

"What would you do?" Borget asked the question Jade didn't need to ask.

"The run to TaLur," he said, gripping his ankles, pressing his nails hard against bone to feel the hurt. "It was too fast—" He looked up quick at Heglit, yellow eyes wide. "No. The crew— Borg—"

"There is danger in this," the Benjor said into Heglit's silence.

Yes, Jade wanted to say. But he didn't know what the danger was.

Heglit told it clean and quick.

Borget listened, looking from one to the other. "It was the outside, confusing the senses, like Shiva Pearls or Dalanth," he said when Heglit was done.

"We do not know."

"And you. Both Linked?" A new thought stirred behind green-flashed gray eyes, brushing Jade with faint guilt. "The Link was good, there was no trouble with the skip?"

"No." Heglit watched, waiting.

"Then the Link is a protection, focusing the self outside, on being other. Is it not?"

Heglit nodded.

Borget smiled full at the Rafalan. "So, Linkmaster, it is for you to say."

Jade watched them, ignored, not sure he knew what was happening, hoping he did not. Heglit finally spoke.

"Linkmen are young trained, and not all Clate can function in Link."

"Heglit—" Jade protested. He had seen burnouts. He did not want that for Borget. "It would be better to risk my capture, to return him to a ComUn port—"

"Jade," soft Benjorspeak. "There is Lista. What chance would there be for this one seeking her alone? The inner worlds do not know us but as things of beauty to use. Let me try to join you."

"I would not have you hurt."

"That I know. Trust the dark one. He wishes us well."

Beaten, Jade nodded. "We have only two chairs," he reminded Heglit.

"There are standard replacement parts." And no reason not to go ahead, not to do the impossible thing.

Like all Linkmen, Jade knew the basic mechanics of the Link system. All too often, on old ships, he had had to repair them. And Heglit, he knew, was a skilled technician. Still, it was complicated work, taking days, even with the aid of the sophisticated internal systems watch computer.

Once the chair (brought up from crew quarters) was installed and insulated, Heglit suggested Jade Link with Borget in N-space to acquaint him with the strange otherness of enlarged awareness. It was a sometimes-frightening experience for new Linkers to find themselves subjectively exposed to space without the familiar boundaries of the ship to protect them.

It was different. Not what Jade expected. He Linked first, to be established before Borget plugged in. It was familiar territory to Jade, the freedom, the gentle photon wind streaming against skin and hair, floating. Then the mildly distant implosion, turning attention in on itself to assess a new complexity of subjectivity. There was none of the bounding power of Heglit, only yielding, reaching, adjusting, and a growing golden joy. He did not so much feel Borget as he felt Borget feeling him, expanding into a new Jade-being he had not known before. And the flush of pleasure was good, shaping a fuller response.

They unLinked easy, relaxed, to Heglit watching from where he worked.

"It is joy-sharing freedom," Borget said to Jade, looking at Heglit, keeping to Benjorspeak. "But it is not so with the cool one. I felt you knowing it."

"Not the same. In Link he is other than he seems."

Borget glanced at him, laughing.

The Benjor Linked alone, getting familiar with the method and sensation, while Jade worked with Heglit. Then there was no Linking while the systems computer was programmed to accept the third Link. And Heglit worked quickly now, quiet, until Jade was pushed to ask why the hurry.

"This channel is not entirely unknown. Rafal knows of it from the old charts. In time they will know that I brought copies of the old charts away from Rafal. They may feel safe in coming here."

When the work was done they rested in the great emptiness between the three suns. But Jade could not sleep. He rose quietly after a time and went up into the control room. And found Heglit. The look in the black eyes could have been a question.

"Questions." He folded himself into a chair, shaking loose his hair, massaging his scalp with slow hard fingers. "Where, Heglit? If we can use the Link system and the device. Where do we go?" Thinking the Rafalan had his own knowledge and plans, and would not speak of them until he thought it was time. And wondering why, after Rafal, he wanted to trust him.

"To Rafal."

The answer jerked his head up.

"There is knowledge there, and something we will need. This ship cannot ground at any port where ComUn controls the beam. But I have a ship."

"The little one?"

Heglit nodded. "No freighter, but fast. And it does not need port beams for grounding."

"Rafal has that?" He didn't remember. And how much more?

Again Heglit nodded. "With a way to ground away from ComUn ports, we can search for Lista. Then perhaps we can learn what Sarn meant us to know."

Jade ignored that, thinking of Lista. And a tiny ship that could ground by itself. He had heard of old and dangerous nuclear-fueled ships that did so. Now they were but expensive toys for the wealthy. Though there were probably places in the galaxy that had not yet come out into space proper that used them within a single system. "Skip-ship?"

"Yes."

"If you can get her— Two ships—"

"She will fit within the cargo hold."

The idea grabbed Jade, exciting, and easier to think about than running always, or the questions Heglit would not answer. "How will we get her?"

"I do not know that yet."

There was no way to address that, so Jade sat silent for a time thinking of Borget and Lista. "The Benjor," he said after a time. "We should find a way to set them free of us. This is not their trouble or danger."

Heglit looked at him, then shook his head.

"But we are a danger to them."

"They are a part of this. We do not know what Sarn

103

foresaw. We can only learn what was meant by accepting the pattern of what is."

He didn't follow that at all, but he didn't ask, not sure he wanted to understand, not wanting the silent look that said nothing. "It must be their choice."

One dark brow lifted slightly. "Yes. Of course."

10

There were no more delays. Borget knew as much as Jade could explain about the skip (but that was Jade's skipping, and so didn't really apply, and Jade knew it). Heglit had plotted their run back from the breakout gate and set the Centra Zar to pilot herself back. Ship control would give them a ten- and one-minute warning call. Jade fitted the Link-mask to Borget, then sat, slightly nervous, as Heglit checked him. And there was no more time.

His finger was too well-trained not to respond to the tone. He went

into brief confusion, strong-gentle, cool-warm, and wondering why he hadn't brought himself. Then he was steady, three-centered, but into the half-skin feel of being out free in N-space, knowing someone else's strength held him separate from the other two of him.

He/they hit the gate clean, shivered with the rich shock of it, flinching a little. Then Heglit (strong, arrogant, glad) caught them up and dove laugh-shouting into the amber flood.

It was— strange. Borget was there, but distant, like a melody once heard returning unexpectedly. He accompanied. The union was like before, Jade and Heglit, strength wedded to agility, iron flowing like water, and joy outgrowing him, opening him up. Easier now than first time, eager to use strength and bold fearless joy, gladdened by a new (not his) pleasure in fluid twists and curves, always with the subtle harmony of the Benjor who seemed to calm even the rage of the Ultra channel.

They broke out, slamming through the gate into stillness, spent, but pleasure-warm. It was Heglit, first unmasked, seeing to Jade, who went to Borget while the Rafalan went to the control room.

"It is joy-sharing of the mind," Borget said, lying back, watching with wide gray eyes. "A way of doing what cannot be done outside. He is not cold, linking, but a warrior loosed from bondage. There is greatness in it."

Benjorlike, he dwelt on the sensory experience, not the channel. Jade shook his head, not wanting to talk of it, not wanting to cage the reality in words, even Benjorspeak. He glanced at the chronometer on the Link-comp. And stared. Eight hours. Coming in it had been fourteen. The first time through took nearly twenty-three. That didn't—

"Jade." Heglit's voice jumped from the speaker, pulling him around, already feeling a tension in his belly. He ran on silent bare feet to the control room.

Heglit stood watching the screen, and his expression was more frozen than controlled. Jade looked, but he was more interested in the Rafalan.

"Heglit—" Tentative.

"Look, Jade." Quiet.

"I did. What's—"

"Rafal." Borget slipped into the room, quick eyes moving from the flashing comp identification to the seven-starred reality in the outview screen.

"It can't—" But denying it meant nothing. It was. His scalp prickled, something in his head felt stretched, pulling him— He shook his head. Hard. "Rafal. The beacon—"

"We are off Dondil." Heglit's voice fell calm over them. "On the wrong side. The beacon has not picked us up."

"But how—"

"We are here. That is enough for now." Mask resumed, Heglit turned away from the outview screen. "We must plan how to get the ship."

Immediate concerns eased the tension in Jade's head, left him tired. He envied Heglit's control. "We'll need the beam to get down," he said.

"They will not allow me to ground." Cool and thinking. "Only Borget has no claim against him here."

Jade looked at the dark face. Dishonesty came more easily to him. And playacting. Heglit did not plot and game. Or did he?

"Could you ground the ship, Borget?"

106

"Help me, them." The quiet voice fell into lowspeak, as it often did when he spoke to the Rafalan. "For reasons, me, saying you are gone."

Heglit thought about it. "They see me renegade and do not know why I did what I did. Tell them I took Jade, then programmed the ship to return to Rafal."

Borget nodded, unsmiling. "Supplies needing. And program. Maybe to C'Erit to barter the ship."

It was insane enough to work, but Jade wondered what would happen if they were found out. This was the sort of thing that would be handled through local regulations, not ComUn.

There was a touch of suspicion when the ship was picked up and identified by the local beacon. And a word of warning. "You will be watched. Do not leave the ship without escort. Rafal is closed."

"Will they search the ship?" Jade wondered, following Heglit down to the cargo hold.

"Yes. We will not be here."

"How—?"

"The beam field holds the ship. It will hold us, if we are close."

"Out?" Jade yelped, then swallowed to bring his voice down. "But there is no air, no—"

"It is cold. But there is air enough. We will have to work our way down to the lift engine flange, or the drop when the beam cuts out will be dangerous."

"Rim. You're crazy."

"It can be done. Come. You do not want to go back to Rafalpha now."

Something in the flat voice made him agree he didn't. But he couldn't imagine going out, either, coming down beside the big ship. He watched Heglit working at the small personnel hatch and wondered why he was going to go along with it. Decided there was no good reason, except maybe that Heglit was going to do it too.

They waited in the big emptiness of the cargo hold, Heglit quiet, thinking or just resting, Jade pacing, nervous, trying to imagine what they were about to do.

"What after?" He asked finally. "If we ground alive."

"We will need out-garb."

"Suits?" He knew the sector watches had them, but he had never seen one close, had never had to go out of a

107

ship in N-space. Like most shipmen he was aware of the danger outside, but it was like thinking of the danger inside some distant star, a fact unrelated to his life.

Heglit watched him. "We cannot bring the ship inside at the port. Borget will lift and meet us."

"Loading outside?" Not that Heglit would repeat it. And it wasn't unknown. In the out-sectors there was still an occasional loss to pirates who cornered ships coming out of the Star Web and forced them to jettison cargo. But it was a lean and risky business, so he'd heard. He looked around the hold, big and empty now, and atmosphered. But there were times cargo was transported in vacuum. It could work. If they could get the primary loading bay open, if they could get the ship together, if they survived grounding . . .

Too many ifs. Too many questions. Nothing but questions from the port on C'Erit. And no fun. He paced out to the center of the hold and looked back at the Rafalan crouched beside the hatch idly scratching the plastic floor with what looked like a thin wire. Why was Heglit doing this? Why everything Heglit did, from taking him onto the Rafalan ship two stanyears ago, to returning now to steal what he said was his own ship. What was he really doing? Did he believe all that skip about a long-gone TreAsh and the holy mission of Rafal? Or was there something Heglit wanted for himself?

The questions weren't new, only suddenly closer. All his life Jade had bought protection and support by the simple fact of his presence. Maybe he had assumed, without realizing it, that he was what Heglit wanted, in his cold silent fashion. Just having him there to make his being less lonely.

Introspection was not a favored pastime. He shrugged and turned away, pacing the width of the hold. He was looking too deep. Heglit had wanted one thing. A Clate partner. And he was honest to say so up front. The rest of this was a thing they were caught up in now because he looked like someone else. Someone important. Someday it would all be done and they would be as before. Only more. Not just Linkmen, but Free-shippers with their own ship (or two) and a crew of Benjor—

"Jade."

The flat voice reached him, scattering his thoughts and he turned back to the hatch.

"We are approaching Rafal. When there is air, there will be a sound here. When the hatch blows, hang onto the edge. Here." He showed him the raised ridge about the hatch. "Go out feet first, down along the side of the ship. We will go out together. Look only at the ship. It will feel fast at first, then slow as we near the ground. Do you understand?"

"Yes." But his eyes flashed yellow as he looked at the hatch, and he didn't want to do this.

There was a change in the feel of the ship, as something outside began to affect her movements. Heglit gestured as he moved to one side of the hatch; Jade took the other, waiting. The sound was a breath, a whisper, a keening like that irritating bone horn of Zander XII, Jade thought, steady, but moving down slow, building tensions.

"Hang on," Heglit said quietly. And Jade, fingers already white, pressed to the cold plasteel wall and tried to grip tighter.

The hatch blew like a big hand smacking them against the wall, then trying to drag them through the roaring hole where the hatch wasn't anymore. Jade clenched eyes and teeth, felt the decrease of pressure stabbing in his ears, then modifying, as silence replaced the roar and air pressure, in and out, equalized. Icy air, ozonic and thin, stung his throat.

"Now, Jade."

It took a minute to force his body to try, to move from the wall and push his feet over the lip into emptiness. Four feet moved out over the edge as Heglit pressed beside him. He rolled onto his belly, lowered himself out along the cold smooth ship's skin, only his right side warm now against the bulk of the Rafalan. Speed. He didn't intend to, but instinct made him bend his head, look down— He gasped. His head said he was falling, fast. But the ship held still beside him and there was no wind. The air here was inside the field of the beam. But he was outside, untethered, too aware of the ground rushing up, flattening out—

"Jade." Hard Heglit-voice close as the warm against his side. "You will not fall. Let go."

"No." Frozen, his hands wouldn't obey his will anyway. "Can't—"

Heglit's arm slid around his back, clasping him to the hard body. Safe. His hands thawed, loosened. And he did not fall. Nor did the arm withdraw.

"Use your hands. Push down toward the flanges. Or the fall will be too much."

Use his hands. Right. Place palms against the icy metal, slide down. It was surprisingly hard to move, but they did. Linked by that strong arm, they descended twice, three times their own length, until the metal flared out in a sweeping curve forming landing leg and engine protection. And they were coming down slow, slowing, drifting into dusk. At Heglit's quiet suggestion they moved down even further, until the metal curve shielded them on one side.

"When we touch the ground prepare to fall."

Then the arm was gone, leaving him cold where it had been.

There was one moment of being down and still held, then the breathtaking release sliding them toward the hard pad. Automatically, Jade rolled, transforming momentum like a tumbler. Heglit fell harder, but was up, moving, angling away from the port offices into the maze of cargo and drydock equipment. Jade followed, dodging about unidentified obstacles.

They stopped finally between large low buildings, breathing hard in the chill thin air. Jade waited, not sure for what, so long he started to shiver. Heglit seemed impervious to the cold wind. Then they were moving again, and he saw the low silhouette of a ground car. Empty. Heglit nodded, stepped away from the wall, towing Jade by silent command. No one shouted, no alarm was raised, and they were in the soft cushioned seats. There was a soft sound of the engine and they were away. Quick and quiet.

Heglit said nothing, handling the car easily, moving away from the port. Jade finally asked where they were going.

"We do not berth the Travelers at the port. ComUn does not know of them. They are beyond the hill."

The hill was a sharp serrated mountain, like a broken knife thrust up against the darkening sky. It took time.

Expecting to be hailed or pursued, Jade couldn't relax, took refuge in wondering how they would complete this idiocy, wondering if after all this Borget would be detained. And if he wasn't, how they would find one another in the big space beyond Rafal. What he finally asked was about getting out of the Centra Zar.

"Did you know it would work?"

"Rafal developed the beam. We played in it as children."

Played. As children. Jade wasn't sure he could believe in Heglit as a child.

They left the car some distance from the Rafalan port and moved through the dark cold too slow to build warmth. There was little sign of activity here, less light. Only vague shapes and Heglit's knowledge of the place. It took some time to find the ship, but like everything Rafalan it was unguarded. Jade clamped his jaw tight trying to still the rattle of his teeth, trying to make cold-numbed hands feel things as they entered the small space. Heglit directed him to a comfortable reclining chair before somehow making a faint light on the control panel.

"Can you see?" Soft almost-voice and breath touching Jade's cheek and neck. He nodded, and in brief words and gestures Heglit explained the controls.

"But—"

The hand on his shoulder silenced him. "If I am recognized— Fifteen minutes. No more. Then lift. The ship could buy Lurz for you."

Then he was gone. Buy Lurz? Run for Burkoze? No. He knew he would not. Not and leave Heglit here. And Borget.

The minutes crawled, then seemed to have evaporated. He hugged himself, shivering in violent spasms. Ten, twelve, fourteen minutes. His heart began to beat, and he imagined himself leaving the ship, going to the Rafalans—

"You didn't program lift." Heglit, scaring him, moving behind the chairs before reappearing.

"Couldn't," he said after a minute. Heglit said nothing. His long fingers wandered over the control board, eyes fastened to a screen glowing with complex Rafalan script. Or code.

A vibrancy swelled through the ship, a silent eagerness and suspense, then the tiny ship leapt away from the port, accelerating in the glow of its own field and beam, so there was a momentary increase of inship gravity. Then freedom and bursting into the light of the distant sun.

"Fast."

"Enough, I hope. Taylon will pursue."

"How far?"

"His choice, and our private ships are armed. I said Rafal would not go as easy as TreAsh."

"Armed?" Jade looked at the chiseled profile. No ships were armed but the few unconverted warships in Centra, and (if Borget was right) the guard near what had once been the place of TreAsh.

There was little time to talk as Heglit moved from one local channel to another, under manual control, weaving out, then back through the complexities of the center of the cluster. Four hours, then five, and no visible pursuit. Heglit relaxed fractionally, threaded a way to the peripheral strands of the Web, and verbally instructed the navicomp to move the ship to a planet near Dondil. There were no life-worlds here, but one large cruel world rich in silvron. Jade watched, fascinated. Verbal command comps were rare, and not considered trustworthy enough for ship command. Another technological victory for Rafal.

But it was Borget who began to occupy his thoughts. "How soon can he lift?"

"Dawn. About three hours ago. Unless they link the ship theft to his presence."

"Would they?"

"At some point they will. If luck holds, after he lifts." And surprising him again. "Are you warm now?"

"About. Borg is different in channel."

"Different?"

"From— Not like a Linkman."

"He isn't. He does not run the channel, only lets it happen. To know it. He could not Link alone in the Star Web without hard training."

And finally the question there had not been time for. "We broke out in Rafal. Why? We were running the same channel."

"I am not sure." Either exhausting the subject or side-stepping it. "You haven't used out-garb. You'd better learn."

There was room, almost. The flat bundle shook out into a surprisingly space-consuming garment. Jade struggled into stiff legs, learning where the closures were, the sequence of fastening to assure an airtight seal. The hood and transparent face-screen gave him claustrophobia. He thought he could not breathe properly, but Heglit assured him he could, and locked in the measured-flow air cartridge. The fabric bound him, and he was sure he would not be able to move, but Heglit was patient, then made him stay suited for over an hour to get used to the feel. He guessed he could survive, but getting out was a relief he didn't try to hide.

Then there was nothing to do but wait for Borget, and wonder what they would do if he was not allowed to leave Rafal.

11

It was a full day and more before the sensors reported a ship in channel nearby, identifying it as a ComUn freighter. It was too far from the standard gate into Rafal to be anyone but Borget. Struggling into the restrictive suit took all Jade's attention, and Heglit's casual reminder that a bad seal would be fatal didn't make him any easier about this part of it. But he kept his mouth shut on his commonsense objections and did as he was told.

Air was drawn out of the interior and stored in pressure tanks, and the suits held, becoming bulkier, but more pliable, as outside air pressure decreased.

Then the massive bulk of the freighter lay beside them, deadshipped. Heglit did something at the controls that seemed to make the Centra Zar drift closer. Then it was time to do it.

Being out felt like nothing, no faint star-wind, no silver-warm rain, just black filled with the mountain of the Centra Zar and the almost invisible Rafalan ship.

Heglit's voice, squeezed thin in the ear-speaker, told him to stay put, and the white suit beside him flexed and dove slow-motioned away from him, not moving (apparently), but shrinking until it touched the freighter. Then the voice speaking to Borget and the miracle of Borget answering, both voices confusingly near Jade's right ear.

The curved side of the great ship split along an unnoticed seam, drifted open on blackness, and the tiny Heglit floated into the great maw and disappeared long enough for Jade to feel lonely.

"Jade, watch for the line."

It came, white-flagged, a slow insane line behaving as no cable in Jade's experience could, holding its kinks

114

and curves, drifting over him to lie above the back of the flier without touching it. He had to move to reach it, and finally did, fastening bulky hands over its thinness. Moving felt like forever falling. Nothing stopped unless he thought about stopping it. Used to a practiced grace, he sweated, felt clumsy and frustrated. But he got the line attached and said so.

"Come along the line first," Heglit instructed, not asking if the line would hold.

Hand over hand, beginning to think there could be some fun in the airless weightless infinity, Jade made his way into the cargo hold. And it felt good to have something enclosing him.

The power winch ran silent, pulling the kinks out of the line, tightening it. But it was a long time before he could tell the small ship was drifting closer.

"Be ready, Jade. It will not stop of itself."

It took only hands and braced legs to handle her, and she rested in the cargo hold, shrinking the great space. A word to Borget and the sides of the Centra Zar drifted together, sealed with a clang Jade could feel through his legs.

Then there was the familiar corridor and being out of the bulky suit and Borget's warm gold embrace welcoming.

Heglit didn't waste time, but set the ship to run for the channel gate twelve hours away.

"Question, me," Borget said, serious after the pleasure of greeting, bringing them baDant juice in the control room. "The skip time was right for us coming to Rafal?"

Heglit nodded, and his dark eyes moved to Jade.

"There were differences on Iron," Borget said.

"How much?" Jade asked it finally, dry-mouthed. He didn't want to talk about this. His head felt squeezed (or pulled) by some effort he wasn't sure he was making and didn't know how to stop.

"Two weeks."

"What?" Jerked from him in spite of Heglit's eyes.

"Figured, me. Having times from Iron before and all runs clocked on the log. Two weeks lacking from Iron time." There was question in voice and face.

Two weeks? His heart beat too hard and the awful

tension in his head pulled, making something he thought was pain behind his eyes.

"It happened before," Heglit said, and Jade couldn't remember if there had been a long silence between Borget's voice and his. Then he wondered if maybe Heglit was talking to him. He felt the black eyes like hands pulling—

"Not— Two weeks." His eyes narrowed against the pain and Borget saw it.

"Jade, are you well?"

"I— No."

"He is well." The cold voice cut through many things, and Jade was mad, hurting.

"Damn you. I hurt—" Eyes stinging now so the gold and bronze figures shimmered.

"You are running again. From the thought. From the truth."

"Heglit." Yellow eyes hidden now behind squeezed lids. "Stop it. It hurts my head." He thought if he opened his eyes they might fall out from the pressure behind them.

"Borget, is it true pain?"

The words touched the taut stretched surface of his mind, mild seismic shivers making very little sense, but he felt cool-warm fingers touch his brow and nearly jerked away.

"Not true pain. But hurting."

The fingers withdrew. The sense of the words wandered sluggishly about his head and he watched them, waiting to see who would drop more words into his head to join them. But it was all quiet. Until that, too, begin to push. Damn them, why did they just sit there? He could feel them there, warm and cool, the glowing warm of Borget to his right and Heglit across from him, sitting—

He stopped breathing, froze away from pain, from anger— Because he really could *feel* Heglit— Dark flame, heat encased in cold— But swift arrogant power and— And the channel-mate laughing, crying, bigger than life—

"*Stop—!*" Afraid (and knowing this was what he had feared before), he jumped up, eyes blazing. "Stop this—" He ran, but there was nowhere to run to, and Heglit's arm flashed out and caught him, held him easily, letting him fight a moment.

"Enough, Jade." He shook him lightly, almost playfully.

Fear ran to anger, but he was helpless and knew it, knew too that Heglit was calm, concerned, vastly interested, and not surprised.

A loud silent sound in his head left him weak, gasping, leaning on the arm for support. Like waking from a nightmare. He shook himself.

"Sorry. My head—" He felt them look at him. But now it was how they always felt looking at him. The—whatever it was— was gone. Imagination, he thought. Too much happening. And he was so tired. Almost too tired to stand.

"Jade." Dark eyes fixed his a long moment, looking for something, finally either finding it or not. Heglit nodded. "You are well." He said it like it was something he wanted Jade to know. "Go rest. It is nine hours to skip."

He woke fast, finding Borget there, the greeting smile, the warmth. It was still a couple of hours to skip. Time enough to wash, to eat, to remember their victory over ComUn and Rafal. And to not think of the strangenesses that were touching them all.

Link-sharing with both was vastly easier now. They had done it and it worked. And there was a sort of pride in Jade about it. They were a unique team, running outside the standard Star Web channels, being and doing things that no one had ever been or done. And now they held one of Rafal's best kept secrets. Wild. And Jade liked it that way. Freer even than Free-men.

And then there was the triangle of stars, familiar now, being safety from ComUn and time to plan. And think. Eight hours. Jade marked his own quick relief at the time silently. Maybe it was all right after all.

Lista was on all their minds. Finding her and getting her back with them. Borget's need (and Jade's) put that first. And Jade wondered if maybe not for Heglit too, remembering that "Would you want me to?" shock.

Heglit was seated at the table in the captain's quarters, studying a thick sheaf of papers. "Rafal Star Web charts," he said by way of greeting.

117

"For?" Jade asked.

"A way to Centra Sector."

"Lista?"

"Tas would have her taken there. To Centra Alzar." The only world (outside Rafal Sector) guarded by an armed fleet. And the Centra Zar was from that sector.

"Would he expect us to come there for her?"

"Possible. He will soon know we were in Rafal Sector."

"They would tell?"

"For the ship. Maybe. They would want her destroyed before ComUn could study her." He said it as he said everything. A fact to be dealt with. Jade picked up loose papers from the table, trying to read the complex Rafalan script. "What does it tell?"

"Position of the Web gates and dates of discovery. Another list, with the gates numbered, gives direction and duration of the channels."

"Is this one on there?"

"It was one of the early ones. Maybe a TreAshal find. I think all but perhaps that channel we ran to TaLur are here."

"And a way to Centra?"

"Many ways. All long. And it has been a long time already, Jade."

He looked down into dark eyes. "Do you think—?" Knowing Borget had said he would know, but—

"I have heard Tas is a cruel man." The dark eyes seemed to weigh him, thinking something beyond the words exchanged.

"And if we do get there, then what?"

"The flier. She is small enough to come down secretly."

"Then?"

"Borget shares a sameness with her." Like that explained it. And maybe it did. But a world was a big place to look for one woman.

"There are ways of looking we could use. On the Zendra three."

"Zendra?"

"The flier. We do name them." Cool enough for Jade not to ask if that was a woman's name like it sounded. But he felt something relax in him. He dropped into a chair facing the table, reached up and loosened his hair, shaking it down, working his fingers into it, rubbing his scalp.

"Heglit, I want to talk. Me. Don't—" He gestured loosely, but watching; the Rafalan picked up the cues, maybe expected this, or something. He leaned back, legs extended.

"When we ran to Rafal we were in the same channel that took us to Ergon."

Heglit nodded, silent.

"But we broke out in Rafal."

"I do not know, Jade. But we wanted Rafal."

Well yes, wanted. But how? Unless wanting— That thought made him smile. Imagine wanting to get from here to Centra Alzar, and doing it in, say, eight to ten hours—

It took a minute to realize he was thinking about it. Then it seemed like maybe it was all right, like this, somehow, when he didn't have to. Eight hours. Except—

"Heglit—" He'd been quiet so long the Rafalan had gone back to the charts. Now he looked up. Jade went carefully, watching himself more than Heglit. "Could it really happen? I mean, could two weeks go by outside the channel while only hours happened to us?"

Heglit saw the quick pulse in the throat, the intensity of the metallic yellow eyes. He was careful, too. "I believe it did."

"Is it part of the other, the getting to TaLur?"

"The reason, I think, the— The way of it happening, yes. The device has to do with it."

Jade drew his hair into two plaits, winding it about his hands, staring at nothing. When he talked again he sounded almost sleepy. "You couldn't believe that without evidence. You're too Heglit. But you don't say what you think or know."

"Because I do not know. I think. And I could be wrong. Better for you to see and think and make your own answers."

Jade made a face. "No brain, me. Only fun and ship-working. Oh, don't look like that. It's just, dammit, it's true. I know the Link system, how to pilot a ship, and the channels. All this other just *feels* to me. It means nothing I can make words about."

Heglit linked his hands and looked at them. "You talk

about it now." Meaning him to remember a few hours ago when he couldn't. Maybe.

"It wouldn't go away. My head got— Something happened inside. There's a thing I keep thinking. Like maybe I peaked. We do, you know. Rafalans don't, I'm told. But I, uh— I could be about to burn." The yellow eyes said this was a true thought. And fear.

Heglit shook his head. "I would know," he said, stressing the pronoun slightly. And for some reason Jade remembered when he could feel Heglit being. His arms goose-fleshed. Heglit noted that and said nothing. Then Borget came in and the talk changed.

Centra Sector. It was the only destination they had. They studied the Star Web charts, plotting times. A long time, Heglit had said. And he was right. A month by the shortest run in straight channels.

A month. "We broke out where we wanted to, once." Jade said, moving away from the table. "Too bad we can't break in where we want, make our own channel. Run it in eight hours and have only eight hours happen outside."

"By wanting?" Borget looked up, glancing at both of them.

"How the Rim else did we get to Rafal?"

"Possible?" This to Heglit, who only shrugged.

"Makes as much sense as any other idea," Jade said. "If true, inchannel us, and go. Wanting."

Jade saw a certain kind of belief in the golden face and didn't say anything. Maybe magic worked on Benjo. Certainly the two he knew from there took some mysteries for granted. Then Heglit caught him off guard.

"It is a thing to try. We could chart a run, knowing listed breakouts, and still hope to break out in Centra."

Jade stared a minute. "Right. And while we want our way there we can want a time outside as well as in." The idea caught him and he grinned at Heglit. "If they know we were in Rafal Sector, they couldn't expect us in Centra in less than a month. They would be watching all the local gates, though."

"There is an ultra channel listed, but not used. It passes above the Triffid, and was difficult when first found."

"Hotter than the run to TaLur?" Feeling bold, able to speak of it and glad, not remembering what had scared him so badly then.

Heglit shook his head slightly, and that could have meant anything, even disbelief.

"Let's take it, then."

And that easily, it was decided. Heglit took the charts to the control room, leaving the two alone.

"Jade, you are twinning yourself, wanting and not wanting, confused and certain. I do not understand this." The Benjorspeak sang sober and the gray eyes watched.

"No, Borg." His hand rested on the hard-muscled shoulder, kneading slightly. "But when nothing is right or makes sense, it no longer matters what is believed. Does it not bother you that we made a two week run in eight hours?"

"Bother? I am only waiting to learn how it was done."

How. Not if. For a minute he had a half-angry feeling that someone was gaming him, like Borget and Heglit knew and were teasing him, making him a fool to be laughed at when he couldn't see. "Heglit could say more than he does, Borg. He knows a way it might be possible."

"Do not blame that one, Jade. He is not your opponent. He is bonded to you by his choice to share your fate."

Jade had his own ideas about that. But it set him to wondering again. He left, going to the Link-room, wanting to be alone with his thoughts, wondering why Heglit had broken the law of Rafal to continue this strangeness, if he did not know more than he said. It was difficult for him to imagine Heglit telling a conscious lie. He was not the type. And from the beginning he had been the means of all their successes, knowing more of many things than Jade. Still, questions lurked in the corners of his mind. Always why, why even the Rafalan being there the second time to save his life. Every answer or partial answer he had from Heglit and his own common sense made sense. Only all together—

He shook his head, staring at the timer. Together, all the truths made a question he could no more ask than answer. He only knew the Rafalan would not throw away a lifetime of loyalty to his home sector (and probably a woman and family he had there) to flash around the galaxy looking for a woman for someone else. But he was here. And it wouldn't be for no reason. So there had to be something Heglit knew that he did not.

The warning tone sounded through the ship. A long skip, he thought, waiting for the others to come down. And wouldn't it be a flash if they *did* break out near Centra?

Share-linking was easy now, knowing the quick identification blending like many flavors, all one but each a part, being the watchful feeling of Borget, bold power of Heglit, and the eager reaching he always brought into the Web, they broke in, diving into the thick amber flood, and went, knowing nothing of time or place outside, running, using themselves up, keeping the ship in channel.

It was a long skip. Muscles knotted and cramped with a fatigue transmitted through the Link. But there had been a worse time. Now Borget brought a strange tempered strength, pulling it from the rage of power in the Star Web itself. And it was enough. The beckoning gate, the desire to stay and go, gave direction, drawing them to a lance, thrust out, exploding into a jewel-blaze of N-space and the clean whisper of the stellar wind. Peace and stillness.

Jade rested, coming down, getting back, still mask-blind, thinking he would raise his aching arms soon, peel off the mask. He took a breath, felt his arms lift, the warm clinging mask peeled away, his feet hard to the floor, thighs tensing to rise . . . *But he sat still! His hands clasp the arms of the chair— What?—* Confusion hurried his thoughts, scrabbling to understand, waiting, wanting unmasked, being unmasked already, but feeling it against his face . . .

"Jade?"

He felt the word form in his mouth, the concern pushing it out. *And he felt teeth clenched, lips sticky pressed together against the mask—*

His arms jerked up, panicked, battered away reaching hands, and fell back helpless as the mask peeled away (only he felt the soft close mesh in his fingers). His eyes blinked up into black ones (or down into yellow). The black closed first. He felt that. Snapped shut. The Link tension in his head stretched thin, taut, splitting him.

He shifted (not moving), twisted, felt power stretching broad shoulders, muscle-laced back, hips, legs shifting to straighten, and a rigid control slipping to form protest, shaping words in a mouth he didn't understand.

"Stop."

Something snapped, loud, in his head, and he pulled in a breath, choking, pulling open eyes he didn't know were closed. But he was still sitting familiar-bodied, and Heglit was bending away, straightening, one hand lifting to his head.

"What—?" Stiff-tongued, he tried to collect the incident, define it. But Heglit turned away.

"The control room." Said to Borget, and the voice, flat and even, had a roughness beneath it Jade didn't know.

"Centra." The word leapt from Jade like an accident. But hearing it he knew he would be right.

Borget threw him a look and left, running. Heglit didn't move, stood looking at the chronometer, eyes veiled. And it came to Jade he was holding himself with an iron will, making himself say nothing.

"Heglit." No response. He got up, light-headed, like from Orziel. He touched the Rafalan, and the arm was like plasteel beneath his fingers. But it got attention. A deep breath and forced relaxation. Not understanding even now, Jade knew he was seeing a test of Rafalan self-discipline, and a thrill of something that might have been fear some place else chilled his lower back when he wondered if Heglit was angry with him. Then that passed and the cast-bronze face turned to him.

"Interesting experience." Flat and easy, but refusing to let Jade pretend nothing had happened. And there was waiting in the black eyes. And something else that made him look away before he recognized it.

"The Link," he said after a little. "I couldn't, uh—didn't—"

"I was out of Link, Jade. Once before—"

"Jade, Heglit." Borget's voice cut between them. They shared a look and turned, heading for the control room. The outview screen showed a view already familiar from breakout.

"No beacon," Borget greeted them. "Checking position me."

123

The navicomp processed the request, flashing the standard star map, major reference points marked. Movements through the Star Web were traced from the log of gates beginning with Rafal. The map narrowed to one galactic area. Centra Sector. But seen from an unusual angle. They were near Centra Alzar. And beyond standard beacon range.

Jade fisted his hands, not surprised, but surprised not to be. He felt them both look at him quickly.

"Will they find us here?" he asked, changing a probable subject.

"I believe they lack the method," Heglit said, probably meaning Rafal had it. "As far as they know, everyone uses the standard gates."

"So this space should be clean except for local traffic."

Heglit nodded. Local traffic would stay in the sector web. To be more sure, he scanned the area, found the local web complex but evenly spaced. He moved the ship into a place equidistant from all near channels, then deadshipped, cutting the automatic ID code broadcast used by all ComUn vessels to key the beacons for travel information and local web charts.

"Twenty hours plus," Borget said. "Still fast, us."

"Very," Heglit agreed, bringing a look from Jade to see if he was serious.

"If it was twenty hours out there," Borget reminded, looking at the brilliant red-gold star named Alzar, "now what?"

"Resting, food, time to plan."

But resting wasn't easy, and after a little they gave it up.

"We have the Zendra," Jade said over hot food. "If we knew where to—"

"Jade. She is here." Quiet Benjorspeak, and Borget not eating, sitting tight as though ready to jump and run someplace.

"Are you sure?"

The golden head bent. "I am sure. There is a— a Link that tells me of it, so I know her being here. She is afraid."

"But she is well."

"She is well. But alone is a cold hurt to her."

Not doubting the Benjor sensitivity, Jade translated

quickly to Heglit, who looked at Borget a minute. "Then we go down."

All three, it was decided. The Centra Zar would be safe. They would leave her derelict, cargo bay open. The flier could find her again easily enough.

"There will be danger," Heglit cautioned. "Tas will not be easy, like Rafal. He will be guarded, and they will have weapons."

"Then we will need weapons," Jade countered.

He was surprised to find out-suits stored in the small sick bay, realized he had no true idea yet of his own ship. But at least the problem of getting to the Zendra was solved. Heglit even brought one for Lista.

12

Centra Alzar, star name, world name, headquarters for ComUn, hub of the galaxy (as far as Clates were concerned), though still distant from the density of galactic center. But it was in a beautiful brilliant cluster of suns, almost within arm's reach, laced by glowing filaments of dust. A sample of what lay within the crowded center. And the red-gold gem that was Centra Alzar, young and vital, surrounded by a family of extremes, pulled eccentric by the greedy reach of more sterile suns. Small heavy worlds so close to the home hearth that rare and precious metals flowed rivers and seas that froze in daily season. Gleaming gas giants alive with an all-but-solar energy created by sheer size and incredible rotation. Together they built the incredible night sky splendor of the life-world Alzar, beloved of the family. By accident of galactic math, or pleasure of the Core God, she held her driftless orbit in a narrow band of peace with all riches near at hand. This lovely jewel of seas and land and the best of climates was the chosen homeworld of Barmalin Tas, Chairman of ComUn. Half the planet lay in his private holdings, balanced by the largest, most populous, city in the glaxay, covering the whole of the second continent. This was the meeting place of leaders from every major world in the Federation, and here was ComUn Council Hall.

The Zendra Three drifted close to the planet in Heglit's skilled hands, and the three watched the green and white orb drift silent, spinning night to day beneath them.

"She is there." Borget's voice held certainty.

"Do you know where?"

Borget's head shook no. "We do not communicate. It is a feeling, no more."

"What does she feel?" Heglit asked the right question.

"Fear and being caged. And lost."

Heglit nodded, eyes brooding on the world in the outview screen. "Tas did not make the Centra Zar public," he said. "The ComUn Council probably does not know of it, or there would have been a ship at every beacon, hoping to pick us up and buy favor in Centra."

Jade agreed. "So he would keep Lista secret also. In his private holding." Narrowing it to half a world, the half that showed wild and natural on the screen after the half that seemed one unboundaried city about the massive building of the Council Hall.

"There is more of Rafal on this world," Heglit said. "Secrets sold only to Tas and his father before him."

"Alarms?"

"Against what they know. Not against a ship such as this. But there are weapons. And certain machines for healing and searching the mind."

"So we'd better not get caught," Jade said.

"What we know and have here could bring war to Rafal. And that could destroy ComUn." Heglit looked at them.

"Truly?" Borget asked.

"We have had three hundred stanyears to remember TreAsh, and to prepare against ComUn's suspicion of us."

Believing him, Jade wondered why he hadn't told them before how much trouble they could be causing. But he didn't ask. Heglit, he knew, told only what he wanted, when he wanted, according to some purpose of his own. And as for himself, Jade didn't particularly care if ComUn went to war with Rafal. He just wanted Lista and freedom from all the mysteries of the past months. He was not, he told himself as they waited for night to cover the hemisphere of their choice, curious enough to want it all answered.

They fell swift and sure into the night, angling over the wide sea, turning in over the continent, searching for signs of life with sensors Jade hadn't known they had. They found what they were looking for beside a wide river, east of a towering mountain.

Heglit didn't approach too close, afraid of alerting a

possible sky watch. They left the Zendra Three in a narrow canyon and proceded on foot, Heglit leading.

"We will have to fight," the Rafalan said once beneath the carnival shimmer of sky. "We may have to kill."

Jade accepted the possibility, but he felt the jolt it gave Borget. The Benjor celebrated life, all life. He will not kill, Jade thought. But he will fight.

Even Heglit, familiar with the Rafalan academy, was surprised by the sheer size of the structure, or complex, they approached. It was castle and city and fortress, built of hewn stone and plasteel and some impossible semi-transparent material shaped into delicate spires and minarets. A nightmare mix of massive strength and flights of fancy.

Two bridges spanned the river, one of great dark blocks of stone, the other a rainbow arch glowing with shifting colors. Which? Heglit looked away from the battlements and towers, turned toward the one of stone. They followed silently under the shining sky, through dark toward the high glowing wall.

Unchallenged, they crossed the river and the wall barred their way, casting a soft radiance across the grass. It was unbroken by gate or door, and they stood looking at it, wondering. It could have been plasteel, but there was a translucence to the material, and enough light from it to throw their shadows behind them.

"Is there a way in?" Jade asked.

Heglit didn't answer, but turned right and started walking in the band of light at the base of the wall. It curved slightly away from the river, but otherwise remained unchanging.

"Walk all night, us," Jade complained finally, tired of the sameness. Just plain tired. "No gate being."

Heglit stopped. He had done the logical thing, and it hadn't worked.

Jade was not particularly logical in Heglit's fashion. He moved toward the wall, thinking maybe of climbing it, maybe only wondering what it was that looked so smooth and impenetrable. But he couldn't get close to it. Three strides, then, as he approached, the glowing surface receded. Or seemed to. To Heglit and Borget, watching, he seemed to walk into it, becoming a dark shadow in the even glow.

"Jade!" Borget called. But Heglit was faster, leaping after, so Borget had no choice but to follow. The wall receded for a few paces, then faded into star-bright night. They turned. The glowing wall was behind them. They stood in a rough-paved alley between dark walls and heard music.

"It wasn't—" Jade began.

Heglit silenced him with a gesture and drew them both close to him. "A projection," he said softly.

"And this?"

"Real, I think. Feels real." He looked at Borget, distant light spilling shadows down his face. "She is here?"

"Is. But where is not known. Only the feel of completeness is."

"She would feel this?"

Borget shrugged.

Jade had moved away, down the alley. Now he returned to them, silent on his soft boots. "Joyhouses," he said.

Heglit nodded. Tales of the pleasures available to guests of Barmalin Tas wove through the galaxy, and Rafal collected gossip, too. But there must be more to this than pleasuring places. And the unreality of the wall bothered him. Almost as much as Jade's luck in discovering it.

In from the great wall, the buildings lifted, bulky or delicate, rising to a center that rivalled the mountain invisible now beyond the glow. There, Heglit thought, Tas would have his private place. And his guarded secrets. He turned and they followed him across the rough paving to a wide street of colored light-fractured shadows. A sweet, slightly wild, perfume wafted from a spraying fountain, like the sound of laughter and music spilling from the brilliant doors along the wide avenue. For a moment Heglit thought Borget reached to touch his arm, then a group of people, all Clate, tumbled from one wide doorway, laughing and talking, ignoring the trio, dancing away to another bright-lit door that opened on loud joy-sounds, then closed.

It was late. There were not many people on the street, and the few there were ignored them completely. They stayed to the center of the wide boulevards, walking through alternating bands of light and shadow, laughter and singing, and interweaving fragrances. The buildings grew higher, more complex, colored lights danced and flowed, creating scenes of delight and curiosities above great carved doors, beckoning pleasure-seekers.

Jade looked around them, excited, breathing in familiar joy-scents, curious, but remembering their mission. He glanced at Heglit, walking erect and stern slightly ahead of him.

Those here are joy-seekers, he thought, knowing the type as Heglit never could. Talk with them could tell much to strangers here. This walking into the unknown could get them trouble they were not prepared to handle. He put his idea to Heglit, who saw the sense of it, but still counselled staying together.

"You cannot. Even for Borget there would be trouble. Stay together and wait for me. If these know where Tas is, they will tell me."

They did not argue his confidence. He turned toward a wall of interwoven lights, pushed through the door. In Centra or C'Erit, a joyhouse was a joyhouse, dim and warm and full of talk and laughter and close half-clad bodies. Only in Centra, local law was ComUn law. Pleasures were bolder.

Coming in alone he was noticed, eyes lifting to where he stood at the top of the stair. He paused there a moment, heart beating, weighing the faces of those who looked. He knew this silent language, knew the difference between buyer and seller in these matters. And what he wanted was one who lived and worked here, not a traveler. One who would know the rules of the place. And the gossip.

Blue eyes and a complicated riot of white hair caught his attention, and rewarded it with a slow smile. He nodded, not smiling, and the others, the knowing ones, looked for other games. She waited for him to come down to her. And she was as beautiful as he thought, smaller, and in no hurry.

"New here, you. Can you talk?"

"If you will speak to me." But the fluid Benjorspeak brought a blank look to her eyes. He tried again in fedstan. "I speak, lovely. And listen."

"And pleasures seek?" Red lips curved, parted to show

sharp white teeth and pink pointed tongue, ripe as baDant fruit. She held out a small silver cup and he took it, touched his lips to the rim, then watched her drink from it. He laughed, and finally drank. It was not Z'Atua, or any joy-drink he knew. But it was good. And joy-giving, splashing heat through him, bubbling laughter warm against his throat. She reached one ivory hand to pour more of the pale blue nectar, the other stirred, lifted to rest against his arm, warm and light.

"A name, Lady?" he asked, raising the silver cup.

"Toyn, traveler. You?"

"Jade." His hand touched the softness of one ivory thigh. The known game. But still thinking of the game she did not know.

They talked, gaming, watching each other or the constant movement around them, the pairings (or more than pairs) and partings. And he learned slow things. That only Clates were here. That this was Tas's house, the whole place inside the glowing wall (to keep out predators, she said, and he wondered how a thing that was not there could do that). And Tas. She spoke the name like "God," and he wondered, thinking suddenly of Heglit and Borget and Lista. And time.

"I would see Tas," he said.

"And you will, Jade. If you deserve."

He thought, but did not ask, how to deserve, looking into blue eyes, finally tasting the warm sweet mouth. And thinking there was something more he wanted now. She was skillful, reading him. It was her game, and he let her play it, enjoying. But not forgetting. So he asked her once, in a quiet time, how she came here.

"Like you. And all here. By invitation. Tas chooses those who will come. And those who will stay for a time. It is the only way here."

He could have said different, but he did not, only laughed, warm against warmth, thinking more of Lista, though her name was Toyn. When he asked of Tas again she pouted, teasing, then said he was here, everywhere, watching all. So it was said.

"Even us?"

"Could." Languid, pouring the silver cup full of pale blue. He drank and watched her drink, and wanted to go back to the crowded main room.

"Maybe some of them know of Tas," he said, pulling on pants and tunic, sitting to pull on high soft boots and knot up his hair.

"We all know of Tas here." Laughing. "And we know more of pleasure."

"Then let us go and find it." Gay now, lightheaded with a growing thirst only the blue nectar could assuage. But the flagon was light and empty. He shook it, turning to ask her—

But the great hairy Clate behind the polished counter held out a muscled palm. Laughing, Jade sat the flagon on it, turned to find the woman, also laughing, leaning away.

"Pay him, Jade. It is custom."

If custom it was, he would. He reached into his tunic, brought forth three metal coins from his neck pouch, and tossed them on the counter. Toyn laughed, eyes sparkling, and took his hand.

"The high glowing towers," he said, letting her pull him through the crowd. "What is there?"

"Pleasures bought dear, I've heard. And wizardry."

"There are wizards?" Thinking TreAsh.

"The one." A soft, deeper, voice spoke at his shoulder. He turned to face the man, found him vaguely familiar, lean and taut with dark hair and darker eyes, warm now with a smile caught from the wide mouth. "The wizard Tas. His magic knows all, sees all. Or so it is said."

"And you believe." Challenge, sharing the smile, gauging strengths and weaknesses as they turned out of shadow to the service bar of carved rindo shell. The broad back flexed hard beneath his hand as his companion dodged a large white-haired Clate who stood unmoving, staring vacantly up.

"Wif," the soft voice said to him.

"But that's—"

"Not here, Jade. This is Alzar. No law but Tas."

Called by name, he paused (but kept moving), wondering. Had they shared names? He felt he should know this one but—

But perhaps the female— Her name dissolved as he reached for it in memory, half turning to look for her, sure she had been just—

His brow smoothed as his hands slid over the warm shell surface.

"Do you know Orziel?"

Jade nodded. "But I do not know your name."

"You have forgotten?" Deep easy laughter stretched the bronze throat. "Come, Jade. The self-name, Dariel."

"Dariel." The rightness of that warmed him.

Sharing a smile they lifted crystal glasses, poured drops of the volatile liquid over tongues, inhaled the delicious explosions of pleasure.

"Tas sees all," he said, feeling laughter behind his Orziel-flavored tongue. "And Wif is legal. And what other pleasures, Dariel?"

"Whatever man has dreamed, or desired to taste and feel and do."

"Have you seen Tas?"

The handsome head shook slightly, tipped back as the crystal glass was raised again. "I do not wish to. This," he gestured about them, "is Tas in a way, more than ComUn. This he does. As gift or reward."

The why on Jade's tongue was buried in the fumes of Orziel. He watched the clean profile a moment, then turned as a short baDant entered his field of vision. Familiar. Like his secret shadowed business. Familiar as his own past.

"Joy-sharer," he said to Dariel. "Chem-links."

Dariel nodded. "All are available here. Through ComUn Tas knows them all."

"Can we go into the city?"

"We are in the city." Dark brows lifted in surprise.

"I mean to the towers."

Dariel shrugged. "There is a new music. From Rio Del, I think, at the White Lur. Shall we go hear it?"

About to agree, Jade saw a crowd gathering near one wall. "What is?"

"Maybe a contest. Come." He took Jade's hand, pulling him along, his excitement infectious. Jade remembered other strength contests on other worlds. A common enough occurrence in joyhouses. And the wagering on them.

They were both heavily muscled men. The test seemed to be which one could overbalance the other and bring him down. They stood locked, hands straining against

133

shoulders, one leg braced, the other feinting and reaching to hook the braced leg of the other. The gathering crowd grew loud, calling out one name, then another, becoming a two-beat chant like heartbeats.

The press of the crowd, warm, life-scented, struck Jade strongly, tangling in the fumes of the joy-drink. He wanted— something. Warmth and laughter, long-ago familiar, wrapped him, but a thin edge of discomfort irritated. Swaying with the rhythm of the packed crowd, helpless in it, he relaxed. It was not his way to fight. Instead, he turned his attention inward, searching. He was—

Thirst rasped his throat. Curious, because he had been drinking. But something more, some—

Eyes closed, he felt himself more real, felt breath and heart and the dull growing pain in his leg. Strange ache, like— something he could not quite remember. This was not unfamiliar either. He knew he could change this, make the pain leave if he just—

Moved his leg, like doing something new and never before done.

"Jade! He's winning. Look!" Dariel's excitement and warm hand disturbed him. But he did not open his eyes. The odd feeling in his leg, bent double and stiff from being still so long— No. Wait. He was—

Never mind, he told himself, beginning to sweat, do what had to be done to stop the hurt. Press hands down, push, lift weight, shift—

The hard rock bruised his hands, gravel slid beneath his legs. But his eyes, opening, saw the people, the bright clad bodies he leaned against. On. One, or the other—

What am I doing? That question, only that, needed answering. Close eyes. *Feel* rocks, chill damp earth, sharp gravel, numb leg. Witholding judgment, he moved his hands, felt something like grass, a cool green feel.

This is not real, he thought. *But which this?*

Chem-skip, he thought. But different. Never mind. This is not real. The leg asleep, the rocks, that was real. Heglit said I could tell the difference, he remembered. The wall wasn't real. None of this is real. Dreaming. But how do I wake up? Opening his eyes brought back the joyhouse.

He worked on that until he could feel the realness of earth and stone in spite of seeing people and bar and floor. It took a queer twist of mind, but not so different from recognizing Heglit or a fight while flying on Shiva Pearls. It was just knowing in a different direction. And very quickly, he was scared.

Heglit, he thought, opening his eyes again, looking around, half expecting someone to try to stop this crazy thing he was doing. People moved and talked, but lacked reality now. Glis, he hoped he was right. He moved his legs, felt himself standing up, unsteady, though he seemed to be walking with Dariel. *No, dammit, he was just standing. And here beneath his left hand was cold hard stone.* What to do? He had left Heglit and Borget— Hadn't he? Or were they—?

He moved his foot, felt it lift, fall, made himself shift his weight— While he moved to sit on a bench beside—

The effort to grasp both stumbled him. Knees slammed the hard ground, wrenching a harsh sound he felt in his throat. No good. Eyes closed he forced his attention to divide, panting. *Feel, dammit, use hands and knees, crawl—*

He crawled (sitting still), hands reaching, scraping, sometimes forgetting to crawl. Dariel (unreal?) said his name and pulled him back, and he had to fight to get into his real body again. Angry. His knee hit rock, and pain made him very real for a moment.

It took ages of shattering effort through conflicting experiences, the simultaneousnesses. Then one hand hooked softness. Fabric. Teeth gritted, he explored with fingers that seemed to hold a stoneware bowl. He felt the hard shape of something— a leg. Yes. Calf, knee, hard thigh, wide belt— Heglit.

He tried to grasp that fact, and for a moment the riot of life and color dimmed to cool blue-green and shadows—

He clung to the wide belt, squeezing his eyes shut. Think, dammit, think! This was unreal. They, all three of them, were in the forest by the river. How could they wake up? Were they seeing, feeling, the same things he was? He needed to wake Heglit. Somehow.

Desperation forced the split. Heglit never chem-linked. He wouldn't know— He felt his way up the hard body,

135

found broad shoulders, neck, face— He lifted his hand, brought it down flat and hard.

"Heglit. Wake up." And again. The body moved, aware. But not to protect itself. The mind was otherwhere occupied.

"*Come, Jade. To the White Lur.*" The voice, laughing, tugged at him. He fought it stubbornly. Once Heglit had ended his trip. He had something (or had had). Something of Rafal. Think.

A muted snap, such as a plucked string might feel if it were feel and not sound, jumped through him, dissolving confusion. It was night, and cold, and the sky blazed a multicolored diadem. And Heglit lay before him, long and very still.

"Heglit." Turning the face to catch the sky light, thinking he had never seen it so still and far away. Wake up, he thought, it's not real. It's a trap of some kind.

Need to reach, to contact, built the bridge. The dislocation hit with a force that staggered him. He split, feeling *himself* lying on hard stony ground, while he knelt over him. He felt a strange play of feeling that was not his feeling (knowing it because it wasn't scared and he knew he was). Not now, he thought visciously, *not now!*

Heglit—

Images, like dream-scenes, rambled through his fear and urgency, but his will outran them until he saw himself seeing Heglit, and the sun was bright and warm and—

But Heglit was seeing him, speaking to him—

"Heglit, *this is a dream, not real. A trap,*" he said, heard himself say, mirrorimaging himself. "*Can't you feel it? You are lying in the dark on Alzar.*"

"*Jade. You cannot be here.*"

"*Heglit—*" Frustrated. Then inspiration struck. "*You said you would tell me how you ended my chem-skip on C'Erit.*"

"*A spore of tangri, collected on Dondil. It protects us from drugging.*"

"*Have you some with you?*"

"*Always.*"

The neck pouch. Hours, or no time at all, happened while he found his way out of that sunlit place to his own cold hurting body. He pushed away guilt and opened the pouch, knowing (even if Heglit had not said) what he wanted.

The fine dust stuck to his fingers, and he rubbed it off over the still face—

Heglit gasped, both hands jerked up, reaching; one found Jade's shoulder with brutal strength, crushing— Then fell back as the long body shuddered, relaxed.

Glis, what if he'd killed him? What if— No time to think of that. Find Borget. Look through tangled shadows to find him crouched against a pile of rocks, head pillowed on one arm. He did not waste time, flicking the dust into the peaceful face, seeing the convulsive change, the sudden total relaxation—

And have time to wait and think, wondering if it was a chem-link that had caught them, and how, out here where nothing was. Unless this wasn't real—

He forced himself to his feet, felt blood trickle down his leg. He had fallen hard on the rock. Both knees felt bruised and swollen. How could Tas do this? Creating this trap for them if he didn't expect them.

Or was it a natural barrier of some kind. Or protection for some secret? Shivering a little, he looked back toward the river, now a scintillating ribbon throwing back the sky-glow. There was a bridge of great square stones. Nothing more. Ahead, toward the mountain where the dream city had been was a wide rock-strewn clearing. Nothing more.

Limping, he moved to Heglit, found him breathing slow and steady. Asleep, or unconscious. At least he lived. And not having that to worry about he became aware of being here in the emptiness of an unknown world, suddenly very much bigger than it had seemed in the Zendra Three's outview screen. Sounds began to come to him, of water washing rock, breeze stirring leaves together, something that could have been movement, something alive moving near the rocks. It was too big and empty and full of threat. He hugged himself and wondered how long the night would last.

13

He dozed fitfully, waking at every real or imagined sound, heart pounding. Once he thought he saw something small and dark and many legged scuttling across the clearing, but he wasn't sure.

"Jade." The single word took his breath. He froze. "Jade?"

"Heglit. You're all right." His leg buckled when he tried to get up. Then Heglit was there, tall and solid.

"Your leg—"

"Nothing. I fell. Borget—?" Heglit helped him up and they went to where the Benjor lay against the rocks. He stirred when Heglit touched him, waking.

"Jade, I dreamed—" He paused, rubbing his face.

"And I," Heglit said, looking at Jade.

"No dream. We were chem-linked somehow."

Heglit looked at him (like Heglit), then nodded. "A barrier." He turned toward the mountain. "Alzar is more than we thought. This is guarded against those of this world. Tas has more secrets than I knew. It will be light in two or three hours, Jade. Can you walk?"

"Yes. It's only a bruise." He looked down at his torn pants, saw the dark stain. It didn't matter. He would go on, up the mountain. He looked into the familiar face, wanting to ask if he was all right, wanting to ask many things. But he didn't. Heglit would tell him or not as he chose. And if the mountain was protected, that was where they had to go, before they were discovered here in the open.

The leg hurt the first hundred steps or so, then settled into a steady ache that he could live with. The land sloped more and more steeply, then became a series of ups and downs, each up longer and more rocky, or crowded with vegetation that could have been low bushy trees of some sort. They walked, silent, looking, but not sure for what.

Light dimmed the stars behind them, tinting the sky violet and rose, shaping sight, but only Borget noticed the out-of-placeness of the great jumble of rocks above them.

"It is not of nature," he said. "Can you not see?"

Jade couldn't. It looked like a dozen other places they had passed in the dimming night.

"What should we see?" Heglit asked, willing to learn.

"No rocks above or below. And no trees. But there is a living thing near."

Heglit looked at the golden face a moment, then nodded, turning toward the massive pile.

The opening was well screened, seemed no more than a trick of shadow among the jumbled rocks until they were climbing into the formation. Then it resolved the play of illusion, becoming a large archway into shadow.

"Lista is there," Borget pointed. "And other living things."

"Dangerous?" Heglit was already moving toward the gate. Half a dozen long strides, and a loud angry roar raced out from the stone, a flash of green and gold exploded through the curve of the arch. Instinct threw the Rafalan aside faster than Jade thought he could move. Then he forgot that, in the vision that faced them. Longer than a man, it lay or crouched against the gray rock, a thing of great teeth and claws flashing back the new sun. Great yellow eyes stared unblinking above gaping jaws lined full with curved fangs. It held there, rumbling, broad flat head moving from side to side watching the trio. Three pairs of stubby legs shifted so claws grated against hard stone, and the sinewy body curved and humped, changing shape as the tail flicked angrily, scales flashing rainbows against the dark hole.

"Is it real?" Jade's voice brought the baleful stare to him.

"Real," Borget said almost normally, and the head moved toward him. "Heglit, do not move. He is guard here, and what he does not know he fears, and so hates."

Moving slowly, but without hesitation, Borget left Jade's side.

"Do not be reckless, Borg," Heglit said, and the beast

made a hard sound, long head snapping around to look at him.

"Heglit," Borget's voice remained calm, but it carried warning. "Do not speak again. You are closest, and I think he can move very fast. He will kill you. I am not being a fool. You trust your knowledge, but it is not of Benjo, not mine." The vibrant voice, pitched strangely to Jade's ear, had captured the beast's attention, though Borget was twice Heglit's distance from it. The yellow eyes glared, tail and claws rasping nervously, rippling scales sent sparks of sunlight against Jade's eyes.

"He will listen as long as I speak, Heglit. When I am nearer him than you, turn and walk by him without hurry. Do not touch him. Do not disobey or he will kill me."

For one quick helpless moment Heglit looked to Jade, appealing. Afraid to speak and break a spell he hoped was building, Jade could only nod slightly.

Borget's voice did not change tempo, but slid easily into the music that was Benjorspeak, talking now only to the angry guardian, telling it of himself and strength and freedom and the sweetness of life. No begging, but equal speech, and the always graceful movements of the golden body became more fluid, almost reptilian, as he closed the distance. The wide glistening mouth narrowed, and watching, Jade thought there was a certain listening attention in the wide yellow eyes.

Half crouching, hands moving in strange slow gestures matching voice-sound, Borget moved near, nearer than Heglit. The Rafalan, as attentive as the beast, waited one heartbeat, then moved, perfectly controlled, straightening, turning, walking quietly through the arch. The beast twitched, but did not look away from Borget, and the great mouth did not open. Heglit disappeared into shadow.

"Jade. Follow him calmly. There is yet danger. Do not look hard at him or touch him. He will let you pass." The voice did not change.

Heart beating slow and hard, Jade began to move, looking at the ground, aware of Borget and the beast from the corner of his eye. The Benjor was almost near enough to touch the beast.

The arch seemed narrow with half the green and hard-scaled body sharing it. There was a strange cold smell in the shadows and a soft metallic gleam of something that could have been a chain. Then they were behind him, and the tall dark shadow that was Heglit was before him.

"Jade," soft voice. "Look."

He turned. In the brilliant splash of sunlight, the golden man bent to one knee, looking up into the savage face of the beast, speaking quietly. Then both hands lifted, lay against the broad snout below the eyes. The whole length of the creature went still.

After a moment Borget rose, one hand resting on the broad head. He spoke something Jade could not hear, then walked past, coming toward them. The beast curved to watch and Jade stifled a warning. Borget entered unmolested.

"Come," he said as he neared them, "he is chained and cannot follow."

They moved back into darkness, and for a time heard what could have been the sound of claws and scales scraping the stone behind them.

"Did you speak with him?" Jade asked, still wondering at the thing they had seen.

"You heard." There was a smile in the voice. "He is a warrior, loving a challenge. But there is no cruelty. And he is lonely."

"Someone chained him," Heglit commented, bringing their thoughts back to the fact of this place and their reason here. At the same time Jade realized he could see a little. The passage curved, and there was light, and a great stair leading down.

Jade moved out into the light, but Heglit drew him back. "There should be guards." He measured the emptiness with thoughtful eyes.

"Perhaps they trust the beast."

"They would not trust one guard, not even one like that." He moved across the passage, looking up along the carved wall, and after a little gestured for them to join him, showing them the tiny gleam of glass and metal that was the spyer, directed at the stair. There were almost certainly others, probably well out of reach against the high ceiling. The chamber and stair were too obvious, too inviting. "There should be other access."

It took a while of searching, back into darkness and along the high stone walls, then a shadow, that caught Jade's eye by being too regular in the broken wall, drew him to take a closer look. Approaching, he found a faint trail, invisible from the main floor. It was steep, but possible to climb.

"Beam shaft," Heglit said, looking into the blackness that was a straight tunnel. Jade knew of worlds where buildings ran high and the port ship-beam had been adapted for use in traveling within the buildings. But he had never used them. Heglit reached into the dark, fingers touching a strange-textured pole. "Come." He stepped into nothing, holding his position with one hand, and began to slide down.

Jade shrugged, reached, grasped the pole his eyes hadn't seen, and followed. It was a peculiar feeling. His body expected to fall, but he drifted, using his hands to guide rather than support. He felt Borget above, and, looking down past his feet, he could see Heglit dimly.

Like dreaming they went down, passing landings leading to other levels. But Heglit did not stop and they followed until they came to the end. There was a grid covering the bottom of the shaft, and a door, palmplate glowing softly, casting enough light to see by. Heglit leaned to the door, listening, as they came down by him.

Jade didn't like being here, closed in. It could so easily be a trap. But they were here, and they couldn't turn back. The shaft only moved down.

Without speaking, Heglit palmed the door, and it slid open on light and space and a wide-eyed Clate. Heglit moved forward, reaching, and the Clate folded to the floor with a sound. Heglit bent and pulled a short metal tube from the limp hand.

"Weapon," he said, looking around. This was an entry-way, from the look of it. There were racks of clothing, and shelves holding things Jade had never seen, plus an assortment of obvious weapons like wide Zondril swords, Algoran knives and light spears.

"Hunting tools," Borget said. "For sport outside. And the way." He pointed to another door like the one through which they had come. The up-shaft.

Heglit paused to search the shelves of weapons, selecting carefully. He handed a small metal ovoid to Borget,

142

showing him how to use it. It protected but did not kill, he explained, knowing more of the Benjor than Jade expected. Jade took up a tube like the one Heglit had taken from the Clate. It killed, the Rafalan said.

"Rafalan?"

Heglit ignored that, leading the way past the clothing and around a corner. There were three doors here. Jade stuck the weapon in his belt, feeling safer for it, and wondered which way they should go.

"Right," Heglit decided, for no reason he cared to give, maybe not having any. The door opened into a long, well-lit corridor, with two doors on either side. Heglit ignored them, moving toward the wide door at the end of the hall. And another beam-shaft. Without hesitation he stepped out, started down. Jade glanced back at Borget and followed. There was a feeling of hurry in the Rafalan's movements.

There were no off-steps this time. The shaft dropped a long way, into soft yellow light and a square room with four doors. Heglit stood a moment, thinking.

"What difference?" Jade asked, feeling caged.

"The bulk of the mountain is that way." Heglit gestured to the door on his right. "One would build in and up as well as down. More than one entrance would be logical."

Jade started for the door.

"It will be guarded," Heglit reminded, checking the weapon somehow in his hand.

Jade nodded, readying his own weapon, thinking he would be scared if they spent much more time here.

Then the door opened and there was no more time. A yell of surprise, violet beams lashing out, silent, surprising him. But instinct took over, he moved, leaping something that could have been a table, giving Heglit room, sweeping the beam of his weapon across the room in front of him, thinking there was noise, but hearing nothing, only seeing movement and men running and falling.

"Jade!" Heglit's voice caught him in mid-stride. He turned as Heglit headed for a door he hadn't seen. Heart pounding, he ran after the two, into more corridor, doors, rooms he didn't really see.

Then another square room and beamshaft and Heglit

143

halting them, breath even and unhurried. "This is a different kind of barrier. We will only lose ourselves."

"Then what?"

"A guide," Borget suggested. Heglit looked at him and nodded.

"We have come down a long way. We need a way up."

It took some finding. Only the down-shafts were open. There were rooms and doors leading to corridors and more rooms until Jade lost track. Then Borget called them to a small door and an unlit shaft. Jade reached in and felt the upward pull. At Heglit's nod he stepped in, began to float up, pulling slightly on the guide pole to hurry. There was one landing, wider than the ones in the other shafts. A space and a door. When all three were landed, Heglit palmed the door open on a large room, full of Clates.

The Rafalan moved first, leaping aside, running, as someone yelled. Then everything moved in confusion. Afraid he might hit Heglit, Jade hesitated. Heglit's own weapon whispered, dazzling the room, and there was no more movement, no cries, and Heglit stood with one black-clad body lifted to his shoulder. The others, not as many as Jade had expected, lay in a tangle near the door.

"Come."

Jade and Borget followed out into a corridor, into another room bare except for shelves of what seemed to be spare machinery parts. Heglit laid the Clate on the floor and rested on one knee looking down at him. After a while the Clate stirred, lids fluttering.

Heglit waited patiently until the eyes opened, blinking, one hand moving to the neck telling Jade how Heglit had got him. Then the eyes saw Heglit and stuck wide.

"Who—?"

"Your name." Cold.

"Godn." The voice shook. "Level nineteen cell-tech."

"There was a woman taken by Barmalin Tas. A Benjor."

"There's none in the cells now. Not for several days."

"He has captives in cells here?" Jade asked, bringing the eyes around to see there was more than Heglit here.

"Captives? Only guests. Is that Benjor?" Godn pointed at Borget.

"It is." Heglit said it flat, bringing the muddy eyes back quick, throat flexing as Godn swallowed.

"Seen none, me. But if one is captive it doesn't go to the cells. Would be up, in Tas's place. If she was got for beauty, she'd be in the hill. He keeps 'em there for watchin' and things."

The tone, the hint of expression, drew Jade forward. Heglit moved imperceptibly, stilling him. "Do you know the way?"

The brown head shook, spilling hair over the brow. Heglit reached out one long hand, lifted the face to him. "You do know. And you will tell me."

"Then I am dead. By law of Tas." Begging. But, looking at the cold eyes, he knew his options. He talked, naming directions and corridors and up-beams. Heglit watched and listened until he was done, like there was nothing but time here for learning.

"Now the truth, Godn."

Jade threw him a look. How did he always *know?* The truth was a stair up one level, and the main up-beam shaft wih coded landings. Heglit nodded.

"Shall we bind him?" Jade asked.

"When we are done."

"But—" He looked to Borget for support, but the Benjor was watching Heglit.

"If Tas hides here, why project the illusion by the river?" Heglit asked the Clate, sitting back on his heels.

"To bring the people. They are free to find it by invitation. It is the place all seek. They come and dream. And they believe the dream. That is the prize. Most are escorted out after the dreaming, and they go out and tell of a place of wonder where all things are allowed, even Wif, and where murder is done and undone."

Because none of it was real. There were guards, the Clate said, who came at daybreak to where the life sensors located the visitors. Some, the special ones, were taken by order of Tas to certain cells here in the mountain, and cared for while dreaming their dearest fantasies. Then they were returned to Cityside full of stories of the wonder of Tas. But they could never come here again. A device was implanted without their knowledge, and by it the guards could find them before they reached the mountain.

"Tas has reason beyond gifting."

Godn nodded. "While they are celled here in the lower levels, he learns, recording the dreams and speech. I have heard they will answer questions though they sleep. All goes to Tas."

"So he brings them here to spy and learn." Heglit stood up finally. Without speaking again he bound the man, left him lying on the floor. They had their direction; now he moved quickly, up the stairs to the beam-shaft, and up, counting levels to the one Godn had named.

The corridors were wider, well-lit, and the doors and cross corridors were marked and titled. Jade tried to imagine the layout, knowing it was bigger than he had thought.

They turned left, watching. Godn had said these levels were patrolled. And he had not lied. Voices came from a corridor to their right, approaching. They ran. Into a small group coming toward them from the front. Violet flashed. Someone shouted, a short hard sound. Then they were to the next turn and running.

"There will be more, now we are discovered," Heglit had the breath to say. He stopped near a door labelled as access to the down-shaft, but Borget caught his arm. "She is here!"

The dark eyes looked to him. "Come then."

The hesitation cost them. Figures appeared in the corridor, black-clad and armed. Heat seared close to Jade and he turned, threw his own violet beam back and saw momentary confusion. Then he ran, following Borget. Turning, running, turning again. And always the chasers behind, or coming from branching corridors, the hot flashes and yells of discovery, then turning, and momentary safety.

Heglit stopped suddenly, one arm halting them. "Wait. Our way is always clear. They are making us go—"

"Rafalan!"

Ears ringing, Jade spun around, met Heglit's eyes. Trapped. And recognized? The corridor was empty but for them.

"Rafalan." Again the voice boomed, echoing through the space of walls. "You are mine here. All my councillors said you would not dare so far, but you have come to my very house to bring me my desire." Cold and cruel,

146

the words beat at them. And for the barest moment the two looked at Heglit. He gave no sign. Then the corridor was plunged into darkness. "Your reward."

One wall glowed softly, shimmered, dissolved, showing a room beyond, a soft-furred couch, and lying on it, splendidly beautiful, Lista. Asleep? Or dead.

Borget's quick breath broke the silence. "She lives."

"Beyond your reach, Benjor," the big voice boomed.

Heglit stood with his hands against the glowing wall like he was listening to something. Then he turned away, toward Jade. "Is it real?"

The question surprised him. And made him think. It felt real. But so had the joyhouses in the city last night. He decided not to take anything for granted but that something he had always to depend on in himself. He closed his eyes, believing nothing but the dark, and walked forward. It wasn't real. It was that easy. The combination of suggestion and visual projection had nearly trapped them again. No longer accepting the unreality, Heglit leapt to the couch, caught up the sleeper and turned.

"Jade, you will have to lead. He may try to fool us again. He will certainly send guards . . ."

The great voice rang through the dark, calling orders, telling where they were. But telling Heglit also. They ran. There was a drop-shaft and dream-like drifting when they wanted to plummet. Then running again and the sound of others running, and new light, and another slow drop, and Lista awake, protesting, running finally hand in hand with Borget.

But it was not enough. They could be seen and they were not certain where to go. And then there were voices and black-clad men ahead and behind. Violet beams lashed out and they could not hope to escape. Unless—

Jade saw the dark side corridor first, smaller than the usual walks. It was the only chance he could give them, knowing Tas wanted him, that he might well let them go. Dodging hot purple, he ran, cutting away from the others. Heglit's voice called once and he turned, met a look louder than any shout and ignored it, knowing he was faster. He sped into dark wanting to put distance between them. Then the voice slammed into him, stopping his flight. He turned, head ringing, saw the wall detach, slide across the corridor, and the voice, more distant now, gave freedom to his companions.

A sound turned him to face a dozen black-clad men, and there was no logic in carrying the fight further. Sighing, he smiled and dropped his weapon. With arms outstretched, he walked toward the one he took to be the leader.

14

"They will appreciate the sacrifice, but it wasn't necessary. I wished them no harm."

Jade had faced all manner of men. The fact that Tas sat above him on a fine chair robed in rich fabric touched nothing but his knowledge. Only the man himself, posture, voice, eyes, all the subtle speaks he used, knowing or not, told Jade about him. And all he saw and heard and felt said Tas was highly satisfied with himself.

"Every logician and thinker said it could not be done, that I could not find one single man in the billions of the Clate galaxy. But you are here. And they will not underestimate me again." He fell silent, watching. For effect, Jade thought. Reese, another Centra Clate, had at least had some spontaneity.

Watching, very aware, he relaxed outwardly, beginning to catch breath and balance. It had come down to this, to one man facing him, and the man, whatever his power and position, was just a man, twice Jade's age, he guessed, still slender and handsome, but petulant, even soft, and, his face said, used to having it all his way. Too easily. That meant he could be understood, even manipulated. Especially if the manipulator had nothing to hide or protect. And certainly he, of all the players in this ridiculous galaxy-wide game, had the least to lose or gain. That made him most free.

Understanding that Tas was trying to use silence to make him speak, Jade turned away from the raised chair, satisfying his curiosity about the room. It was large and richly furnished. A glow behind heavy embroidered drapes hinted at a window and sunlight. Outside. It figured. This was the top of the mountain. For some reason that made him think of Lurz.

"You are younger than I expected," Tas said finally.

149

Controlling a smile of success, Jade looked at him over his left shoulder. Nonresponsiveness would lead Tas to quick vindictive anger, he thought. Now he was curious, and Jade, certainly as curious, felt it would be to his advantage to build bridges.

"Should I be older? Or only appear younger?"

Tas frowned. "Is that a question?"

Jade turned to face him, hands thrust into his wide belt. "I thought you could—" He let his gaze fall away. "I do not know my age. Or parentage. Perhaps I am older than I appear, older than I think I am."

Tas leaned his cheek on one hand, looking down at him pensively. "Your Rafalan mate did not tell you?"

"My age? Does he know?"

"Perhaps. Almost certainly Gandar does. If you were the Clate they tried to hold on Rafalpha. You don't take the opportunities to learn much, in your wanderings through the limbs. The Rafalans do better. I will tell you now that you cannot perjure yourself in this room without my knowledge."

Jade hadn't given that any real thought. He knew, of course, that there were sensors good enough to pick up changes in pulse and respiration, perhaps even muscle tension. They were a part of law enforcement on richer ComUn worlds, even out in the limbs.

He felt Tas watching him, or perhaps watching something else watching him. "Well," he said finally, "do I?"

"You were the one to catch the illusion on level nineteen." Tas ignored the question, seemed almost to be talking to himself. "Perhaps I should have kept the Rafalan."

Frustrated, adjusting enough to this place to begin to feel anger, Jade decided to take some initiative. "Did you arrange this, Tas? Or were you really trying to get me killed? Like Lurz said."

"Lurz?"

"Of Burkoze. He tried to buy me."

"Lurz." Unexpectedly, Tas laughed, a soft whispering sound in the space between them. "You have a good opinion of your skin value. Perhaps he was trying to buy me."

Jade bowed slightly, acknowledging the possibility. "What is my value to you, Tas?"

"None."

"Two years and more of your seeking me says there is some reason." He would not bow too low. "I have caused you no injury or loss. I have nothing of value you could want."

Tas held up a white hand. "My wanting you dead should have killed you. Yet you lived. You have done too much of the improbable. You were an inconvenience. Now you have become a riddle through what you don't know. More interesting by far. I am indebted to your renegade Rafalan."

"How could this one be an inconvenience to Barmalin Tas?"

"Not by wishing to be. A combination of probably unrelated items, of ideas even, that likely have no interest to you. Have you noticed any particular similarity between us?"

"One. Our eyes," he admitted after a pause, wondering where any of this was going. But Tas did, indeed, have eyes of a color like his, called yellow, but more metallic.

"Yellow eyes. And only in the family of Tas. And then rarely more than once or twice in a generation. Of my seven known sons, two had the eyes, my successor and his brother who did not live to see his seventeenth year."

"You wanted me dead because of my eye color?" It wasn't really a question, just surprise. As far as Jade knew, there could be a hundred worlds that spawned yellow-eyed Clates.

"Only Clates of our blood line are so marked."

This was too much. "You think me to be your son."

Tas ignored that. "You were spoken of several stan-years ago by an ambitious shipmaster who owned you for a time. His father was on the ComUn board, and when he came to visit me brought tales of you to Alzar. The Council is well acquainted with the legends and beliefs of the sectors we touch, and there is one such legend that tells of a time of trouble for the Federation, when there will be a warring between Clates. It is said there will be a new order built by a man of no loyalty. A man with the mark of leadership."

Tas watched and Jade watched him back. He knew how intrigue and fable spilled out of Centra, washing the outer sectors in waves, changing and spreading. He didn't imagine Tas believed them. But there was something of the texture of the Rafalan idea threaded through this tale. He said nothing, waiting.

"I do not believe the legends either," Tas said. "But others do. You appeared rather inopportunely, with the Free-men uniting against ComUn. Twenty-three worlds have contracted to Free-shippers this stanyear, breaking quotas on export items that are in great demand in Centra and cluster worlds. They will grow rich in a short time."

"Let them."

"They do not understand how control holds the Federation together. There will be rivalries, and the trouble will spread. Already there is a lack of balance when they concentrate their freight in the luxury areas and neglect the staple items many inner worlds depend on. If they succeed in uniting many more worlds, they will endure only long enough to shatter the ComUn worlds and the Federation. Then they will have destroyed themselves."

Jade looked up at him, arms folded, daring to half-sit on the edge of a carved desk to take the weight off his still-sore leg. He found what Tas was telling him interesting, but what did it have to do with him?

"They cannot unite easily without a focal figure. Already there is a striving for superiority among the wealthy Free-men."

Listening, watching the man, Jade felt something that said this was only talk, that the real happening for him here was something else. He thought over what had been said, looking for clues, discarding this fancy. If Tas believed there was some danger to ComUn from the prophecy or legend, he would have kept Heglit, surely, for he must know of Rafal's interest in ComUn's collapse. Maybe. Tas was talking to him, Tas wanted him here, for some reason.

He looked up to find Tas watching him closely, yellow eyes thoughtful, saying—

Yellow eyes. The thought came from somewhere unexpected and he nearly jumped up in sudden excitement, then buried it deep. But the cold thought remained. Not about why Tas wanted him, exactly, but something else, maybe something important to him. He had only once before seen eyes to match his in color. In the information

152

center on Rio Del. Jadriel Sarn. The last of the TreAshal. Supposedly the last. But Heglit had told him of the offer made by the military command of the Federation. Maybe some of the TreAshal were not the heroes Rafal believed. If some had escaped, or defected, to the military—

A door opening behind him broke into his racing thoughts. Tas looked up, annoyance washing his face. A deep voice said something in a speak Jade had never heard before, and Tas leaned forward, answering in kind.

Listening closely, trying to hear, Jade felt a cold tension growing, like sticky sand in his head. He shook himself quickly, aware again now of hunger and thirst.

"Jade." Tas called his attention back. "I have enjoyed our visit, but business presses. We will continue this later."

"Food and drink, even for captives, is common courtesy," Jade reminded.

"Indeed." Tas said something in that other speak, and four large Algoran types appeared. Jade went with them quietly, knowing something had changed but not sure what, or in who, only that it would have some effect on him. He just hoped someone would feed him. He was so hungry he felt lightheaded.

From the richness of the mountain top to a small cubicle of plasteel containing a couch, a table, a washer, and nothing more. The door slid closed behind him and he was alone. Locked in. He tried not to think of the smallness of the cell, but it pressed in on him until he retreated to the washer. The few minutes the wash took didn't do a lot to help. Neither did having to pull his stained clothing on over his now-clean skin.

There was a tray on the table, and that made him nervous, until he found the hairline crack in the tabletop that gave away the trick. And then he wasn't much interested in anything but the food, a thick gruel that somehow tasted like Lursteak, squares of bread filled with something spicy, and a tall bottle of cold water. That helped a lot.

When nothing else happened, he lay down on the couch, eyes closed, wondering about Borget and Lista, wishing he had been there for their reunion. He annoyed himself by wondering if Heglit had joined in, decided to forgive him in any case, and found himself remembering the last

153

he had seen of the Rafalan, and the look in those black eyes.

He was tired. He wanted to sleep. But being here, locked up, got in the way. Damn, he was tired of being locked up. Everybody he met anymore wanted to put him in a cage. And wanted to find a father for him. Shaking loose his hair, he sat crosslegged on the couch, frowning, working his way back to his thoughts about Tas. A TreAshal?

The more he thought about it the more right it felt (and the less he thought about the smallness of the cell). If someone had left TreAsh during the last days or hours they wouldn't have been missed. Not from a world preparing to die. And that was probably why Tas wanted him. He could be afraid others had survived and would find him out and let the Clate worlds know ComUn was headed by a TreAshal. That had to be the best-kept secret in the galaxy. Maybe Tas didn't even know the truth of it. Only the danger of people with yellow eyes that were not of his family line. The eye color had to be a racial trait. He recalled that Reese had been intrigued by his eyes. And he had talked of his joy-skinner here on Alzar, and Tas had learned of him. That had to be the reason for this. Tas wanted to know where he came from.

The first time the urge to leave touched him, he dodged, fastening on his thoughts about Tas. But it came back, an urge to get off the couch and try the door (again) to, to— He shook it off. Then suddenly found himself at the door, looking for some kind of latch or pressure plate.

Fool. He pushed back his hair with both hands, knowing the door was locked. Still, the urge grew, like panic, needing release in action. To calm himself, he tried to think how the door was fastened, touching it lightly with his fingers, though he hadn't meant to. He watched his hands as though he wasn't connected to them, beginning to feel a different kind of fear. Then that passed, and for a little time he felt nothing much, until he noticed somewhat lazily that one place on the door felt warmer, almost sticky beneath his fingers. That should be important, he decided. And after a while it was. He knew when the time came he would do something about it. Just now his right arm was growing, thickening, swelling out from his shoulder, throbbing with a mounting power. He watched it draw back, thought this was probably a mistake, but he couldn't seem to do anything about it except close his eyes as his arm shot forward, smashing into the plasteel door.

The pain made him gasp, blind for a second, hugging the hand to his belly. He blinked away the fog, trying not to voice the whimper in the back of his throat. It hurt so much he was afraid to look at the hand. So he looked at the door. It was caved in, and the hairline crack about it had widened enough for him to get the fingers of his good hand around it. He pulled, and the door slid back until the dent he'd made stopped it. But it was open wide enough for him to slip through.

The corridor was empty. He tried to remember how he had come here with the guards, but impulse turned him to the right. He started walking, bent over, cradling his right hand tenderly, sweating with the wash of pain radiating up into his shoulder.

A different kind of urgency flared in his middle, and he moved faster, finally trotting awkwardly, surrounded by hurt and the need to go on, all reason tattered by pain and confusion. He turned, turned again, came to a door and palmed it open with his left hand. A downshaft. The little sense he had left tried to pull him back. "No," he whispered. "I can't—"

But he did, stepping out, reaching for the pole, falling into dark, and falling, thinking he was going to be sick—Then thinking nothing, hardly touching the guide pole, just going down, floating, like in N-space, growing and growing, pulling away from the pain . . .

He stirred, thick muscular ripples moving down his length, trying to reach. But the arm was connected wrong — Left and right rested solidly on the ground. He blinked his eyes open, saw dim green, steaming, deliciously warm. He breathed in, felt the huge cavern expand inside the ribs, turned his head, and his neck bent and bent until he could see—

He would have screamed then but the mouth he felt suddenly terrified him. The long thick loops of him he saw (and felt) coiled, tail lashing, short legs churning in the warm mud— He closed his eyes—

felt the guide pole cool in his convulsive grip, right hand stuck on his arm like a nova.

Jadriel Younger. The thought whispered up through fear and pain, siren call promising peace and strength and help. If he could only—

I have you safe. Come.

Who are you? Then his feet touched the floor and the shock folded him, dropped him on his right arm. He yelled quietly against his left hand and tried to get up.

Let me help you.

Who are you!? He knew he hadn't said it out loud; his teeth were clenched too tight.

Come back. I can hold the pain.

The desire to do what the whispering voice suggested, and knowing how, floated up like a bubble, bursting knowledge and agreement against his brain. He gave up with a faint sigh, leaning against the wall.

Warmth and comfort and knowledge of power beat in him with a slow double pulse. He knew this. Eyes closed, he watched the distant figure move away from the wall, stagger slightly, then begin to walk. Coming (he knew somehow) close to this place.

Me, he thought, bemused. But around that, knowing vast thoughts of why and how and purpose tangled into a structure that wouldn't fit his head. Only a great and complex desire to have that figure come here was understood.

There were other doors, heavy, that had to be negotiated. Stairs. The figure stumbled, fell twice, and Jade, watching from outside, felt new pain in his sore knee and savage protest in his right arm. But it was over there somewhere. The Jade out there got up again, came on through the last great door, and down wide stairs into the warm steamy air.

Only then did he begin to wonder, if that was Jade crouched over there on the wide stone stair, *where the Rim was he?*

He shouldn't have asked. All too quickly he was the Jade crouched on warm stone, shivering, coming to, wrapped in tangles of pain and confusion and long black hair. "How—?" He started to say and see at the same time. Pale green glow (familiar?), steamy smell of vegetation. Memories tangled him up. He pulled his hair back with

156

one hand and sat up, peered out into big foggy space. And wished he hadn't.

The beast at the gate. Only forty times the size. And it was looking at him with huge unblinking eyes. The humps and coils of its body shifted, gleam of scales winking away into dimness. One great foot moved toward him—

"No!" The yell whispered through numb lips. Not real, he wouldn't accept this . . . He looked away, down to his right hand. That was real. He felt a queer looseness in pelvis and inner thighs. Swollen and purpling, the hand hung useless, only the thumb recognizable. He touched it, grunting through icy flames of hurt, and felt the knuckles like coarse gravel. Shattered. Wrist, too . . .

Man. You hear me.

The words whispered like star static, feeling them said, feeling the saying, like with Heglit, only—

He pressed his good hand to his eyes. Hard. "Stop it. I can't— dammit, I can't—!"

Man. You fear what you see.

He shook his head. He was, he thought, beyond fear. None of this was real, except his ruined hand, so nothing mattered. Comforted by that odd thought, he opened his eyes.

"Are you the speaker?" he asked softly. And felt agreement in his head or mouth.

"Who are you?"

The translation of feeling overwhelmed, losing him for a moment in the sensation of being that great beast.

You are in pain.

"Yes." He wondered why he was talking out loud when all this was taking place inside his head, then decided it was better that way, to keep track of who was speaking. He nearly smiled at that kind of reasoning. "My hand is broken." Understatement.

I could find no other way. There was an essence of guilt in that, pulling Jade's eyes up to the great yellow orbs.

"Do you have a name?"

And he knew it in a tongue he could never hope to speak.

We are two.

That made as much sense as anything else just now. He didn't ask two what.

Man. The pain can be done. The damage repaired.

"I wish."

Do you want? The word sounded (felt) like want, but it was bigger, more complex, encompassing desire, need, pray, and other things he didn't know how to do.

"Yes. I want."

Trust is needed. We can. But I must touch you.

Jade looked at the great flat snout, the half-hidden white of teeth, and he thought of the beast at the gate. He shuddered, realizing he wasn't as far from fear as he thought. "Shall I come down?"

To the last step. You may touch me then.

Right. After a minute he started down. And the beast moved, approaching slowly.

Do not fear. I will not devour you.

Humor? Then it didn't matter. He leaned forward as the great flat head lifted. It felt cool and moist beneath his hand, and very hard. Relief at being able to do this thing and still be safe washed through him, grew into a delicious euphoria. He leaned further, bent over his knees. His breathing slowed. And the dreams began. Pleasure dreams swirling like smoke, of places and people, and finally of Linking, skipping the Star Web in joyous freedom.

He woke lying on his back, confused.

Man. It is well.

Glis. He had thought the dream was over. He turned his head and looked into great yellow eyes. "You too," he said after a minute. "You have yellow eyes."

That is the key.

"What?"

The eyes of TreAsh. You are right. Tas is of TreAsh.

That brought him awake, sitting up, right hand automatically protected. He looked at it. Still swollen and purple, but— he touched the knuckles. Very sore. Still, there was a difference. Healing. He imagined he could feel the bones knitting, and something in him blocking the pain he could remember. "How was it done?"

The whole pattern is. Knowledge of togetherness. It needs only to be freed. The wanting stimulates, and the parts desire to become a oneness. We spoke to it.

Jade didn't know all that much about medicine, but he thought that was rather out of the ordinary.

"Dragon," he said suddenly. "You look like the old dragons of man. The old wise ones. I dreamed of you a while ago."

With us, Jade.

Whatever. "You belong to Tas."

No need of ending it.

"You know of TreAsh. You said Tas was one of them."

Their seed. Of the one who brought us here.

"Brought you? From—" Intuition hit, and he knew it wasn't something he had known before. Then he denied it. "You can't be. Three hundred—" The huge eyes blinked and Jade knew finally what he was talking about. "You're a Traveler."

All are travelers.

Philosophy, yet. "You knew the TreAshal during the war."

Knew, and friended, and agreed to wait here for the time.

"Wait. I can't follow you. You were friends of the TreAshal, yet you are— different." To put it mildly. "You know what happened to them, to TreAsh?"

TreAsh is a thought forgotten for a time. It will remember.

"You, here with Tas— I thought the Travelers all disappeared."

Returned. Tas, the first of his seed, brought us. We agreed with all. We would know. There was to be a watcher for safety.

Other meanings, like echoes, made full chords of the words, and Jade wasn't sure he understood. Except that this was a Traveler. And Tas was TreAshal.

"You helped me against Tas. Why?"

It is our being-reason.

Jade shook his head, trying to find sense in the huge words. "Couldn't you escape him?"

We were to be here. To help build togetherness until the memory is recalled.

There was a period of silence, then the great body shifted, head lifting over Jade, scaled loops of body and tail rising from the misty depths as the head swung away, jaws opening. Jade's heart pounded. He could almost walk into the gaping maw.

The strong warm one is returning. Are you together enough to go?

"Who is coming?" Dry-mouthed, Jade got up as the head swung back to him, tilting to look down to where he stood on the steps.

The togetherness in the Star Web. He comes angry and willing conflict on Tas for you. He will enter soon. Go now to him.

Heglit? But where would he be? And how to find him? "I don't know where I am."

I will show, Jade. Trust us. And remember my greeting inside.

Trust? Why not. He started up the steps, half running, and felt a strong impulse turn him left, to more stairs. There would be guards searching for him now. He felt like he'd been down here a long time. If Heglit came into them—

He hurried, but not so fast he forgot the need for a weapon, so when he passed the rack at the top of the steamy green cavern he stopped, choosing the same type of weapon Heglit had shown him, hoping his left hand would cooperate.

Twice he held back instinctively as black-clad men passed near, and he hoped the dragon understood his gratitude. Then he ran, feeling good, waking up. This was real, something to do and feel, pulling him out of the mystery and drug-dream feel of the dragon's chamber.

Panting from the long run, he climbed, using the beam-shaft only twice. Then something seemed familiar. He paused at an intersection, momentarily confused by the twin feelings, knowing he had seen this place before.

A shout spun him around to face three men. He lifted the weapon and the satisfying violet flash helped. Heart pounding, he ran again. But the hesitation had trapped him. A quick heat seared his shoulder and he ducked aside, thumbed the tube, sending violet fire at the group behind. And heard a yell ahead of him. He was quick, but they were many. Three dropped, but one rolled, came up, hand lifted—

Something very heavy squeezed Jade's body, taking breath and heartbeat. His head rang and his arm wouldn't work, for all his desperate desire. The corridor faded into dull red and he couldn't even protect his hand when he fell.

"Jade!" Hard voice, pulling his eyes open, protesting. He looked up into the dark familiar face.

He wanted to wake up, to be sure. And it was Heglit. Only different. The dark eyes blazed down into his. The loose blouse was torn, baring one thick-muscled shoulder, and the dark bronze was striped with a dark slash that dripped crimson to the floor.

" 'Glit." Lips rubbery. "Sorry."

"Time, Jade. They will return." The strong arm pulled him up and held him until he could stand, and there was the barest tremor in that strength.

The corridor was a charnel house. His weapon had killed quick and clean, but there were other bodies, dead by older, crueler weapons. A sword weighed Heglit's dark hand and evidence of its strength slicked the floor. Jade glanced at a face, walked several paces before realizing there had been nothing else, only the head, alone. He did not look back, but was very aware of the cruel, kindled eyes beside him. There was an up-shaft and he went first, depending on Heglit's strength for guide, holding his weapon in his good hand. But the guard there would never give the alarm.

They ran the last corridor, breathing hard. And then there was the wide stair, the well-lit chamber, the black tunnel.

And the beast. Heglit paused, preparing, but Jade walked on. "There's no danger now."

Heglit let the sword fall and came after, and the beast shifted and rumbled and watched them come.

It was twilight as they made their way down to the river. "You're hurt," Jade said, remembering.

"And you. Come." The familiar flat voice, but there was a memory now of Heglit wearing his warrior's face, fierce, and willing him to be alive.

"The dragon healed me," he said on the bridge.

Heglit looked at him and walked on.

It was full night when they came to the Zendra Three, and Borget was there, warm strength, helping them, and Lista, song-speaking, and time to sit down, trembling and feeling Heglit's eyes. Time to reach and touch the cruel hand, feel it turn and grip close in gratitude for the un-nameable.

"Borg," Heglit's voice, commanding, and the golden man turned to the controls. In moments the tiny ship leapt from the world like a spear, and threw herself into the blazing sky.

15

The gate through which they had entered Centra Sector was not marked on any ComUn map, but the position was logged in the navicomp. Borget ran them out through the local web to the proper coordinates, then dead-shipped, cutting everything but life support systems and external visuals. Unless someone came very close to ramming them they would be undetectable.

There was time for sleep and washing and clean clothes and food, and being together again, victorious.

Lista had tended their wounds, and the white dressing ran stark across Heglit's muscles as he pulled on a clean blouse. Jade's hand, still swollen and tender, opened and closed and felt whole.

"What now, us?" Borget asked, watching Lista.

It was the question Jade had asked himself on waking. They had Lista, they were away from Alzar. Now what?

"We have supplies for a month," Heglit said. "No port will allow us to ground when word gets out from Alzar."

"The Zendra—" Jade began.

"For supplies. If necessary. But we cannot always live on board, running and hiding."

True enough. And another thought struck Jade from somewhere. "We only have the three Links."

"There are two ship-Links on the Zendra Three."

"Will that work?"

Heglit nodded, fairly certain that the only protection necessary with the somehow modified skip-system was a cancellation of normal sensory contact during Star Web skips.

"Knowing a world, us," Borget said. "Safe for going to and unpeopled on Grio."

"Grio?" Everything Jade had heard of that world said it was the least safe of places to be.

"It only does not like reapers, Jade." Lista smiled, singing Benjorspeak. "We have seasoned there since childhood."

"It has a ComUn port," Heglit said, making her meaning.

"ComUn station for loading. Not import. And contracted to Benjo for keeping."

There was no available option, as far as they could tell.

"Charted run?" Borget asked in the control room. "Or wanting us there?"

Jade shot him a look, bringing golden laughter.

"Both," Heglit said, not looking at either of them.

It took time. The Benjor had to be fitted into the Zendra's Link-system; then Heglit programmed the Centra Zar to enter the Star Web automatically.

"Grio is a long way," he said to Jade. "We will not have Borget's strength."

Jade knew loss of control would deadship them in channel. They could get lost. They opted for long runs in the ultra channel, hoping wherever they broke out they would not have to contend with ComUn beacons or ships.

Then they were ready to Link and Jade thought this would be different, a thing of himself and Heglit, alone again, sharing.

And it was. They did not have the instinctive grasp of the Benjor, but they had their own greater knowledge now, and an ease binding them into a unit running free and strong. And sometimes in the urgent joy he thought he knew this Heglit too.

It took five long skips, with time for eating and sleeping in between, while the ship crawled from one gate to another, around the edges of busy sectors, or lay dead in N-space just giving them time to catch their breath. The Benjor were safe, linked only to one another in an extension of an always condition between them.

Once, while resting, Jade spoke of Tas, but Heglit silenced him, saying this was not the time.

Both hovered on the edge of exhaustion when Grio was a world close enough to see. Borget brought the ship into a port staffed, as he had said, only by Benjor, and there was greeting but no questions.

The port was little more than a small grounding pad and beam, surrounded by dull warehouses, a few odd-shaped ships Jade assumed (correctly) to be Benjor, and a few unlabeled buildings. The Benjor, male and female, were quiet and calm, asking for no explanation, but seeming to understand they needed sanctuary. They offered to stock the Centra Zar with ComUn supplies, and, at Borget's suggestion, Heglit agreed to move the ship off-world immediately and dead-ship out away from the world beam, returning in the Zendra, that could be grounded beyond the port and safe from any chance encounter with a ComUn ship.

Too tired to think much about it one way or another, Jade agreed when they offered them a house, and by late the next morning he and Heglit were following the Benjor out into the humid and oddly-scented jungle.

The house, a small hut, really, was built of stone in a small circular clearing. There was a spring for drinking, trickling into a pool where they could bathe (no autos here). And they were warned not to go out into the uncleared areas without a guide. No animals had developed on this world, but the plant life had evolved in complex directions, approaching sentience. It could be dangerous (the Benjor said, and Jade thought they would know) to those who were not familiar with it.

Jade had heard of stranger things on unpeopled worlds, and he had no desire to go exploring, though Borget told him there were protective suits at the station for the use of non-Benjor who came sometimes and wished to go out unescorted.

Jade noted that the Benjor themselves wore little more than sandals and briefs.

"But Grio knows us with pleasure," Borget smiled, and left without explaining, returning with Lista to learn what was known at the station.

Heglit, preoccupied since grounding, seemed to relax when the Benjor had gone. He examined the hut and clearing, then stripped to bathe in the pool below the spring. Jade watched, not sure it was good idea, but after a little he, too, entered the water, glad to escape the clinging heat of the air.

Drying on soft cloth (not as quick or efficient as a

blower, Jade thought) he wondered what they were going to do now. "How long do we stay here?"

Heglit straddled a stool made of some unpolished local wood, and leaned back against the stone wall. "That depends on what happens."

"What can we do? Turn pirate?"

Heglit let that pass. "I don't know yet. Since the TaLur run, all things seem to have moved to bring us here."

Jade didn't see how that made sense, and said so.

"We should talk of what you learned on Alzar." Heglit's unexpected switch to Rafalspeak caught Jade out of his mood. A long exhausting run and weeks of distance from Alzar without speaking of it had dulled his urgency to share the experience. He was no longer sure how much he knew and how much was fantasy, done to them or made up in his own head.

"Tas," he said finally. "Maybe I know something of him now that could hurt ComUn and help us. I think he's TreAshal."

Heglit leaned away from the wall. "Evidence."

"He wanted me because I have yellow eyes. So has he. And only in the record of Sarn did I see another."

Heglit listened, thought, leaned back. "I would have said it was not possible."

"Only if the history of Rafal is true." Jade told the thoughts he had had that some escaped TreAsh, and maybe ran to the Federation. "From a whole world who would know?"

"It would be seven generations. Does he think this?"

Jade shrugged. Tas hadn't said, and now he thought it didn't really matter. But the idea led to a more personal thought, one that could explain his own eye color (if yellow eyes were, in fact, a sign of TreAsh). "There could have been others. Or I could be of his blood."

"The possibility of survivors was considered on Rafal-pha. The tests left no room for doubt."

"But the time—"

Heglit's look said they would not argue the point again. "Leaving Alzar you spoke of a dragon."

"Oh. That. I don't think it was real." But the memory warmed him like a mystery and delight from childhood, and he looked at his hand. Almost healed now. And be-

166

cause he liked the idea (even if he didn't believe it), he told what he remembered.

"He was bigger than any life I've seen, or I thought he was. I thought he called me to him, showed me how to escape from the cell Tas had me in." He held out his hand, telling how he had broken out, and of the painful journey through the maze to the great cavern. Heglit's eyes held to him, listening.

"You doubt your memory."

"Now, yes."

"You did escape the cell. I would have said that was not possible. You must accept the things that are."

Jade shook his head, running fingers through his still damp hair. "Then explain it so it makes sense to me."

"Will you listen?"

Jade nodded, sighing. But not necessarily believe you, he thought to himself.

"The door was plasteel, the locking mechanism hidden inside. You would not, of yourself, ruin your hand in the hope of breaking the lock. Rather, you would wait to deal with one who had caged you. Whoever helped you had a reason. He might have told you of it."

"But how could he even know I was there?"

"I don't know. Maybe by the feel, like Borget with the guard beast. He could have reached you, a linking—"

"Heglit—" His heart jumped, taking his breath.

"Jade, don't. We must speak of that. Why does it trouble you?"

Jade didn't know, and the quietness of the Rafalan voice only added to his tension.

"The share-Linking," Heglit said after a minute, watching. "It made a change between us, a sensitivity, so there have been times we built a sort of knowing between us, outside the Link-system. We both know it." The dark eyes pinned him, forcing the truth to be acknowledged. "Not only on the ship. We did not speak of the night on Alzar, but you somehow learned of the tangri spore and how to use it."

"You knew?"

"I thought of it on waking. I know the effect of the spore. And until that night you did not know it existed. What of the dream was real I do not know."

Truth. And he was sweating. But Grio was hot.

"If the dragon linked with you in such a way, it explains itself."

"But is that even possible?"

"The Benjor have knowledge of a thing like it. We will ask them." Calm. "The dragon had a purpose. He spoke to you."

Jade nodded. Searching his memory, he tried to remember what had passed between them. "A lot was said, I think. Little of it made sense."

Heglit got up and went to stand against the open door, looking out into the clearing. "You remember some of it."

"That he wanted me away from Taş. But so did I. And I think he healed my hand while I slept. But maybe it wasn't so badly damaged as I thought." He closed his eyes and remembered the feel of that great hard head, the not-voice pouring words and other meanings over his thoughts. And as he looked and tasted memory, it expanded into meanings and truths he (or the other) had willed forgotten.

"Oh," he said, surprised, yellow eyes flashing to Heglit with a knowledge he wasn't sure he wanted. But knowing Heglit, more than anyone, deserved to know. If there was truth to it. But how could he know? Silenced by his internal questions he looked at the Rafalan.

"What is it?"

The yellow eyes blinked, looked down. "He spoke to me in a voice like I never dreamed. He told me Tas was the seed of TreAsh. That's how I knew it. And—"

"And?"

"And— dammit, Heglit, it was—"

"Jade."

"I think he said he was a Traveler."

Heglit's total silence brought Jade's head up. The Rafalan stood as before, but now the big hands were pressed flat to the door, the dark face gone strange.

"Heglit."

"You waited until now to tell me?" The quiet intensity of the voice crossed the room like a blow.

Jade drew back. "So much happened. So much not real. I couldn't tell if— maybe it didn't—" Under the blaze of those eyes he stammered, heard the defensiveness, the cowering in his voice. And he was angry.

"Stop it! Dammit! Enough!" He jumped up, kicking over his stool, letting his rage cast him free of the cool logic of Rafalspeak. "Why should I have told you? What's a Traveler to me? I'm not Rafalan. I'm not anything but me, Jade. Or I was, until that gleesting run to TaLur. Now I'm a fugitive from the whole damned galaxy, hiding out on a world that could kill me just for being. And for what?"

He stood before the Rafalan, lean and taut in the dark cloak of his hair. "You tell me nothing! Go here, go there— For what? I don't care about three hundred stanyears ago, or the TreAsh, or the Travelers. I never heard any of it until a few months ago. And I want it to end. Now. Do you understand? It is enough. Finished."

Heglit listened, head down. He heard the man out, then waited a moment more.

"It cannot be done by wanting, Jade."

"For me it can. I am not chained by your loyalty to Rafal and its dreams."

"Nor am I chained now to Rafal, but to TreAsh." There was a new look in his eyes. "You are angry with me, thinking I know more than I tell." The switch to Rafalspeak forced a change in attitude, purposeful, perhaps. He gestured to the stools and came to sit near where Jade still stood.

"You are only partly right. There are things I know that I have not told you because I lack the proof you would need to believe me. There are some things I guess or hope without evidence. I am as caught in this as you are. And as homeless now."

"You have enough knowledge to believe something is happening to us." Not eager to be pacified, Jade finally relented and sat on a cot, pulling his feet into his lap.

"There is a reason for the things that have happened to us, Jade. The dragon. Did he tell you why he was there?"

"I think he was captive, but had no reason to escape. He may have told me that. There was something about a need to watch, to wait, to keep or hold a togetherness of something. But I don't know what he meant. I thought he meant he had been there since the others, the Travelers, left. Returned, he said."

"Returned?"

Jade rubbed his ankles absently. "His words were so *big*, like a lot of speaks all saying the same thing and meaning a lot of other things too. He was chosen, I think, or offered, to wait."

Heglit bent forward, hands clasped between his knees. "Did he speak of TreAsh?"

"No. Yes. He said TreAsh was a thought forgotten, but it would remember again. That can't be right. I wish I could— there was so much."

"I think you will remember. Surely you must see that all that has happened to us fits a pattern, all building on that run to TaLur. While we seem to be following our own desires, I don't think we have any true choice of action. Even the search for Lista. That only took you to Alzar to learn of Tas and speak with the dragon. I think we are following a path laid out for us."

"By?" Challenging. Then his face changed. "Oh," he said again, and his eyes were brilliant in the light from the open door. "He said they helped me against Tas because it was their being reason. Do you understand that?"

About to answer, Heglit paused, looked to the door. And, though Jade heard nothing, in a moment Borget and Lista came into the clearing, calling out to them.

"Z'Atua and food," Lista smiled, producing packages. She looked from one to the other and stopped smiling. "Talking, you," she said, in lowspeak so Heglit could follow. "Leave us for later?"

"No." Heglit gestured them in, taking the wine. "Maybe you can help us."

They filled the room with calm and golden beauty, and Lista chose to sit beside Jade, making him glad.

Heglit put the question while Borget produced bowls and poured Z'Atua. "Between you is a bond. You, Borg, you shared the Link with us. Is it the same?"

"Of a kind, yes. But differing. A knowing was there, and being oneness. It was not unfamiliar."

"And the Benjor know of this kind of linking with other kinds."

Not quite following, Borget nodded, looking to Jade. "Not talking of it," he said, finally. "Being a thing of Benjor, as you have things of Rafal."

"Not trust-breaking." Lista spoke suddenly, touching

170

Jade's thigh. "These are brothers of a kind, for all they do not know it yet."

"What do we not know?" Heglit asked.

"The sharing between. It is, but unsaid and ignored. Only the feel is."

"How do you know this?"

"My brother shared one time."

They looked to Borget, who blushed, looking at Jade. "It was very loud, and became anger for both. I did not understand the not wanting."

"Do Benjor share with other life?" Heglit took the eyes from Jade.

"Of course. Or Grio would not allow us."

"But how does it work?" Jade wanted to know.

"Feeling. All life feels. It is the beginning. And wanting. The basis of all things."

Long ago, Borget said, the Benjor studied the sameness of all things, the feel of life and wanting, and the nature of thought. Their studies turned inward, much as Rafal's turned out, to the doing and learning of things.

"We do not hide inside, so all is like sharing the Link between Benjor."

Explaining, maybe, why the Benjor here had asked no questions of them.

"Wanting is force," Borget said. "So the traveling within the Star Web has built questions in us also."

"What does the Star Web have to do with this?" Jade asked, lost again.

"The Web is traveled in the mind, is it not?" That brought Heglit's head up a bit.

"It is, in a way," he agreed.

"The question built now, by us only, in reaching Centra, is about the nature of the Web. If it is an outside place, how do we travel it wanting?"

Good question, Jade thought, meeting Heglit's eyes and seeing something there.

"If it is a place where mind and outside touch," Borget continued. "Could not all learn to travel it, wanting?"

The golden voice wove the question into silence, and Heglit still watched Jade.

"Can the Benjor way of sharing be learned?" Jade asked, knowing Heglit wanted to know.

Borget shrugged. "Maybe like speaking. By wanting

171

and learning the feel of it. No one has asked before." He grinned suddenly. "Would you want to learn from us? Here?"

"Could we learn from you outside?" Heglit countered.

"There is more life to feel with here. And Grio is a wise world of feeling."

Wise wasn't exactly the word Jade would have used to describe Grio, but he kept quiet, feeling a little outside the conversation.

The Z'Atua relaxed him inside, and he wished they would stay, but Heglit shared the hut, so they went back to their people at the port saying a ComUn ship was scheduled to ground in a few days.

"Borget thinks it is possible to learn the Benjor way of sharing," Heglit said, closing the door on a quick nightfall. "Perhaps this is the thing we are to do here."

"Talk plain."

"The most probable answer is that TreAsh created the situation we are in." Crisp Rafalspeak brought logic.

"Through the device, Tas, and the dragon."

Heglit shook his head. "Tas is not part of this now. His part is done."

"Evidence." Jade knew the game too.

"The Traveler said. He and Tas, his family, were to see to the formation of a stable Federation."

Jade blinked. He didn't remember the dragon saying anything like that. He let it pass, reaching for a slice of fruit the Benjor had brought. "Only the device, then."

"You, Jade."

He thought of that. And it was impossible. "You're back to that glis about me and Sam. Maybe that dragon lived three hundred stanyears. Not me."

"No. But I believe I know how it could be possible."

"Evidence," Jade snapped, goaded by the unbelievable stubbornness of the Rafalan.

Heglit nodded slightly, following the Rafalan rules. "If I am correct, the clue is in what we have done in the Star Web. Perhaps it is the device. Sam could have brought you here."

"How?"

"Wanting."

The word fell into the room like a smooth stone, and

in the dimness Jade wondered if the wide straight mouth curved a little.

"Right." Jade knotted his hair with a quick hard motion, quitting the game by dropping into lowspeak. "Wanting ahead three hundred stanyears, him. Bringing his child here to leave him. Came up wild, me, Rafalan. No home, no father." His own bitterness surprised him.

"You survived." The cold of that logic couldn't be argued, or the inference that perhaps Sarn had not, that there could have been more sacrifice on the other side.

"A reason, Heglit. Something I can understand and believe." As anger ran away from him.

"I do not know, Jade. Only that there is one. Maybe the Traveler told you."

"No. He said he helped me because it was his reason. Or his reason for helping me was— Dammit, I can't remember. Is it possible, Heglit? I mean, if you weren't Rafalan, would you believe what you believe now?"

Heglit shrugged, almost invisible in the dimness, and got up to light the primitive fire as Borget had shown him. Crouching there, as the flames grew slowly, he reviewed the evidence he saw, the appearance of the device, the too-short skip to TaLur, the interest of Tas, the genetic study on Rafalpha, the seemingly impossible distances covered in a short time while a longer time went by outside, then the apparent real-time speed-up and the ability to get where they wanted to be, when they wanted to be.

"From the first, Jade, on the TaLur run, we expected to get to TaLur. What if we had wanted some other place? And we lost two weeks going to Rafal. But when we wanted outside time to match ours, it did."

All true. But thinking (trying to think) about it pulled his head in strange ways. He looked down at the flame-burnished face and was reminded of the Heglit in the underground corridor, the savage warrior, so unlike this Heglit, the cool thinker. The warm one, the dragon had called him. The Benjor called him cool.

What would the Benjor say of Heglit's logic, he wondered. Had Heglit already spoken to Borget about it? And Heglit thought they were here for a reason. Like once before, he had said they shouldn't send the Benjor away, that they were part of the thing that was happening. But what part? Of what? What had Borget said of the Star Web? That it was traveled in the mind. And it was, in a way. Linked, he knew his body was in the chair, monitored by the computer that was ready to pull him out if physical symptoms of stress hit a critical level. He even accepted that what he experienced in the Web was imaginary. But it worked, it took him (and the ship) from here to there. And no one knew how. Or even what it was. Heglit said it was a gift from the TreAshal, who discovered it. But now they were doing things that shouldn't be able to be done in the Web. Maybe Borget was right. It was a place where the mind and outside touch.

Heglit got up, moved away from the fire, but the novel dancing flame held Jade's eyes. His thoughts drifted. Mind-touching, wanting, and how had he reached Heglit through the drug of Alzar except by wanting? (Even before, some secret part of his mind said, share-Linking. He enjoyed the sharing, the experience of that Heglit. And he didn't want it to end. So once it had not.)

He felt Heglit's eyes on him and glanced up, full of fantasy, wondering if this, a way to use wanting, was what the Benjor spoke of teaching. But fantasy locked itself up behind his face, as always, against the solid practicality of the Rafalan.

"Borget spoke of teaching us a thing."

Jade started slightly when the flat voice touched so close to his thought. But it was a thing Heglit sometimes did. He swallowed and nodded, watching Heglit pull off his blouse, muscles bunching and swelling as he moved, preparing to sleep. For a moment Jade touched his own shoulder, remembering the quick reflexive strength that had nearly crushed him in the dark confusion of the Alzar night. He stirred himself finally to strip and slide beneath the soft Benjor blankets.

16

Grio. A week and he hated the clearing, hated the heat, hated the unchanging wall of green that hemmed them in, away from the rest of the planet. Heglit's always silence and always reading or writing didn't help. Even Borget and Lista didn't help. For one thing, they never stayed in the clearing. And Heglit was always there.

"Lift, us," he said finally, after promising himself he wouldn't be the one to bring it up. He had bathed in the pool and his damned hair wouldn't dry, and there had not been a word exchanged between them during the entire day as far as he could remember. "Doing anything, Tas. And us not knowing."

Heglit looked up with no readable expression, knowing the reason for the lowspeak, seeing frustration in the restless movements. "We are safe here."

"Better doing than safe, maybe," Jade grumbled. Knowing Heglit was right didn't help his mood. "Safe for what? How long, Heglit?"

The Rafalan put aside his papers and came out to the spring to drink. "When the time comes we will go. From Rio Del we have been guided. We are being led toward something for some purpose."

Jade whirled to face him, hair whipping about his narrow waist. "Did you ever think you could be wrong?" Cold clear Rafalspeak said he was angry. "Did you ever think there was nothing to your theory, that all we have done is our doing, that we could go on and do something?"

Heglit ignored the question for a moment. "Go where and do what?"

"We could go to Lurz. What we know of Barmalin Tas would be worth a lot."

"It would destroy ComUn. The Free-men cannot

175

hold the worlds together without controls and restrictions. They can only function within the ComUn structure."

The reasonable tone didn't soothe Jade. "You sound like Tas," he snapped, rubbing at a slight headache. "Sorry."

Heglit nodded and finally answered the other question. "I have wondered if I am right. Evidence and logic say I am. We will not know for certain until something more happens. The waiting is hard."

"For you?" He could have bitten his tongue, but the Rafalan answered without hesitation.

"Yes. I do not like waiting and not knowing."

He didn't act like it bothered him, but Jade kept himself from saying so. Anyway, the quick anger had eased him a little. He wished Borget and Lista would come. He spent an hour trying to decipher the Rafalan script Heglit had agreed to teach, but his mind wandered in the enervating heat, drifting around Heglit's explanations for what was happening to them, traveling back to Alzar and the dream-like memory of the dragon.

Time dragged. Heglit worked quietly, talking only when he had something to say. Jade exercised, sweating, hated the constant heat, and finally the Benjor did come, and there was talk and wine and different food brought from the port. It was the pattern of his days.

Once Borget brought Shiva Pearls (he had mentioned them, hoping), but the chem-link was a confusion of dragons and the jungle of Grio. Borget laughed at him, saying Grio had done it, that the chem-link opened him up to all the being things here. He wasn't sure he liked that. But it made him think of Grio differently.

"You said none could go out into Grio alone," he reminded Borget. "Could I go out from here with a guide?"

"Of course. Not for reaping, but to see and learn. I will take you."

"Would Lista come?"

Heglit heard, and looked at them, saying nothing.

The gold head shook no. "With a female, only. It is Grio's way of meeting. We will go tomorrow. She may join us after a time."

Jade wondered why Grio cared who went out, but it didn't matter. He was glad to have something to look forward to.

Borget returned early, greeting them with fresh fruit and news of a ComUn ship to ground in two days. "Out of C'Erit last, come to load the spores we have collected. They will hunt no contraband but old T'Chal dust for pleasing the crew on the long runs in to Rio Del."

"If there is news out of Centra they will know," Heglit said. Borget agreed. The Benjor was aware and would learn what was known.

"Come, Jade. Let us go," he said when they were done eating.

Jade had been thinking of some kind of protection and maybe a pack of some kind for supplies. Borget laughed at him. They would take nothing.

The tumultuous green swallowed them quickly, hiding the clearing, the white sky, everything. Jade kept close to Borget, moving as he moved, and there was silence for so long that he began to listen to his own heart and the soft whisper of their passage through the thick growth. It was hot, and the exertion brought sweat. The golden form of the man an arm's length ahead was the only relief from the constant green of the world, and Jade was some little satisfied that that flat muscled back was glistening with moisture also.

"Where are we going, Borg? Or do we just walk?" he asked finally, beginning to think too much of the jungle and the warning he had heard.

"There is a spring. We will rest there." Plainly he did not want to talk, so Jade continued silent, walking, wondering if Borget was also thinking.

The monotony of movement, of green and the gold of the figure ahead of him merged with his thoughts until, though he felt full-headed and occupied, he was not really aware of thinking anything. There was just a not-unpleasant constancy and quiet. When Borget stopped, Jade was so wrapped up in the experience that he bumped into him before realizing they had stopped.

"Where are we?" He looked around, seeing individual things for the first time in a long time. There was a sound of water running, a fall, a pool, a mossy bank and the absence of thick undergrowth. Pale flowers gleamed back in the denser shadows and there was a subtle fragrance in the air, over the smells of water and heavy dark soil. He looked up at the narrow waterfall, and for a moment stared, unbelieving.

"It's a tree," he said finally, someplace between a question and an exclamation. The mountain he had felt, rather than seen, down which poured the whispering stream of water, was no shape of rock and earth, but a single tree, too big to understand. The trunk lifted thick and rough, so wide there was only a hint of circumference. Looking up, he saw great branches thrusting away from the trunk, curving out and out, then down again to root and support the mass of the tree.

"ChatkarJ'Mur, the father tree," Borget said, smiling up at the tree. "All the tall growth on this land are his daughters. The shape and strength of his roots have formed the land itself from the shallow sea."

"You *know* this tree?" Wiping sweat from his eyes, Jade tried to understand.

"It is our way, Jade, as Heglit said, to know in a way much like your Linking. A wanting thing. Come, let us drink." He led the way down to the pool and there was a silver cup on a small shelf of what must be a tree root. "We thought of what you asked, and have some thoughts on the Linkmen. We do not think all can yet travel the Star Web. Perhaps all Benjor, had they the desire for it. Certainly all Rafalans and your kind. But not all men always, until they learn to look inside, to know the ways of being and believing that are not from the skin. When they begin to fear the inside warring with the outside they can no longer Link."

"Benjor don't usually Link, do they?" Refreshed by the cool water, Jade rested on soft moss, looking up at the tree, thinking it was nice here.

Borget smiled, reaching to fill the cup again. "We do not need to. Few of us go out into the Clate galaxy, and then only to find out what is there, to feel it. We thought Star Web Linking was a different thing than it is, a thing of machines and science."

As he bent to the water, three stripes of lighter gold laced his bare back. Scars, Jade thought, from the Algorans on Rio Del. He reached and touched them lightly, found them slightly raised from the smooth sweated skin. Borget smiled at him over his shoulder.

"It should not have happened," Jade said, remembering, wondering if Heglit saw this as another part of the pattern they seemed caught up in. "We should have sent you away after grounding."

"But you did not, and we have become part of a greater thing, touching the mystery of the Star Web, hearing legends the Benjor never heard, passing through the gate of a new adventure. Only you hold back, Jade, trading joy for anger."

"I'm being used."

"Better not to be?" Borget laughed, eyes dancing, and Jade knew he was teasing him. The Benjor, he thought, probably didn't realize how serious this mystery had become. Then he thought of Rio Del.

"Why me, Borg? I don't know what's happening. I always knew what I wanted, why I did the things I did."

"Now you don't?"

He looked to see if Borget was teasing, but the eyes were level and serious. "Not if Heglit's right. He says there's a purpose, that everything since—"

"I have spoken with him, Jade." He smiled again, looking to the incredible tree. "If he's right, is that so bad a thing?"

"I don't know." He had half-expected Heglit to speak to the Benjor; now he found he didn't like the idea that he had. "What are we here for?"

"You are angry now." Borget lay back on one arm, looking up at him.

"No. Not really. It's just— Heglit said we were meant to come here."

"Being here is part of you now." He rolled over onto his back, hands linked behind his head. "Grio is not as bad as you expected."

"No. But it's too hot." And because it was not like Borget to avoid a question, he asked again. "What is it we are to do here?"

"To be here, to talk a little, to learn something of Grio, maybe."

Jade didn't see how that could help anything. He wondered if Borget was being intentionally uninformative. He looked at him, at the complete relaxation, the half-closed eyes dreaming on the massive tree, and it occurred to him that he did not know this one as well as he thought. A loneliness brushed him, a cold rare feeling.

With a sort of shock, he felt he was poised between things, all the familiar on one side, on the other a new and strange experience. With a sort of vague panic he opted for what he knew, turning back to thoughts he knew he could deal with.

"Lista should have come," he said.

"Pleasure thinking, you." Borget laughed softly. "But Grio is a pleasure world, and she is here as you wish."

"Where?"

A golden hand lifted, pointing, and he turned to see her step from the crowding greenery. "You followed."

"No." She laughed. "I came to be with you."

"For pleasure?"

"For joy." She let him pull her down and reached to loosen his hair. And that was good and right. He lost himself in their responsiveness, used and using, hot and steamy as the jungle surrounding them, slowly violent until they released him, let him lay back and learn to breathe again, glad of the soft moss, riding sweet lethargy toward sleep.

Once in the dreaming silence he had a thought and voiced it sleepily. "With this between us why should I have Linked with Heglit? Surely we are closer."

"Maybe the ship-Link," Borget answered softly. "And with us you chose skin-linking before self-linking."

"M-m-m." Jade squinted up at the tree through his lashes. "Explain."

"Like you know how I feel to you, you don't know how I feel to be me, like you know how it feels to be Heglit."

The drowsy voice anchored him against the sweet heaviness of sleep. "What does being you feel like?" he asked, or thought he asked, seeing only the tree through closing eyes, foggy.

There was a small movement of air flowing across him, deliciously cooling his damp skin. He smiled, felt it curving his sleepy lips. ChatkarJ'Mur was a great wall before him. So big to be a tree, he thought.

"We should wake and go a bit further, Jade."

He heard the words, soft golden sounds and meanings, and he thought, yes, that they should go, and in a while they would. But now he was so comfortable, so easy—

When Borget spoke again he sighed, moved to rise— and could not. Curiosity moved through him slowly,

180

without fear. Why could he not move? He pulled his drifting lethargic mind into himself, exploring. He stirred, felt the great pressure of massive sinews and

What?

The feelings were something he had never felt before. He knew his body so well— He tried to reach down, slow and dream-like, very different from his desire to do—

Brown, he thought, dark cool, reaching out and down, spreading, bunched and knotted down through dark and damp to the solid muscle of—

What?

Bending, jointless, was a smooth elastic stretching, an all-overness— Too many places uncentered, all oneness moving, many touchings into—

What?

Interested, vaguely, thinking (in some nearly unreachable once-familiar place) that Borget was waiting, he tried to open his eyes, feeling a laugh loosen him up inside. He would look up and say he couldn't move. He would—

See?

At first he thought the sun had come out of the white overcast, then he realized he was seeing, all-seeing, full round and high-low, deep in dark, high in warm white light, and through a hundred greennesses all alive, awake, seeing back, happy-glad—

Where was Borget?

And he knew-saw him, small, distant, down (or over), crouched naked gold beside—

Jade?!

Wait!

Jade is me!

I am—

Slow massive memory dwelt behind thoughts he tried to hold and recognize. He knew with a vast certainty that he was *not* Jade. He was—

Well, he was. There was that. And something like excitement waiting to happen somewhere, and a pleasure too vast to be called joy.

This is being me. Great hard suppleness, alive, all parts seeing, being, feeling, knowing, growing—

Too big for Jade only.

I am ChatkarJ'Mur.

The tree?

And without protest he slid into knowing that, and becoming aware all at once, rooted deep, branched high, growing. He smiled (?), felt himself melt and seep into the slow life-fluid of ChatkarJ'Mur, touching a foreverness of being.

Lazily thoughtful, Borget suggested moving on, seeing more of Grio before they had to turn back. He smiled as Jade smiled, willing to wait a while yet, at peace here with Grio and Jade and Lista. A soft rustling in the thick growth about the spring was no usual sound; there was a quality to it, rousing him.

"Jade—" He bent to touch the shoulder of the sleeper, but a stiff spiny growth swelled out of the soft moss, brushing his other hand. The woman, watching, halted him, and he held still, looking down at the new thing. He felt no fear; he knew Grio. This was a message in the way of the world. He did not reach for Jade again, but went very still, listening in a way his people had learned long ago, being aware of the othernesses about him. And he felt intent and desire with a peculiar pointedness.

He waited a long time, not entirely sure and trusting in his own thoughts. Jade, after all, was not Benjor.

Lista, female and more receptive, spoke first. "Grio has taken him." She turned slightly, looking toward the tree, and Borget followed her glance. Always, the huge presence of it hallowed this place, building safety and subtle raptures for them who lay here. Now that slow awareness was coalescing, drawing to the mossy hillock, reaching. He could feel strands of attention weaving through the warm air, wrapping the quiescent form of the man.

"ChatkarJ'Mur." Her word was a breath as their eyes met. "Do you feel?"

He nodded.

"He is more aware than we knew, my brother. I thought him slow-lifed. There is a desire here, not a pleasuring, a purpose."

"For Jade. I should not have brought him here." Dark gold brows drew together slightly as he tried to decipher the great slow waves of attention pouring through the forest.

"Perhaps it is only that he is new, and come unafraid."

But Borget shook his head. "No. I feel a greeting. There is no evil, but ChatkarJ'Mur will have him."

As though to prove his words, a new rustling moved through the heavy surrounding brush, like a wind, though no air moved. Borget looked up, watched the great outer branches stir. A new marvel. He had thought Chatkar-J'Mur too big and old to be mobile, as some of the smaller life was on Grio. But the great branches were curving, reaching down from above, trailing thick vines, curving in from the sides, slow. It would take time, but the movements were inexorable and mysterious.

"The Rafalan," Lista said, watching. "He spoke to you of a purpose in coming to Grio."

"He guesses only. There are more things at work here than logic, I think. But he must be told. Jade is his also. Go to him, my sister."

"You?"

"I will stay with Jade."

She hesitated a moment, looking from him to the tree, wanting to argue. He could only stay if Grio allowed. And Grio brooked no argument. They knew this. And she knew her brother. He would give his life to protect one as dear to them as Jade. Also, there was a bond debt for her rescue from Tas. No matter that the Rafalan put another purpose to it.

"ChatkarJ'Mur knows me," Borget smiled. "We will not battle. Go to Heglit." He kissed her and let her go.

Alone, he sat beside the sleeper, noting that the small prickly plant had vanished as Grio became aware of his motives. Perhaps it was a sign he would be allowed to stay. He watched the encroachment of the branches and vines, wondering, feeling only desire, not explanation. And the presence of the great tree fell over him like chords of sound, mesmerizing.

A touch on his bare thigh stirred him and he looked down at the curved tendril brushing his skin, new and tender green. He stroked it with a finger, smiling. It was a greeting he had exchanged before. But now there was no reciprocal caress. The shoot thickened, hardened, butted against his leg insistently. The message was clear.

He was to move. He stood and looked down at Jade, saw the vines and firmer branches had reached the lean body, new tendrils lay against ribs and hips, pressed slow fingers through the tangle of dark hair.

A gentle bump on his ankle told him again to move, and he was torn between protest and acceptance. But he moved, turning to the mountainous base of the tree. He crossed the spring and climbed to sit in a hollow formed in the roughness of the bark, where he could watch as vines and limbs wove about Jade, circling legs and thighs and waist and chest. Jade did not move. Soon he could not if he wished.

"ChatkarJ'Mur," Borget said softly, "he is flesh, not tree. Be gentle."

There was no response, and Borget sat quiet, chin on knees, as the body was lifted slowly, drawn up into the thick green roof of the jungle.

17

"A tree, Lady?" Heglit looked at her frowning slightly, wondering if he heard right.

"Not a tree, shipmaster. ChatkarJ'Mur, the father tree. Willed it, him, and Jade went. Grio would not let Borget wake him."

"He is there, but he sleeps."

"Was. Yes." And anticipating him, "Not chem-linking. This is Grio's will of him."

Not for the first time, Heglit wished for some of Jade's talent for communication. Lowspeak was a poor language for explaining any but personal action and reaction. And Grio was unknown territory. Rafal had heard little more than that it existed and was dangerous as well as valuable, supporting a type of plant life that appeared to approach intelligence. Watching the female, he was sure she was not alarmed by what had happened to Jade. And Borget had stayed with him, so whatever was going on was probably not threatening. But he didn't like it. First a dragon, now a tree. If it was, he supposed it was, but his education and training was firm-based in realism and logic and the fantasy-feel of current events was unsettling, for all there were probably reasonable explanations. He sat down at the rude desk, frowning more. Probably not threatening. Probably explainable. Not very acceptable conclusions.

"Should I go to him, Lista?"

"Try. Maybe. Grio lets or doesn't."

He had spoken to the Benjor of the alleged sentience of the plant life, not sure it wasn't a function of Benjor sensitivity. The Benjor insisted the plants possessed an intelligence rated far beyond simple response and were able to act on their own. He accepted that. The galaxy was full of seeming impossibles. But he had to wonder if

185

this could be something else, something to get at Jade.

"Borget will bring him back," Lista said, maybe sensing his worry. "Jade is being new here and we are known to ChatkarJ'Mur. Wanting to know him too, is all, maybe." She smiled and touched his hand. "Stay here me, waiting?"

He nodded, aware of her beauty, but untroubled by it. ComUn restriction forced physical discipline of Rafalan Outgoers as rigidly as the Rafalan Council on Rafalpha. There was no question, it simply was. He accepted it. They talked of Grio and Alzar as time passed, and she ate with him, bringing fresh fruits from beyond the clearing.

"Jade is not mad with you," she said once, out of a silence. "Only afraid, him."

"Afraid of what?" He leaned back against the wall, thinking of time.

"Too much. Of not doing him for him. Over reaching. Borget said the thing you thought for him, for Jade, of being TreAshal. And of things happening for reasons. If it is being done to you, outside, could you not undo?"

"I don't know. Maybe. But we would never know why, Lady."

Arms clasped about long golden legs, she smiled. "For learning we have all ComUn after, and it still doesn't answer."

"Not yet. But there is reason to it."

"For running to Grio."

"I hope so."

"But worry you for him, shipmaster."

"Yes. I am part of it. Perhaps when we learn why I will learn what part." He was worried. They had been here together for several hours. It would be dark before long. He walked to the door, stood looking at the thick growth around them. "I would go to them, Lista."

She appeared at his side, silently. "Try us. Come."

She led the way across the clearing, started into the jungle, seeing no path. Heglit followed. She moved quickly, finding a clear way until they could see nothing but leaves and limbs. Then she hesitated, seemed uncertain, finally stopped altogether and looked back at him. "Grio doesn't want us," she said soberly, and there was a new look in her eyes.

186

Heglit believed her, but he wasn't sure how she knew. He asked her the way and moved past her, meaning to try. Branches crowded the way, roots and vines tangled his feet, and he thought he felt a sort of denial. Then he was sure. His eye caught movement as obstacles formed, branches curving down, vines, untouched, falling to tangle about his legs. He stopped and nothing moved. When he turned back he felt a subtle release of tension and it seemed a way was made clear for him.

"Grio knows intent," he said, and Lista nodded, keeping silent until they reached the clearing.

"Not you only," she said, looking back. "Also me. I am not to go."

So they waited. And the bright sky faded, and Heglit thought of the jungle about them, and built questions of methods and awareness and intelligence.

As night fell Borget came into the clearing. Alone.

"Jade?" Lista asked quickly, saving Heglit the trouble.

"Grio has him. Chatkar]'Mur." He looked at Heglit helplessly. "I was sent back. I don't know why."

"Is he in danger?"

"I did not feel it."

Which could have meant there was no danger, or there was no danger Borget could feel. Heglit looked at both of them, thinking, knowing it was a thing they didn't like either. But he had a feel of the jungle's power and they could do nothing but wait.

He asked them about the tree, and they told him what they knew of it, but there was nothing they could say of purpose or reason.

"You came, waiting for a thing," Borget reminded. "A thing has happened."

But was it accident or design? Only time could tell them. In a silence Heglit thought of the Zendra Three and certain armaments. Then he remembered how the jungle had reacted to intention before action, and he did not think of that again.

18

Growth and reach and memory of time made by happenings. Jade felt it, felt himself feeling it with curiosity as remote and present as his (?) downreach into Grio and outreach into rooted othernesses.

Jadriel Younger.

Satisfaction sighed like slow wind, stirring his elastic branches. No, wait, he thought. Not mine. Yours.

I knew before. The elder and seed.

Meaning flowed, dark brown resonance against a belly big as a mountain, stirring skyreaching limbs, and a soft gold that he knew someplace was pleasure, but that the Jade of him found more strange than pleasing.

There was a knowing of you when you were before, and a bond made with the Speaker Prince. You are here for the gifting, as said by Vril-Atalba.

Not sure if this was information given or his own memory, Jade waited. He could remember not being what he was now, being softer, fleeter, more together. But that tangled with a memory of being a foreverness of this always expanding feeling of growth and calm. And memory, long and long, solid as his reach down into dark earth.

He remembered—

The Benjor coming, new and good and full of warm joy, meeting and learning and sharing a pleasure never known before. A gift gifted in return, so all his parts moved to protect and love them.

He remembered—

A time of pain and anger against small life and hurting sharpnesses slashing, burning, killing, and his anger was created slow and irrevocable against the Reapers of new life. And the sure wisdom of stopping that, of learning how the small soft life could be made to cease.

He remembered—

Silences and reaching, and the slow joy of seeding the swampy soil to become more, and reach further.

He remembered—

A people of dark hair and yellow eyes. The Speakers who sat long before him, unmoving, dreaming dreams of touch and wonder and sharing a new experience, a pleasure time of learning, and the new freedom of knowing he learned and felt feelings only small life had, things he had never known. He remembered his waking.

And a last time he remembered—

A small silver seed leaping down from the hard hot sky, bringing one known, the joy-bringer, the Speaker Prince.

Memory-pictures grew, and Jade was divided by intense interest (his) and nostalgia (a different his), and someplace in the head he didn't really have he felt a pressure building, a pain that was unable to reach him.

No, he thought.

Yes, he knew. The face of the man clad in dark green tunic and trousers, seen once (and everyday familiar), and a voice never heard (and beloved) spoke a speak he had never heard, making meanings he knew like the flavor of his own thoughts.

"Vril-Atalba say talk to you, Chat," the voice said (or was remembered saying). "They will only say to bring the boy to you, that there's no other way. You know I don't trust this solution."

And he (the he that wasn't him) did know that, knew the frustration and angry fear in the man as well as the bold decision and swift action. He also knew it would work (but he didn't know what *it* was). He told the man in a speak of feeling that he must follow the plan. And soon.

The lean face looked up to him. "I could stay, too." There was held-back hope in the yellow eyes.

He could not, ChatkarJ'Mur (the tree he was now) said in his own way. The doing was upon them. He was bound to his people in a way he could not undo. The child was not. Yet.

"But he is my son, Chat. So young—" One hand rose, protecting the back of the child held close against the green-clad chest.

Someplace very far away Jade's head roared, dimming the connection, reaching even the vast tree he had become. But that part of him accepted that.

Your seed will survive, he reminded the man in his way, Vril-Atalba has shown you that. You must go fast to Rafalpha. They will seek you and must find you there. And you must leave the signs. Go.

"Yes. All right. But— Will he remember?"

In time he will remember. He will learn from us and he will remember even this day, Speaker. Leave him.

No— The Jade locked into the vaster being would have protested. But the pain wound suddenly tighter, higher, and in some distant green place the cool white body in its cradle of vines writhed, hurting, cried out once . . .

Remember— *Man-smell, dark green against face, warm strong hand, and secure deep-toned laugh*

Remember— *Soft speak and no pain, only a pure crystalline clarity on all levels, feeling, knowing*

Remember— *Big face pressed against his, soft touch of lips, warm cheek salt wet, and words*

Remember— *Cold of no arms, no dark green and aloneness, alone*

Drifting in the warm green shadows, held secure by the vast power of ChatkarJ'Mur, the man lay quiet, slow breathing, pale as death. But diamonds welled through dark lashes, gathered, slid across blue-veined temples to fall and hang glistening in the dark hair. He slept. And he dreamed a dream three hundred years old as Chatkar-J'Mur gave him back to himself.

"Jadriel Younger, seed of the Speaker, you are whole. You have survived. It is time now to begin."

The voice did not come from him but to him. He roused slowly, drifting, reached out and touched warm moss, felt the hand and arm, the legs and body. The other was a dream, then.

"Jadriel Younger. You are aware, you remember. As the Speaker was told, so it is."

"ChatkarJ'Mur?" He swallowed in a dry throat, and looked up at the tree. "You talk like the dragon."

"It is time for you to begin, Speaker-seed."

The vast word-sound echoed like another voice and tendrils of memory stirred, wanting to be claimed. He touched the dream and recoiled, closing his eyes, feeling a weariness great as the voice rooting him to the ground.

"No more," he whispered

Remember, Jade, the warm face, the hands, the kiss— He actually felt the caress, raised a hand to his face. He remembered. And wept.

He woke from a dreamless sleep, hurting inside someplace. He drank at the spring and watched the tree and knew how it felt to be so vast, to be root and roof of a continent. But there was no pleasure in it yet. He recalled too well being small and helpless and afraid. He looked down at his body and wondered, then forgot to wonder as other memory thoughts flashed and teased.

"ChatkarJ'Mur," he said, and his voice was rough and hoarse. "How could I forget that?"

"I took the memory to keep for you, Speaker-seed. For your safety in the Clate worlds, until you should come ready."

He accepted that, beyond reaction. Beyond much of anything but weakness and a dull hurt someplace inside.

"Begin what?" he asked, some time later.

"Vril-Atalba will tell you of it when you are safe."

That meant nothing. But it didn't matter. He was too tired to think about it. He rested against the tree and perhaps slept, and learned a little of what he knew.

"TreAsh," he said at dawn, and misty memories shifted. "It didn't die. Tell me."

But he felt the tree not knowing (or not saying), and knew there was danger in his knowing. But it was the right question.

"Does Tas know?"

And he thought, no, Tas did not know. But having seen Jade he would be thinking, and his thoughts could lead to TreAsh, and there was somehow a danger in that.

He was not aware of time passing. He slept without sleeping as the multilevel connection with the great tree was unravelled, and he didn't particularly care. He didn't want to think of that anymore. Or anything. It was too much. In some deep untrusted place he knew everything had changed. He had ended in a way he didn't understand. It was time to begin, and he didn't know how. He only knew danger, and that three hundred years separated him from him and it was too long. He was too alone.

Alone. That thought lasted through the day before he recalled that he was not alone. Maybe. Not now. He wasn't really conscious of rising, moving across the spring and away from the tree. It was a thing that happened. Something separate from the jungle his mind had become. But he wanted desperately to be alone no longer.

Time was a different thing to ChatkarJ'Mur, and sustenance an always thing, so he did not fully understand the needs of small life. But the thing that needed doing had been done. He let the man go, feeling a need he did not comprehend.

Jade was weak, so the walk of a morning became a dim torture pushing him toward his own kind. He walked, and sometimes fell, not really aware of the stroking fronds and tendrils that knew his hurt and tried to ease it, not seeing the miracle of movement that opened a path for him.

He came into the clearing at twilight, a long white blur in the green dimness, naked in the tangled cloak of his hair.

The Benjor knew of his coming and met him, warm hands and arms and gentle speak soothing. He felt their worry and wanted to tell them he was well, but it was too much effort . . . They took him into the water to bathe, caring for him, and he let the hands wash him, having perfect knowledge of his skin and hair. He drifted on pure feeling, bouyed up by the water, knowing it all had to end, and the beginning he had found would become all there was. But not yet, not yet.

Time passed in what could have been sleep, but it felt no different. It felt like nothing. He knew they came and looked at him from time to time. He heard them talking quietly about him, and he thought that when he woke he would tell them he was all right. But hours spun out, utterly still and empty.

The waking rippled through him like wind bringing storm (he knew neither well, but Grio did), and he watched it, wondering, felt his lungs fill, mouth unlock—

"Dariel." He heard the words, puzzled, wondering why

he had said that particularly, and felt Heglit beside him, bending, eyes strange.

"What did you say?"

"Dariel. The— other you." Prying words up like deep roots. "Once I knew. I learned a thing—" The vision drifted back, and outside he felt his eyes sting so the dark face above him shimmered.

Staring down at the drawn face, the yellow eyes glistening and wet, Heglit held silent, knowing only that something had happened, and it had cost Jade something. And, in a new and not entirely trusted way, he felt the focus of attention wandering away again, fragile and vulnerable.

"Jade. Tell me of it," he said quietly, thinking Borget, standing behind him, could do this better.

The voice was anchor and reality. Jade paid attention again, and spoke, voice drifting. "The dragon named me, too, Dariel. There is too much—"

Heglit watched the effort, felt the gulf separating Jade from Jade, and dared. "Speak plain, Jade." He made his voice stern, and felt Borget stir behind him. But the yellow eyes flickered with something like waking, the long body stirred, pulling in a deep breath.

Someplace in the brilliant space of being, a thread was woven, a familiar offering. Between one beat and the next he grasped it, dove down the long distance to a thing he remembered before or after this being. And he knew it was begun, finally.

"Heglit." He really saw the Rafalan now, the shadows and angles of the face, the stern lips parting to speak, then closing, silent. "How long?"

"Seven days."

He did not remember the time passing. Lista appeared with a bowl, and he sat up, curiously light and clear. But his hands shook so badly she had to hold the bowl. He drank the warm broth and tasted the herbs of Grio and felt better. And Heglit stood solid, waiting.

"You were right," he said, wiping his mouth. "The thing you thought would happen here. The tree, Chat-karJ'Mur. He knew me. There was a reason— They knew it would happen, and they knew I would come back."

"Come back? You've been to Grio?"

"Once. It started here. You were not wrong. There

is a purpose. I was brought—" Memory brought the warm touch, the taste of wet salt against his face, and he looked down to hide his eyes. A dream, a memory, but the hurt of it, his and others, was real and aching inside for all it was three hundred stanyears (or only twenty-eight) ago.

"Jade—"

He lifted a hand, stilling the Rafalan. "ChatkarJ'Mur took the memory and kept it to give back now. I know him. My father, Speaker Sarn, he brought me to Chatkar-J'Mur."

"To the tree."

"Vril-Atalba. They told him. They knew I would survive. And TreAsh is in danger. Was—" He looked into uncomprehending eyes. "There is still danger, but even without knowing all of it yet, I have to go, to find TreAsh."

"TreAsh is gone," Borget said softly from the shadows.

He stared, wondering, working back to where they didn't know—

"Yes. Taken. Vril-Atalba can help, when I am—" Their blank looks snared him, tangling his words, and their disbelief brought quick anger. He stood up, too fast, and was dizzy. And that angered him, too. He swore softly and sat down again.

"You are not well, Jade," Lista said, coming to him.

"Dammit, I am well. I—" The hurt in her face shut him up. He reached out and drew her down to the couch. "Forgive me. I am weak, is all." He kept her by his side and looked at Heglit, reading only watchfulness in the dark face. And he knew the Rafalan did not understand what he was saying. He pulled in a breath and let it out, remembering a time when calm was a truth of being ChatkarJ'Mur, ancient and young at once, knowing only growth and not age. For a little, he felt small and frantic and fragile. Then that passed.

"Heglit, I would speak with you. Will you listen?" He asked it quietly, in Rafalspeak.

Heglit followed the formula, still watchful.

Speaking carefully, calmly, he told as much of the story as he could separate from the oddly tactile memory shared with the tree. "My father knew Grio. He was a Speaker, and he shared with the tree in long dreams.

194

He left a thing here, something I must get. Maybe a thing of TreAsh, for finding it, or a thing of the Travelers." He saw the change in the eyes and held up a hand. "TreAsh, as Borget said, is gone. Not destroyed. Gone. Like, I think, we are gone from Alzar. It is why I was brought here and given to the care of others, without a memory of the thing that happened. Knowing would have been a danger to me before. There is still the danger, but I was meant to find—" He fell silent, feeling suddenly that there were things he knew he should not speak of, even to these. Not yet.

"Jade," Heglit said into his silence. "It is not only the people gone. It is the world."

"Yes. I know."

"How could a world be gone as you say?"

"Wanting." He did not smile as he used the word once used against him. "Maybe a thing of the Travelers."

"Where is TreAsh?" It was the logical question.

"I don't know. ChatkarJ'Mur does not know. Nor did my— Sarn. But there is a way to find it. In TreAsh Sector, I think. And there will be help for me."

"And danger there. There is an armed fleet patrolling that sector."

He had forgotten that; not that it made any difference. "I will go, Heglit." It was a thing he had to do. It was his reason.

"Then I must go with you." The dark face didn't change. "There is nothing else I can do. You should rest now and regain your strength."

It was easy to take that advice. For all his head was a racket of confusion and ideas, his body was weak, and pulled him down like a great weight. And that was all right now. He had told Heglit and they would be together. He didn't know why that was so right, but he thought the tree would be pleased. He lay back, letting Lista tend to him, and slept before he could smile his thanks.

He slept a long day and a night, and the three watched and talked, and once Borget went out into the jungle and returned with herbs.

"I have been with ChatkarJ'Mur," he told Heglit. "Lista and I will also go with Jade." He did not ask. It was a thing he knew.

"He says he remembers," Heglit said thoughtfully. "He believes TreAsh still exists."

"And you do not believe."

"Believing is not knowing. I only know that, if we continue, we may learn what reason there is to this."

Borget nodded and looked down at the sleeper. "He remembered his father and there was pain to it."

Later, after he had eaten and bathed, Heglit came to Borget. "Will he sleep longer?"

"I think he will wake and eat, then sleep again."

"Will Lista watch him?"

"Yes."

"We may have trouble ahead. I need your help and supplies from the port."

19

A week of regaining strength, of seeing little of Heglit and Borget and not really noticing them through the oddly brilliant memories, glad for Lista and her easy warmth. Then he knew it was time to go out into Grio one last time. He had seen the place he was to go (from a rather unusual angle), and he knew the way would be made for him. Since his time with ChatkarJ'Mur even that did not seem strange.

Lista wanted to come, but he refused. This was a thing for him to do alone. He stood at the edge of the clearing, thinking of the tree, of the vastness of it he knew so well once, and he felt a calm, a greeting. Or imagined he did. For no reason that came to mind, he reached to loosen his hair, shaking it down against his back. And he saw the path. He didn't think about it, he just went, walking lightly on the dark moist soil. No branches crowded his path, no roots thrust up to trip him. Even the constant heat seemed less, here in the leafy tunnel. It was a long way, but there were springs (created for him, he thought without surprise) and occasional ripe fruits hung near at hand. He ate and drank, and once he lay down to rest and dreamed that a lovely female of green and gold sang wordless songs and combed his hair and shared deep slow pleasure.

He found the hill that was not a hill but a great root thrusting up from the ground, and he circled it, found the dark opening high up on the steep side. He began to climb without thinking about it. Even when he reached the rough black opening and moved into darkness, he just went, feeling a rightness so big it had to come from ChatkarJ'Mur.

The tunnel was long, a confusing series of twists and turns and ups and downs, but there was light of a sort, a pale blue-green glow built of some fungal growth, and the air was deliciously moist and cool. Walking, he wondered, not about what he was doing, or why, but if the tree was aware of him down here walking around in one of his roots. Then the tunnel ended, and there in the shallow depression in the wall before him lay the multi-faceted crystal he had once seen from a greater distance than he could easily imagine. He picked it up, feeling the cold hardness of it, and something like a fragment of memory or anticipation. There was an irregularity on one side, marring the perfection of shape. He noted it, but it didn't matter. This was what he had come for. He turned back, retracing his steps to the green-white day.

Heglit was waiting in the clearing, not entirely trusting Borget's assurances that Jade was safe.

"Are you well?"

"Yes." Jade smiled and held out the crystal. Heglit took it, looked at it closely, running long fingers over it to learn the shape. Nothing of what he might be thinking showed in his face, and Jade was distantly disappointed.

"It fits," the Rafalan said after a minute.

"Fits what?"

"The other is part of it, see?" He showed him the depression in the jewel and Jade took his word for it. He felt Heglit watching him, looking for something, and, slightly annoyed, he reached to knot up his hair, turning to where Borget and Lista waited near the hut.

He did not speak of where he had gone, and they did not ask. It was a thing of Grio. At least the Benjor knew that, and if Heglit didn't, entirely, he was willing to trust their lead. There was food, and Heglit and Borget talking, telling Jade of the fourth Link rigged in the Centra Zar. But a smooth easy calm held in Jade. He heard and remembered, but it didn't seem to matter, except that things were going pretty much as they should.

There was also news from the ComUn station. Another freighter had grounded for a day, and someone in the crew had said there was trouble making of some kind. The Restricteds from Rafal Sector were being called back. The shipmasters were angry, liking Rafalan Link-men for the long jumps, and there were a lot of complaints going in to Centra.

"Is it Tas?" Jade asked, stifling a yawn.

Heglit didn't know, but he rather thought it was the Rafalan council, either trying to find some information about him and the Zendra Three, or there could be some trouble building between them and Centra Alzar. Maybe Tas had gone asking questions and Rafal was learning things.

Sleepy, Jade could tell Heglit was concerned, but there didn't seem to be any problem for them. He fell asleep with his head in Lista's lap.

"Jade." The strong hand shook him again, and he opened his eyes to see Heglit. It was not yet full light. "Come."

"Come? Where?"

"To TreAsh Sector."

"Now?" He sat up, swinging his feet to the floor, feeling a strange reluctance to begin.

"Dress, Jade." Patient, Heglit waited, and Jade saw that everything was gone from the hut but his clothes. The Benjor, Heglit said, were at the Zendra Three.

He really did not want to go, but Heglit's cool patience kept him from saying anything. Then there wasn't time.

He came into the ship, seeing the severe mechanical perfection of it with a sort of shock, like it was alien and strange to him.

The Benjor watched him and shared a look as Heglit turned to the controls. The ship hummed, gathering herself, and leapt up away from the jungle. Jade watched the screen, thought he might have seen the upper branches of the tree, then lost them in the shrinking curve of the world becoming an emerald, dwindling to insignificance beside the brilliant sun. A soft tone sounded, and the screen flashed panvision as they entered the local web, running for the Centra Zar.

Jade's smooth peace lasted until they were in the familiar rooms and corridors of the freighter. He went to the captain's cabin while the others checked out the ship. There was a stone bottle of baDant juice, bringing memories beyond Grio tugging at him.

He was sitting crosslegged on the couch looking down at his glass, when Heglit came in. He looked up, bright eyes flashing to the dark face.

"Lista is female."

"Yes." Seriously. But Jade felt teasing in the voice.

"Females don't Link," he said, wondering why he hadn't thought of it before. "You plan to have her Link with us."

"For her safety."

"But share-Linking—" He gestured, not sure how to say it. "There's a reason females don't Link. Or they would. What will happen?"

Heglit looked at him, seeing the lethargy evaporate, and was eased of some unvoiced worry.

"Jade, Rafalan women have linked at times. It is different for them, but possible."

"But Rafalans are—"

"Of human stock. Like all Clates." Old point, often made. "You do not want her sharing with us."

"Oh, come, Heglit." He protested, angry, and knowing it was because Heglit was (as usual) right.

The Rafalan ignored his protest. "You were different on Grio after the tree."

About to protest that too, Jade stopped and thought. The last weeks were slow and dreamy in memory, Clouded. "Sleep-walking," he observed aloud. "Inside, it was all slow and easy. But right. It was Grio." And, thinking back, he found other questions. Like how much of anything happening inside had he told them.

"That you had come to Grio before. With Sarn."

"I was so small." He felt the memory again and pushed it down, with the pain that was sharper than he remembered. "Some, most of the things I saw or remembered, meant nothing to me. Only the speak. I never heard it before, but I knew it. And there was a . . . something said to me. I think someone is going to help us."

"You spoke of a Vril-Atalba."

"Words. I don't know what they mean." His eyes flashed to Heglit's, saying he doubted. "Could it have been a wish-dream?"

"Was it?"

"I don't *know*. If it wasn't—" He shook his head. "A tree, Heglit."

"A tree. And a dragon."

"Do you believe this?" Asking for reassurance, maybe.

"I believe we must act on it. And remain watchful,

201

not fully trusting all the things we see or feel. There is nothing else for us to do."

The practicality of that was anchor and annoyance. "And if we do find TreAsh?"

"If. Then it will be because they want us to. And they will know what comes after." He got up. "We must chart the run to TreAsh Sector. It is in the southern limb. A long way."

"Did you— did the crystals fit together?"

"They fit. I did not put them together."

Jade was glad for that. If the crystal he had found also affected the Link it could cause more complications than they needed in the new four-way sharing.

The Rafalan ultra channel chart showed strands of the Star Web that bypassed the denser sectors of the galaxy, but some of the skips were weeks long, impossible without dead-shipping in channel, something Jade, like all Linkmen, avoided instinctively. He had done it once, that was enough and more.

"Slow-thinking," Borget laughed. "Wanting us is doing."

Heglit looked up at him, then back to the star map displayed on the navicomp. "Not direct to TreAsh Sector," he said. "We could want ourselves into trouble."

Like the Federation war fleet.

"Lista needs to learn the Link system," Heglit reminded, looking at Jade, either giving him a way to become used to linking with her, or because he and Borget could plot the course and Jade had the time.

She met him in the Link-room, lovely in pale green, and happy, eager to learn and full of questions. Her mood was infectious.

"Head-linking, not skin-linking, us," she grinned, looking at the chairs. Heglit had done a good job, everything looked like it belonged. He explained the system to her, stressing the importance of remembering that, whatever it felt like, it was all in the mind. The body was safe here in the chairs, and constantly monitored.

Borget, she said, had told her what it was like in the Web. She did not think she would be afraid. He sat her in the chair to his left, automatically assuming they would use the chairs they were used to, with Heglit across from him, and Borget to Heglit's right. He removed the pins from her hair before fitting the Link-mask, making sure it fit, snug and comfortable. Then he Linked himself in, and they were suddenly outside, knowing N-space.

Nothing unusual happened, and he relaxed a little, enough to feel her there, no longer beside, but sort of *inside*, so what he felt, the whispering wind of solar energy, the silver rain, the flowing hair, brought a sort of now-flavored nostalgia and deeper wonder. He didn't end it quickly, but let her get the feel. Like Borget, she was more restrained in Link. He wondered if they could talk, well, sort of talk, like he had with Heglit, or share the feel. Heglit had been surprised by the hair-feel, and once he had thought he wore Heglit's skin . . .

He didn't do it intentionally, but suddenly he had a different kind of awareness, definitely physical, a blend of unusual erotic sensation and structured alienness. The warm-cool pressure translated as breeze flowing across hard-nippled breasts—

Once he would have pulled away. Now he went still, reaching, becoming acquainted, like once before with ChatkarJ'Mur. Only now it was subtler, a change of balance at once clumsy and more graceful. When he finally did break Link he felt mildly guilty. But her dark-eyed laughter eased him.

"You are different from Borget, my Lord Jade."

"Not so much, Lady. A man only."

"But more aware, and perhaps arrogant, in a man's way." Her eyes, moving on him, made her meaning and he laughed, looking down at himself, unsecreted.

"Surely that is not different."

"Enough." Her eyes danced, teasing him.

"There is no time for pleasure games in the Star Web," he cautioned her.

"But to share with three men, even if one is as cool as your Rafalan, surely I may take pleasure in that, knowing only and not interfering. It is so with the Benjor at times. Knowing a thing is not to use it up." She slipped from the chair and came to him, kissing him lightly. "Beautiful Jade, it is not so different from sharing with our kind, for me. Do not worry. I believe I can watch with my brother and forget the Web if it troubles you in channel. It is the feeling otherness you think about. And our time on Grio shows us that."

She was right. He had found a similarity with the tree, only more complete because there was nothing else to do, only share being different.

Walking down to the galley with her, to prepare a meal to take up to the control room, he thought of the time spent with ChatkarJ'Mur and for the first time wondered if the tree had simultaneously experienced being him. How small he must have felt.

Looking at Lista in green, he remembered another thing. "Lista, when I went to find the thing Sam left with ChatkarJ'Mur, did you come to me?"

"I stayed with Borget. Why?"

"I rested in the jungle and— maybe it was a dream. But I thought someone came to me."

She looked at him. "Benjor?"

"I didn't think so. Not so gold and warm."

"Colored like the forest, with cool green hair, singing and bringing peace without words." She saw the answer in his face. "She was not Benjor. Or human, Jade. A different kind of realness. I have heard of them."

"Them. Who are they? I thought Grio—"

"We do not know. They are male and female, or seem to be. We think they are his, the father tree's. All those who have been with them are bound to Grio." Her look was thoughtful for a moment, then she smiled and took up a tray. "Perhaps you will return there."

Which reminded him to wonder if he (or any of them) would return from wherever they were bound.

They chose a short skip, five hours, for the first, to learn the feel of the four-way Link. As far as any of them knew, multiple Links had not been done until Heglit and Jade took the TaLur run, but as Borget pointed out, it was not too different from the plant-linking of Grio, or the unique psychic bond of the Benjor. Except those were in real space, not an experience constructed through the sensors of a ship.

It was easy from the first, and mostly fun. Lista, as she had said, focused more on her brother, finding a familiarity she expected, but sharing a sense of wonder and excitement that they all felt. Only once, approaching the sensory paradox of the breakout gate, did her feelings overpower her, flashing a sort of fear through the Link, and a strong desire to *not,* creating a sudden drag until Heglit overrode it with superior strength, grabbing them up and bursting through.

"I was afraid, not knowing," she admitted. "Only feeling a thing would happen beyond my strength."

They were in a star-poor area with the north limb of the galaxy a sweeping arc of radiance behind them and two fainter curves of silver dust ahead, misting the dark foreverness. They ate and talked and rested, and Borget suggested trying to cross the void in one skip, urging speed and distance. And it was time to try. They chose a sector on the edge of the east limb, sparsely settled, as their goal, but for safety's sake also plotted a way through the ultra channels that would be long, but not the longest they had made.

Their danger lay ahead, in the fleet maintained by ComUn. They would have to spend time in TreAsh Sector, not knowing yet what to look for there, or where, and they were almost certain to be found out, with all traffic banned in that sector. But by staying out of ComUn active sectors until they were actually in TreAsh territory, they might have an edge. Only Rafal knew of the ultra channels. But both Rafal and Tas wanted them.

The sudden appearance of a ComUn ship near their breakout gate was a shock. The gate supported only non-Clate worlds, poor and not worth a ComUn run. And there was no beacon. But the ship was there. And close. The Centra Zar's sensors picked it up before they were well out of the Link-room, but it couldn't tell them more than that a ship was near. Their delay in acting was nearly fatal.

For the first time for all but, possibly, Heglit, they knew what it was like to be attacked in space. A barrage of colorless light set off alarms Jade hadn't known existed. And they were without defense. They ran, but they could not hope to escape for long. There was only one option, and they took it. Setting the ship to run herself out along the edge of the local web, they Linked, following Heglit's command, and leapt for the nearest gate, not sure what direction it led. Fear and the need to escape gave them impetus, the Star Web itself gave direction. They skipped hot and fast and grabbed the first gate out.

Into emptiness so complete there were no referents to tell them where they were. No stars, no galaxy patterned on the screen. Nothing.

"How long?" Heglit asked, pulling out the Rafalan charts.

"Six hours. Not long." Jade ran a back-check to confirm previous position, and the navicomp had had time enough to identify it. In standard channel six hours could not have taken them too far out.

"Wanting away," Borget reminded. "To safety."

"Well, this should be safe enough, Jade thought sourly. It was damned near nowhere at all.

"The sensors aren't strong enough," Heglit decided. "We might learn more through the Link."

It was worth a try. Jade went down to the Link-room with him, leaving the Benjor in the control room.

"Surely we didn't *want* ourselves here," he said.

"We didn't want anywhere. Only away," Heglit pointed out. "It's something to remember."

He couldn't argue that.

Linked, they flashed into the sensors and were out in N-space.

Nothing. Total emptiness. Frightening because there was nothing to respond to at all. Jade kept wanting to ball up and hide, but Heglit was there, so he looked, reaching for some clue to direction, wondering if the sensors were working. He found nothing but the texture of Heglit, steady, curious, there.

Maybe it was a trick of the sensors, that faint dust bordering one area of no-direction. Maybe it was hope burning his eyes. But he felt Heglit's attention. And it was all there was.

As Jade had not thought to do, the Rafalan fixed position relative to the ship. Galactic directions didn't exist any more for them. Then he broke Link and Jade followed him out.

They weren't yet out of the chairs when Borget's voice called them to the control room. He sounded worried enough to pull a quick look from Heglit.

The Benjor sat before the control console, watching

a readout, and he looked more worried than he'd sounded. "The Web sensors," he said when they came in. "Either they do not function, or—" He looked up, wide-eyed.

"Or?"

"Or we are beyond the Star Web. The sensors record nothing."

"We can't be beyond the Web," Jade said. But he looked to Heglit, who was frowning slightly, looking at nothing in particular.

"We got beyond the stars," Borget said quietly.

All right. In a way, that was true, and Jade knew it. But they had got here somehow. By wanting, he thought, then wished he hadn't. Not that it mattered. With no Star Web evident, all the co-ordinates in the universe couldn't get them back to their galaxy in their own lifetimes.

"The rest of the crystal," he said suddenly, remembering. But Heglit shook his head.

"We didn't use it to come here." His dark eyes held Jade a long time. Then he changed the subject. "That ComUn ship should not have been there, waiting for us. Only Tas could send an armed ship."

Jade didn't see what that had to do with their present problem, but Heglit usually knew what he was doing.

"Couldn't know, him," Borget said, watching the Rafalan.

Jade started thinking again. Borget was right. Tas couldn't have known where they would break in to N-space. They weren't using any channels ComUn knew about. "Rafal," he said. "Tas has gone to Rafal and they're helping him. He must have the Star Web charts, all the channels. Would they give that to him?"

"Maybe." Heglit tapped lightly on the control panel, thinking. "He's learned more of us than that. We ran too fast even for the ultra channel. But if he knew we could by-pass sectors like we did— I would guess he knows our goal is TreAsh Sector."

"How could he know that?"

"Logic. If he has heard that you are Sarn's son. He would not believe that, but he might think you do, and he could anticipate our actions."

"Rafal would—?"

"It's the only way he could know."

ComUn couldn't have just had a ship there. It would be asking too much of coincidence. Somehow Tas was getting ahead of him. Jade paced, restless, pulled two ways. The new thing in him, part pain, part hope, insisted he go to TreAsh Sector. A need as big as the hope of a man in dark green speaking to a tree in a steamy jungle. But if Tas knew that was their goal, they would have no chance. They would be attacked and destroyed the moment they broke out of the Star Web, whether they came through standard channel or ultra channel. It was an impossible situation. Nothing in his life had prepared him for something like this. He had traded pleasure for pleasure and survival. But to go knowingly to his death was beyond his comprehension. ChatkarJ'Mur had known so much and left so much unsaid, he thought. Like the dragon on Alzar. Leading him on.

"They expect us to run for TreAsh Sector, then," he said to Heglit's silent waiting. "We could run the other way." But saying it he knew it wasn't possible, and he knew Heglit knew it too.

"Is it possible they could have foreseen this too? I mean, if this is all—" He gestured vaguely and Heglit nodded.

"If there was a Traveler on Alzar. Perhaps."

"But even if they planned it all, they couldn't know so well what we would do, Heglit." Something brushed his mind and he moved to get away from it, uneasy. He turned toward the door and Heglit followed him down to the captain's cabin.

"There is time to rest and think, Jade."

He didn't answer. Tension crawled across his skin, pulling it tight. Frowning, he unknotted his hair, massaging his scalp with stiff fingers.

"What is it, Jade?"

"Nothing." But he was lying. A coldness touched his spine. He caught his breath against it, yellow eyes flashed to Heglit to see if he had noticed. He tried to ignore the strangeness, lifting his arms to knot his hair when the pain struck, crushing his hand. He cried out, clutching the hand to himself, bent double in familiar agony.

"Jade!" Heglit leapt to him, felt the tremors of pain before he saw the hand. "Borget!"

The call rang through the ship and the Benjor came running, halted at the door.

"Is it real?" The hard Rafalan voice slammed across the room, breaking the spell holding them.

"Yes. But—"

Jade went suddenly limp in the hard curve of the arm supporting him. Heglit lifted him, laid him on the couch, and stared down at the gray pain-sweated face. Then he saw the hand, and disbelief stood in his eyes, bright and sharp. The hand hung useless, crushed, purpling, swelling—

It could not be.

It was.

Muscles knotted along the dark jaw. There were drugs on the ship that could ease the pain of the ruined hand. But dared he used them?

"How did he do this?" Borget asked quiet, looking more at the Rafalan.

"He did not!" The words hissed and snapped through the room as the Rafalan approached anger, more fierce for lack of a target, and the Benjor felt that more acutely than the new, feeling, voice.

"He is injured." Even in this strangeness, Borget knew his bond to Jade was greater than personal fear.

"He cannot be. We were talking. Then it was. It cannot be real. The hand was healed." Logic no longer performed, shredded away by this last assault of fantasy, and Heglit held his anger loosely, seeking answers out of habit. "It is the injury done on Alzar. By the dragon of Tas. But the hand was well."

Borget frowned, bent over the man as lids fluttered, lips pulled tight against teeth with pain.

"Heglit, help me—" Yellow eyes opened, brilliant but not seeing. "It hurts. Please—"

Borget reached, feeling the hurt, needing to help.

"No!" Heglit struck the hand away. Borget glanced up at the bigger man, but Lista came forward, face tight in response to the feelings loosed in the cabin.

"Borget my brother. Wait. It is another thing, not a realness of here. Put away anger and listen." She held his arms, insisting with her eyes. "Listen. And you, shipmaster. There is a thing."

Her intensity netted them. Heglit felt a change in them and it unbalanced his anger. "What is it?"

"Reach," she said softly. "You are one of us here. Reach out as he did to you."

"For what?" Dark and doubting, he stood over them.

"For Jade. There is—"

He turned his attention to Jade, reaching, letting himself know pain and fear and something besides. His attention and will were his own to control. He reached.

And like a thing forgotten he thought of the crystal from Grio. A moment he doubted, then let impulse rule logic. He turned, running from the cabin.

21

The crystal lay where he left it, cool blue on the dark shelf. He reached for it, hesitated, then, without knowing why, he turned to the wiring panel, disconnected the smaller crystal first. He brought it to the shelf, lifted the larger—

They leapt together, the larger turning in his grip to present the hollow. There was a moment of tension too fast to react to, a loud sound or feel, and the crystal was whole. Fused. He turned it in his hands and there was no evidence of fracture or joining. It was one, and it was whole with a soft blue warmth.

"Heglit." Borget's voice startled him away from his study of the crystal. "Please come—"

He went, carrying the crystal, not sure what he would find or what had happened, except that they were irrevocably committed to whatever Jade had brought from Grio. The original crystal no longer existed.

Jade lay on the couch, no longer pale and hurting, only asleep.

"What?"

"The hand." Borget spoke, and Heglit looked. The hand was impossibly whole and well, lying open against the other.

"He did not speak, but the pain is gone."

"Borg." Jade's voice, sleepy soft, pulled their eyes. He stretched, rubbing his face, smiling. "I dreamed—"

"No dream," Heglit said, feeling his own muscles relax, seeing Jade look down at his hand.

"This was, Heglit. My hand was broken again."

"Yes." Flat-voiced again, being Heglit. "We saw it."

Jade looked at the others, doubting, but they nodded and Borget spoke. "We saw the injury and felt the hurting in it. Then there was a feel and a sound and it was whole."

Impossible. But any more what wasn't? Jade sat up and pulled his feet into his lap, reaching to knot up his hair. "You fixed it," he said to Heglit around his up-raised arm, indicating the crystal, still clasped in the dark hand.

"It is together," the Rafalan agreed, sitting, examining the crystal with eyes and fingers. He did not trust anything now, but the pointless attack on Jade seemed to be ended and the change in the TreAshal device demanded some study. Beyond what his eyes could tell him, he knew the thing had changed, was something other than it had been. And the changing seemed linked to the unexplainable thing that had happened to Jade. A thought brought his eyes up to study the man. Was Jade also changed?

Jade felt the eyes pulling at him, and stared at his feet, rubbing his arches, resisting, until he felt the look move away to the Benjor, who were standing quiet by the door, keeping their own counsel about what was happening. He looked at them, too. "It was a dream."

Lista's golden head shook no, and they both looked troubled.

"What are you thinking?" Jade asked quietly, wishing he knew what the Rim was going on. Then remembering they were already beyond that. For a small moment he fought against feeling how far out they were, then the feeling passed.

Neither Borget nor Lista broke silence, only looked to one another, two golden statues.

"Lista—"

But Heglit was faster, rising, moving toward them, alert to the unnatural stillness. Then he stopped, looked back toward Jade, dark face faintly puzzled. He did not move again. The blue crystal glowed steadily in one dark hand.

Ice flowed down Jade's back, roughening his skin. He opened his mouth, then closed it, feeling the muscles work, reassured by that subtle normalcy. All right. Wait. People did not freeze into statues. So this wasn't real. Timestop. He'd been here before, or someplace like this, surprised in the strange chem-states he'd visited. He pulled in a breath and closed his eyes to safe dark, hear-feeling the loud beat of blood in his ears, whisper of breath in nostrils. Familiar. Maybe, like on Alzar, he could—

Jadriel Younger.

No. He would not look.

But his eyes snapped open, seeing nothing but Heglit, and beyond him the Benjor. Everything was as before. Except the crystal. It flared a cold blue flame in the dark hand. He watched, refusing to believe, as the crystal freed itself from the fingers and floated away. Toward him.

"Stop it!" he snapped, sounding as angry as he was scared. The crystal halted in mid-air. This was too much. He wanted to laugh, but his throat felt like screaming, so he kept quiet, frowning against a subtle and growing pressure in his head. Too familiar. Trying to avoid it, he wondered if he was actually moving ahead in time so they looked still, or if this was hallucination.

Waiting only, Jadriel Younger.

The queer inside-out voice reverberated and his head began to ache. No more games. He knew that voice.

"Who are you?" His own voice surprised him.

We are Vril-Atalba. Or ChatkarJ'Mur. He couldn't be sure.

No. Wait. He was falling for it. Never mind. It apparently wasn't going to end soon.

"You're the dragon on Alzar."

Were.

"There's nothing out here. We're beyond the Rim." But whether he was arguing with the voice, or trying to convince himself, he couldn't have said.

Need brought. Help seeking and knowing the way from ChatkarJ'Mur, World-Seeder.

"Need brought? You mean wanting?" He rubbed his head absently. "Can't be here, you," he decided, annoyed.

Speaker seed.

For an instant he felt rooted and huge, taste-smelling dark brown, moist—

"You too?" Glis, was it never over?

Then he remembered. ChatkarJ'Mur had said Vril-Atalba would help him. Damn, he wished Heglit would blink or look away.

213

"What are you doing to me?"

Calling. You came seeking and would not know it even now. Life being is strong over blood being, and you would not accept the gift of World-Seeder.

"I didn't come here on purpose. We were all Linked—"

You knew.

"Knew what?"

To come.

Sure. Jade closed his eyes, wishing he could break out of this. "I did not come. I don't know where here is. Or you are."

Below thinking you knew it.

That defeated argument. "What did you do to them?"

Waited them. You are our link. Their help would break it.

"Why did you hurt my hand again?"

The silence following that touched puzzlement.

We would not. Hold. More silence. *Not us. Jadriel, we have less time. If you would succeed, you must accept us so we may free your friends. You will need them soon.*

There was clear warning in that.

"I— How? I mean—"

Do you touch our realness?

If that would get things back together he was willing. Except he didn't know how.

"Vril-Atalba—" The silent explosion behind his eyes made him gasp and grab his head, surprised because it felt so normal between his hands and it was suddenly so *big* inside—

The blue jewel hanging free in the middle of the cabin began to swell— no. To approach, steadily. He had time to wonder if he really wanted to do this, time to see the frozen trio beyond, time to think he didn't believe in magic or spelling. And time. And his thoughts echoed around the vast space in his skull, and that scared him.

Then he looked at the blue crystal an arm's length from his face and forgot it all. The crystal smoothed, opened misty gates, and drew him out through his eyes, falling—

How—?

It didn't matter. He felt-tasted the broad current— cool blue, not amber, but he knew it, balanced in it instinctively. It was his element more than any other he had known. There was time to savor the wild icy warmth, forgetting to wonder how.

This is the way to us.

The message was woven into the flavor of this blue channel swallowing him.

Danger is, and quick. Bring yours through with wanting and AzlurEor cannot follow.

Gliding quicksilver through the powerful blue flood, he absorbed that without interpretation, caught up, racing toward a golden portal that pulled like every promise of union.

Breakout shredded the spacious freedom in his brain. He was still raising his hand to grasp the blue crystal, blinking against the memory of a loud feel. The crystal dropped lightly into his palm, cool against moist warmth. The Benjor said something about a strangeness here and Heglit resumed his movement toward them a moment before realizing there was no more need. He halted and turned back to face Jade, quick dark eyes seeking clues, noting Jade's expression before seeing the crystal.

"There is a wrongness here," Borget repeated, moving away from Lista, toward Jade.

"The crystal," Heglit said, not moving at all, demanding explanation.

Jade looked down at the thing in his hand. "The crystal?"

Heglit ignored his tone. This made no sense to him.

"Heglit, what about the crystal? I have to know." His yellow eyes moved up to Heglit's, sharing something the Rafalan didn't expect.

"A moment ago I held it in my left hand. I got up to—" He glanced at Borget and fell silent.

"Heglit, please—" Biting his lip at the sound of his own voice, for no reason at all he thought of a word, AzlurEor, meaning danger.

"You know what happened." Heglit wasn't accusing, only cool and right.

"No." But he told it, or tried to. And they listened. "I went through. Into a— this." He held up the crystal. The three of them watched him. He felt it, really felt it, so hard he wanted to tell them to stop it. Then he looked at Heglit and saw something touch the dark eyes. He felt that, too. Like on Centra Alzar. And he felt-saw the Rafalan start to deny it, sample it, pause—

"This is part of it, Jade?"

Half of him wanted not to understand that. He looked at the dark face and thought that someplace behind that well-schooled mask Dariel waited to laugh again, or fight, and he wondered why he thought that.

"Jade."

"Yes." Finally. And getting rid of that he found a jumble of knowing, waiting for him. "But you know it. You know more. It's the crystal and the Travelers. You knew to put the crystals together, to finish it."

Heglit thought about it. The Benjor watched them both. "It was a thing to do. When I tried to reach you in the Benjor way."

"You?"

The dark head nodded. Once.

Jade looked to Lista who also nodded. And Borget. He believed. He wanted to ask Heglit about it, but found he couldn't. Not yet, anyway. Maybe later. "The Travelers told you somehow."

"Is that why they hurt you?"

"They didn't." He believed that now, and found memory to back him up. "The Travelers aren't all. AzlurEor. Someone or something. It is a danger and it wants to stop us."

"Why? What is it?"

"I don't know." Enemy, he thought. Danger. A danger that couldn't follow through the crystal. *Through* the crystal? That's what they had said. He was to bring these three with him through the crystal. He told them that. And felt them look at the jewel in his hand. Heglit finally moved, coming toward him. He reached out his hand and Jade laid the crystal in it. It didn't stay. As the dark fingers curled over it, it bounded up, repelled, and drifted back to Jade.

Heglit said nothing, fisted the hand tight, and did not reach again. Jade closed his own hand over the thing and it nestled there, cool and heavy.

"You aren't sure of it," Heglit observed like nothing had happened.

"They said we could go to them through it."

"Or by it." Bringing logic to nightmare.

216

Jade shrugged and finally got up. Wondering what would happen, he placed the crystal on the table. It rested obediently on the dark wood. At least it wasn't going to follow him around trying to get back into his hand.

"Linking," Lista said. "Together us, wanting. And Jade touching through it."

Heglit thought about that and nodded. There were things happening here that needed thought and understanding, but life went on. He suggested a meal and Z'Atua.

Postponement prodded Jade with a sense of urgency he couldn't find any reason for. He wandered up to the control room, feeling the need to do something, but not sure what. He looked at the nothing on the outview screens, checked the ship functions, even played back the log, but there was no information there for him. When the nothingness on the screens began to push at him he retreated to the captain's cabin glad for company and Z'Atua.

"They said I came here," he said, remembering. Heglit looked at him like he expected him to remember.

"They said ChatkarJ'Mur told me. That I knew where to find them. You knew?" he asked Heglit.

"Wondered. We are not near any channel we can find with our sensors, but we had to get here somehow. You were the logical answer."

"But I—"

"Jade!" Lista's cry of warning jerked them around an instant before the ship moved, bucked, shuddered throughout her length. There were sounds of things moving, shifting, falling. Impossible sounds.

"Hold." Heglit's hard voice caught them, held them against the beginnings of terror. The vibration died away, but the message was clear. Out here beyond stars or worlds or life, something had touched their ship.

"The control room." Heglit led the way to their only eyes, the outview screens. Following, Jade reached instinctively for the crystal and it seemed to leap into his hand. The screens, no longer black, glowed a hard emerald, flooding the room with strange light. Heglit checked sensors and ship status quickly, but his voice was level. There was some kind of charged field about

217

them. And they were moving. Jade's eyes flashed to Heglit's dark ones, then to the Benjor, seeing the glaze of disbelief. But Heglit was again first and fastest to react. "Zendra has weapons. Tas—"

"No." Jade grabbed the hard arm as Heglit moved toward the door. "Not Tas. AzlurEor."

The black eyes pinned him, speculating, demanding explanation, and maybe blaming him. He felt the muscles stir beneath his fingers and wondered if he would have to fight (and lose). Then the ship shuddered again, more gently, and the feeling they were being taken somewhere grew.

"Not Clate, or any known life thing, but being outside is," Borget said through the tension.

"You were told." Heglit relaxed, glanced from the deepening glow of the screens to the man.

"The crystal. They said to bring you through it, that AzlurEor couldn't follow."

"The Link?"

"Yes. No! Look at it." His heart bumped as he held up the crystal, saw-felt the change in it. And he knew— he felt the swift-rushing icy warmth, clean and blue and safely beyond the growing lurid green pouring through the screens. The structured energy of that place reached out to him, calling, promising, becoming a flood through his nerves.

"The screens. Off—" he whispered, unable to pull his eyes from the jewel, not wanting to, wanting only to go, and feeling the lack of conviction in Heglit holding them back.

"Stop it, Jade."

There was authority in the command, grating against a newer knowledge. He needed help, from Lista and Borget. It was a matter of faith only, and Heglit could not believe without reason. The ship rang distant, beyond the blue siren song on the crystal, and, forcing his outside to function, he spoke to Borget in swift Benjorspeak so the golden hand flashed to the control panel, blanking the outview screens. The glow of the jewel flooded the room and he felt the Benjor reach out to him, giving acceptance and strength.

"You've got to help," he told the Rafalan. "Now. Just this once be Dariel—" Spoken or desperately wished he

218

didn't know, only felt the shock of that and out of the hesitation a strong and arrogant attention. Yes. Like that. Reach for me. Follow me. Stay with me—

He let go outside vision, awareness of everything but the rising power of the jewel, yielding to a desire in himself for the blue, or it for him. Entering was glass veils shattering. He dove into the Star Web channel four strong, and some unconcerned corner of his mind felt the instinctive adjustment orientation, flavored from memory of the strength and berserker joy in flight that was Dariel-Heglit. As one they clasp the Benjor and raced to the core of the channel, and it was pure and clean and power beyond any Web skip ever shared.

Dark hair glowed, scattering tendrils of electric flame over back and hips, and the free Rafalan laughter bounded down the halls of flight.

Jadriel Younger.

The great chorus of meaning compassed but did not still the tumbling gaiety of their vision. And he found answer somewhere, acknowledging a command he understood like his own joy. But he was caught in the flood of movement and too weak. Until his desire bound Heglit, created analog, and strong arms caught and held. Power was freed by need and his grace flowed into Heglit's strength, made lever of motion to become something other—

Now, Jade! Dive— Soar up, over, buffeted, tumbled, shooting across blue to rose and crimson, black-laced, where cymbal crashes of heat and danger forced care. Where? And knowing, struggling toward the sensed hurry-up promise of gold that was a gate. They leapt toward it yelling defiance through phantom pain, burst through to lay stunned, panting, too spent to respond to anything but stillness and dark and being done.

He woke quickly, feeling time passed and danger, before remembering escape. Confusion bound him until he realized the pillow under his head was a dark-clad arm, beginning to stir. He opened his eyes and saw Heglit, or Dariel, and the black eyes focused, seeing him. It was Heglit. The physical weakness of prolonged skip didn't fit his memory of what had happened, but it was real and affected them all. Borget and Lista still slept.

He got off Heglit's arm, wishing for a drink of something, and watched him reactivate the outview screens. The room was flooded with a dull red glow.

"Where are we?"

Heglit didn't answer that, and in a moment a slice of sullen red slid onto the screen. A world, bombed out and lifeless, from the look of it. There were a lot of that kind throughout the galaxy. Heglit keyed in sensors and asked the navicomp for comparison with planetary descriptions on the chance it might be one of the ones listed.

"We didn't Link. I mean, the Link-system—" Heglit looked at him over his left shoulder, the still face he could never read. "Dammit, Heglit, the ship. How did we get the ship here?"

"Wanting it." Borget's voice startled him. They were awake and Borget was looking at the crystal lying forgotten on the table. He reached out a hand and touched it a moment, as though expecting something. Then he looked up, smiling. "It is not living."

"Unrecorded," Heglit read off the screen. "The ship doesn't know where we are."

"Vril-Atalba brought us."

"No, Jade." Borget said it. "You brought us, wanting, and through a new thing. That other was beyond. A teacher."

"He's right." Heglit spoke without turning, punching in requests for sensor information and maps of the galactic area of the closest match. "The Star Web was different."

"To you too?" Obviously, or he wouldn't have said. Heglit ignored the question.

"You have, or are, the gate key to a different Web, I think. Not like the one we've used before. Not knotted to the stellar loci. It was bigger."

"Blue being," Lista spoke finally, hugging herself. "Like the jewel from Grio."

And for no reason he could think of, Jade knew where they were. "It's TreAsh Sector."

Heglit nodded, not surprised, waiting for the screen to list the anomalies the sector was noted for, anomalies of imbalance not yet accounted for by drift.

So they were here. And so, somewhere, was the remains of the Federation war fleet. Fine. Now what? He glanced at the crystal. Ask it? Could he?

"Could it be more than a Link device, Heglit?"

The broad shoulders lifted a fraction. "We did not come through any known gate. The patrol may not know of us for some time. But if Tas can get word—"

"Not Tas. AzlurEor. He's—" Something dangerous. But what? He didn't know, only that Vril-Atalba had said something that might have meant AzlurEor was not bound by the same rules as Tas, that somehow he (or it) could find them, could even be helping Tas. Maybe. He could find them, had found them out beyond the Rim. Why he wanted them, or wanted to stop them, was something else. The only certain thing Jade knew was that there was more to this than Tas, something that probably went all the way back to TreAsh.

The three held quiet while he thought. He wished he had their faith. The crystal held his attention. Borget, who would know, said it was not alive. But it acted. And it brought them here. It should know what happened next.

Crystal, he thought, feeling silly, come to me.

The jewel rocked slightly, lifted and slid through the still air, flashing back the orange glow from the screen. Skin roughing lightly, Jade held out his hand and the crystal nestled into it. He wasn't sure he liked this, but he felt better knowing it would answer him like that. He wanted to know if he could reach Vril-Atalba through it, but he felt the others watching and that made it hard.

Watching him, Heglit felt his ambiguity, remembered it was getting ever easier to feel what was happening to Jade. He put that idea away for later consideration and asked Lista to go to the galley for Santo tea. Borget he sent to feed a few pounds of atmosphere into the hold. If they had to run for the Zendra Three, they wouldn't have time to suit up for vacuum.

"Shall I go also?" Heglit asked when they were gone.

The dark head shook no, yellow eyes flashing thanks and maybe curiosity.

He meant to speak aloud, but somehow didn't. Intent became a spear of blue flame pinning him to the jewel. He gasped with the surprise of that, and went unnaturally still. Everything happened inside his head, like being turned inside out, making a bigness inside that scared and exhilarated.

Within, Speaker-seed. Touch knowing.

ChatkarJ'Mur, he thought with distant clarity, feeling a big something looking up. This was memory then? And yes, it tasted like it.

"Jade."

He heard Heglit, dim and dual-imaged, moving away. Stop it, he thought, trying to be here and there both. And it stopped. I can't understand this, he thought inside himself.

Hear us, Jädriel Younger. Even now AzlurEor's eyes and ears seek. If you are found we must leave you. Go to the yellow star close where the force is strong. The crystal will know. Come to us. We cannot again come to you.

But how? Come to you how? The answer to that came in violent flares of solar radiation and colors that yelled through the cold blue inside his head like hunting horns in full cry. Understanding nothing of that, he shrank back from the onslaught and clenched his teeth on the silent implosion of his brain returning to familiar size.

"They're so loud," he breathed, rubbing his forehead, pressing hard fingers through his hair until it fell loose around his shoulders. Someone put a cup of hot tea in his hand, and he looked up into Lista's face, glad of her there. But he could feel Heglit waiting, and finally turned to him, looking over the rim of the cup.

"The star?" The Rafalan voice was a shade too quiet. "You heard it?"

"Part. Maybe. Run to the sun, I think, where the local web isn't tangled, where the solar force holds it steady."

"They should talk to you." The tea helped, but Jade wondered if the inside of his head was as tender as it felt.

"They can't. They aren't here, except through that."

"How close do we have to get to find the web steady?"

"Close, I would think. Maybe inside the orbit of the nearest planet. The patrol will almost certainly spot us on the way in. And they know the territory."

"The eyes and ears. That must be what they meant.

222

Once they see us AzlurEor will know where we are. He's not part of the patrol, but he uses them."

Heglit looked like he might ask about that, then didn't. "Once we leave the cover of this world we must go fast."

"AzlurEor was the feeling of wrong beyond the stars," Borget said. "Knowing it, us, if it comes." He moved to the console beside Heglit, reached to monitor the local web.

Jade looked at the crystal in his hand, a little surprised now at how small it seemed, and cool, all its potential locked up beneath the faceted surface. He heard Heglit and Borget talking, knew they were plotting the run in, but he didn't listen. He knew if it was left up to him alone, in spite of what had happened so far, he would not go. The vision he had had of their goal looked and felt deadly. He wondered how much of it Heglit had seen, and whether he was as calm as he looked. Lista's hand on his shoulder beneath his hair felt good and warm.

The web drawn on the screen wasn't just tangled, it was three-dimensional chaos, with flares and smudges of interference where the lines of force were drawn too close together. Heglit studied it, arms folded, mentally tracing some careful course as straight in as possible, avoiding the obvious trouble spots. There was no way of knowing exactly what would happen in those tangled areas, but it wouldn't be pleasant. And if the web was knotted the ship could get caught and go dead, unable to skip out, even manually.

Once he decided he didn't hesitate, he punched in the pattern, waited the short second necessary for confirmation, then turned his back on the screen to drink his tea and look at the others, especially Jade. He was ready.

Jade wasn't. The burden was his. Like the crystal. Once they left here it would be up to him. He would have to know when they reached whatever it was they were supposed to find. Before they got too close to the star. He had never approached a star, at least not in N-Space. All he knew was what he'd heard of heat and pull and some invisible danger from radiation. He wished someone would say something. They didn't. He stared at the blue crystal and felt fear and cold in his lower back and wetness in his palms. He didn't really think he could do this.

He nodded before he really had time to think about it, to decide, and, as quickly, Heglit's hand jumped out to the control board. They went.

22

Heglit had plotted the run well. The Centra Zar blinked out of N-space, appeared briefly beyond the red world, then out and in again, and again, short skips so she seemed a silver hyphen dashing nearly straight in toward the star. The four inside her held silent, watching the outview screens. Except the Rafalan, who watched Jade sitting between the Benjor, face white and set, right hand clasped about the blue jewel to the point of pain he did not feel. The star grew, but there were hours to go. The screen blinked with the choppy skips, compensating for changes in perspective.

Jade thought he would feel something, but it was (except for his fear) like coming into any system.

The first tangle in the web sent them sideways, and on the next quick skip they flashed back to N-space directly behind two patrol ships. There was a flare of brilliance on the screens, but too late. They were already away, breaking back in out of range. Jade changed the jewel to his left hand and rubbed the right on his thigh. Two more quick leaps in and there were the ships again. Waiting.

This time alarms hooted and scattered lights flickered across the board. Heglit studied them, and then they were away again, but somehow damaged. And there was nothing they could do, only run in. And hope.

"The hold, Borget." Heglit's voice unchained him from the screen.

"Breathable."

"Sensors are damaged on the left section."

They leapt into a blaze brighter than the nearing star, and the ship stumbled, shuddered, shrieking only a second of her wounds before Heglit cut the alarms. Knowing did them no good. He bent over the controls, manually overriding the programmed skips, hesitating for the barest instant in the hope that the patrol would advance one skip and get out of synch. It would give them a few minutes. Unless they were following in sequence. But it was all he could do. That and hope the chasers didn't realize just how far in the Centra Zar was going.

Then they ran for the hold and the Zendra Three.

Urging the others aboard, Heglit waited by the controls that would open the wide loading bay. With luck, he could set it to open and still have time to get aboard before the walls separated.

He made it. Barely. The ship shuddered again. The patrol had found them. Too late, hopefully. Heglit punched in the program from memory and powered the flier, waiting through another short skip, another flash of brilliance flashing through the open bay. The little ship slid out and skipped seconds after the freighter and her attackers. Then he leaned back, watching the screen.

"They may believe they breached her," he said after a moment of welcome silence. "And Rafal may not have told them all of it."

But it was a slim hope, and there were yet ships not involved in the attack. Their course had been discovered and they would still be visible as they threaded the Web. But there was nowhere else to go, and they had to go now.

They flashed in and out and in and out to confront a pair of ships and an expanding cloud of vapor and debris that had been the Centra Zar. They leapt away, not daring to hope they had escaped detection, hearing the soft clang of something hitting the dull black outer skin. A muted tone from the board told them something had followed them into the web. Heglit took a chance and deadshipped for a long minute, letting the other break out first and continue the run ahead of them. It worked.

The web straightened, strengthened, and in the brief moments of N-space the yellow star swelled. They flashed out beside a blindingly white cloud-world. And a crowd of ships. Outguessed. A dark hand jumped to break the command that would send them into the web, knowing this many ships could lock them in, strand them in the local channel, helpless, to be drawn out and crushed at leisure. Three of the waiting ships guessed wrong, vanished with the eye-wrenching sparkle of breakin. Two did not go. They attacked.

The Zendra bucked, shivered, and the long Rafalan hand moved to a different part of the console. Lights flashed across the board. Violent purple beams leapt across the screens, away, one great ship glowed red, blue, white, burst in an expanding cloud of debris. Again the purple flare. The second ship exploded. And Jade thought he heard Dariel laugh. But the dark face was closed and hard and fierce as he had only seen it when the strong arm wielded a bloodied sword.

They leapt into the web, toward the blazing star. "They will not follow." Heglit's voice was calm like back in the time before TaLur and Sarn. "The web goes closer to the star than we can survive." There was nothing in the voice that said Heglit was talking about their impending extinction.

The ship skipped, skipped, and there was a brief flash of the tiny inner world. And Jade was scared again, knowing they had too much faith in him, and he didn't know what to do. It was getting hot. Salt sweat burned his eyes, but the crystal was cool, flashing back the flares and million-meter-long tongues of flame the star sent toward them. And Heglit would continue. This was a course decided, he would follow it, trusting now even something he could not understand. And the crystal had brought them here.

Jade looked at the dark face, smelling heat, dazed by the violent glare of the star growing in the screens. He knew they were here because of him. And he was here because—

He scrubbed stinging sweat from his eyes and felt Lista's hand on his shoulder, calming. He looked down at the crystal. Help us, he thought, Vril-Atalba, Chatkar-J'Mur, whoever you are. Help us.

The tiny ship sparkled out of visibility, leapt toward the swelling golden furnace, close and closer, a moth daring the greatest of all flames.

The crystal burned like ice in the hot hand, pushing knotted fingers away.

"Heglit—!"

There was no need to call out. The jewel lifted over

227

them, throwing back shards of light from the blazing screens. And it grew, swelling, bringing from great distance the sound of many voices, becoming blue sound, a mist falling cool over them like mercy and joy and the single hope of the pure rushing blue of the great Star Web. They reached for it, greedy. All but Jade.

"No." And again, "No. Heglit!" But it was too late. They weren't hearing. He struggled alone and couldn't remember why—

Lost in blue torrents of getting someplace else, tossed, twisted, forgetting to control the skip, he was swept along like froth on a wave, cresting against heat and pain, slipping free, caught again, bounced and buffeted. Only the clear pure negative held his thoughts, the no, and nothing before or now. Rafalan strength fought for him, brutal and careless, and won, and even Lista yearned for the golden gate to finish this, for they were all suffering his pain and he dare not let go of that great no to help even himself.

It ended in dark cool stillness. A shock because he expected pain or attack or—

"Jade."

Heglit's voice, worried. Dariel, then. Heglit didn't worry. But was it him? Light burst up from the dark hand on the control board and Jade jerked, forced calm, and looked into the dark face.

"You didn't—" Didn't what? Skip? Link?

"No," he said, finally getting it heard, feeling his lips stick together, and the cool air wasn't wet enough to help, wasn't even— What?

"Jade, we are safe." Dark eyes watching, worried. Dammit, don't look like that. You don't ever look like that.

" 'glit, no." Tongue like dust, lips burning salt. "Not. It's not."

"Not what? Talk sense, Jade."

The words came slow and easy, good sense, and Heglit wanting to help. Wrong. He had to hurry, to do something. Believing. That was it. Heglit had forgotten he would know. And he did. He knew. Because the crystal wasn't here now. Fighting to breathe, to speak, he held out empty hands.

"Gone. Lies. Lying. Don't accept anything—"

228

"Jade? What's gone? I can't help you if—"

"Stop it!" But not said to Heglit. To the other, locking him up, killing them. Holding them back. "Damn you, stop!" Screaming (maybe), he reached out, filled clumsy hands with damp hot cloth, a rat shaking a lion. Heglit took the hands away. He couldn't believe, couldn't understand.

Vril-Atalba. Last chance. Last hope. Act of doubted faith. But he didn't want to end here. Not now. "Vril-Atal—"

Unseen, a mote against the flaming nuclear cauldron of the star, the tiny ship burst into N-space. And vanished.

No time. No heat. No feeling at all. Then there was a hardness in his hand. The crystal. And really cool air against his throat, telling him he was breathing again, and that for a time he had not been. And finally wet—

He jerked back and water trickled over his chin, fell cold onto his chest. Looking into Heglit's eyes he didn't notice. The Rafalan looked like hell, haggard and rusted with exhaustion.

"Jade?"

"Right. All right. I think." His throat hurt, felt seared. "What happened?"

Heglit sat down, long hands rubbing his face before falling together in his lap. "I think it was a bad skip. In the blue Web. You were fighting me. You hurt."

He remembered. Enough. "It wasn't real. I mean, it was real enough, but it was a trap. AzlurEor." He saw Heglit hesitate, caught on that word, full of questions and deciding not to ask them.

"I thought— I was too eager to go. When the crystal changed I accepted it. I nearly killed you."

"Not you." He looked away, suddenly tasting the hot metal smell of the air, uneasy because Heglit was never wrong, never had to apologize. "They couldn't warn us until the last."

"But you knew."

"The crystal. It wasn't there. And it's a thing AzlurEor can't touch." He drank tepid water and felt better, and noticed that Heglit's blouse was wet. He wondered how close they had come to the star, but did not ask, then he wondered about the Benjor, and did.

"Sleeping. They have more strength than they seem."

"Weren't fighting it, either."

"I did not mean to hurt you." And finally the thought behind that first look. "When I woke, you were not breathing. I thought—"

Jade reached to touch the hard leg. "It was shock. And maybe Vril-Atalba. Do you know where we are?"

Heglit hesitated a beat before answering that he did. "But I don't know that I believe it."

"What?"

"We're still in TreAsh Sector."

"What?"

"The description fits. Except—"

"What?" Jade realized he was repeating himself and chewed on his lower lip.

"There are nine worlds. TreAsh is here. But not as it was. Nor is the system quite the same." He showed the comp-display, which meant little to Jade, then punched for the outview. The world he called TreAsh hung in the screen, blue and white. Jade stared at the beauty of it.

"We found it."

Heglit shook his head.

"Dammit, Heglit, what are you trying to say?"

"That I don't know. Logical interpretation of the information says this is TreAsh. But the dating is wrong. Unless we're off by a factor of approximately two hundred million stanyears."

Jade clenched his teeth on another what, and stared at the sapphire world. Two hundred million meant nothing. Hours, even weeks, of out of phase time could scare him, had scared him. Millions of stanyears meant nothing, it was simply a phrase. He watched the world turn peacefully in the screen and knew Borget was awake and listening.

"Is this what we were supposed to find?" He asked finally. And knew the answer. That long ago TreAsh, as world of the TreAshal, didn't exist. No one said anything. He drank more water and wished he could wash the salt off his skin. "Vril-Atalba brought us here for a reason, I guess. Should we go down?"

"You will have to say." Heglit threw the ball back to him. Just as well, for, asking the question, he knew the answer. They would go down.

"What is there?" Heglit asked, watching him.

"A dragon." He grinned with sore lips, maybe joking. But Heglit just nodded and turned his chair toward the controls.

They went down through soft white-gold light, big wet clouds, and blue air, dropping easily on the ship's beam.

And the dragon was there at the foot of a low hill, lying in the green steamy swamp, raising its massive head, shifting the loops and coils of scale-plated self as it moved toward the firmer land where they stopped.

Jade felt Heglit pause and look at him, but he kept his attention on the great yellow eyes alive in the rough-scaled face he remembered.

"Jadriel Younger." It was a voice, he felt the others hear it. And it was a greeting to him.

"Vril-Atalba," he answered, giving back greeting and hearing how small his voice sounded. "You are the dragon of Alzar."

"Were. You have come safe here."

"Why here?"

"A place AzlurEor cannot come yet. For your deciding. So it will not be known beyond us."

"Is this TreAsh?"

"To become."

Jade guessed that fit. "This was it, then? Getting here?" He asked it, already knowing there was more, that this was nothing.

"Who, or what, is AzlurEor?" Heglit spoke aloud, and the great reptilian eyes moved to Jade's right, where the Rafalan stood, arms folded.

"That is for later, warrior of Rafal. We have only a small space here, and the question must be made and answered."

"What question?"

"If the Speaker-seed will continue as his blood commands."

"Continue? There is a choice?"

"You are a free life. You only can decide your fate."

There were echoes behind the voice, giving it strange dimensions that distracted almost as the manner of speaking.

"I have to choose if I want to find TreAsh?"

"TreAsh does not need found."

"What? Then what is— Where is it?"

"Knowledge can harm. Not you alone. Learning comes with choosing."

"And if I choose not to continue?"

"You will return to swim the Star Web as before. You are you."

True. He looked at the great flat head and began to think more clearly than he had in some time. He couldn't quit and go back to before. Because of what he knew about Tas. And Barmalin Tas would get him for sure. And not only him this time.

"If I choose to continue?"

"There is danger. We will help as we may, and are bonded to do."

Which told him exactly nothing. He looked at Heglit, but for once the black eyes were not watching him. He was going to get no help for this. He should have expected as much. He wanted to talk to Heglit, quiet and reasonable, but the situation didn't allow for that either. He could feel the Benjor on the other side of him, thought how much had happened to bring them all here. He didn't want to go back to just being a Linkman again. He couldn't. Unless—

"If I quit, will I— we still remember?"

"You will remember. It was ChatkarJ'Mur's bond with Speaker Sarn that you would remember him."

The words brought a taste of rich dark growth and still unplumbed depths of memory. But the dragon wasn't giving out any information to make it easy. There was just a feeling of complexity and danger and not-too-patient waiting. Even his companions were waiting on his answer.

"There is tension here. Our time is ending. You must choose."

And now Heglit looked at him, and Borget, standing with an arm about Lista, reached to lay a hand on his shoulder. He took a breath and let it out.

"I will continue," he said, feeling cold and committed. "Now what?"

"While there is time, Speaker-seed, we wish to come with you."

"With us? But the ship—"

"We. Vril-Atalba. Not the dragon." A strange distant humor touched the broad voice.

"But how—"

"Through the life-touchers of Benjo. We would become them for a time, beyond AzlurEor's knowing."

He didn't understand that for a minute, then he thought he did. "Oh, no. You don't take them."

"Jade." Borget touched his arm again. "There is no harm to it."

"How do you know? No. I won't—"

"It is our choice. They have spoken to us. It is a union for a time only, as with the dragon. When they leave him he is dragon still. As he was before. We have accepted."

"You can't. Heglit—" He turned to the Rafalan for support and got none. "No. I won't let you. If you have to become someone, be me. It's my game."

"We cannot. You are blood bond to TreAsh and Sarn."

"Jade." Heglit's voice cooled him a little.

"But what if—?"

"It is done, Jade." Lista's voice poured ice down his back. He didn't want to look at her. But he did. And she was Lista, smiling at him. And something more. And Borget's arm moving about his shoulder was as warm, as familiar.

"We have not become dragons, Jade," he said. "But the dragon has become himself, and he is hunter here. Let us go to the Zendra Three."

Jade looked at the dragon and it was different. There was a new tension in the loops of body behind the head, and an attention that carried threat. The great mouth opened, become a dark cavern flashing ivory swords and glistening trails of wet— He might have stood staring long enough to become a meal, but Borget's arm drew him away and they ran for the ship.

"Now what?" Jade asked, and remembered he had just asked that question.

"Lift. Our time here is done and we must remove ourselves." Borget spoke highspeak, pulling a look from Heglit. But this was not the time for interesting observations on change. They leapt away from the surface and

233

as the blue planet dwindled, Heglit automatically punched in the Web sensors.

"The red world," Borget said behind him. "It remains stable."

They ran for the red planet, away from the yellow star. Once, in the series of short skips, there was a turbulence that forced reprogramming. Jade watched the dark hands do the things that needed doing, then rest, open, on the padded arms of the chair. He wanted very much to talk to Heglit about what was happening, but he could feel Borget and Lista behind them and was afraid to say anything.

Heglit finally broke the hard silence, being practical. "We cannot go far. We lost our stores with the Centra Zar."

"If we're in the right time, there should be a ComUn station and supply base near."

"Not necessary, Jade." Borget's voice stirred his nape hair. "For a time let them believe we fell into the star. There is a ship near. Unknown. It will supply us."

Us? "Your ship?"

"A Traveler." Borget made the distinction with a laugh somewhere in his voice.

"They haven't found it?" Heglit glanced at Jade, who shut up.

"They do not have the sensors necessary to find her. She is in the Rock Belt, and looks like many other large rocks."

"How do we find her?"

"Jade can find her with the crystal."

"Me?" He finally turned to look at the golden couple and his eyes and something more said it was Borget and Lista there, close enough to touch, and their gray eyes held understanding. As a sort of side issue, like something learned once, he knew how to find the ship. But he asked anyway. "Can't you find it?"

"We could. But our doing so could be a thing AzlurEor would know."

He nodded, accepting that, willing, for the sake of wanting the ship and the comfort promised, to accept his part in finding her. He was tired and badly in need of a place to wash and lie down and sleep without running.

234

"How long since we came into the sector?" he asked.
"Eighty-two hours plus."

No wonder he was tired. Even Heglit looked beat. They keyed into the local web, hoping the patrol would be busy elsewhere, and began to skip. Still not sure of himself, Jade looked down at the crystal in his hand wondering about the ship they would find. And it happened so fast he missed it. One skip and they were near a large jagged asteroid, another and they were in the dark.

"Inside," Heglit said, and it was just a word with no particular expression. "Is there air?"

"Yes. The ship knows us."

It was too big to call a ship. Space echoed to their steps and a soft light sprang up as though keyed to the sound. The Benjor led the way from the big space to a door that sort of folded open as they approached and unfolded closed behind. Then there was corridor, soft carpeted floor, and rich colors, rather than standard gray plasteel. And there were doors at irregular intervals opening into rooms of many sizes.

Lista pointed to one room containing a wide couch and two large chairs with a table of what might have been blue-green glass between them. "We are safe here, for now. There is a washer, and we will bring food. Then we can rest and talk."

And talk. She was so lovely, looking up at him like he might strike her, and willing to accept it. "Lista—"

"Wash, Jade, and rest first. And do not be angry at us." Soft sweet words, and her hand cool and lingering on his cheek before she turned away.

He stripped, shook down his hair, and stepped into the washer, accepted the warm spray with a shiver of pleasure, feeling salt and tension sluice away. The blower took away the wet so his hair slid heavy silk over his clean skin and he was ravenous.

There were clean clothes on the couch, crimson pants, soft silver tunic with wide sleeves, a wide black belt. The unfamiliar fabric molded his lean frame perfectly. And there was a brush for his hair. Perfect. He'd ask later.

He was seated crosslegged on the couch, brushing his hair when the others came in, and they were also clean and new-clad. The Benjor brought trays and a silver flagon that teased memory briefly before the smells drove away thought. Real food, not basic stores. There was Lursteak and some kind of fish and a sweet crusty bread. The silver flagon held a bubbly drink like nothing he had tasted before.

They ate and drank together, and Jade relaxed, yawning, content, needing nothing but sleep, and glad to be there with the three of them. Even Heglit leaned back, long legs pushed out into the room, dark eyes looking at not much of anything.

"We need to sleep," someone said, rousing Jade, who was near to dreaming where he sat. Probably Heglit, he thought, yawning again. Then they were gone, and he stripped and gave himself up to the softness of the couch. He thought once of the Benjor, but drifted to sleep before the thought became more than a path into dreams.

23

No ship he'd ever seen or thought about was like this, Jade thought, walking through the colorful corridors, looking into uncountable rooms and areas that served purposes he could not imagine. It was more building than ship. He moved down curving ramps and stairs, but found nothing even vaguely resembling a power room or control room. And there was no sign of Heglit or the Benjor. He didn't know where they spent the sleep time. In fact, he'd been so busy exploring he wasn't sure he could find the room he started in.

"Jade."

Lista's soft voice spun him around, and she laughed at him, a gentle singing too sweet for anger. "We thought you slept."

"I woke," he said stupidly, wondering if he was hearing Lista or the Traveler, and not sure he should ask or even think of that very much. He asked instead where Heglit was.

"With Borget, waiting for you to wake." Her hand reached to touch his arm, but he moved a little away before it made contact, not looking at her.

"Jade." There was a puzzlement and something like hurt in the voice.

"You are not Lista," he said, and felt ice in his throat. "No gaming, us."

"I am no less Lista than I am. Do you see any other here?" Forcing him to look at her. And that touched anger in him.

"The Traveler—"

"Is with me for a time. As Borget is always. As you have been with us, and sometimes with Heglit. No more."

"But Vril-Atalba came back. You are—"

"I have told you, Lord Jade. But you wish to be angry."

237

And he learned that Benjorspeak could sting gently. He reached to take her hand, defeated, and let her lead him to where Heglit and Borget waited.

Borget greeted him with a smile, Heglit with a look that said he guessed about the meeting with Lista. But when he spoke it was about the ship, saying it was not the same as the Federation found during the Traveler War. "It is built for human types, but I think from outside."

Borget nodded, looking pleased. "It was gifted to the Travelers, and is here for our using."

"Then the Travelers do need ships."

"For bringing you to, yes." Which could have meant they probably didn't need ships for themselves, or he was speaking of this particular ship, or maybe their idea of a ship was not something you could bring people to. Jade wandered about the room trying not to get tangled in his own thoughts.

"So we're here. This is what it was all about." He sounded edgy, and he was. After the business of getting to a TreAsh that had been longer ago than made any difference, it occurred to him that the Travelers could have just brought him here without all the games on Alzar or Grio and out beyond the Rim. He said so.

"We can do nothing to you, Jadriel Younger. But think for a moment if we had. You would not have the knowledge or the ability to do the thing you now can do."

"What is it I can do?" He made the mistake of looking at the speaker (Borget, his eyes said).

"Choose. And remember."

"I already chose. Didn't I?"

The golden head nodded.

Heglit looked at both of them for a minute. "We are here. Our being here has to do with TreAsh."

Borget smiled his golden smile, knowing the Rafalan's motive. "TreAsh. The reason. And the reason for all that went before. Yes. It was necessary that the one choosing come to where we were to learn of Tas and me, also that he return to Grio to speak with World-Seeder ChatkarJ'Mur and find the crystal."

"If I had known something—"

"Your knowing before you could act would have

brought danger. AzlurEor would have learned of you in time to act."

"AzlurEor," Jade prompted.

"Yes. It is time to speak of AzlurEor. Our brother."

"Brother?" Thinking shared flesh and parentage. But Lista saw his misunderstanding and explained.

"Not brother in your meaning, or the meaning of Benjo. This is a thing of the Travelers. He is of a kind with us, and from our life island." Which could have meant world, but very probably didn't.

"Now he is your enemy." Heglit's hard voice lay the mildest stress on the pronoun, perhaps making subtle accusation.

"Adversary," Borget said, as if there were an important difference. "And not alone ours. He seeks to delay the Web spinning or break the thread as has happened before. We are the ones who first taught AzlurEor of the Star Web. It is our responsibility, though the doing was done before we understood the true nature of the Web."

Jade listened impatiently. Becoming the Benjor had improved the speak of the Traveler, but it didn't make him any easier to understand.

"What does this have to do with TreAsh?"

"AzlurEor cannot work against the knowledge TreAsh is building about the Star Web. It was he who directed the first fear of the people to TreAsh and sought to destroy them."

"And you helped them," Heglit said, hoping to bring the subject back to their situation.

"As we could, making use of AzlurEor's error as TreAsh planned to weave the several worlds into a oneness through fear of a common enemy. In that they achieved the thing that demands growing and learning and building a pattern within each island of life."

Jade dropped down on soft pillows, wondering if Heglit understood more of this than he did.

"Then what happened to TreAsh was intended and Jade was supposed to find out."

"He already knew, but he could not be allowed to know in full until he could come to the place where he could do the thing himself."

"What thing?" Jade sat up, thinking they might finally get to it, but Heglit gestured him quiet.

"Rafal and Alzar and Grio. We had part of it, and ChatkarJ'Mur. The part of the crystal in the Centra Zar was another clue." Heglit nodded and leaned back, folding his arms. "All preparation for what?"

"TreAsh is safe. But not of this space. It became possible to be elsewhere when the probability occurred that the attack by the Federation would succeed."

Even Heglit had to admit he didn't understand that.

"If a world is, the probability exists that it will remain, only changing with the parent star's change. When forces act to make a possibility that the world will not continue to exist, then there is also a probability that it will not exist beyond a certain point."

Heglit looked at Borget (who was Vril) a long time before nodding. "You helped them use a probable. But how?"

"It is of the nature of the Star Web, and so unexplainable," Lista apologized, bringing tea or something like it on a wide tray. "We have learned a thing since AzlurEor. The nature of the Star Web grows as the Web is woven, and abundant knowledge does no good thing for the Web."

"Then the Star Web is not finished?" Heglit asked, watching Borget close, hoping for what they said they would not give.

Borget laughed lightly, sounding altogether too much like Borget, and raised his steaming cup. When he had drunk he changed the subject.

"TreAsh is no longer of this space, but Jadriel Younger is. Put simply, by being of both he can form a path, make a certainty of the probable continued existence of TreAsh. The probability of its non-existence is also possible, for there has been this time that it did not exist in its rightful place. But it was not destroyed by the Federation. So, the probabilities are balanced. Which becomes the firmer reality here, is dependent on Jade. He can establish either. His choice was for TreAsh. To make the probable actual, he must himself return to TreAsh. It was for this reason we chose to wait. We cannot go, but we can build a safer path for you, and aid you to some degree."

"We will go like we went to— back to where you were?"

Vril shook his head. "It will not be so easy. AzlurEor

will not be fooled so twice. He cannot find us here, but he knows you now. When you leave here he will be watching. It is necessary that you do not know the true place of the path and we do not know how you arrive at your destination."

And that, Jade thought, was absurd. He started to point that out, but Lista's soft laugh shut him up.

The impossibility is in the words, Jade, not the thing itself. It is a thing you have done before. The two realities simultaneous, the one accepted, the other acted upon."

"Like on Alzar?" He didn't quite look at Heglit.

"In that manner, yes. But the path will be traveled by all."

"All. Then you— then Borget and Lista will come?"

"Of course. You chose them for it, as Dariel said before Rafal."

Dariel. This time he did look, but the Rafalan wore no different expression.

"AzlurEor." The hard Rafalan voice kept to the priorities. "You say he is a danger. What can he do?"

"If he discovers your path he will try to stop Jade. He could influence you in ways that would prevent your success."

"He knows of me?" Jade asked.

"He may not yet know the truth of what you are, but he does know you. He had you once in his present being as the one from the Burkoze Sector."

"Lurz?" Thinking for a minute Borget had meant another kind of thing, Jade laughed. "Then he's Clate."

Vril did not laugh. "As Atalba and I are Benjor. And he has been other. Many would lease themselves for well-being and power and wealth."

Jade shook his head. Lurz. He had no great respect for the man, but it was unsettling to think he was something more than a handsome down-limb Clate with ambitious ideas.

Vril-Atalba had unspecified tasks to tend to, leaving Jade and Heglit free to explore the ship and speculate on its origin. And to wonder, without yet speaking, about the things that were happening to them and the Benjor. They came into what seemed to be some kind of exercise room, and the equipment brought a comment from Heglit that the builders had been more than like human stock. They played with the strange devices, using up energy, discovering how they could be used for tests of strength and agility.

The Benjor were more serious when the two rejoined them, as though they had learned something.

"AzlurEor knows of our being here," Vril said over another excellent meal. "He is seeking us, hoping to find you. He will not discover this ship, so he will move out, beyond the sector. It is then you must go. It will take time to reach TreAsh, and when he does not find you he will take action to harm the Star Web."

"But the Web is. What can he do?" Jade asked over the taste of something hot and crisp and sweet.

"Many things." It was no kind of answer, and he saw the look Heglit gave the Traveler.

When the meal was done, Borget asked Jade for the crystal and he went to his room to get it.

"What is it?" he asked, dropping it into the golden hand.

"The Star Web." Then, seeing the look on Jade's face, he laughed. "As the same nature on one level, and not to be explained yet. The knowledge will come, unless AzlurEor has his will of this island."

AzlurEor again. And no, Vril (sounding like Borget) said, he didn't know of the crystal.

"We will need supplies for the Zendra," Heglit said, either to his glass or to everyone, or just thinking aloud.

"You will not take the Zendra Three," Lista said, as though he should have known that.

"Not this, surely."

"No ship, shipmaster."

Jade couldn't think of anything to say, so didn't. Heglit waited a couple of beats, still looking at her. "Perhaps you should tell us how we shall go."

"We do not know. Only that you shall go." Lista as herself would never meet that dark look so levelly. "And the crystal shall go with you, returning to Speaker Sarn."

Returning to Speaker Sarn. Jade didn't really think of that until he was lying on his couch waiting for a sleep that eluded him. Sarn. She couldn't have meant what it sounded like she meant. Not after three hundred stanyears. It could not be. The doubts that had held back since the flight toward the star came back, pushing sleep further away.

He did not want to be alone. And he did not want to be with Vril and Atalba ("We are two" the dragon on Alzar had said, and he finally understood that), who were too damned much like Borget and Lista. He got up, finally, and went to find Heglit's room, telling himself he would leave quietly if we found the Rafalan asleep.

"What is it, Jade?" The voice was alert, almost like it expected him, though the room was dark.

"I would talk." The clear Rafalspeak sounded strange in his own ears. He had not known he would use it.

The light swelled into the room to show Heglit sitting up on his couch, bare to the waist. He gestured to a chair near the couch, and Jade dropped into it.

"There are too many things I do not understand, Heglit. I hear them speak and it seems they are putting too much faith in me. And leaving too much unsaid."

"It is not faith alone. This was begun long ago."

"For them." He linked hands and looked down at them. He knew himself for what he was, and it wasn't anything begun back during the Traveler war, nor had it anything to do with his parentage. Biting his lip he dropped out of Rafalspeak. "Not smart, me. Joy-skinner and lucky, is all."

"You are afraid."

That didn't need to be answered. He pulled his feet into his lap and shook down his hair, pulling it into plaits wound about each hand. "Before TaLur it was Linking and joyhouses and chem-links when I got the credit. All this— It is too much."

Heglit watched, picking up clues, measuring what he saw against what he knew of the man. "You think yourself less than you are. And you are not alone in this."

Not alone, true. But—

"Heglit, when we go, will you—" The dark hard-planed face and black eyes could not be asked about Dariel, not now. He left the question unasked, wondering why he wanted to, and Heglit didn't pursue it.

"What do they mean, no ship?" he asked after a time.

"They will answer that in time." Heglit didn't seem

243

concerned. "I think they don't want us to know very much until it is time to use the knowledge."

"Because of AzlurEor."

"Lurz, they said. And he is trying to harm the Star Web."

"He is working against ComUn."

"So that is a danger to the Web. Somehow. On Alzar they said they were helping keep the Federation together. Not for the Federation or ComUn, I think. The Star Web is their concern. I think TreAsh knew more of it than Rafal ever guessed."

But Jade was more into personal thoughts. "She—Atalba said the crystal would return to Sarn."

"There are answers we will only get by going to Tre-Ash."

"AzlurEor has gone beyond the system," Borget greeted them. "Two standard hours gone he Linked into the fourth level of the Star Web, bound up the limb."

Fourth level? Jade didn't ask, knowing he wouldn't get a real answer. Anyway, it was probably the standard commercial channel. "Then we go?"

"Soon. Yes. Before he begins to know you did not leave this sector. The path is chosen and stable. Once you begin it will become an established reality."

"Like Linking?"

"Of a kind. The doing will be of all of you. The goal is known. Your doing on the path will not be known to us, only if you stray. There is that danger that you will too-fully accept. Another danger is that AzlurEor will trace Jade. To make him less visible the journey will be a series of goings, not a continuous thing."

Frowning, Jade looked at Heglit, wondering if he understood what was being said. The Rafalan sat, thoughtful, legs extended, clasped hands resting on his chest.

"We go, then," Jade said when Borget had been quiet for a while. "We leave here and just go into it and try to get to TreAsh. When?"

"Now. While you are rested and AzlurEor is moving away in the Star Web. One thing we will tell you of this journey. Though it is linked to the Star Web it will not be as you now think. Do not mistake it. Remember always, from the time you leave until you reach TreAsh, or confront AzlurEor, you are on a Traveler path." Vril rose. "The place of departure is three levels down."

Walking through the corridors with them, Jade watched the calm golden faces, holding the thought that these were more than Benjor and wondering what it was like for them to be so close to the Travelers. Then he remembered that Borget and Lista would come with them, but not the Travelers.

"Vril," he halted at a door they had not seen before, and the gray eyes touched him, questioning. "When we leave, the four of us, where will you go? AzlurEor will be back."

"Your concern is pleasing, Jadriel Younger." A warm hand pressed his shoulder and slid away. "We will not tell you of our going, for your safety and ours. But we go to a familiar being-place where we may aid you yet."

The door opened. Blue hit their eyes, fast, radiant, and present like the bubbles in Orziel, tingling skin and hair as they moved onto the hard polished floor. There were four chairs, equidistant about a low table holding a— He couldn't decide if it was a decorative piece or a container of rich blue shot through with threads and ripples of red-tones, blending into violets and purples and colors he couldn't name. He looked around, but the walls were hard to see, like motion on the edge of vision, pulling his attention a dozen ways.

Jadriel Younger. The echoes were back. Dragon voice. And Borget's (or Vril's) mouth did not move. He glanced at Heglit, but he was looking at the room and did not notice anything else. So it was not the voice they could hear. He started to pay attention.

This is gift and talisman for you. It cannot be harmed where you go and it spins a thread to us. Wear it, keep it always with you until it returns to Sarn.

Borget moved the step toward Jade. "He is gone," he said softly in Benjorspeak. "He gives you this."

It was the crystal, set now in a lattice of some blue-white metal, finely worked, and fastened to a heavy chain of the same material, woven in complex links. The golden hands raised the chain, slid it over Jade's head, and for a moment the pendant slid cold against his chest.

245

The hands stayed warm on his shoulders, and he studied the unsmiling face.

"He— they are gone," Borget repeated.

"Yes." He knew it. "And you?" He looked at Lista. She nodded.

"Do you remember?"

"Yes."

"Jade, there is not much time," Heglit called him back to the moment. "The chairs."

The chairs waited and he felt the weight of the crystal against his skin, no longer cold. He touched it, glad it was there even if he didn't know what good it would do them. He wished for time to have the Benjor back, but Heglit was going to the chairs. Not letting himself think about it too long, he followed.

Without plan, they assumed the seats they had had in the Link-room of the Centra Zar.

Then they waited, tense, wondering what to expect. Nothing happened. The walls wearied their eyes and more and more frequently they looked to the unusual blue construction on the table. Now, as Jade had time to study it, he thought it might be a solid crystal. The motionless colors were a soothing stability and relief from the mobility of the walls. Jade thought about saying something about the colors and design, but did not make the effort. He was too tired, not weary, but relaxed, content here with his three companions.

They all stared at the blue, drifting, lulled. Breathing slowed, deepened, and none was aware of the slow changing rhythm of the room, walls pulsing like heart beats, matching, bonding the internal physical timers, until four hearts and the room pulsed to the same measured beat. There was a sound, distant and unimportant to the four, like something torn, a beat, an intense flash that blinked the staring eyes to black. And they fell long and long, rushing away to the place they were going.

24

"Up you, sleeper! Leaving us for Kaldon."

The teasing voice and rough hands disturbed a kinder dream, and Jade protested, groaning, half numb, tasting the bitter of a night's Orziel and Skyweed.

"Come, Jade. Up."

Insistence pulled him far enough out of sleep to mumble something unkind in harsh and explicit Zoarspeak, bringing a laugh he knew well. Slippery Lurweb tangled his legs, twisted about his hips and under him like fetters, irritating. He fought free and forced aching eyes to open, to see Clarant Reese already washed and dressed.

"Come, Jade. I promised you a qualifying run this time."

He remembered, but it didn't heal the hangover. He sat naked on the wide couch, hiding in his hair, wanting nothing more than to step into the washer and get clean. In a minute he would be up and—

This isn't right. I'm not—

take the job. It was only a small run, and Reese had let him Link often enough.

"Linker, me," he told the fat Clate. "Wrote him for getting QL papers."

It wasn't standard, but a letter with the Reese seal was high credit. He could have asked for a pilot's apprenticeship and had good reason to expect it with that letter. But that would be ComUn and he didn't want that. Not if he could Link.

The clean fat hands held the packet, but the eyes, deep in little folds and rolls of skin, looked at him. The round head finally bobbed up and down. " 'Prentice then, with our qualified Linkman. Make it, you, I'll code for licensing."

It was enough. He could skip the Star Web clean to

HarCon and RioDel, he had done it often enough. But he needed the QL. He knew well enough now that an hour's worth of his time and effort would buy it for him. And maybe more. Then he'd be free, able to sign for runs to—

This is not right! Happened already, and Heglit was—Heglit!

The Benjor . . .

He pressed hands to his face, felt it real and alive, eyes blinking and not seeing . . . Hands slid down and over throat, familiar, felt chain, pendant—

Blue flashed against his eyes, solid and real, and the shadows were Heglit and the Benjor, sitting very still, eyes open and watching nothing he could see.

There had been something there, where their eyes were focused. A table. And something— But he couldn't remember. Heglit sat so still, frozen, his unseeing eyes masking him, making too much distance.

Jade got up, surprised at how easy that was. He went the three steps toward the Rafalan, reached to touch the broad shoulder, then hesitated, thinking of that other time he had tried to wake him and nearly got his neck broken. He grasped the shoulder lightly, shaking it.

"Heglit."

Black eyes blinked, did not see him.

"Heglit." He put authority into it this time.

The eyes closed. And stayed closed a minute. The dark throat flexed, swallowing.

"Jade?"

"Yes. You were, uh— dreaming?"

"Yes." Only that. Then the eyes opened and saw him, held a moment, then flashed to the Benjor. "Wake them."

The calm voice was power to act. He needed them all with him now, more than he needed to remember the places he had just come from. And it wasn't time to wonder what dreams Heglit had had that he hadn't wanted to leave.

He touched Lista, gentle, and they both woke, telling him they had been together in their special way, sharing.

"I thought—" Borget did not say what he thought, but shared a look with his sister before unleashing attention to what was real. "Where have we come to?"

Jade shook his head. He didn't know, but it wasn't

what he had expected and he felt a little cheated. It was still blue, like the room they had left (if they had gone; maybe the walls were just holding still). Then his eyes adjusted to distance, and distance increased, giving him the odd sensation that looking was creating distance, until he stopped looking for and started looking at.

They were on a sort of platform slightly above the floor, and beyond their immediate area great columns lifted toward the ceiling. Not that they could see a ceiling, there was just a feeling of being enclosed. Rows of columns colored in shades from pale ivory to deep rose and every shade in between, marched away into distance, creating an illusion of corridors. The combination of colors irritated Jade with a memory he couldn't quite grasp.

"It's a building," he said at last.

Borget moved to the edge of the platform and jumped down. "No harm being," he called up to them. "For safety is. Protecting us."

"Someone had to build it."

Heglit looked at him and followed Borget, so Jade took Lista's hand and helped her down to the sapphire floor. It was as smooth and hard as it looked.

"Not built," Heglit said, looking to Borget, who nodded.

"But—" Then, looking up, he remembered the table and the thing on it. A chill roughened his back and flanks. "It can't be."

"It is. We got inside, somehow."

And it was. Jade knew it. For one wild minute he felt trapped, betrayed. The urge to run swelled up in his belly, tensing thighs and shoulders. Heglit saw it.

"Jade. We have begun the journey. You know what must be done. It was decided."

He knew. Or what he thought felt like knowing (and could as easily have been wanting, it was hard to tell). Borget was right. It was safe here. Once they left here they were— What? He wasn't sure, but it scared him. "We have to leave here."

There were no true directions. They just started walking between rows of colored columns. Once Jade glanced back to see how far they had come, but the platform and chairs was not there. He toyed with ideas of mechanical explanations, imagining they had been sleeped and

249

lowered to some other level of the ship, and now that they were away from the platform it had been raised. But he could not manufacture any reason for that sort of thing. Anyway, this place felt even bigger than the ship. He grinned at himself, thinking the truth was stranger even than he could invent. They were actually inside the crystal on the table. And that was something smaller than the ship.

There was more time for thinking strange thoughts than Jade needed. A big block of it had been tied up in walking and nothing was changing.

"Lost, us," he suggested, stopping.

The others stopped too, and he caught a look in Heglit's eyes that annoyed him. "Well, how could we know? It's all the same."

"No. The colors." A hand gestured about them. "There is no more white or red."

He was right, of course. Jade gnawed his lower lip, realizing he had not been paying attention. "The blue. When it matches the walls, or whatever, we go out."

Heglit nodded, like of course, waiting for him to get to whatever he wanted to say.

"I don't know what will happen. It might be like before we woke up, dreams like real, and all this forgotten. Except getting to TreAsh. Or trying. If anyone knows anything we should talk now, before getting out."

"They said even they did not know," Heglit reminded.

"Do you remember?" Jade asked the Benjor. "I mean having him, them, with you?"

"Yes. A little." Lista laughed her soft golden laugh. "Like Linking, us. Knowing them, but not all, only knowing them knowing us."

"Shared good and safety for us. But not their knowing or doing in this," Borget added, knowing what Jade wanted.

"If we will not remember there is no reason to speculate," Heglit pointed out logically. "And AzlurEor will be coming back to find us."

That was something Jade would rather not dwell on. But Heglit was probably right. All he was doing was postponing the inevitable. He shrugged, nodding, and they went.

The wall was blue light, not bright, but solid-looking.

Heglit reached out a hand to touch it, and it wasn't there. Like the wall on Alzar. Only this tingled almost pleasantly. He looked back at the others, then stepped into the light, feeling them follow close behind. There was bright blindness and a swift rush of euphoria and invigoration. He paused long enough to explore his reaction and conclude that it was real and physical, an infusion of energy absorbed from the light itself, bringing him to optimum strength. He meant to mention this to Jade, but there was something in the light that prevented sound. No matter, he would ask when—

25

Sunlight flashed against their eyes, bright hurting jagged flakes of it leaping from the surface of the river, solid bars crashing down from the colorless sky.

Hands on hips, Heglit surveyed the dense purplish jungle growth, then turned to Jade. "We can't use the river to get any closer."

Jade reached into a pocket for the navimap, flipped it open. The bright green lined north, straight away from the river. He pointed at the tangled growth. "That's the way."

He turned to look back at the water skipper, frowning slightly, feeling an un-namable sense of wrongness, trying to pin it down. Borget and Lista were coming aground, dressed, like him, in the light but protective suits necessary on a trek like this. Even so they were graceful. He was glad they were here. Daneb III was a big unfriendly world and he was already wishing they had bartered for a ComUn team to look for the old city. But speed was essential now, and only the first there could stake a claim under the law.

Glis, it was hot. And still early. They pulled on their packs and armed themselves with Zoarknives, light broad blades they would need to clear a path. Heglit took first lead, silent and efficient, and Jade was glad for the time to think, to chase down the feeling of not-quite-rightness.

There's more to it, he thought. Something bigger. He chewed on the thought, finding no answers in the thick growth pressing in around them, watching Heglit's broad back bend and straighten as he cut through the brush, opening a path for them. It wasn't anything here, he was sure of that without being able to make sense of it. It had something to do with him and where they were going. There was danger. Not the sort he could face or plan against, but something dark and shadowy . . .

Lost in thought he tripped over a vine. For a moment, feeling the damp soil beneath his palms, breathing in the smell of earth and damp growing things, he was struck by a memory so strong the purple-green jungle faded to a greener-green, memory of a bigger dark brown being . . . ChatkarJ'Mur! He nearly said the name aloud. Wonder swept away all sense of heat, of fatigue, and in its place he felt-tasted blue, pure sapphire and turbulence and speed. The glorious freedom of the Web. But—

Heglit stopped, straightening to wipe sweat from his dark face, and Jade bumped into him. Shocked back to reality he grabbed the dark arm that reached to steady him.

"All right?"

"Yeah." He apologized absently, losing tatters of memory to heat and annoying sweat. But inside, the cool blue memory stayed, and he was glad for it. He turned to look back the way they'd come and there was no sign of the river.

"Let me lead a while," he offered. "We may need your strength later."

Heglit nodded and he took his turn, swinging the blade a little clumsily at first until he learned the necessary rythm, glad that Heglit didn't offer to show him how it was done. It wasn't all that hard, but the cut and step was constant. There wasn't one foot of clear space. But that was all right. They were pushing on and working was better than walking and worrying. He felt better now, and someplace inside the cool rushing blue buoyed him up. This is a dream, he thought once, very clearly, and laughed aloud before remembering the others could hear him. But no one asked.

It was a long day. The heat forced them to rest when the blue-white sun hit the top of the sky and started down. They came to swampy areas and brief grassy meadows that gave vivid relief from the jungle. There was tepid water to drink, and bitter little capsules that were supposed to give them energy, and by the time the sun was lying on the horizon they were working up a steep hill and thinking about making camp.

They didn't need the fire, the nutritabs would do them

as much good chewed dry and swallowed with a mouthful of water, but it was more satisfying to heat the water and make a broth. Jade rested against his pack, wishing his muscles would stop jumping so he could really relax. He dozed, and woke when Lista brought him a cup of the broth.

"Anything out there mad at us?" he asked, trusting the Benjor to know.

"Nothing large, or near. Not liking people, them."

Good. Very good. Tiredness wrapped him up like warm gruel, and looking over to where Heglit sat watching the fire, he gave up and drifted down and down, into rushing blue.

"Jade." The hard hand shocked him out of dream and he dove up, surfacing, dripping silver blue, being both places at once for a moment before time came back. Muscles protested stiffly as he moved. Crazy, he thought. He should tell them they didn't need to do this, be this, when—

The dawn-dusky mountains wavered as he looked at them to the north. He opened his mouth to say something, to warn them—

The world steadied, smoothed into rolling grasslands, humping away into illimitable distance. He frowned, one hand moving unconsciously to the pendant, clasping it through the coarse cloth of his blouse.

"No one out there," he heard himself say, and remembered why he thought there might be. The Homers had found out they were here, without invitation. And that made them legal sport. Damn. He should have known better than to trust that Burkoze Linkman. Still, if there was a pre-Federation city on Home—

He turned to look north again, wishing they had the ground car. But it was gone, lost in one of the chasms this freaking world called rivers. The land continued its slow climb toward what, on this world, was a chain of mountains. Beyond, if the scanners were right, lay a large lake basin, headwater for all the rivers in this area. And beside it, the ruins of the old city.

The others were ready. He shrugged on the pack and started to walk with them, casting a quick look back down the rolling plain to the southwest. Nothing moved. Yet. But they would be there before long, the riders on their plodding tireless dramels, sun flashing from curved naked blades. The Sportsmen. It was world law, null only on the ComUn owned port land. And he had known it before they started.

Exercise warmed the stiffness out of his muscles, and they all moved faster, hoping to reach what looked like more broken land to the north before the sun spotlighted them. He found a rhythm balanced between pain and agony and listened to his own breath rush in and out, already wishing for a drink of water.

"Jade." Heglit's arm halted him and he looked up beyond his feet. They were in a shallow dip hidden from the lower land to the south. Safe. But directly in front of them lay a black shadow. For a moment he couldn't decide what it was. Then he knew. Another river. Or stream. A steep-sided cut in the depthless fine black soil of the world. He moved closer, about four steps, and realized it was right there. No more than three meters wide. And forty or more deep.

He looked back. The dip widened like a funnel and the lower end was bathed in rose-gold light. They couldn't go back.

"Jump, us," he suggested softly.

Heglit flashed him a look and stayed quiet. They both knew it wasn't a problem for him. But for Jade and the Benjor— He turned to them.

"Jump," Borget said, and Lista nodded.

"There is swift danger behind," she added, telling them their track had been found, and all the ground gained in the long night walk was being taken away.

"Throw the packs first," Heglit said, slipping his off and moving to the edge of the narrow gorge.

They obeyed quickly, feeling the light creeping up behind them. It wasn't any problem to get the packs over. They bounced and lay waiting on the coarse deep rooted grass. Jade looked down, hearing the sound of fast water, feeling damp rise against his face. To his right, soft light struck down on just the right angle to touch the smooth ruffled surface locked between the dark walls. The water glowed blue and deep. He froze, staring, leaning, caught by a strange desire to be part of that rushing blue stream. He could almost feel the power, the clean shouting joy—

"Jade!" Heglit's hand drew him back, leaving him breathless and dizzy. "Do not look down. We must go. Now."

Go. Yes. Jump. But that wasn't what he wanted. He wanted— Pulling air hard down into his chest, he nodded, stretched to unlock muscles. His body was trained to grace and agility. He moved back a few paces to give himself momentum, ran forward, and leapt lightly across the chasm.

Coarse sand slid beneath his feet and he fell forward, feeling the roughness score palms and knees. Hard white light stabbed up under his narrowed lids.

So soon?

The question rang in his head like a big bell, and he closed his eyes, sitting back on his heels. So soon what? Think, dammit! He rubbed sore hands on his thighs and licked lips that tasted of salt and felt like old dry wood. Think. You just jumped over a river crack on Home. That was truth. He still felt the push and extension in his muscles. Remember. Home. Green rolling plains, aging red-gold star. The Sportsmen. Right. But he was sitting on what felt like desert. And he had wanted something. The water? The blue. The Star Web. Excitement knifed him under the ribs. He should tell them before—

"Heglit—"

No answer. He forced his eyes to open, to see the harsh white and black land. Solqar, he thought. Memory crashed through his eyes telling him how they had got here, forcing down the other important thing in his mind. Gripping his thighs, he scrabbled about in his head until he recalled the Star Web. Something about reaching a place and—

"Heglit!" Desperation sharpened his voice, but white heat and silence ate the sound. He whirled around on his knees. White sand and black rock. Alone.

"No. This is not real. Dammit, Heglit, you were right *here*." Hot dry air scorched his throat. There was water in the packs. They had thrown them—

But his hands were wiser here, reaching up to loosen the straps, slide off the pack. His back felt briefly cool as trapped perspiration evaporated. He unclipped the water bottle, lifted it to his hurting lips and let a scant mouthful of water wash his tongue. He savored it slowly.

"Not real, this," he muttered, putting away the water, pulling the pack on. He got to his feet, frowning, ignoring the land, the heat, the knowledge insisting on his being part of this. "Jumped, me," he insisted doggedly. "From there to here."

Eyes closed, he could remember, could hold off the ideas that tried to be real for him. He had jumped. But had the others? Or were they still back there? *Could he get back?*

Pressing sandy fingers against his eyes, he struggled to think. He had jumped well enough to land maybe a meter beyond the far edge of the chasm. The place was right there, he could feel it. Carefully, balancing between ideas, he felt back. It was there, grass beneath his legs, Heglit's hard strength close and watchful, Borget and Lista, the packs lying close together. Holding his breath he concentrated memory about his companions. "Borg, Lista—"

"All right now, him." Borget's voice (please be real) close and worried. "Jade?" And the weight on his back was not a pack, but a strong arm, and he was no longer kneeling.

"Borg?" And eyes, straining open to be sure, touched the golden face. "Heglit?" Scared again for a minute, he struggled to get up, saw the big man standing near with Lista. They all looked worried.

"Rest, Jade." The caring hands drew him back and he was content to lie against the thighs. It was all right. He wasn't alone. He heard them moving near, preparing food. He smelled the fire and meat roasting.

"What happened?"

"You fell. On the hill there." Heglit's voice, closer than he'd thought, pulling his eyes open. "You did not wake."

He remembered. The smell of meat made him hungry, and he sat up, looking around. The great rocks were shadowed in the dusk light beneath the broad-limbed trees and he could feel the bulk of the mountain rising behind them. Beyond the fire the sky still glowed pale green through the branches and he remembered how far it was down to the valley floor where the ship lay. Quite a distance from the formation they had spotted coming in, but it was the closest place level enough for a safe grounding. The sun had been high, casting bright sharp shadows when they came by here on their way up the mountain.

"We lost half a day," he said to no one in particular. "We could have been over the mountain."

Lista called them to eat and there was Santo tea from the ship, and meat that was unfamiliar, but golden brown and sweet. The Benjor spoke of the life forms on Glendon, comparing them with other worlds they knew, but Jade paid little attention. He was annoyed with himself for the stupid accident. They were gambling everything on this run. If a ComUn ship heard about the city before they got there, they would be out of it. There was no way they could hope to win out against all the resources of the ComUn. No Free-shipper could. He frowned at the fire, wondering how far it was to the ruins and how they could make up the time he had cost them.

Heglit got up, moving into the darkness growing beyond the fire, and Jade watched until he returned, feeling there was something he should tell him. But it had slipped his mind.

"Jade." Lista stood near. "It is warm and there is a pool for bathing beyond the rocks."

He looked at her and warmth rose in him, loosening him. Then he thought of Heglit and hesitated, but only for a moment, before yielding to familiar temptation. Rising, he took her hand and they moved away into shadows. Beneath the big tree he drew her close and tasted her warm mouth, and a strong warm hand came against his back, saying other things.

Twin moons silvered the rocks and drifted restlessly over the surface of the pool. They pulled off clothes and the Benjor were quicker, laughing softly as they slipped into the water, shattering the restless moons. Jade grinned, lifting the silver chain from his neck. He put the necklace on the rock beside his boots and shook down his hair. Then, turning, he dove cleanly into the cool water.

The pool was deep, much deeper than he expected, the water clear as crystal, and sweet. They swam and dove and played, splashing diamonds of brilliant moonlight as they broke the surface. But their gaiety had a goal, their game became closer, more serious, touching delicious extremes of flesh warm and water cool, more and more silent as tension crested and they came together, drifting down beneath the crystal water glowing deep and blue under the brilliant moons, pleasure holding, sweeping aside every outer thing to be, opening to it in the wild clean blue, becoming motion becoming sensation, rushing, swept up yet controlling the cresting flood, all dark falling away in the glorious tide. Then multiplied abruptly, so it was joy and right that a dark and harder strength should catch him up, dive down and down the urgent flood, close, closer than mere pleasure, racing free and wild and closer than being allowed. Breathing in the crackling vivid blue, they soared, leaping from crest to crest on the rich victorious laughter he knew only here where violet flames raced over skin and hair, flashing toward the golden portal to a doneness that exploded all senses into nothing.

He lay on the soft moss a long time trying to breathe deep and slow, wondering if it was real, knowing it was and was not, knowing the other three were there, close, but not too close. Other three? *Heglit?* Against his will his eyes opened, head turned. The Rafalan sat dark and silent, wet skin looking more metal than flesh. The hard-planed face, supported on one hand, brooded on the still-rippling surface of the pool.

"It was the Star Web," Jade said, to himself, really, wanting to hear it. "You—"

"Hush, Jade." The dark face turned to him, eyes catching the cold blue light of the moons. "You nearly drowned."

Drowned? But those eyes killed the question and protest. His flesh and nerves knew what had happened, but the eyes looked at him with concern, and for a moment some other thing, deeper and less likely to be seen again. Jade wondered, over the sudden beating of his heart, if it was knowledge, and if so, knowledge of what?

Never mind. Dammit, he had been in the Star Web, had breathed in that blue storm, raced down the broad current sharing a familiar strength. I heard you laugh, Heglit. It was the Star Web.

The watching face bothered him and he closed his eyes. After a time he heard the Rafalan leave. He lay still until he heard Borget and Lista stirring. They came to him and he opened his eyes. There were soft Benjor words and touches, but they were subdued, overcome with some knowledge they would not discuss. When they were a little drier they pulled on clothes and returned to the dying fire, and Heglit lay already asleep. Or seemed to.

Dawn came gray, with a wind that scurried up around the rocks, raising dust clouds. They ate quickly and prepared to leave. Heglit thought they could reach the place spotted from the ship by the end of the day. With luck.

The path led up from the grove of trees into a jumble of great jagged rocks, difficult walking, but offering some protection from the wind. Jade led the way with Lista at his side, and he marveled at her quick grace. She smiled when he looked at her, and that was good too. He turned once and looked back and down, saw Borget and Heglit, climbing easily, and below them the restless shadows of the trees. Further, small with distance, was the valley where the ship rested. A long way down. And there was still a long way to the top.

The path curved out of the rocks and the wind tugged at them as they climbed, then they were back in shelter, looking through a narrow passage that turned sharply between rocks so close he had to turn sideways. One step. He reached for Lista's hand, took another step, and there was nothing. He yelled, and instinct tightened his grip on her, pulling her forward. He fell on soft warm grass, and she fell on top of him.

Grass. No wind. It's happened again.

He closed his eyes and remembered climbing, remembered, and remembered that if he opened his eyes he would remember something else. I should be scared, he thought, but this is right. This is the way it should be. He just wasn't sure why.

Lista's laughing mouth touched his.

"Come, Jade." Heglit's voice, but somehow different. "This is no time for pleasure games."

"Fell down, us," Lista laughed, moving finally so he could get up.

"Heglit," Jade said, not opening his eyes. "Where are we?"

"Half a day away." The strong hand caught his and pulled him up. "Longer if you keep lying down."

Something in the voice jarred him. His eyes snapped open. "The rocks—"

"Rocks?" Teeth flashed white as Heglit smiled, and fear turned Jade to stone. "There are no rocks here."

"Not here." Lips stiff, he stared at that face and his belly felt loose and cold. "Stop it."

"Jade—"

"Stop it!"

"Stop what? Talk sense, Jade?" But he did stop smiling. He frowned.

Lost, fighting to remember, Jade reached to his chest for the familiar (if now unreasonable) comfort of the—

It wasn't there!

"It's gone!" He turned wildly, staring at the flat forested land. "Heglit, I've got to go back."

"Back where?"

Where? Where had he last had the stone? The pool. "Down the mountain. I left it there—"

"Jade." There was sharpness in the voice. "What's gone? What did you leave?"

"The stone!" But how could he get back? How had they gotten here?

"The stone." Heglit laughed and Jade felt panic crawl up his back. He shivered. Heglit opened the neck of his dark blouse. "You gave it to me to keep for you when you bathed last night. We both forgot." He slipped the chain off over his head and the crystal flashed pale blue sparks in the sunlight.

Not knowing why, Jade felt almost faint with relief as Heglit placed the chain over his head (except, he thought in some deep place inside, Heglit would have handed it to him).

"We can reach the city by nightfall," Heglit decided, adjusting his pack. Looking at Jade a moment, he asked if he was all right. Jade nodded and turned away, the reasons for his peculiar feelings fading as the four walked through the sun-dappled forest. He didn't really remember giving the necklace to Dariel, but he was glad he had. More than once in their friendship, Dariel had helped him out. There was a time in some joyhouse or other, he had bet on a contest of some kind. There had been trouble— He frowned, trying to recall exactly what had happened. All he could remember clearly was Dariel being there and warm companionship.

It was a pleasant day, but something lurked behind it and Jade was increasingly nervous, watching Dariel, expecting something. He clasped the stone through his tunic and felt some small measure of comfort.

"Tas will melt down when we register this claim," Dariel said, laughing his rich strong laugh. And Jade's skin shivered along his shoulders and spine. He felt sick and wondered if he was . . .

The forest shimmered, flashed into aching brilliance. "You cannot stop here, Jade," Borget said, shaking him lightly.

"What?" Stupidly, shuddering in the fierce wind, blinking against the bits of ice driving into his face. Borget, shrouded in dark fur, looked worried. And there were two dark forms, moving away in the white madness.

"Jade, come. It is warm down the mountain."

He nodded, deafened more by the howling inside his head than the storm outside.

They had been walking in warm woods. He knew that. But he remembered climbing through the icy snow, losing sight of the ice river that held the ruins of the old city—

This is not real.

His body ached, and he moved beside Borget, head down, feeling the energy leak out of him. They needed shelter, warmth, food.

Did they remember?

No. He was certain they did not. So why did he? Or was he remembering? Maybe the warm sunlit forest was a dream in which to escape this numbing cold. We could die here, he thought, and was scared again.

"How does he know where to go?" He had to shout to be heard over the wind. Borget shook his head. His eyes were dark-circled, mouth drawn down with pain. The Benjor were not meant for this land, Jade thought. Lista. What must it be like for her?

He tried to move faster, to catch up with Heglit, but he was not so strong as the Rafalan. It was hard. He was panting and dizzy when he finally came close enough to touch the fur-clad arm.

"Heglit, where are we going?"

"To the city." But it was not Heglit who looked at him, not Heglit who was leading them. He opened his mouth to say so, then shook his head against sudden confusion.

"It's ice up there. We must go down."

"We're almost there."

"No!" Shouting up at the dark face he saw impatience and anger there, and shivered against something more than the cold. Heglit did not argue. Ever. "We go down. Now."

He turned from the angry face to Lista, felt a strong hand, hurting even through the furs—

And turned, blinking in the lurid red light, hot and panting.

"There must be shade somewhere," he complained.

Hearing himself, he struggled to embrace this new area of experience. Lista's hand slipped from his grasp.

"Rest, us." Borget's voice was hoarse, like pain, pulling Jade's eyes from Heglit.

"Rest. Yes. We can't go any further."

"The city, Jade." Heglit's voice was strong. Heglit was strong, standing straight, hands on hips; he seemed to tower against the blood-red sky. "We must find it, Jade. I am stronger. I will help."

"No." He closed his eyes. This was insanity. The last time he was in a desert he had been alone. Last time, last time. Last—

Stop it, he ordered himself, hiding in the hand-made dark. Last time. Memory seeped up, cool blue; ice, forest, mountain . . . The changes were coming faster. That meant something. Maybe. But the last. And this—

Unasked, he remembered a day and a night on this red world. The reason, the search—

Not true. Or, not truer than the others. Except now they were exhausted and out of water. Danger. And the time before. Not danger like being chased or being too slow. Danger from the place itself. That was wrong. It didn't fit.

In here in the dark he could almost see it all, the patterns, the layers of memory . . . What was different? Was the wrong in him? Ask Heglit, he thought, yearning for the clear cool Rafalan logic.

He opened his eyes. Heglit was bending toward him, reaching for his hand. Instinct made him accept the help.

"Which way?" He felt lightheaded. Heglit looked at him a moment, then pointed. West. He kept hold of the strong hand and began to walk. A few hours. That was all. Then they could rest. The sand burned his feet and he thought of baDant juice.

"Thirsty," he said through burning lips.

"There is no water." Cool firm voice. But wrong. Borget had some water. He turned, pulling against the hand, and looked back across the wide empty space. Borget and Lista. Gone. He almost remembered they hadn't come here, that they—

No!

Four. He had chosen. That was one true thing. All together. Forgetting he held the dark hand, he started back.

"Jade."

"Come on, dammit! I won't leave them."

"Leave who?"

Before he could answer that, he slipped, fell heavily. Water rushed into his nose and he splashed wildly, choking.

Water?

"Don't like water, them," Borget said quietly.

Jade wiped his eyes and studied the dark shapes ranged along the banks of the river. They looked like rocks, irregular shapes, all sizes, some even sporting patches of moss and lichen. But they moved with intention, guarding the pass that led to the city.

"Are they alive?" he asked.

"They might as well be," Dariel answered dryly when Borget hesitated.

"Living, them," Lista said. "Killing and eating."

And Jade remembered the small furry creatures, looking bipedal, out on the plains, racing in confused panic from the rocks.

That didn't happen. We just got here. In spite of memory, he knew that.

264

"We could go upstream, around them," Dariel suggested. "Come, while it's still light."

It wasn't easy to walk over the smooth wet stones, and soon everyone but Dariel had fallen. The water deepened as the banks rose, and the current grew stronger.

"Watch your step," Dariel warned, reaching out a hand.

Jade looked down, saw the hairline crack appear in the glass-like rock. He moved quickly before it could grow wide enough for the wiry tendril to lash out. He'd been too slow once and his leg still ached dully. If it hadn't been for Dariel's blade—

"Plant or animal?" he asked, watching the ground.

"Both, I think. The theory is that it's just one thing living under the rock. Carnivorous. The crust was built by it. It's a trap for the animals that need to get to the water."

The only water in the area was a spring in the pass ahead. It was also the only way to the old road. Another crack appeared and Jade leapt away, following Dariel closely. The edge of the crust was far ahead and he wished his leg would stop hurting. He threw a quick look back and felt vague trouble. There was nothing there, and he knew it. But he felt there should be. He was sure that if he could just stay still for a minute he would remember what. He shouldn't have let Dariel talk him into crossing the glass. They could have gone through the hills, even if it took longer.

Why had he followed? He was supposed to choose the way. The thought came so sharp he paused to look at the tall figure—

"Jade—"

They weren't doing this right.

"Jade!" Dariel called, turning, starting back for him. Jade heard the glass crack near him but he dared not look or move or he would forget.

"No. I can't follow you."

"You did." Dariel laughed, and the sound grew, blotting out sky and glass and sound. Rushing like a giant wind, the laugh erased everything. The world dissolved and he fell miles, spinning aimlessly, away and away from everything.

26

Black. Inside and out. And now what? It felt like a long
time before he began to think, and now there was plenty
of time. Nothing but time.

How had he got here, wherever he was? He worried
that around a while and found a small kernel of hurt and
betrayal identifying a certain memory as Dariel. He
did it, he thought. He put me here.

Answering that satisfied for a day or two. Then he
started wondering why. Shards of memory lay scattered
around him and he began to pick them up one at a
time, looking at them. A slow pattern started to form.
They had been on a Traveler path. Fine. He could
remember that. And the reason. To find TreAsh. He
would have smiled if he could have found his mouth.
The city was allegory. Like the whole path. All the
journeys they might have had on worlds they knew.

The changes?

That was harder. Maybe something in them, or the
nature of the path. Like breakout gates. He worked on
that and wasn't satisfied. Something didn't fit. The jump
to Solqar. Alone. He was not to be alone.

And the way the changes started to come so quickly
after the mountain.

When he started following Heglit.

No. Dariel.

From danger to danger.

But Dariel was Heglit.

He looked at that bit of fact a long time, wondering
what it meant. Why would Dariel (or Heglit) take the
lead? When had he?

After the pool. After they— He jumped that thought,
found one that related. When he had left the jewel and
Heglit found it. Then he had become Dariel. And from

then on he had tried to separate them from the Benjor. But why would he want to do that?

Because he wasn't Heglit.

The truth of that finally shocked all the bits and pieces together. I lost Heglit first. When I lost the crystal. That's why he laughed when he gave it back. It wasn't Heglit or Dariel. It was AzlurEor. He found us. All the changes after that were his doing. Keeping to the pattern just enough to fool me. To— What?

To get me here. Lost. Not even real anymore.

No. I am. I can feel myself knowing that. I am. I have the jewel. He knew he had it even if he couldn't touch or see it. He wondered why AzlurEor had given it back. Probably to keep the Traveler from knowing what was happening.

But where was he?

There were no clues. There was nothing. Just thinking. It took him a while to decide that was enough to decide, not to accept what seemed to be real. He started looking inside, seeking clues, examining thoughts and memories. And after a little he knew he had a body. He could feel the distant mild discomfort of being. That calmed more than anything. He knew he was real.

It took time and concentration to make the arm move, to slide the hand up over a chest he knew was his (he could feel the hand), but it was a long way from where his knowing was. Finally he felt the jewel in its decorative setting. A thread to Vril-Atalba. Did that mean they knew what was happening? No, he decided. They said they wouldn't know, that he would be safer that way.

He would have laughed at that some other time. Now he just wanted to get back to himself, to Heglit and Borget and Lista. And he was very sure he would have to do that himself. Somehow.

It was too big. The black was too pervasive (or too empty). He didn't know enough. There must be a logic to this, a method. But he didn't know it. He just hung there, helpless, wondering where they were, knowing they must still be on the path, wondering if they knew he was gone.

Or had AzlurEor become him?

That idea appeared with all the force of conviction. And he got too mad to be scared. Mad enough to kill.

Mad enough finally to begin to think. And he began to understand. No wonder he felt so far away from himself. He was locked up in his own head. He wasn't over there someplace lightyears away. He was all around himself. *And he wanted out.*

I have eyes, he thought. I can see. He reached for the function, becoming aware of his face, the bone and flesh fact of it, feeling himself breathe— relief poured strength into his effort. He was right. The force binding him in gave way grudgingly, but he was master here. He was him and he knew himself better than anyone.

Shaking with strain, he sat still, exploring every area of self, every physical sense, every kind of thought and memory. He was back. He lifted his eyes and looked around at the pleasant little glade. He was really alone. He did not recognize the place, but he thought he was still on the Traveler path.

There was a spring near, and he drank cool water, feeling more tired than he could remember. He sat on soft grass and tried to force himself to think. He (as AzlurEor) had left the others, but stayed on the path, he thought. AzlurEor wanted to reach TreAsh. At least that made some kind of sense. So, how could he get back? He must have made several changes since the fall in the river. And if they had gone on they would have made changes too.

He shook down his hair, massaging his scalp with nervous fingers. Glis, he was tired—

Movement snapped his eyes open. "Lista?"

But the lovely female figure standing back in the shadows was not Lista. Pale green, she gleamed softly. And he knew her. She had come to him before. Heart pounding, he watched her, and she did not move until the light faded. Then she stirred, moving on bare delicate feet to come and kneel before him. He did not move, afraid she would vanish.

"Jadriel Younger." Her voice was like sweet wind in tall grass, a thing of feel more than sound. "The father sends me to companion and guide you."

The father? "ChatkarJ'Mur?"

She nodded and reached cool hands to lay against his face. "Rest safe."

He did not intend to sleep, but he did, a sweet drifting

268

peace that restored him to himself. He woke in late moonlight and she was there. There was something he wanted to ask, but she touched his lips and motioned him to rise and follow her. Not at all certain, he did as she bid. And in some ways it was his strangest journey.

Her hand rested cool in his and he stepped from moonlit grass to harsh rock, and in a few steps to a world of howling wind. Another few steps and a bright blue sun in a purple sky lit a world of gracefully swirling semisolid forms. He watched her and she neither looked at nor noticed the changes until they came to a dark forest and the scent of a summer night. There was a gleam of what could have been a fire through the trees to the north. She gestured toward it and took her hand from his.

"Wait. Your name—"

"Daughter." She did not smile.

"How did you—?"

She listened gravely, and he thought she wasn't listening only to him. Then she spoke. "Father says to the man, you are not lived long enough to know the Web ways, but you may learn them as you will. AzlurEor is an otherness of no danger to the father's being. Strength and long life, Speaker-seed."

She slid back into the shadows and was gone, leaving Jade to puzzle over the cryptic message. How had ChatkarJ'Mur found him? And why? And maybe that was a thing TreAsh could tell him. He turned toward the red glow.

The fire had burned down to a bed of coals casting up a red glow. Heglit sat beside it, arms clasped about his knees. Two dark forms lay nearby in shadow. Jade approached quietly, but before he could speak Heglit turned toward him.

"Jade?" He rose to his feet in one smooth motion as Jade came into the light.

"It's me, Heglit." He held out his hands and felt the familiar firm grip, wondering for one brief second if he dared trust this reality.

"We could not find you."

It was Heglit. "I got off the path."

"AzlurEor?"

"You remember?" And remembering that he also re-

269

membered, he wondered why he should be surprised.

"When I found this." Heglit reached into his blouse and drew out the necklace.

"But—" Jade's hand jumped to his chest. The stone was not there. "But you already gave it to me—"

"No." He placed the jewel in Jade's right hand and drew him toward the dying fire. They sat down and there was hot Santo tea, and Jade was glad for the familiar taste.

"We came through two places thinking we followed you," Heglit said. "Then we knew we had to wait. There is more mystery here than I expected."

Jade agreed. The clarity of Rafalspeak felt good in his mouth and ears. "Borget and Lista?"

"All right." Heglit glanced toward them. "They have been afraid for you. Put the jewel on."

He slipped the chain over his head. "AzlurEor became me. The changes came so fast. And I thought you—" He shook his head. "ChatkarJ'Mur helped me find you again."

Heglit glanced at him and said nothing.

"Is there a city we're supposed to find here?"

"No."

"Then how—?"

"The Benjor say they know where the gates are. Maybe it's a way of wanting. Probably why you chose them to come with us. They knew when we got here. We have to go on, the path does not go back."

Jade nodded, knowing that, and they sat together watching the fire die, hearing the forest wake about them with the approach of dawn.

"Free-shippers, us," Jade said suddenly, voice small in the dark. He felt Heglit stir beside him and thought he would comment on the lowspeak, but he didn't say anything.

"It's a long time since then. Like I can hardly remember," he continued after a little, in highspeak, maybe explaining.

"Not so long," Heglit said finally.

The Benjor were awake before dawn, relieved and glad for Jade's return, looking thoughtful when he told them of his escape and the guide who brought him to the forest.

"ChatkarJ'Mur held the crystal. He is wise in the

270

knowing way, so it could have a sharing with him," Borget suggested, as they moved away from the campsite, walking north. Jade accepted that explanation for lack of a better one. He didn't particularly care. He was more interested in the Benjor's new ability to sense the time and place of the changes, those instantaneous skips into other places.

Lista, hand resting in Jade's, tried to explain the knowledge of the gates. It was, she said, similar to the inside feeling of the Star Web gates, but more subtle. One had to reach out and explore for them. She thought he might be able to find them himself with a little effort, but he doubted it. He had come through many changes with the lovely guide from Grio and he had felt nothing. But then he didn't have the talent born into the Benjor and the life of Grio.

They fell silent as the day ripened. It was a good land for walking, pleasant with clear light and scattered birdsong. They left the forest for a grassy hill dotted with rocks and flowers, the sun pleasantly warm along their left sides. Borget was slightly ahead, leading, by silent agreement, over the hill and down into a shallow valley where a clear stream tumbled over smooth stones.

"Past the fall," Borget said suddenly. "The change is."

"What fall?" Jade asked. No one answered and he shrugged, adjusting his pack, and returning to his solitary thoughts about AzlurEor. At least he supposed it had been AzlurEor. He had touched nothing he could identify. But looking back, he was sure he could trace the pattern of interference. Something must have changed when he got himself back, something basic to the nature of this journey, or the Traveler wouldn't have changed the path enough to let them remember.

They rested by the stream at the edge of the meadow, eating dry wafers and drinking cool water.

"You know what's next? Through the gate?" Jade asked, eyes flashing yellow as he looked up toward the distant fall visible through the trees.

Borget shook his head. "The gate only."

Jade guessed that was better than nothing, and hoped it was as easy a place as this.

They stepped from water spray and high sun to cool red-gold sunset and the strong voice of a sea breaking

271

below the cliff on which they walked. The breeze brought a taste of salt Jade had known and relished on a dozen worlds. It was beautiful.

He glanced at Heglit, who said nothing, only looked around, seeing the place. The Benjor moved up the path and Jade started after them, but Heglit hesitated, looking from Borget to Jade, seemed about to say something, then changed his mind and followed, face burnished bronze in the fading light, mouth set and thoughtful.

They walked and rested and walked and stepped into other places and continued until Jade called a halt. They were in another low basin surrounded by high cliffs jutting up into a star-rich sky. Only Heglit did not look ready to drop from exhaustion. They had to stop and sleep.

"The gate is a little beyond the water," Borget protested gently. "It might be the last."

The last. Muscles jumped in Jade's thighs. The last. Or maybe there were hundreds more. He looked at Heglit who was looking at Borget, frowning slightly.

"You would speak?" he asked in quiet Rafalspeak.

Heglit hesitated. "Why has AzlurEor stopped?"

"I have the same question. And no answer." As quietly, feeling trouble swell up beneath his fatigue.

"Jade, I do not believe we will get to TreAsh this way."

"Evidence."

"I have none. Only you can tell if this is right."

Jade looked at him sharply, but the large bright moon had risen, and the black eyes were hidden in dark shadow. "I cannot, Heglit. Not now. I can only believe."

The shadow masked face nodded.

After a moment Jade turned back to Borget. "One last gate, then, if it is close, before we rest."

Lista sighed softly and Jade smiled as he gave her a hand up. She smiled back tiredly.

They followed Borget's lean figure through silver air and dew that sparkled in delicate flashes as they brushed through tall grass making their way to the shadow of the enclosing walls. There was a gleam of silver through shadow. A spring, Jade guessed, as they moved toward it. He glanced at Heglit's impassive face and felt worry tighten him. You would know, he had said. And he felt something was wrong. But what? Or am I missing something obvious?

He watched Borget pick a way across a small stream and felt on the edge of knowing something important, but weariness dragged at his thoughts. Something obvious. But they were doing what they had done since this damned journey started, walking and changing from place to place.

Light flashed against his eyes from the right and he jerked his head around, heart beating. The spring. The moon had risen enough to strike full on the gossamer stream sheeting over the smooth rock. Beautiful, he thought automatically, pale blue-silver, glowing like— It pulled his mind like his eyes, the urge to move toward it stronger even than weariness. Peace and rushing blue, free and—

Heglit's hand on his shoulder shocked him awake.

"It's like the pool," Jade said stupidly.

"The pool?"

"Yes. The one we—" He stopped, struck dumb by the insane truth. Once they had traveled another path. The right path?

"Borget!" His voice rang back from the rock, and the Benjor stopped, turned and started back. "No gate," Jade said to himself. "No more gates."

"Jade." Heglit's voice was solid beside him.

"You were right. By the Rim, you were right. I do know the way. But we've been following him. That's what you meant." He was no longer tired. Just mad. "You all remembered, after I got back, away from him. But it's not all true."

"Jade. Talk sense."

"It doesn't make sense." He stared at the handsome Benjor face. "I know you. It won't happen again. No more." He shrugged off his pack, hardly aware of it, and started forward. Heglit's hand caught his arm.

"Jade, we do not understand—"

Both were caught unprepared as Borget attacked, hurling himself at the half-turned man still restrained by the Rafalan. A trained and knowing hand struck for the throat, attempting a fast decisive blow. It would have killed if it had landed as intended, but Rafalan reflexes are fast. Heglit shoved Jade to the side, and the hand

273

glanced off the bone below Jade's ear and was caught in an unbreakable grip. He struggled, but Heglit held him easily, trapping both hands, pulling them together behind the straining back before Jade could recover enough to get to his feet.

"AzlurEor?" Heglit asked the obvious.

Jade nodded, rubbing his neck. "Lista?"

She stood poised, alert. "He hid well, Lord Jade. But Borget is overshadowed now."

Even the familiar handsome face had changed as the ruse became known, and Jade felt cold and murderous. If Borget was harmed— he gritted his teeth, knowing there was little he could do to protect him. Unless—

The fall sparkled, catching his eye, making up his mind. "Link with me. Both of you." He grasped the pendant inside his shirt, willing himself to do it, reaching in/out for them. He did not really feel Lista, but Heglit— the shimmering water wavered, became a torrent that engulfed him as he released being and became doing. The jarring shock of superior power reached out, grabbed him up— They were in channel. And another thing was there also. They dared not travel the Web, not now with AzlurEor here. He knew the Web too well, he could use it. They had no choice. They attacked.

In the nowhere not-being place of the Star Web their brains created allegory to deal with unreality. Anchorless in the swift current, Jade felt a dark and knowing power pull him from the center to disharmonies of danger near the boundary of the Web. He resisted, and a bold strength drew him back to safety. Heglit. Together they dove through various currents, seeking the enemy, nearly missing it until a golden song of warning drew them together. A violent whiplike tongue of sound like angry horns crackled about them, slicing through the Web. Jade twisted away, dove clean through the coils of pain, glided up a rich harmony of bass and string, and with impetus from an agreement that felt like his, he fought the eddies and cross-currents, seeking a source, a point of wrongness that could not act here unless it was here. Blue deepened to purple, red-flashed, a tongue of black fire licked across his back and thighs and he wanted to curl up and run. But a stronger desire held him, helped him. He dodged, curved, darted through shrieking whips of hurt, until the banks of the Web were near enough to sear his skin.

His hair snapped along his body as he fought to maintain his position and safety, seeking, sliding helpless toward a vast black thunder threaded with red spikes of danger and destruction.

There! The knowing felt cleaner and more certain than himself. Lista. He laughed with Heglit's laugh of victory. There, nearly hidden in a twisting nest of red and black, drifted a small orb of brilliant green. He reached for it. Lightning scored his arm, rang like gongs against his sight. But he knew it now. He danced. Bracing himself with Heglit's strength and Lista's faith he lept forward, tasting black, drawing agony in with full hands. He clasped the green point. It bit like ice, sounded shrill and metallic like the taste of danger. He endured the pain, knowing victory, and felt the crystal cool against his chest. With a strength he could never match or master he drew back and cast the thing against the shouting edge of the channel. There was a roar like crying and death, a flash of purple and a single cry through a distance so great it scared him.

He opened his eyes and lay still until the moon hung steady in the glittering sky.

"Heglit?" He pushed himself up to look for the Rafalan. Heglit was on one knee, Borget lying lifeless on the ground before him. Jade made his body get up, travel far enough to bend down and search the pale face. "Borg?"

"His body lives," Heglit said. Jade didn't doubt him. But Borget, the real one? He touched the face numbly, felt Lista press close against his side, reaching to touch—

"Jade." The voice warmed him with relief. "I did not know."

"Nor did we," Heglit answered, and there was some gentleness in the voice.

"The other is gone," Lista said, touching her brother lightly.

"But not destroyed." Borget moved to sit up. "Mad him. And knowing our place."

That was a truth they had to deal with, and Jade knew it. Knew, too, they had only one option that made sense. And it was now or never.

"We have to use the Star Web."

"Yes. Before he returns," Heglit agreed.

There was no better time. Maybe no other time at all. Jade sat crosslegged on the grass, knowing they were watching, waiting for him. He could feel their attention like hands reaching to him.

He closed his eyes, reaching for memory of the blue current of the Star Web, felt it pulling at him, felt himself sink down, melting into the strong flow to be joined by the darker strength and richer joy. This was the way. This was where they had always been, soaring free and strong through the tumultuous harmony of the Web. He gave himself up to it, meeting curves and twists and eddies that trapped them playfully until strength and joy cast them free into a distance that had no meaning.

The gate gleamed gold and urgent, drawing them to a fine point, exquisitely sharp, stretching toward the final consummation of doing, being fun and necessity and delight. They burst through, done, complete, and drifted in a pure and perfect peace of stillness.

27

Distant words struck sound against Jade's dreams, waking him to confusion and knowing someone had been speaking near by. He saw enclosure and brief panic pulled him up on one elbow to see Heglit sitting on the edge of a near couch, himself just waking. They were in a large airy room. All four of them. The Benjor lay asleep on their own couches.

"Someone was here," he said to Heglit.

"I heard. I did not see them."

He didn't ask the obvious, wondering where they had gotten to this time. Pale light came through a curtained window, but he couldn't tell if it was dawn or dusk. He completed the process of rising and went to the Benjor.

"Someone brought us here," Heglit said behind him. But Jade wasn't sure he agreed. They had come to some pretty unlikely places without help in the last while or so.

A sound by the doorway pulled his head around, and he looked into eyes as yellow as his own. Shock held him frozen.

"Greeting." The man smiled slightly, but there was a guarded look about him. He spoke fedstan. Jade began to breathe again. For a minute he had thought the man was Barmalin Tas.

"Who are you?" he asked, feeling Heglit's look saying that was the wrong first question.

"Ruyalon Tas."

"Tas!" He whirled toward Heglit, whose face gave nothing, then turned back to the man. The yellow eyes danced, and Jade had the feeling he was being laughed at.

"How did we come here?" Heglit's cool voice took the laughing eyes away, asking the question that would give them the most information. But Ruyalon Tas wasn't playing the game.

"My question to you, wanderer. Your companions are waking. When you are ready, there are people waiting to talk with you." He showed them the washer and other facilities, including fresh clothing, and told them he would be back when they were ready. None of the four had much to say after he left them. The name the man gave was indictment enough as far as Jade was concerned.

True to his word, Ruyalon Tas returned by the time they finished dressing. It was time to go.

Not yet, Jade thought, feeling anger push against curiosity. But Heglit warned him with his eyes. Defeated, Jade shrugged and obeyed the man's gesture to leave the room. He didn't miss the veiled curiosity in their guide's (guard's) eyes as he walked past him. Yellow eyes. But Barmalin Tas had yellow eyes. And he had sons.

They walked through halls, roofed but unwalled, so the soft breeze brought them the scent of lush gardens and the great mountains in the near distance. But Jade still wasn't sure which end of the day it was.

There were steps of gleaming white stone going down into the garden, and a sound of water played with the solitary strand of melody some unseen player drew from a wind flute. More steps, wider, leading up through an arch, an open space, and people at the far end, so Jade did not really look at the room. People, standing together, talking, dressed in a wide variety of styles, from long loose robes to the tunic and skintights he himself preferred. He paused, uncertain, and suddenly Heglit's hand closed on his arm hard enough to hurt, his black eyes fixed on the group, leading Jade's to the central figure who turned to look at them. For a minute he thought his arm would break in the Rafalan's grip. Then he forgot it, stood transfixed by the one face he never thought to see.

Something was said by Ruyalon Tas. Jade didn't hear it, heard nothing beyond the peculiar roaring in his ears. This could not be. It was some trick of AzlurEor. But the stone burned cold against his chest, stirred by the slow hard beating of his heart. He shook off the weight of Heglit's hand and walked forward, reading question in the yellow eyes, saw the rather wide mouth open to say something never voiced. For now there was only this, the two of them and the question and the out-of-place memory of green and dark brown power and vastness that had once been a part of this, and a beginning to it.

Holding the unblinking yellow eyes, Jade clasped the silver chain, lifted it over his head, held it like shield or offering, as he took the final steps. The eyes wavered, dropped to the stone, leapt up, wider, to the lean face. And the lips opened finally to form words in a speak Jade had never heard except in the great memory of ChatkarJ'Mur. "Jade. My son."

Complete and perfect silence surrounded them and the golden eyes shimmered as Jade raised his hands, placed the chain about the waiting head. Falling on the other's chest, the stone flashed vivid fire, darkened to a rich deep blue, and there was nothing more to do.

For a time Jade knew only a strange anesthetic numbness, then the waiting hands reached out, drew him close, and it was the same, remembered, like warmth and dark green against his face, and the taste of salt.

The silence about them was broken by a muted gale of voices, but there was attention only on the doubly-familiar face, and Jade's first question brought a smile beyond the humor of it. And the answer that this was, indeed, Tre-Ash, freeing him to hear other voices, and finally to make introductions.

There was the sanity of the day's first meal, set looking over the garden, and only eight of them there, the four companions, Jadriel Sarn, Ruyalon Tas, and two golden-eyed dark-haired women. And there was time to watch Sarn and be watched by him, and to know that being watched by him was not too different from being watched by the Benjor. Jade could feel the bonds, secret and sensitive, and never touched before.

It was Heglit, still cool and watchful with his dark eyes giving nothing, who spoke first of Sarn's surprise.

"You did not expect us."

Sarn measured the curve of his glass with slow fingers. "We believed you would come. But only twenty-eight years have passed."

"It is three hundred and two stanyears since the Federation attack on TreAsh," Heglit said levelly.

The TreAshal looked at him through a long silence. "I have no explanation. We had planned on three hundred years to allow the Federation time to grow and solidify. It could be a function of our existence here."

"The Traveler knew," Jade remembered. "He told me to give the stone to you."

Sarn looked down at the pendant, now a deep glowing blue in the early light. "It was made here, long ago. A sign, we thought, so the ones here would know you. Vril didn't say anything about the time span. They didn't tell us many of the things they knew. So we assumed—" He looked up at Jade.

"They seem to feel there is danger in explaining too much," Heglit observed.

"They learned that from AzlurEor." Ruyalon's voice pulled their attention. "They feel responsible for his actions in our galaxy. I see Vril told you of that. He's mostly the reason for this."

"For what happened to TreAsh?" Jade asked. "And what did happen? I mean, we know about the Traveler war and the attack on TreAsh. But how does AzlurEor come into it? Vril said, I think, that he was a danger to the Star Web. But he didn't explain."

"It gets a little complicated. There's time to get into it. There are so many things to show and explain, and so many questions to ask. But first things first." Ruyalon pressed a napkin to his lips and stood. "We weren't expecting company for some two and three-quarters centuries yet. I imagine they could use me at the Academy."

He offered to show Heglit and the Benjor around, leaving Jade and Sarn together.

"I'm not sure I believe this," Jade said self-consciously as they moved into the house that was his father's.

"Believe?"

"Any of it. A whole world just gone, but not gone. There's so much that isn't known all through the ComUn. I mean about the Travelers and TreAsh and AzlurEor."

"Knowing things beyond the obvious usually has little value for most."

"But they're like— like I was, being blind and deaf. It was so far beyond what I knew could be. I didn't believe, even after Heglit had most of it."

"He's a good friend."

280

Jade grinned wryly. "Cold him, and distant. Unless he's being Dariel."

Sarn laughed aloud, a good strong sound. "The Rafalans. They wouldn't have changed much in three centuries. So well disciplined on the outside. Even to the use of their names. Self name, common name, blood name. D'you know the whole of it?"

"Dariel Heglit D'Othiel."

"D'Othiel? I knew his— Couldn't have been father, someone further back. He was a friend, too. Interesting coincidence."

"He put the pieces together. The ones we had. I hadn't even really heard of TreAsh until a few months ago. Then I went to Grio. The tree—"

"Chat. Old World-Seeder." Sarn nodded, smiling. "I met him first in my twelfth year. When I learned to speak with him we became friends. He's wise. And he has ways of knowing we may never discover entirely."

"And mysteries." Jade told him of the one called daughter.

Sarn nodded again, eyes focusing on memory, unexpectedly shared, so Jade knew he had met that one (or one like her) three times. Once at the beginning of this.

"I did not expect to see you again," Sarn said quietly, sharing a look and a sort of pain, speaking finally of what both were thinking. And Jade was again touched by a feeling outside himself.

"ChatkarJ'Mur kept his word," he said as quietly. "I know how it was for you that day."

"He gave you *that*?"

Jade nodded, struck finally by the fact of being here.

"You must have wondered why," Sarn said finally. "You should know from me before you meet the council."

"Know what?"

"I am, by birth and will of the people, ruler of TreAsh. Or such as we have here. I could not ask the people to do what I would not. There were other children suitable, having the qualities we and the Travelers decided necessary. But only you were a prince of TreAsh."

Prince of TreAsh. The words made strange echoes in his head. Prince of TreAsh. He stared at his father dumbly and thought of the last sleep on the Traveler ship, the talk with Heglit. I know what I am, he thought, joy-skinner, Linkman, chem-skipper, Free-shipper. Prince of TreAsh. He swallowed against a sudden laughter, then gave up. Prince! It was too much.

"Sorry," he managed, ashamed of his reaction. "It's just that, of all the things I have been and am, a prince—"

Sarn looked at him and smiled slightly. "Perhaps, Jade, your ideas of being a prince differ from ours."

There was no possible answer to that. He leaned against a window looking out on the garden and wondered what his companions would say when they knew.

"If Heglit knew who you were he knew this," Sarn said behind him, answering the unasked.

"He never said. He's like the Travelers sometimes, not saying all he knows." Turning back to the man, Jade saw a full-dimensional portrait on the table beside him. A lovely woman near his own age. Sarn noted his interest.

"Gloyin. Your mother," he said.

Mother. That was another one he hadn't thought about. "Does she know?"

"Know? Oh, I see. No. She died in the attack."

"Attack?"

"By the Federation."

"But I thought— I mean, you left, or whatever."

"We did. But it wasn't so simple as it sounds. We could not leave until it was within a certain area of probability that we would no longer exist here. Or there, I should say. Vril and the others of his kind helped as they could, but the doing had to be ours. We had to synch with the attack as closely as possible. We were four seconds too late. Not long, but long enough." The slow voice carved traces of memory Jade couldn't avoid.

"The Traveler didn't say anything about this."

"I don't know how much they knew of those last moments. They couldn't follow, of course. But in that last instant every major city on the planet came under attack. Nearly seventy percent of the people gone. Gloyin was in Thens as acting head of the council in my absence. Our parents, your sisters and brother— All lost."

"But you—"

"I couldn't return in time. I was taken by the Federation off Rafal."

"Right. I heard that from Heglit. But how did you—?"

282

"That I don't know. I should have been left behind like Duran Tas and his family in Centra. I remember being on the Federation ship, under guard. Then I woke up here, alone, remembering nothing."

A small bell sounded, interrupting them. Sarn went to a desk Jade hadn't noticed, did something to a small screen, and a picture of Ruyalon Tas appeared. There was a mutter of conversation Jade could not hear.

"They want me at the Academy. Your arrival here has created a lot of activity. Come along, your friends are already there."

The town was random and widespread, the low buildings separated by vivid gardens and stands of tall trees. It was the political and scientific center of TreAsh, and it was all open to them. Ruyalon Tas offered to act as guide while Sarn was occupied, and he took them through the area in a quiet vehicle that reminded Jade of the ground car on Iron.

Beyond a low hill and a large stand of timber the pastoral beauty ended in the ruins of a once-large city. Work was going on here even now. Salvaging and cleaning up, Tas said. It was a sobering sight, though he was familiar with it. He remembered the day of the attack and told them something of it.

"It nearly succeeded, but we had enough faith, enough will to think we could do the impossible. We moved the world to where they couldn't reach it."

"To where?" Jade asked. "Where are we, really?"

Ruyalon looked around at the sky, the sun, the land, then he grinned. "Sort of between things, I guess."

Which explained nothing. "And we were supposed to come here, to help you get back to TreAsh Sector."

"This is TreAsh Sector," Heglit said, reminding Jade that the others had been at the Academy while he spoke with Sarn, and Heglit had said he visited the observatory.

"But—"

"But not really," Ruyalon said. "And we'll have to start becoming reality again before long."

"Or?"

"Or the other possibility becomes the dominant reality."

The possibility that TreAsh had been destroyed.

"The four of us. I don't see how we could make any difference."

"That gets a little complicated. Let's get Tar Bulyn to show you what we're talking about."

Bulyn, a tall thin man looking even taller and thinner in his loose robes, met them back at the Academy near Sarn's house. A teacher, Jade thought, more serious than either Sarn or Tas. He ushered them into a large room containing a number of chairs, arranged about a large screen flanked by two smaller ones and an impressive array of hardware. The Logic Construct, he said.

"Your question about our location was the same we asked that day," he told Jade. "We continued to ask it for some years."

The general Link effort had been successful, he explained. At least the attack had ceased immediately. But nothing else changed. The sun still shone, the weather was the same, and the seasons, the night sky exactly as before. Once the shock of the attack faded, the scientists began looking for explanations. Ships were sent up. They lifted, moved out beyond the orbit of the satellite, and vanished. There was confusion and some fear, but it was finally accepted that the difficulty was with their relation to the Star Web. The Web existed normally for some distance, then ended. Or was twisted in a way that made passage through it impossible.

Jade thought of the confusion of the Web in TreAsh Sector and looked at Heglit, knowing he was thinking the same thing.

TreAsh knew, of course, that they had salvaged a probable existence for themselves by vanishing from the time and place of the Federation attack. But they were obviously someplace, and wanted to know where. Work was begun on the computer that would take every bit of information known and build a visual construct of their situation.

"When we had given it everything, even unrelated data, we asked the logical question. This was the answer."

Bulyn turned to the console beside him, and the room darkened as the screen lit up. "The primary information on the system is from our own firsthand experience." His voice stirred the shadows as images appeared on the screen, a distant look at TreAsh Sector familiar to them from their own navicomp information, but incomparably more detailed. Each planetary orbit was defined by a pale line in a relationship that gave good dimensional effect. Each major constellation was named and outlined for a moment. Then the travel effect, passing over the outer worlds, scanning, in past the giants, the Rock Belt, the red world. Movement stopped, held on a second rock belt, great hunks of debris flashing a hundred minor eclipses. A pale green label appeared across the bottom of the screen. Probability A-1.

The screen blanked, made the run by the red world again, homed on the glorious sapphire world of cloud and water and russet land mass, with the distant tan and dun cresent of its moon. A second label flashed. Probability A-2. Jade leaned forward, intent on the screen as Bulyn posed the logical question.

"Based on all the information available, what is the position of TreAsh?"

The image wavered, lines and forms scattered, coalesced. The beautiful world, gone pale and ghostly with the tumbling debris visible through it. Double exposure.

"Which probability is most likely?"

"Neither." The perfectly modulated compvoice expressed mild interest.

"Which probability is least likely?" Bulyn persisted.

"Both."

"That is a paradox," Bulyn pointed out.

"Yes."

"Can the paradox be resolved?"

"It is self-resolving," the computer assured them. "One existence will become more probable through duration and establish an overriding acceptance of being."

"Which?"

"Probability listed A-1."

"What will determine that establishment?"

"The force that binds the field called Star Web. There is insufficient data at present to analyse the components of that field."

The screen blanked, erasing the ghostly double exposure as the lights came up.

"And that," Bulyn told them, "is our position to date. Or up to yesterday."

28

Sort of between things, like Ruyalon Tas said, Jade
thought. They were back out in the warm sun, and he
was glad for the blue sky after the dark of the room.
Heglit stayed back to talk with Tar Bulyn and the
Benjor walked out into the garden. For a while Jade
held back, but there was nothing he could add to the
technical discussion developing behind him, so he went
down to join the Benjor, walking over the cool grass
away from the others, feeling Lista's slender waist beneath his arm.

"You feel good on this world, prince and shipmaster,"
Borget said in the soft song of Benjorspeak.

"Yes. It has a feel to it, a beauty like no other world."

"Your flesh is of it, Jade. It is home here." Borget
did not smile now. "Should it come to an end, it will
be a pain to you, and not only for the people lost."

"And maybe there's nothing I can do to prevent it."
Jade dropped down on the grass, shaking loose his hair,
and lying back so the sun was a warm weight pressing
face and chest. The Benjor sat on either side of him and
he touched them with reaching hands. "It seems written
somewhere that I have to try to do this thing."

Borget took his left hand, turned it palm up in his,
bending to look into it. "Not you alone, Jade. We are
bound to it through you and because of Grio."

Jade closed his eyes against the vivid blue of the
sky and thought maybe Borget wrote something lightly
across his palm with his finger, then rubbed it away.
And Lista did the same with his right, warming him,
giving him reality as a bond between them. He drifted,
feeling the bigness of the sky over him, the softness of
the ground, the earth. He imagined he could feel down
to incredible depths, and out, surrounding the vast

286

roundness of the planet, aware instantly of all or any of its parts, the hidden mineral, the compressed and stable core, the breathing seas and deep-rooted mountains. TreAsh. Alive and real.

"Jade." Soft voice reeling him in, pulling him back into his man-skin, the place where his eyes were. "Jade," Borget said again. "Sarn is seeking you."

"Yes. I was dreaming. I—" He saw it in their eyes. "You know."

"We know."

"You didn't—" Thinking they might have somehow.

"No." They smiled. "It was a thing of your flesh, a coming together again. A goodness."

Sarn was waiting with Heglit when Jade and the Benjor joined them, and Heglit looked thoughtful.

"The Traveler said the beginning of it was the Star Web, the thing that TreAsh knew and taught Rafal before the beginning of the Federation," Heglit said to Sarn. "The nature of the Star Web. They didn't explain. But the Web is bound up with returning TreAsh and with all that has happened to us."

"The Star Web." Sarn nodded. "We don't yet know as much as the Travelers, but we've been working on theories. Some we got from them, some are extrapolation, logic, or just plain hunch. But it seems the Web is both the cause of our problem and, maybe, our salvation." He led them toward another building, or another part of the same one; Jade couldn't tell.

"When we worked with Rafal to learn how to use the Web, we were only interested in use and exploration," he told them. Only after the arrival of the Travelers had they begun to think in terms of nature and philosophy. From the Travelers came the first hints that the Web did not exist of itself, that it became a fact as it was discovered, which was to say its development caused its discovery. Confusing.

But, for the sake of argument, say the Star Web was created, or brought into being, by the same force that stimulated the development of intelligent life and sentience on a world. As life developed, multiplied, became aware of itself, the threads of the Web were woven, becoming a palpable force when the number of sentient beings expanded awareness and communication to all its members, becoming in essence a planetary unit of self-aware-ness. Almost inevitably, this planetary consciousness turned outward, first with curiosity, then with hope, reaching toward other worlds. The desire to know began to grow from the mother world to sister worlds, became a self-concept embracing an entire stellar system.

When the system itself became familiar territory, and so a larger unit of self-knowledge, curiosity expanded, reaching out to other stars, and the hope and curiosity of other races. This cast the first thread of the Star Web. With luck another race would be doing the same thing, and the two lines of curiosity-hope-desire formed a bond, stimulated occasionally by more mechanical signalling methods.

The first strand of the Web would be the hardest to establish; also the straightest, forming the ultra chan-nels. Once contact was made, a long-term process de-veloping on the lowest psychic levels first, it became easier and easier to believe in the process, whatever conscious analysis was used.

"We've had twenty-eight years to restudy the Star Web in the light of what we learned from the Travelers, though we are cut off from it," Sarn said. "This is the visual result. The map." He touched a control of some sort, and the empty room was plunged into total dark-ness. With shocking suddenness a bold amber line raced across the darkness near the ceiling, where it hung, glow-ing and stationary. "The channel from TreAsh to Rafal. The first."

The line brightened, other lines sprang out. Two. Then four, then dozens, darting from point to point, sometimes forming clusters, sometimes long solitary lines branching at one end, some thick and strong, some deli-cate, racing to lace the darkness until the pattern glowed a radiant complexity of geometric perfection, bound and supported by the heavy amber strands that were the ultra channels. It was a breathtaking display, and they looked around at it, bathed in the amber light, turning slowly to see all the design. And each felt a vague and haunting familiarity, some memory that could not quite be reached. Glancing at Heglit, Jade saw the look of puzzlement on the gold-brushed face.

"That's another thing we don't understand." Sarn's

soft voice did little to disturb the atmosphere. "From the time the map was done we have all felt that touch of recognition. It reminds, but no one knows of what."

"You touch feelings like the Benjor," Heglit said, still looking at the map, nailing down the particulars of the moment automatically. Jade didn't know if he said it to have it admitted or because it meant something else, but Sarn wasn't disturbed.

"To a degree. We think maybe all Linkmen and potential Linkers can. Or maybe the Linking itself creates a sensitivity."

"And maybe a reason why so many Clates lose the ability after a while," Heglit mused, almost to himself. Then he changed the subject abruptly. "The Travelers say AzlurEor is a danger to the Star Web. How could a thing like this be destroyed?"

"By breaking a strand. Or more than one. Say several ships are lost on the standard run from C'Erit to TaLur in quick succession. Word would get out, a doubt would be created. Faith in the Web would diminish, draining energy away. Fear would kill the Web more quickly than faith built it."

Logical answer. But Heglit pointed out that his people had come into Rafal Sector long before the Star Web was used. Curiosity and hope would maintain contact between worlds.

"They came in sleeper ships," Sarn reminded. Too slow for commerce. There would be no outreach except for reasons of conquest or exile. Worlds, cut off suddenly from intercourse with other worlds, would turn in on themselves, build in and use up their resources and energy, and finally cease. Life would go out of the galaxy.

"It has happened in other places, the Travelers say."

"Then the Star Web and intelligent life are interdependent," Heglit said, not quite making a question of it.

"Apparently." With a touch, the map collapsed in on itself and was gone.

"There are more channels on your map than were in use before the Traveler War," Heglit observed as they came out of the dark into mellow sunset, surprised to find the day ending.

"Based on trends," Sarn explained. "Is it fairly accurate?"

"Yes." Nothing more than that, but Sarn looked pleased. It was time for a meal, he said, and there would be a number of guests at the house, scientists, for the most part, willing to ask and answer questions.

It was a pleasant meal with good food and talk and laughter. The mood touched Jade, tried to make him part of the feelings of relief and excitement and new beginnings. But he had too many questions unanswered. Like how their coming here had changed things for TreAsh.

"The coming," Bulyn answered, leaning to pour more wine, "proved it could be done, balanced the probability. With the fact of your arrival added to the construct, both probabilities are stable."

"Then nothing is changed." Silence ran around the table as the others listened.

"The theory has proved out. And you have established the reality of TreAsh to yourselves. When you return—"

"Return?"

"Yes. Of course. That will make your knowledge a part of that reality."

Jade held silent, not looking at Sarn. He had not thought of returning. He supposed he had known they would, sooner or later, but he hadn't thought it would be part of this, of helping TreAsh.

"The force that binds the Star Web," Heglit said to someone. "According to the construct Tar Bulyn showed us, that is the key to the survival of TreAsh. So, in fact, the more who know you exist the more real you become in that reality."

"Indeed. Well said," Sarn applauded.

"Becoming part of that reality again might not be so easy for us," Jade pointed out.

"You should have no trouble. We could not enter it because we probably aren't there, but you are already an established fact there. The Star Web will be no barrier to you."

"Not the Web. We're fugitives, hunted in every sector, including TreAsh. The ComUn, at least the Chairman Barmalin Tas, tried to kill me before I even knew of TreAsh."

"But surely Rafal—"

"Can do nothing," Heglit told them. "Except as Link-men, we are restricted to Rafal Sector by ComUn law for our support of TreAsh during the Traveler War."

"We have made errors," a woman said into Heglit's silence. "We assumed Rafal's position would be secure in the Federation. You say the ComUn that was the Federation wishes to destroy Jade. Is there a sector not loyal to Tas that would give you sanctuary?"

"The Free-shippers aren't loyal to Tas," Jade answered, feeling Heglit's look. "They follow AzlurEor."

"AzlurEor? Surely not after three centuries."

"It is AzlurEor. Vril told us. He is, or has become, a Clate called Lurz, of Burkoze Sector. He is working against the ComUn. He had me once."

"Had you?"

Jade told of his brief abduction. "He may not yet have been AzlurEor, or he would have kept me."

"You didn't have your memories then. But the timing was close," Ruyalon mused. "Someone must have tied you in with TreAsh. AzlurEor would have ways of knowing what was going on."

"He didn't want me, except to use against Tas. Until after Grio." He told of running from the battleship and getting lost beyond the Rim, and how he first met the Travelers. Tension ran through the room like wind.

"He is like the Travelers," someone said. "He may be able to know of them and where they are. Maybe that's why they couldn't come here."

Heglit, dark and calm and thinking, agreed. "When we came to them they avoided AzlurEor, not wanting him to know of them. But I do not think they fear him for themselves." He told them of meeting the Travelers on a TreAsh of distant time after the attack by both ComUn ships and AzlurEor.

"He was in the sector?"

"Vril said he was. He even attacked after, when we left the Traveler ship to come here."

"We assumed too much," Sarn said finally. "We thought the union of the sectors would strengthen the Star Web enough to contain AzlurEor, and that Rafal would be a major factor in the growth and expansion of the Federation. Instead, it seems AzlurEor has learned enough to make his own predictions, and use out nature against us. He has waited until the crisis period to act. As did we." He rose from the table. "We've learned more than we hoped tonight. I suggest we find out how it applies and what it implies."

He asked Ruyalon Tas and the woman Jarlon Dar to see to the comfort of his son and guests, and called the others to return to the Academy with him.

Star Web thoughts tangled Jade's head long after the house was dark and quiet. Too much information, too little understanding. And the trouble their news had brought to TreAsh. Questions plagued him. How had they really come here? And how could they get back, especially now, knowing how important their return was to TreAsh? And could AzlurEor really destroy the Star Web?

He drifted to sleep on that thought and was brought awake by a vision of TreAsh gleaming pale and ghostly among the shards of its destruction. *This isn't real yet.* The thought kicked him like panic.

Shadow-scared, he thought, sitting up, waiting for his heart to slow. I am here. I know I am here. I remember coming here. Still, the double picture hung in his mind. He wanted logic and knowledge, and he thought of Heglit. But when he left his room his steps turned him toward Lista's.

He wasn't too surprised to find a second golden head on the pillow, and he might have left them, had not a strong hand reached to grasp his wrist and pull him down to a murmured harmony of pleasurespeak.

"You do not want to go back," Lista said sometime before dawn.

"Going back may not be so easy. We must use the Web and it is that which AzlurEor attacks."

And later, as the sky paled to lime before the pink of day, Borget spoke, deep-voiced with sleep. "In the map of the Star Web there were no blue channels."

Jade yawned, thinking about that. "Maybe they only use the one color."

"Maybe." Borget got up, naked, to open the window wide to the dawn breeze, and slid, cool, back under the light cover. "There is another thing we found here. A tree, gifted to TreAsh long ago. A seed of ChatkarJ'Mur."

"Here? Do they know?"

"Ruyalon Tas said it was gifted long before Sarn's birth, when TreAsh received many gifts. It is happy here and already a great tree."

29

The sun was well up when Jade found Sarn and Heglit in the garden, deep in conversation. For a moment Heglit's dark eyes looked at him, and he felt a swift irritation. How did he always know? He avoided the eyes and accepted a cup of some dark fragrant beverage.

"We must leave soon, Jade," Heglit said without preamble, waking him like icewater. He glanced at Sarn.

"Tar Bulyn said our coming—" He began, then picked up on the expression in the golden eyes. "Something happened."

"Only knowledge, and the pattern built on it that says there is less time than we supposed. We were seeing AzlurEor as a potential threat, not an active adversary. He almost certainly knows your purpose and will try to stop you."

"He tried to stop us before and couldn't. Our chance of getting back should be at least as good as our chances were for getting here."

"There is more to it now than getting back." Heglit's voice had a tonelessness he had heard before. He didn't like it so much he felt his muscles tense against hearing it. He looked at Heglit, but he was watching Sarn, and his face said nothing at all.

"The High Council met before dawn to study the situation and consider possible actions," Sarn said after a while. "There is little we can do from here, obviously, except advise and prepare you."

"For what?"

Sarn linked his hands on the table and looked at them. "The facts you brought us last night were added to the logic construct in the hope we could anticipate the effect AzlurEor's actions would have on TreAsh. One particular pattern shows as a statistical certainty, and it effects the Federation, or ComUn, more directly than us. At least in the short run. It could mean that all of this has been for nothing."

Jade frowned, not at all sure Sarn was answering him, less sure he wanted to be answered. He nodded for Sarn to go on.

"You said Tas was after you. AzlurEor was also after you. It would seem he found a way to aid Tas, to let him know where you would break out of the Web on your way to TreAsh Sector. If this is true, he has contact with Tas. So he could arrange for Tas to leave his fortress on Alzar and direct the hunt for you in person, and so be present in TreAsh Sector for the end of the chase."

"Why would— Oh."

"Right. AzlurEor's hope is to destroy the unity of the Federation. This way, whether he found you or not, he could achieve a major victory. He would simply dispose of Tas, perhaps putting the blame on you and your companions. This would disrupt the ComUn and strengthen the union of Free-shippers."

Jade admitted the logic of what Sarn was saying, but it sounded like a whole lot to figure from what they had said the night before. He didn't say so. "Wouldn't the ComUn Council simply appoint another chairman?"

"They have always been of the house of Tas, have they not?"

Jade remembered his conversation with Tas on Alzar and nodded. "Tas was afraid of successors. There was one surviving heir."

"That would fit. Logic says the house of Tas will fall, if it has not already. AzlurEor would know of the son."

"Suppose it does fall? What does that have to do with us?"

"Tas must have some means of assuring his family's position in the ComUn. Some legal provision. The Council would most likely accept an individual with the family characteristics."

Jade agreed again, wondering how AzlurEor could make use of that. He looked up and saw both Heglit and Sarn watching him, waiting for the obvious to occur. It did. "Oh now, wait. You can't know any of this hap-

pened, or will happen. Wouldn't work anyway. I'm—"
They just sat waiting for shock to pass.

"You can't know what happened," Jade repeated forcefully, trying to make certainty work. "You can't be sure."

"They are sure, Jade. It's a science with them. They would choose another way, if there was one." Heglit's dark reasonable voice pushed at him.

"AzlurEor will try to stop you if he thinks you survived to reach TreAsh," Sarn said, like continuing a discussion. "But if you can get out of the sector and to Centra, you could claim the chairmanship by right of blood."

Claim the chairmanship. Of ComUn. Sure. Jade shook his head. "Can't. You don't— Anyway, they have me listed fugitive."

"You are afraid," Heglit said, looking at him. "You think it might work."

"No." He got up. "Crazy you. Both. Needing a Heglit for that. Not me. I'm just—" He turned, wanting to run, and collided with Ruyalon Tas.

"Prince Jade," the man greeted, bowing slightly.

Caught by timing and accident, Jade gritted his teeth and turned back to the table, feeling hot blood in his face when he saw Heglit's expression. He only vaguely heard Tas say that Sarn was needed at the Academy, scarcely felt the hand on his arm as Sarn left.

"Your wanting, or his, won't make it work," he said through a strange feeling, looking down at Heglit. "It's space dust. Crazy."

Heglit took a breath, held it a moment, let it out. "Think clear, Jade." The lucid Rafalspeak forestalled angry argument. Jade sat down.

"I can't see what's happening. How this came to be."

"You do not see your part in it," Heglit corrected patiently. "Only you can achieve the necessary end for TreAsh, and perhaps all the rest. This is the way."

"Evidence."

"You are TreAshal. And related to Barmalin Tas through your father's sister. Without one of Tas's blood, the ComUn Council will be divided. They are too ambitious to agree. Your appearance is TreAshal. To them that means Tas."

Jade thought about it. It was almost insane enough to work. At least that part of it. But achieving that was nothing. The rest of it was ridiculous. "I would only accomplish AzlurEor's end, Heglit. You know that. I know nothing of the authority and administration of ComUn."

"The Council does. So does Rafal."

"You are fugitive from Rafal."

Heglit nodded, leaning back. "It is that your father and I discussed. The council of Rafalpha does not act without thought. I will be given a hearing. If you succeed on Centra I would be going to them from a position they would have to recognize."

"Heglit, we're talking about the ComUn, the chairmanship."

"Yes."

"You can't just—"

The arrival of the Benjor interrupted him, just as well, because he didn't know how to say what he wanted to say.

"Smart talking, you," Borget said, laying a hand on Jade's shoulder. "Troubles are."

Briefly, Jade told them of Sam's plan.

"Fitting, is, Prince Jade. And bold. But danger is." Borget didn't sound surprised, and Jade wondered if he was missing something.

"There is hope for success, my brother," Lista said in soft Benjorspeak. "Speaker Sam would not easily lose his only son again."

And that was a thing Jade hadn't thought when he heard the idea.

"There is fear in the people," Borget said. "And hoping. And wanting the waiting done."

Jade watched the handsome face, seeming to listen, reaching, and in spite of himself he felt a subtle explosion behind his eyes, a reaching out he didn't want. There was a growing tension, restrained but pervasive, like a scent carried on the wind from the mountain. Eyes blank, he let it happen to him, waiting, sampling it, knowing this was what Borget and Lista knew of their world. And knowing below even that, on some level beyond interpretation, it was not the people, not entirely. There was a vaster thing, a thing that bound him and

297

left him free, all at once. The majestic and vulnerable fact of the world itself, the serene blue jewel hanging before the golden star, wanting to be, with a kind of wanting he could not define, only feel. He shivered lightly, aware of his own insignificance and fear and inability to speak of this. With a subtle shift of focus he pulled away from that knowing, and looked up to meet Lista's gray eyes.

"You are also Speaker and Prince, Jade. It is what you are from the beginning."

And I don't know what those things are, he thought, but didn't say because someone was coming from the Academy with a message from the Council chairman.

30

The day dragged out, going too fast. Heglit was off talking to people, and Jade spent the time answering questions he didn't understand, thinking mostly that they had to leave very soon and these people (and Heglit) seemed to think he could just drop in on Centra Alzar and become Chairman of the ComUn Council. Just go there and take over for Barmalin Tas. It was a joke, and not very funny. His answers became more and more abrupt as his tension increased, and finally not even the presence of the Bertjor calmed him. He wanted away, peace, and being alone with nothing to think about but pleasure and sleeping. Then Sarn sent for them.

He was waiting on the steps above the garden, and Heglit was with him, and Ruyalon Tas and Bulyn and Jarlon Dar. They all looked tired and Jade thought Sarn probably had not slept.

"The time difference bothers us most," Sarn was saying when Jade joined them. "Twenty-eight years against over three hundred. Every day here could be that much longer there, giving AzlurEor time."

"You have as much information as we can give you," Heglit said, looking greeting and something else at Jade. "You have an estimate of our chance of a successful return."

"Only probable," Sarn said, and smiled a little grimly at the word. "A fifty-point-two percent chance of returning safely, if there is no interference." He glanced at Jade, then away, but Jade was too busy with his own reaction to notice. That was no kind of chance at all. They might better not bother.

"Not acting makes the alternative a certainty," Ruyalon said, as though he had heard Jade's thought. "We must do what we can. You must leave today."

Jade gritted his teeth on a sudden anger he didn't try to analyse, wishing he could say or do something that would get control of things. He looked around for Borget, saw him sitting on the low wall above the garden, staring intently at nothing. He turned, feeling Jade's look, and beckoned him in Benjorspeak.

Jade went to him. "You heard?"

"Yes, I heard." He said it like it wasn't important just now, making Jade frown. "There are other things fitting into this, Jade. They speak of your position, and belonging to both realities, but it occurs to me there is another here of both realnesses, part of one who has helped before."

Jade followed the brief gesture, looked across sunlit lawn to the shadowed temple-like structure on the first slope of the hill.

"The tree, Jade." Borget laughed lightly, turning to him.

The tree. Tall and broad-limbed, casting its shadow over the buildings at its feet. The seed of ChatkarJ'Mur. Jade stared at it and forgot the others as pieces fell into place in his mind, pieces he hadn't known he had, building a cool obvious structure. He studied it a moment, then smiled and returned to Sarn and the others.

"I think there is a way back AzlurEor wouldn't know."

"He knows the Web," Sarn countered, puzzled by the change in mood.

"But he didn't know of me. Not until Rafal, or after. And he didn't know of your journey to Grio."

"No."

Now Heglit was watching, close.

"What you did had already been done," Jade told Sarn. "By ChatkarJ'Mur. The tree here is his seed. Isn't it?" Excitement sharpened his words.

"It is, yes," Sarn frowned, glancing at Heglit. "It was a gift before my time."

"Jade." Heglit's voice demanded some explanation that made sense.

"Just listen, please. When I was with ChatkarJ'Mur he came close to telling me. I mean, he told me enough so I would know when I got here. He must have known the Benjor would find out about the tree here. He called me Speaker-seed to make the link between us, and the tree here."

"But Chat is—"

"A mystery in some ways. You said as much. I was with him, I know he knows the Web. Probably better than any warm life, because he's had so much time all in one piece. I think he uses it. The Web, I mean. That's how he sent me the guide when even I didn't know where I was."

"You were in the Web." Maybe calling attention to the way the Web was traveled and the mind's ability to create allegory, but it was more a thought than an argument.

"All right. Maybe. But there's more. Like how you got here from the Federation ship." That had some effect; he could feel Sarn thinking about it. Jade went on quickly. "What you told us of the creation of the Web, of the first strands reaching out, makes sense. It builds, doesn't it? I mean, a system Web would be built before two systems would make contact and create the larger Web."

Sarn nodded, still puzzled, but willing to listen.

"So how did the Travelers get here?"

"You mean ChatkarJ'Mur?"

"I think so. Yes. The Star Web of this galaxy isn't complete yet, but it's a lot further along than when the Travelers came. We weren't thinking that far yet. But there is another kind of Web, a sort of blue channel that is too long and fast, too different."

"Blue." Sarn's eyes jumped to the tree, then back to Jade, yellow as the sunlight. "There is a thing I remember, a blueness. It meant nothing. I thought I dreamed it."

Heglit looked toward the tree. "Jade, why would a tree build a way to other worlds and sectors?"

"Desire, I think. Maybe like the Travelers thought, a desire of the world before the tree, or even of the parent star. Grio did not make a life that could build ships. But the need to know, to reach out, is in the tree. We know that." Saying it, he knew it was true, knew Sarn and even Heglit believed it.

"Then Chat has been part of this from the first, or before, and you can go safely," Sarn said. A soft wind stirred the silver wings of hair at his temples, and he looked at Jade sharing a secret sort of relief, but there was something in the eyes like hands wanting to reach out and grab and hold. And a thought that wanted to stay secret longer.

Jade swallowed under the impact of that look, helpless.

"It's for a bigger thing," Sarn said finally, to both of them, speaking to the knowledge he knew Jade held.

Jade agreed, knowing it was true. But it didn't get any easier this second time. He knew Sarn's thoughts like they happened in his own head, saying they would not meet again. He refused to believe it.

"You thought three centuries last time," he said in the old tongue. "It wasn't."

"Was and wasn't," Sarn corrected, looking away.

"How long do you think it will take?"

"There's no way to tell. Until the knowledge and belief are enough to make us real to there. And there will be danger, and many things needing done when you return." He took a deep breath, let it out slowly. "We knew it long ago, Jade."

Which didn't make it hurt less. Borget was right, he thought. I don't want to go. Not yet. There hasn't been enough time here, even to tell him it doesn't matter.

Heglit's hand on his shoulder scattered his thoughts, and Borget and Lista were there beside him. The sun was sliding toward the edge of the mountains, just gilding the top of the tree. There was no reason to wait longer, and many reasons not to. Just please, he thought in no particular direction, please let this be right.

31

They went unescorted up the dusk path toward the tree, and it was the Benjor who knew first greeting, drawing Jade in through the gift of their sharing. But it was Jade's memory, and a knowledge gifted before the crystal, that held the truth, knew the likeness of being between this, the seed, and the father, differently nurtured, but sharing a bond of sameness and memory in a depth experience couldn't reach, only build up. He had time to wonder about that a little. Then he felt the dark brown force being what World-Seeder was, and that was a very private sharing, drawing him out of being Jade with a desire he was too small to resist. He flowed, power accepted and turned in on itself, plumbing depths inside he would never remember, drawing the him that was to a point beyond reach until fear and need to be was an ecstasy, forcing him up and up, knotting him whole and more than whole, joining golden singing threads to a him he yearned for, and weaving in that dark bold strand of power, racing them toward the no-time no-place of blinding blue song, creating passage and joy for their four-souled oneness.

So fast! Going, getting there, bursting into gold and down and down, struggling, a yearning oneness torn apart and grabbing fast and hard to maintain union, but separating, fractured, split into—

Two?

Strength, broad binding muscles flexing—

Get out, Jade. Dark voice, cool and stern and something more. It was like being clubbed between the shoulders. Jade got, scurrying, scrabbling for a hold on being Jade and nothing else.

Breath (his first?) crashed into his chest, familiar flavored. He gasped, hugging himself. What was that? he wondered. He calmed, felt this was the right feeling, more suited and pliable, not— Heglit?

"Jade?" Heglit's voice. The outside one.

He opened his eyes. "I, uh—" I came back in the wrong place, he thought. But Heglit's eyes, knowing him, said that wouldn't be funny. "I didn't mean—" He started to apologize, then knew he wasn't going to talk to Heglit about that. Not yet.

Then he saw where they were. "The Zendra? We made it, then. Where—"

"The Rock Belt."

"Not—?"

Heglit looked at the controls in front of him. "No. Beyond." He reached out to check the sensors, to be sure there were no other ships around. His eyes scanned the screens, finally went to the chronometer. He frowned.

"What?"

"Forty-two days and seven hours, plus."

"But it wasn't for us . . . the time on TreAsh—"

"They were right to worry. AzlurEor has had a long time."

"We don't know he planned to act against ComUn."

"We don't know he didn't."

Which meant they either still had to worry about ComUn being after them, or they didn't. "How do we find out?"

"Grio." First and safest choice.

A long way. Unless— "We don't have the crystal."

"It wasn't the crystal." Lista's voice brought relief before he realized he had worried about them. He turned to see two pairs of gray eyes watching him. He opened his mouth to ask what she meant, but his brain was faster, outpacing his words, running clear lucid thoughts through the smoky veils of his confusion. The crystal was only a talisman. It did nothing. But it kept them from knowing what they were doing when there was such a chance of failure, of AzlurEor knowing too much about them. The crystal was for them to believe in, and a message to Sarn. Nothing more. It hadn't helped. He thought he felt a vast warm laughter somewhere around them. And he knew how to get to Grio.

"The Link system will work. Enough to keep us to-

304

gether," he said (and apart, he didn't say). "We'll know the way."

The Link-mask, familiar-strange, comforting like the sanity of Heglit's deft hands fitting it. They had set the ship for the nearest Star Web gate, running a little blind but believing. They leapt out into N-space with the warning tone, felt the gate—

Wait, Jade thought-said, resisting the tension, using Heglit's strength to not go until their muscles burned with the strain and the gate grew loud, adding octaves of being there, calling, changing, reaching bright hot gold—

He leapt broad-winged into the sparkling blue flood, free and wild and laughing Heglit's laugh at the pleasure of being here and capable of this miracle, cresting against the flaming gold that drew them out fine and helpless to the silver-dusted black of N-space holding the brilliant stars of the cluster.

It was the right sector, the navicomp said so, and Jade accepted it, lying back in his chair thinking of something else, of coming back here, inside the ship, and being Heglit (Get out, Jade) and Heglit knowing it. How had that happened?

Maybe it was because he was so much Heglit (or Dariel) in skip. He wanted to look at the Rafalan, but he didn't. It didn't matter.

Except for that cool, precise "Get out, Jade."

And there was Grio, cool green from up here, welcoming them like it knew, and Heglit saying they would come in secret. Down easy, and liking to be here, thinking wouldn't it be funny if none of what had happened had happened. But it had. He wasn't Jade anymore, but something less simple. The fact of it lay in the back of his head, heavy and present like the knot of his hair. Jadriel Younger, prince and Linkman.

Interesting thought. Linkman he was, but the word said something about him it never had before, something about what he Linked.

So, they would find out how went the ComUn. And then what? To Alzar, probably, to probably get killed.

He stepped down off the ramp into air like a damp warm blanket thrown over him, and for a moment he tasted the air of that long ago TreAsh, home of dragons. And he remembered with a sort of a shock that his father, his people, survived. Almost.

They had grounded beyond the dawn belt and light was just now happening to the sky. Borget and Lista left them at the familiar clearing and went in to the ComUn station.

Heglit looked around, not restless, just seeing what was there, then he came back to where Jade stood by the door of the hut and looked at him.

"We've changed," he said with no particular expression.

Jade listened, thought about saying a lot of things, didn't, wished Heglit hadn't said it, but knowing he would have sooner or later. "The Linking?"

Heglit shrugged slightly and turned a little away. "Maybe that. But the thing done to you to keep you from knowing has been undone. You think differently."

"Not really. I have more to think about."

The dark head shook a brief negative. "I can feel a difference."

Feel? His eyes flashed yellow to the dark face, then away. "Don't."

"Think about it, Jade. None of this can succeed if you don't." Dry and calm. Being Heglit. And Jade couldn't answer, because Heglit was gone, walking away to the spring, squatting, pulling water up to his face to drink or wash.

Changed? And dammit, he would think about it because Heglit said to. And he was always so rodding right.

But had he changed? He felt the same. He felt different. He was—? Chewing his lip, he frowned into the unfocused greenness of the jungle. He was different now than when he first came here. Then he'd just been Jade, loose-Linked to everything but himself and maybe the Benjor. Heglit was something else, beyond that. Maybe. So what had changed? He was still Jade. All he was. The sum of his experiences.

Not quite. This time coming here he was a prince of TreAsh. In spite of himself, he smiled at that, at the sound of it. Somehow he had been added to. He could feel that, a solidness backing what Jade was, something that reached beyond the him he was. Was that what Heglit meant? For no reason he had a sudden vivid

306

memory of Sarn, tasted the sunlit breeze that stirred silver hair against dark, saw the look in the golden eyes. It hurt. He moved away from it, or tried to, and remembered Heglit had said *we've* changed.

The bright white day wandered by, hot and stupefying, full of silent thought and rare talk.

"If AzlurEor is acting against the ComUn, what will we do?" he asked once.

"Go to Centra Alzar. To the Council Hall."

"You think he got Tas, don't you?"

Heglit looked at him over his left shoulder. "Do you?"

"Yes."

And later. "Linking into the Web isn't what everyone thinks, is it? I mean, getting in channel isn't what the ship does, it's the Linkers. They're more than pilots, aren't they?"

"It seems so. Not that it matters, if it works."

Not now, but later, it would be necessary to know. When TreAsh got back there would be work to do in that area. When. If . . .

The Benjor returned before he got the tangles out of that.

There were no ComUn ships at the station, had not been for more than a month. The last ship to ground on Grio had been a Free-shipper. "Claimed cargo, them," Borget said levelly, but Jade felt a hard and surprising anger in him, and some hurt in Lista.

"The cargo is ComUn contracted with Benjo," Heglit said. "They were pirates."

And Grio was half the galaxy from Burkoze Sector. There was trouble.

"Do they know why ComUn left?" Jade asked.

"A ship came, there was talk, like credits not being honored, and cargoes spoiled, and in a few days they left. All."

"And what else, Borg? What upset you?"

The answer came in low Benjorspeak, telling him the Free-shippers had seen the Benjor, they had fought for the cargo, and four had been killed. Another five were taken by force. "For using, and selling later. One was of our blood. Her father is dead here, and there is hurting and fear in the people. They know it will happen again with ComUn gone."

And it would. The products of Grio, difficult to get and mostly illegal, were incredibly valuable. Up to now the presence of ComUn controlling the grounding beam had kept the illegal trade down to what a few individuals could grab while their ship was down. Once word got out there would be an attempt to harvest the spores and plants on a large scale. That would mean widespread invasion and destruction of the jungle.

"Heglit, we can't leave the world open."

Heglit had already thought of that. "Are there Benjor ships here, enough for the people?"

Borget nodded. "Enough."

"Is there anything you need from Grio?"

"Only being here."

"But they can leave. For a time."

Again the nod.

"Go tell them to get ready to lift. All of them. We can shut off the beam, and it will be months before a lander can be brought out here to check it."

That easy, thought Jade. And when they found out the beam had been shut off after all the ships were gone? Only Rafal had ships that didn't need the beam. Moving through the jungle toward the station, Jade wondered if ChatkarJ'Mur knew what was happening. The question brought its own answer. He did. And he was not helpless, either. Jade wasn't exactly sure he understood that. Or wanted to.

It took half a day to get the Benjor off-world, and one couple insisted on remaining. Grio would care for them, they said, and no one doubted it.

Then Heglit took Jade down into the small generator room and showed him how to cut power to the beam: Just a couple of dials, a switch to pull, and no more ships could ground. Ten minutes of easy work put the power plant on standby, and the planet was effectively off-limits. Jade was a little surprised that the system was so vulnerable.

Then it was time to think about Centra Alzar. And Heglit (like always, almost) was right. Alzar was the only place to find out what was happening.

"The four of us," Jade said, standing by the small ship, looking at them. "All of us will be in danger on

308

Alzar just being us. A Rafalan, two Benjor, and me. None like us there."

"Or anywhere," Heglit pointed out. "But the real danger is to you and me. The Benjor have a different value, especially there. And they know about TreAsh. So there is hope, even if we are taken."

A different value. Jade looked at the golden couple and wasn't comforted. Heglit could talk about different values, he'd never lived the life he was talking about. Bad enough for one, but these two— being together was their life. And their staying alive was TreAsh's life. So there wasn't any choice after all. As usual.

32

Centra Alzar. And heavy traffic in the sector. Maybe more than usual, Jade couldn't tell. They had made such plans as they could, knowing everything depended on luck, and there was nothing they could do about that . . .

They dared not show the small ship in a port, not if Rafal was still keeping her secrets, and there was no place on the city-filled continent to ground the Zendra secretly. It would have to be Joyside, the vast wilderness surrounding the fortress and home of Tas. Heglit pointed out that there would have to be transport to Cityside. That was logic.

Jade commented that Tas might be there too. That was fear. And there was no more time for that.

There was no marker near the fortress, no glow, no phantom city, but the mountain itself was distinctive enough. They came down near the base of it, below what Heglit said looked like a small landing field near the rocky peak.

Nothing happened as they grounded, calming Jade's sudden fear of alarms. An irrational fear, Heglit pointed out, since all but Rafalan ships needed the port beam to ground. Any logical precautions would be taken against airships coming in horizontally.

Fine. If true, Jade thought, as they left the ship and started up the steep slope. He was reminded briefly of another walk, but put the thought aside and tried to remember this was not in fact a mountain. The last few meters up to the landing space was a muscle-pulling straight up. And they had company. Heglit saw them first, signalled for silence and disappeared into shadow. Jade stayed back with the Benjor and listened to his heart beat over the sound of their breathing. Looking at them he decided he was the only one scared.

A rustling snapped his head around and Heglit was back, reaching down for Lista's hand, pulling her up, then Borget, and finally the big hand closed on Jade's reaching wrist and he scrambled up onto the paved level.

Heglit gestured toward two machines parked under a protective rocky overhang, but before they could go to them there was a flash of red light, a signal of some sort, Jade thought, pressing back against the rock. The light flashed out along the edge of the pavement, running the width of the field.

"One's coming in," Heglit said, but didn't start for the edge again. Instead he led them back along the rock to a dark hollow space, and stairs. Wondering if this was a good idea, Jade started down. A door slid open. Auto. And they were in a dim room with three corridors leading away.

"One is private," Heglit said, looking at Jade. "Which?"

How the Rim should he know? But his mind ignored his self-pity and annoyance. This was the opposite of his first entry, so the Chairman's private quarters should be to the west. He remembered windows—

"Left," he said, and they went. Jade didn't need Borget's whispered information. He knew Tas was not here. It was dark in the corridor, empty. They came to a door, high, wide, and solid. He felt over it for something that would say how it opened. Nothing. But in the silent dark a memory rippled through him, settling in his shoulder and arm. Oh no, not this time . . . But his fingers stroked over the flat surface anyway, curious, feeling for—yes, a sort of something, hard and brittle.

"Locked," he said, against the unreasoning fear that he would suddenly draw back his fist—

"Stand aside, Jade." Heglit's voice, his hard bulk moving up as Jade moved back, sweating. There was a piercing white flash, a smell of heat and something bitter, and the door swung open.

They moved over carpet, around things that could have been furniture. And another door, open, and a square of brighter darkness that, as their eyes accepted it, showed the rich blaze of the night sky. A window.

Heglit found the light control near the door, and they looked around, momentarily dazzled. It had to belong to Tas. It was like him, rich and vivid. A sitting room maybe, a place to meet with friends and talk. Now it was very empty. They explored, found a room of screens and machines more suited to a ship than a building. Jade brushed his fingers over glowing squares on a panel, and several of the screens came to life, showing a corridor with a trio of guards standing together, talking; a room, bright with lights; and a group of Clates talking and laughing, drinking together, all silent.

Heglit, more knowledgeable, found the sound control. They settled on the room and listened to the tiny babble of voices.

"Mardel shouldn't have gone," someone said clearly.

"You heard the report. He's off-world. Gone hunting."

"Ha. Not roddin' likely. Unless he found another bastard to erase."

"A month, Darl? And Mardel said there was trouble Cityside."

"Looking for trouble, since Timli found a new rod-man."

"Glis, and you know it. I don't blame him for wantin' to find out. Roc's a rich sector."

"He'll be back. A day Cityside will—"

Heglit cut both sound and vision and leaned against the wall, arms folded. "Tas is not on Alzar. The chance is greater that Sarn was right."

"So we go to Cityside. And?"

"We go to the Council Hall."

Just like that. Jade looked at his companions, torn and dirty from the long climb. "Like beggars, us." And on the sophisticated inner worlds that meant a lot. Reese had taught him that. He realized that memories of Reese had been tugging at him since entering this apartment. The same essence of wealth and power held here. He shook off the feeling and went to look for a wardrobe of some kind.

It surpassed his expectations, but then, he had never seen a Council Chairman's wardrobe before. There were styles and fabrics from everywhere, and jewelry to match. There was even a selection of female styles, and Jade smiled, wondering. All right. They wouldn't appear on Alzar like beggars.

He chose a wide-sleeved thigh-length tunic of some translucent silver white stuff over maroon skintights, a wide black belt, and knee-high black boots, topped with a knee-length cape of rebofur.

They took turns in the washer, and Jade inspected them critically after they dressed. The Benjor couldn't help being beautiful, but they called attention to it with pale green and gold, becoming elegant. Heglit was most changed. Pulling on a dark crimson tunic that left his arms and broad chest bare, black pants that molded his powerful thighs, he looked savage and beautiful, threading the edge of violence.

"Wanting you for skin games," Jade told him, half-teasing.

Heglit smiled faintly, choosing a heavy gold chain and settling it about his neck. "We are not always somber on Rafalpha." He strapped on a long dangerous-looking knife, and suggested they all go armed, even Lista. Jade agreed, picking up a large goldstone pendant and slipping the chain over his head, thinking a theft like this could get them in trouble. Then he thought that was almost funny. They couldn't be in any more trouble than they were. Until they got to Cityside. There was a delicate and deadly jeweled dagger for Lista, and a sharp blade for himself. Borget chose his own weapon, a narrow-bladed short sword, and he handled it like he knew what it was for.

Then they were as ready as they would ever be.

Either no one had missed the guard yet, or security was lax with Tas gone. The parking platform was empty except for three machines, telling them someone had indeed come in. Maybe Mardel. The machines, Heglit said, were basic Rafal designs. The controls were simple. They lifted lightly, turned to the west, and darted off toward the ocean in the star-silvered dark.

Heglit insisted on showing each of them how to operate the air car, not saying the obvious, that some of them might have to run back to Joyside where the Zendra Three waited. Then there was time to talk.

"If Tas is not known dead, I better not show up at the Hall," Jade said. "We have to find out what's happening."

"There will be talk in the joyhouses," Heglit countered, leaving Jade wondering if he had thought out all the steps in the near future. He entertained a brief hope that Tas was alive and well and meeting with the Council.

313

Then he realized that that would not solve the real problem. And he wasn't at all sure what would.

A sudden brisk voice shocked him out of his tangled thoughts.

"Joyside car, we have no destination logged for you. What is your destination?"

"Sorry," Jade responded, looking at Heglit. "Going to Council Hall."

"That field is still closed, Joysider."

"What's closest, Lander?" He kept his voice light, only slightly annoyed.

"Ring two, plot north seventy."

"If that's closest."

There was a muffled sound of cursing. "You want us to bring you down there, Joysider?"

"Yes."

"Switch red and we'll handle it."

Heglit reached out and touched something, and the control panel glowed a solid red. The ship stumbled a bit, then steadied.

"Got you. And next time, Joysider, hire a pilot."

The coast came up fast, and the unending blaze that was Cityside stretched to the horizon in three directions. There was nothing but that to see (and no talking because they could probably be heard) for over an hour, and it seemed the sky was full of the bright white lights of other air cars.

They circled twice, going nowhere; then the car came down fast in a spot of hard white light. Around them other cars landed and took off and spots of light flashed on and off. The night traffic of Alzar. Jade thought it was a minor miracle they didn't all crash.

Field men came out to open the car, stood aside while they climbed out, then pushed the car away. That was that. They looked around, found a marked path leading to a well-lit avenue, and started walking.

Crossing the field was the last time they were alone. The street teemed with people, milling, walking, talking, laughing. A roar of noise and movement that closed them in. He tried to see everything, but there was too much, it came to him in sharp unrelated cameos; a man, open-mouthed, eyes squeezed to slits, face red; a woman, dyed in narrow blue and yellow stripes beneath her scanty

314

red tunic, head thrown back in laughter (or pain); and lights flashing every color, moving life-like tri-dee advertisements promising every sort of pleasure.

He half-turned to speak to the Benjor and a staggering weight crashed into him. Spaced-out shipper, he thought, automatically slipping aside. Then he felt the hand clawing at the chain about his neck and instinct sent his own hand up, fingers sinking into the warm moist juncture of neck and shoulder. The man jerked up, eyes rolling to white, and Jade stepped aside, letting the body crumple to the pavement. He walked on, pretending disinterest, heart slapping madly in his chest.

They brushed by knots of people and Jade noticed that Heglit had moved slightly ahead of him, and Borget was behind Lista. Van and rear guard. Right. Sure. Reese would have hired guards. He drew Lista close to him, sliding his left arm about her waist to make it look realer. He could feel a fine trembling in her.

"Afraid?"

"There are so many here," she replied, great gray eyes wide.

A dark arm reached out to halt them and Jade stopped, looking around. They were near the entrance to a joyhouse whose sign was a tri-dee of dragons fighting, realistically bloody. The entrance was blacked by a knot of men, several of them in uniform. ComUn.

"That's glis!" Someone shouted. "Been there me, and seeing it. Broke up the bid-center, them Free-men. Fired the store. No cargo coming off Dagon since."

"Lies!" Another voice. "Free-men needs the ports same as us."

The four moved closer, listening.

"Tas went to Dagon for seeing it."

"You don't know it. Even the roddin' Council don't know, or ain't sayin', where Tas been goin'."

Heglit shot a look at Jade, who nodded. With Heglit to break trail, they cut through the crowd, getting looks and muttered curses. One broad-bodied half-spaced shipper held his ground until the calm dark hand grasped his shoulder in an almost-friendly gesture. Then the broad face went pasty pale and he fell back. Heglit never paused.

Inside was crowded, but quieter, as if the walls cut off most of the street noise, offering security. They pressed through the many-smoked dimness and found a stand table. Jade pressed the service tab.

"They know Tas is gone," Heglit said, looking around the room.

"Afraid them," Borget said. "Wanting safety and help here."

"Dagon Sector is halfway up the limb. The Free-men must be stronger."

"Or trying to start rumors of strength. A few could disrupt a port if they worked together."

"But they need the system, Heglit."

The dark head shook a brief negative as the service man came to take their order. Jade called for Orziel with bread and cheese and fruit.

"They could easily believe they do not," Heglit answered. "Greed."

They were all hungry, and glad when the food arrived. The fumes of Orziel loosened Jade a little, enough so he began to take an interest in his surroundings, tried to hear what was going on through the rise and fall of general noise. For all the size of the crowd this was familiar ground. A joyhouse. The same moves, and countermoves, the same games. He watched them, wondering how much of it the others saw. Then he made a quick decision. Unclasping his cape, he handed it to Lista. "Heglit, stay and watch them."

The dark eyes questioned the wisdom of this, but he would stay, freeing Jade to move through the din, to listen. To talk. To play the games. He knew how to get attention, holding a long calculating look until eyes snapped up to his, then looking away, feigning disinterest, broken by a covert look sure to be waited for. He was offered a glass of Z'Atua by a blue-clad Clate. He accepted, noticing the uniforms at the table. He laughed lightly, implied much and promised nothing, managed to make his questions appear innocent, and learned the men were shipmasters.

"Been out?" one asked, looking at him with red-webbed eyes.

"Times, me. Hear there's trouble out now."

"A few roddin' Rim pirates. Gonna mash 'em good when the Council gives the word."

"Council in it?"

"No way." The blue-clad man sounded annoyed at the attention Jade was paying the other. "Wantin' to have it like that ain't gettin' it. It's Tas. They're meeting to find out what happened to him. All them roddin' smarters up there got their heads up their tails. Tas is gone gone."

"You know it?" the uniformed captain asked.

"Do. Why I came in. We ripped a crew of Freeshippers on Tallant. After our cargo, or maybe other things as bad, so we mashed them. But a few cuts and one tells us Tas was lost. Out of TreAsh Sector."

Jade felt a coldness in his middle around the Z'Atua, but his face belonged to him. "TreAsh?"

"Gleesting true, skinman. The Star Web broke."

"Web can't," Jade said, feeling the shock in the others at the table.

"Did. Word is, one channel out in Burkoze went. Took two free ships."

Damn. Sarn was right. AzlurEor knew the Web and he knew how to hurt it. If these stories got out, the fear would spread, growing . . .

He put his glass down and stood up. The blue Clate reached out and grabbed his arm. "Slow it, skinman. Night's waitin'."

"Not for me, shipper." Cool and superior, he looked down at the watery eyes, making no effort to pull away. "I strongly advise you to keep any and all stories about the Star Web to yourselves."

"Now look—"

"You look. Remember where you are. This is the Council's world." The hand on his arm snapped open like it got burned, drawing conclusions from the cold highspeak, the implication of position. Jade smiled. "That prop from the Free-men is supposed to scare us out of the limbs. There's nothing else to it. Think about it, captains."

But the feeling he took back to Heglit and the Benjor was a cold helpless one.

"Sarn was right. He's attacking the Web the best way possible. And word's already out Tas was lost in TreAsh."

Heglit nodded like he expected it. He had hired a

room for the remainder of the night, expensive, but if they failed here their credits wouldn't be worth anything, anyway. Jade was grateful to have the next step postponed, if only for a few hours. He had no trouble sleeping. He was committed. Things would go the way they would go.

33

The ComUn Council Hall was probably the largest single building in the Clate galaxy, thrusting out of the geographical center of Cityside continent like a mountain. Two rivers had been tapped entire for its water system, and it was said (and probably true) that it used enough power in one day to run an entire planet for a year out in the limbs. Inside the ever-growing structure was private housing for the presidents, governors, whatever titled rulers of every major ComUn-linked world, and in the center, the foundation of the Hall was built around the largest data-processing center known. Here the schedules of transport, the economic structure, the quotas, were established to maintain balance in the empire. Here, too, were the inconceivable lists of employees and individual credit bases. The huge and always expanding computer complex was the brain and nerve center of the ComUn. Detailed information on every world explored, including the non-Clate, could be gotten here (if one understood the retrieval system), as well as the Star Web gate and beacon system and map. There was no end to the information available, most of it filed and forgotten, building a constantly shifting super-detailed picture of the ComUn.

The Council of a Thousand was chosen from throughout the galaxy and answerable only to the High Council of a hundred seats, chosen by the planetary leaders (in theory). And they in turn were accountable only to Barmalin Tas, who ruled the ComUn by virtue of that complex knowledge system.

And it was all possible by the impossibility of the Star Web.

Walking toward the Council Hall, Jade found it too big to comprehend. Like what he proposed to do. He just looked at it and felt absurdly insignificant.

There were guides and travel-strips inside, or sheer size would have paralysed the system. They read the maps, were carried along the busy corridors, up crowded chutes, always up, always in. And the crowd gradually thinned, but became, if possible, more frantically active. And they were beginning to attract attention.

"Jade." Borget touched his arm. "There is a wrongness here."

He felt it, explored it, but if Tas was indeed gone, if they were without a Chairman, and faced with the new and mysterious problem of the rebellious Free-men, then there would be confusion and anger. He tried not to think ahead to what would happen when—

"Stop, Clates. You are out of the public area."

A big yellow-haired guard stood in the center of the hall. Above him a decorative seal glowed in mid-air, identifying this as the way to the Council Chamber.

"We have business with the High Council."

"So do a million shippers, you ask them." Cold voice not caring. "They sit in closed session. You have to petition."

"No time," Heglit said, stepping forward. "We found—" He held out his hand, his left, and Jade tensed as the guard stepped forward to look, bent his head—

Heglit's right hand flashed out and caught the head under the chin, snapped it up hard enough to lift the big man clear off the floor. He fell and lay still. Heglit bent to him, but Jade thought it didn't matter, they had all heard the sharp crack, and there was a thin trickle of blood from one ear. It couldn't matter, not now. They went on without the travel-strips. Heglit's hard heels struck the floor evenly and the sound echoed through the hall. The dark face showed no expression at all. Jade was thirsty.

The corridor ended in a high circular chamber with large ornate double doors directly before them. The Council Chamber. A long-robed Clate appeared magically beside them, white-haired and stooped with age.

"The Council sits," he told them softly.

"At what business?" Jade asked, wondering if this one had a way to call guards.

The old face drew together in a frown, not used to questions in his ritual position. "The business, I think, is that of setting aside the succession law. The House of Tas has ended."

"Did you know Barmalin Tas, old man?"

"Oh yes, of course, they all pass here."

"Then look at me. At my eyes."

The old face peered closely, bringing a faint sour smell. Then he pulled back, one hand rubbing at papery lips. "A trick—"

"Of a sort. We will enter."

"No. You cannot. No one—"

"You will open the doors." Jade's voice held cold authority, and, hearing it, he wondered why he was doing this. Once the doors were open it was all luck and insanity.

But the robed figure moved and they followed. "How shall I announce you?"

"You won't. We go in alone." He saw that Heglit approved of that. The Benjor were silent.

The great doors swung open on bright light and a broad stair leading down, a vague hint of figures surrounding them, not yet looked at as they started down into the babble of voices. Swift silence as they reached the round fenced space with two great chairs. The speaker's place, Jade thought numbly, feeling Heglit behind him. The light came down through a great stained glass dome, the top of the Hall, dazzling. But as his eyes adjusted he saw the councilmen were seated in a semi-circle about the walls, slightly above him, each behind a wide curved desk. Safe and secure, he thought, keeping their distance from the petitioners. The chamber itself was splendidly barbaric.

He waited silently for some reaction, feeling shock and anger and a growing curiosity someplace outside himself.

"What the Core is this?" someone said finally, and Jade learned there were voice amplifiers.

"What are you doing here?" Another voice.

"Who is that?"

"The Council is in closed session, Clates." This voice had authority. Jade looked for the speaker, found a strong face frowning beneath a crown of iron-gray hair.

"The Council is about the business of selecting a Chairman," Jade said, clear and slow, glad his voice was steady.

"It is a closed session," someone repeated.

"Am I not right?"

"You are. But—"

Risking a lot, Jade interrupted. "There are laws of succession."

"Useless to us, now."

"Barmalin Tas was murdered in TreAsh Sector." Jade kept his voice steady, heard a patter like surprise rippling through the bright air.

"Tas is gone," the speaker agreed, in essence. "His only son was found dead a month ago. Now, please state your business here." That last had the ring of command.

Jade took a breath. "I am of the House of Tas."

The rustle of sound rose to harsh staccato.

"Silence!" The sheer volume of that command shocked the sound away. "Tas had one heir. He is dead."

"Tas had one public heir," Jade said clearly, making the distinction, hoping someone here was as familiar with the gossip as the guests in the mountain fortress on Joyside.

"Jesta, enough of games. Call the guards and end this." The voice was strong and female.

"Peace, Ronde. He does not sound mad, or entirely fool. And he did save us some trouble by coming here rather than going to the people in the City." And to Jade. "Your presence denies certain things we believe true. Have you a name?"

"Jade."

"Only that?"

"I am forbidden the use of my blood name."

"Have you proof of your claim?"

"My presence."

"You will submit to a medical examination?"

"I demand it." Calmly.

"Then I suggest—"

"Jesta, I protest this foolishness!" A strong ringing voice, and for the first time Jade felt a chill rush of real personal danger. "This is some move to delay the vote. Nothing more."

"Do not be overeager, Gritor." There was humor in Jesta's voice, and maybe a touch of strain. "A few hours will cool tempers and give us time to eat, while resolving this interesting development. Guards, escort Jade and his companions to the medical wing."

They hadn't heard them, but four burly Algorans stood just behind them. They went without argument.

He was taken alone to the small white medical chamber. A pair of blank-faced Clates, in loose white, applied instruments, took samples, tested. And he was released to dress and wait in a comfortable office of some kind. He was tired, worried about Borget and Lista. After a while a female Clate brought a tray with food and drink and he asked after his companions, but she might have been deaf, for all the attention she gave him. He ate, lay back in the comfortable chair, returning to his thoughts. He had done all he could for the time being. If he had failed he had failed entirely. But Borget and Lista worried him. They would survive, he was sure, if only because of their beauty. Heglit? He didn't know. A Rafalan, restricted . . .

"Comfortable?"

His eyes snapped open. He had been nearly dozing. The gray-haired Councilman Jesta stood in the doorway smiling slightly. "You have your share of courage." He came in and closed the door. "The test results will be back soon. Each member will receive them simul—" He stopped, staring at Jade, who stared back, confused.

"By the Core god!" Whispered. "We couldn't see it in the hall."

"What?"

"Your eyes. The color. It's the same—" He regained his composure rapidly, came to sit on the edge of the desk, looking down at Jade with even more interest. "It is a genetic characteristic of the Tas line."

"You don't think I would come into the High Council chamber if I were lying."

"People do strange things for high enough stakes, Jade." Jesta was silent a moment, thinking. "Even if the med-scan gives you a position to make claim, the Council will fight. Especially Gritor. He's being considered."

"I expect that. What about my companions?"

"Well, but worried. Especially the Rafalan."

"You knew he was?"

Jesta smiled again. "I have been to Rafal Sector. They

323

are hard to mistake." He rose to leave. "You will be called soon. I look forward to hearing your story, Jade."

"Jesta," Jade said impulsively, halting him at the door. "The ComUn has enemies. Powerful ones."

"Yes. I find that easy to believe after the last few weeks. Thank you."

He waited, and sometimes he thought the tension that knotted his middle wasn't his, but something from outside. Then the guards came, leading him back to the big doors, and Heglit and the Benjor were there, waiting. Borget and Lista looked troubled.

"There is some danger here we cannot name," Lista murmured to him.

The council was more subdued, but the danger Lista warned of swirled like smoke, speeding his heart.

"All members have received the report," Jesta said, beginning the session.

"All lies." That strong voice again. Jade looked around at the faces watching him, found the speaker, blond and angry. Gritor. He caught the eyes on him and a surge of immediate danger drowned out everything but that look. He opened his mouth to warn Jesta, to— Pain crashed through his right hand, blinding savage pain. He wanted to curl up around it, to scream if he could catch his breath. He didn't have to look at the hand, he knew what it was like. Sweat broke out, icing his skin. *AzlurEor! Here in the Council!*

Blinking the red fog out of his eyes, he hid his hand inside his cape. The bold face was laughing at him. He drew a breath, fighting for it as waves of black crested over his brain. Not now. He dared not fall, dared not fail. Heglit's warm presence moved up beside him, a hand reaching to steady.

"AzlurEor," he said aloud, ignoring what, if anything, was being said and not heard through the roar in his head, the tempting waves of black that tried to pull him down into his own brain. "Jesta. The enemy I spoke of. Here."

"Who is it?"

He wanted to say. But before he could, the point of threat leapt away. A woman laughed. Cruelly. Jade's hand flamed, and sweat stung his eyes like tears. He bit his lip and tasted hot salty blood. Again the focus of evil purpose moved.

Help me, dammit! Trying not to moan, wishing for strength, for— *Heglit. Dark savage power, controlled—* It flowed over him like water, pushing back the pain, putting it somewhere else. And surrounding that superb strength came warmth and depth and a different strength. His vision cleared, became more than clear, became so vivid the hall seemed bathed in sparkling blue light. He watched, poised on the brink of some illimitable discovery. There! The green haze rising from a frozen figure, drifting toward—

No you don't! AzlurEor. I know you here.

It was Linking and not Linking, both and neither, but a part of he-them reached out through the blue fire, ignoring the hand that screamed agony someplace else—it didn't matter. Not now. He-they reached, clasped the searing green, squeezed and squeezed until it collapsed. Remembering another time he-they summoned strength, cast the green out and out, away, into the flaming boundary of the Star Web. . .

Peace shook them apart. Jade was shaky, but the pain was only a memory, leaking out of his nerves. Total unnerving silence filled the hall.

"Jade?" Lista's voice. "What is here?"

She didn't mean AzlurEor. He most certainly was not there. He looked around, caught Heglit's eye, and remembered when he had heard this silence before.

"The Travelers," he said softly. "They're here, close. They waited them."

"Waited—?"

But Jesta's voice interrupted, began in mid-sentence. ". . . side our internal disputes is there any logical reason not to accept the evidence? We did not know all Barmalin Tas's private affairs. Gritor?"

"I, uh— I withdraw my objection." He sounded confused.

"Vote it." Jesta's voice sounded confident. He smiled, watching something on his desk. "Ninety-one accept. Jade, it is the will of the Council that you succeed to the Chair under the rightful law of succession. Have you any comment?"

He took a breath, wondering how he was going to feel

325

about this when he could feel again. "Only that I would like time to learn about all this before it is made public."

"Well said, and granted. Our action will go before the General Council tomorrow . . ."

A month of learning, of talking long hours with Jesta, speaker of the Council and assistant to the chair. A Jesta who was not too proud to talk with a Rafalan as an equal. A month of meeting with the other ninety-nine of the High Council. A month of being tied down, held back, of seeing the Council reform about the threat of the Free-men and the unexplained hints that there could be a bigger danger to the ComUn than a few dissatisfied Free-shippers. And the first hesitant mentions of real conflict.

They needed Rafal, the technical ability, the strength, and Jade recommended an end to the ancient restriction. The Council accepted the idea unanimously. And that was the first step in the bigger thing, the thing the Council could not know about yet. Heglit went to Rafal with Jesta and returned thoughtful, bringing word that Rafal would send a delegation to Centra soon, but would retain their closed status for a time. It was enough.

A month gone. And Jade finally asked for some time to relax, time for himself.

"Of course." Jesta laughed. "Joyside is yours. There is complete communication with the Hall, even a tie-in with the computer. And you don't have to ask, you know. You are the Chairman."

Maybe someday, Jade thought. He still hadn't come to terms with that idea.

But now there was time to steal, time to do a thing that needed doing. And the Zendra Three was on Joyside.

Word went out that the ComUn Chairman was resting, taking a well deserved vacation on Joyside, as the Chairman had always done. Alzar drifted back to normal.

But in a joyhouse on Everwait Twin a slender man with dark hair to his hips and strange yellow eyes moves from his solitary table to stand beside a Clate wearing the ComUn uniform with the sleeve badge of cargomaster.

"Drink you?" the yellow-eyed man asks pleasantly, weighing the face and manner of the older man.

The cargomaster looks, grins slightly, accepts the Z'Atua. He asks the standard question.

Long dark hair ripples as the head shakes no. "Free-man me. Linker. Bound out?"

"In. And booked, Linker. Want out, you?"

"Down-limb. Word is TreAsh is contracting when the Restriction lifts."

"TreAsh?" Quick laughter dies under the yellow eyes. "Heard it was burned up."

"A world, man?" Laughter, and cunning not too well concealed. "ComUn says, right?"

"You with Burkoze?"

"Free-man, me." Yellow eyes laugh above the glass, then the Free-man excuses himself, leaves for the port. To find a run down-limb, he says. Toward TreAsh.

A day later a free licensed Linker with Benjor companions signs the work list on Algor, asking for a run out, toward TreAsh Sector.

"Cheap runs, them," the ComUn portman observes. "More runs in, and better pay."

"Now, maybe," the Linker agrees mildly. "Us for getting down toward TreAsh."

"Dead sector," the portman insists. But curiosity has him now. The strange yellow eyes dance with laughter, knowing a secret. "TreAsh gone, Linker. In the old war."

"Yeah. That's why they guard it, man. Keeps out lookers, right?" Then they leave, giving an address where they can be reached if a run comes in going their direction.

On Grandon a non-union Clate-Rafalan team signs the available-for-work list, but turns down seven offers. Rafalan Linkman are still scarce, they could almost name their own price, but they want a run down-limb, to a sector bordering TreAsh. They ignore the high-bonus offers.

The scene is repeated with variations on a hundred worlds within a few weeks. Worlds in every limb, both ComUn-loyal and free. And word will spread because that is the nature of the shippers. A new world opening up, a new and major contract run. And it is possible, of course, with the new Chairman. Hadn't he lifted the Restriction on Rafal? He is young, they say. Even the

Free-shippers, greedy, and hungrier than the ComUn, will hear and talk and plan, and dream their dreams of riches, helping in spite of AzlurEor, in spite of everything. It is their nature.

And the delegation from Rafal will be in Centra soon.

In a joyhouse on the edge of the ComUn port on C'Erit a dark-clad Rafalan and a dark-haired Clate with yellow eyes sit drinking Z'Atua, waiting for dark so they can leave the port, go up the hill to the north, where a beautiful Benjor couple wait in a tiny ship.

"Go home us, now," the man says over his glass. "Wait for Sarn, us."

The Rafalan looks at him a minute. "Jade," he says, "talk like a man." Then, hearing himself, he laughs quietly.

SCIENCE FICTION AND FANTASY
FROM AVON ◬ BOOKS

THE BEST IN SCIENCE FICTION
AND FANTASY FROM
AVON ⬢ BOOKS

URSULA K. LE GUIN

The Lathe of Heaven	43547	1.95
The Dispossessed	51284	2.50

ISAAC ASIMOV

Foundation	50963	2.25
Foundation and Empire	42689	1.95
Second Foundation	45351	1.95
The Foundation Trilogy (Large Format)	50856	6.95

ROGER ZELAZNY

Doorways in the Sand	49510	1.75
Creatures of Light and Darkness	35956	1.50
Lord of Light	44834	2.25
The Doors of His Face The Lamps of His Mouth	38182	1.50
The Guns of Avalon	31112	1.50
Nine Princes in Amber	51755	1.95
Sign of the Unicorn	30973	1.50
The Hand of Oberon	51318	1.75
The Courts of Chaos	47175	1.75

Include 50¢ per copy for postage and handling,
allow 4-6 weeks for delivery.

Avon Books, Mail Order Dept.
224 W. 57th St., N.Y., N.Y. 10019

SF 7-80